RES GESTAE

II

Res Gestae Series

Actium's Wake
Agrippa's Wake

PRAISE FOR *AGRIPPA'S WAKE*

An epic story that delves deeply into ancient traditions.'

Reader's Favorite

'Highly exciting and entertaining. Jackman does an excellent job of weaving together the different aspects of historical fiction, evoking the exoticism of the ancient world of the Mediterranean, a poignant love story with a beautiful woman...and situations of desperation and danger that would fit nicely in any Hollywood blockbuster.'

Portland Book Review

'This fast-paced, event-filled novel is a gripping read, crisply told, with a sure grasp of historical detail. The portrait that emerges of Agrippa is one of the great strengths of the novel.'

Val Morgan, Author

AGRIPPA'S WAKE

BOOK TWO
OF THE
RES GESTAE SERIES

RALPH JACKMAN

SACRED EAGLE BOOK PUBLISHING
Norwich

The Chapters, Norwich,

NR15 2EB

First published in Great Britain and the United States in 2014 by Knox Robinson Publishing

A CIP catalogue record for this book is available from the British Library.

ISBN HC 978-1-9999638-0-4
ISBN PB 978-1-9999638-2-8

Typeset in Book Antiqua
Book Cover Image by Egisto Sani

Printed in the United States of America and the United Kingdom

www.sacredeaglepublishing.com

To Becca, Esme Rose, Rufus, Mum and Henry

For my father

Andrew Jackman (1946 – 2003)

And my sister

Ellie Jackman (1972 – 2020)

AGRIPPA'S WAKE

Happy Reading

Reading the inscription on my gravestone is a haunting experience. According to the skilful carving, I have been dead now for long past a decade. It is true that many times I have been close to death, and it is because of death that I sit down to write once more. But not mine.

Owls flit through the streets as I write, in numbers never before seen. Lightning strikes sacred places. The night sky is lit by a comet, a baleful portent; all around there is fear. And well there might be.

For Rome is in grave danger.

Before my 'death', I wrote about Octavian, Rome's first king for hundreds of years, about my personal ruin at his hands, and about my beloved Republic's fall. My proclaimed role at that time was to be the man who did not flinch from the truth. I step into that role once again.

Octavian is still the king of Rome, though he does not use that title. He has changed his name. Several years ago the senate in their sycophancy granted him the title of Augustus, marking him out as greater than mortal. I still call him Octavian.

Marcus Rutilius Crispus, meanwhile, well, he is dead; no status, no rank, no influence, and the Republic he loved is nothing but a memory.

But I, I am still very much alive. I have been on a journey worthy of an epic by Virgil, though, unlike Aeneas, I am no hero. I have done many deeds I am ashamed to have done, thought thoughts I reflect on with regret, but I still have a chance to become a good man, worthy of the Rutilian name I lost, worthy of my father, and worthy of my family.

I suppose that my suicide is where this account should begin.

I

It was Octavian who ordered me to die. Most men have reasons to be ashamed, have deeds that do them no credit. Perhaps the greatest stain on my character was that I could not fall on my sword. A lack of courage? Maybe. A sense of injustice? Certainly.

I could not accept that Octavian, who had carried out more and bloodier deeds than the world had previously witnessed, would sit on a throne as sole ruler, while I, with justifiable faults driven by desperation, should be forced to die by my own hand.

Nevertheless, on that cold and windy evening, with Octavian's agents closing in, I walked into the sea expecting to drown.

But the sea was cold. Very cold. Too cold. I could not do it. I could not go into the deeps. I could not force myself to die.

I looked behind me. I had to think of another plan. I knew I did not have much time. As I began to shiver uncontrollably, I had an idea.

I could escape. If I could slip away unseen, it might just work. Whether I carried on into the water to my death or ran away, one crucial fact would remain.

They would find a pair of sandals on the beach.

As quickly as I could, I waded back to the shore. I can still feel the pain in my body from the chill. I tore off my wet clothes to get them away from my skin, preferring to be naked, even with a night time breeze.

I stood on the shore, a former senator stripped of everything.

I gathered the wet bundle of clothes into my arms and ran through the shallows to avoid leaving a trail of footprints.

Octavian's agents would only find that pair of sandals. I hoped that would convince them.

I swam out to the boat and clambered aboard. It rocked as I hauled myself in, scraping my naked flesh on the side. Afraid that Octavian's agents would arrive at any moment, I fumbled for the anchor and heaved it in as quickly as I could. Within moments, I was sat at the oars, frantically rowing to escape the shore.

It was not long before I had rowed as far as I could. My arms, legs and back were burning with the effort. I shipped oars and drifted, directionless, hopeless, in the lap of the gods. After a while, I decided to find out what else I had been fortunate enough to acquire in my new fishing boat.

I sliced my finger on an iron fishing hook. Despite the pain, I was delighted. With a fishing hook, as long as there was a line as well, I might eat. But there was no bait: no flies, no spiders, no worms.

It was as I pulled my tunic back over my head that I kicked what felt like a pile of stones with my unprotected toe. I confess, I swore. But this too was good news. The pebbles were attached to a net, a small drag net, though in the dark I could not see what condition it was in.

If the fates were kind to me, I would be able to fish. And if I could fish, I could survive. My father had taught me one crucial lesson about the sea. If ever I was stranded without water, I should drink fish blood.

'It may taste foul,' he said. 'But it will keep you alive. Whatever you do, don't drink the sea water. You'll be dead in hours.'

So began one of the harshest, most painful episodes of my life. When it was over, I believed it had lasted only a couple of weeks. In fact, it had been nearly six months.

I had no intent of direction, other than to avoid land at all costs. So, I went out to sea until there was nothing in sight, whichever way I looked.

I was weary. I could not row any longer. And so I gave up, allowing the sea to take me wherever the gods intended. Day after day, the sun poured down on me mercilessly. The sea and sky merged into one deep blue. My skin burned, then developed rashes. As time passed, it dried out and began to crack. From time to time I would plunge into the sea to cool off but the water stung my wounds. I learned to make sure my tunic had dried before the evening. Because no matter how hot the day, the night was cold.

I managed to catch small fish with the lines, and in the first weeks, I can remember beating the surface of the sea with my oar to scare a shoal into my net.

But with time, I had no energy left to lift the oars.

The small fish I did not eat. Instead, I used them as bait to catch something bigger and better. I dreamt of catching a mullet, like the ones I had tasted so many times, and seen painted so life-like on so many walls.

But no mullet was forthcoming.

Aristotle believed music would lure fish or crabs, but I had no flute.

It seemed to me that fishing was going to be like so many other things in life I had set my hand to. Something I would fail at.

As the days passed, and by some miracle the gods preserved me, my eyes began to hurt, especially on sunny days. The reflection from the water dazzled me, until I felt that I would not even be able to see land if ever I did come across it again.

Just as I felt my skin would destroy me, and the pain of the boils and rashes on my hands, elbows and legs was growing too great, Neptune sent a rain storm. It nearly sank the boat, but it soothed and preserved me. Until I began to feel sick from the rocking of the boat. And that sickness lasted for days.

So it was that I stranded myself out at sea in that stolen little fishing boat. Delirium set in and I lost track of time, track of my mind, track of anything.

I can still feel the pain of my cracked lips and just how dry my mouth became. It was a torture of the most painful kind. Long-lasting, enduring, with no end in sight.

Looking back, I see it as punishment for my selfishness. I had allowed my slave-girl Whisper to be subjected to torture. In pursuit of money, I made her submit false evidence in a trial. As a slave, she had to be tortured for her testimony to be accepted. Whisper suffered greatly.

Now, I know her pain. I know the shadow and scar of wounds which will never heal.

On one occasion, I can vividly recall wanting to die as the sun had been baking me for so many hours, but a squall and a storm came, drenching me in rain. The cool drops of water were probably saving my life, but the anguish of having no means to capture any of the water to store for later was excruciating. Rain never fell frequently enough.

Bearded, burned and scarred, I collapsed in the boat, with my drag net floating hopelessly in the water, and my line of small fish dangling as feeble lures for bigger prey. It felt tragically ironic. I had achieved committing suicide after all.

But it was not my time to die. One day, land appeared on the horizon. I did not know where it was, or how far away it was. I just knew that if I did not get the boat to that shore, I was going to die.

For the first time in weeks, I lifted the oars back into position. It took nearly all of my strength to achieve even this. My legs had no power left in them, and my arms had wasted away till they looked as thin as a young boy's.

With everything I had left, I hauled at the oars, guiding the boat slowly into land with the tide. Slowly, oh so slowly, the boat beached. I slumped out of it, feeling the relief of hot sand on my face.

I managed to drag myself towards the trees that were just off the shore, seeking shade from the sun. There I rested for a while.

I do not know how long I slept, but I was woken by the sound of music. At first, I thought it was a dream, but I could see the flicker of torchlight. It was a villa, and I heard the sound of plate and cup. Someone was dining.

I staggered to my feet and headed towards the music, propping myself up on tree trunks until, at last, I made my way step by step up the path to the door.

I knocked, and was greeted by a burly doorman, who seemed surprised and unimpressed by my presence.

I suppose I must have smelt terrible, looked unkempt and was wavering on my feet. He concluded that I was drunk and, without a word, shut the door in my face.

I tried again, desperate to speak and show by my language that I was not a vagrant. But the door was not answered.

I lifted my face to the heavens and called on the gods.

'Help!' I bellowed. 'Help!'

Still the door did not open.

Distraught, defeated, but determined to try elsewhere, I tried to make my way back down the path to seek another house.

I did not make it. Half way down the path, the world spun one too many times and I collapsed.

The next months were a blur. I was rescued by the curiosity and kindness of the lady of the house, Aemelia. She had seen my faltering approach to the house through the window. When the doorman reported on me, the dinner guests debated on what should be done. In the end, Aemelia concluded that she lived in so remote a place, it was bizarre for a beggar to be lingering there. She did not even know that I had collapsed in her garden when she sent out slaves to recover me.

And so it is that I owe Aemelia my life. And I hope she knows how much I appreciate what she did that night.

Then came the questions. How long had I been sailing? Where had I come from? Who was I?

The first I could not answer. I guessed at a few weeks.

The second I kept simple. From Rome.

As for who I was, well, Marcus Rutilius Crispus was dead. So I took up the name Sextus, my late friend and comrade who fell on that fateful day in Actium, where my destruction began.

I distinctly remember a conversation about my boat.

When I suggested I had only been sailing for a few weeks, my answer caused consternation.

'He can't have been sailing for only a few weeks. Have you seen the barnacles on that boat? To have that many he must have been at sea for months...'

'For months? But that's impossible.'

'Not impossible, clearly, but certainly improbable. He's a lucky man, this Sextus.'

That was the first time I had been described as lucky in a long while. Perhaps I should have considered it a new beginning. But that came later.

A few weeks passed and I was strong enough to stand. I had to deflect the endless questions, well meaning though they were. My story as a fisherman was too vague. I could see them doubt that I was truly a man of the sea. So as soon as I could, I took my leave of that household. With new clothes and fresh supplies to set me on my way, I would go wherever the gods took me. I did not care. I was just grateful to be alive.

And that is how I failed even to kill myself; the last in a succession of failures.

Or perhaps not. For when I disembarked from that boat, Marcus Rutilius Crispus was, indeed, believed to be dead. Within months, a gravestone declaiming his life's achievements stood tall beside that of his wife, Olivia's. All that remained of him was a nomad, travelling under the name of Sextus. The last mark of my old life was the scar on my left cheekbone from the battle of Actium.

Oh, the battle of Actium. Another of Agrippa's great successes, but the scene of my demise. When I wrote that history, all those years ago, I did not have time to tell my tale of Actium, to explain how I made my mistake, the mistake that cost me everything. My sole purpose then was to reveal the nature of Octavian, Rome's king.

Now, I wish to justify, or at least explain, that I was not always a bad man. I was a senator, a commander of a fleet, a good husband to Olivia. But the wake of Actium swept this all away and more. Even the Republic died that day.

Years have passed since I stood aboard the *Triton* at Actium. Nevertheless, I can recall the day's events with absolute clarity.

'Is she a witch then, sir?' My comrade and dear friend Sextus stood beside me.

'Come now, Sextus,' I replied, 'surely you don't believe that? You're far too pragmatic to believe in such nonsense. She certainly is different though.'

'Well, if she's not a witch, then Antony's no Roman,' sneered Sextus.

'I've heard he anointed her feet, in public. A true Roman

wouldn't do a thing like that.'

'No indeed. But there's something about Cleopatra. Even Caesar couldn't resist her. I wonder what he'd think about Antony becoming her lover. Not quite the loyalty he expected I'm sure.'

We stood, side by side, as we had stood so many times, looking out towards the harbour. There, two towers had been strategically constructed on either side of the bay, guarding our prey. We had them trapped, and it looked as if, at last, after so many years, there would be a decisive outcome.

'What are the latest reports, sir?' asked Sextus. I can still picture the weariness in his face, his worn breastplate.

'The news is good,' I said. 'The storm last night upset their fleet much more than ours and they say their troops are suffering with dysentery. The gods appear to be favouring Octavian.'

'Rutilius old friend, you don't seem to believe in any of this, in what we're fighting for...'

I knew that a wavering mind in battle was useless, and it was not a good example to my men.

'Sextus, I want peace as much as anyone. Peace and loyalty. If there were more loyalty in our world then maybe we would not be suffering such strife.'

'But don't you hate Antony?' Sextus asked.

'Hate is a strong word, Sextus. Of course I disapprove. Of what he's doing, of what's he done. But no one can deny that he's under Cleopatra's spell. Lust does strange things to a man. He was a great Roman. Things could have been very different.'

'But sir, he ponces around the streets like a poxy king. He even dresses like an Egyptian.'

'So they say,' I replied.

'And what about his will? You can't ignore that, trying to give Cleopatra the eastern half of the Empire.'

'No, of course not.'

And there was the power of politics. In Sextus' mind, there was no doubt about the validity of the will that Octavian had read out in Rome.

That document gave Octavian his pretext for war. Who would dare to suggest it might have been a forgery?

'If I'm going to risk my life,' Sextus said, 'then it's got to be worth it.'

If I had truly believed that Octavian was going to restore the Republic, then I would not have had my troublesome doubts.

'It is worth it,' I said. 'And with Agrippa in command, we cannot lose. I must check on the men.'

I paced along the deck. Beneath me the rowers sat, layer upon layer, rank after rank. Lives as much as oars lay in their hands. The oarsmen chief had reported that all were fit and well, but the heat under the deck must have been stifling.

When I reached the stern, I nodded at the helmsman, who stood by the rudder. Even that grizzled campaigner looked apprehensive.

'Have no fear. Victory will be ours,' I said.

He stared out at the bay. When would it begin?

I marched along the deck inspecting the marines, their armour, their weaponry, their attitude. All acknowledged my presence. A few were gambling. Most stood or leaned against the side of the ship in silence. My confidence grew as I looked in the eyes of each man and knew that they believed in the cause. They were Italian legionaries, the best kind. Their armour gleamed in the bright September sunshine.

I had never been involved in a battle on this scale. Our fleet stretched out as far as I could see, and beyond. All around I could hear the creaking wood as we sat, waiting.

I walked to the bow of the ship, fully one hundred and twenty feet from the stern. Soon, the entire deck would be teeming with war. At the front of the ship stood the 'grip', Agrippa's brilliant invention, a variation of the catapult. Five years ago, the 'grip' was unleashed for the first time at Naulochus. Our enemy that day was Sextus Pompey, son of Pompey the Great. He had had no answer.

Now, once again, the heavy grapnel was locked in position, laden with the weight of our expectation. The four marines in charge were checking the ropes and lines attached to the winch.

'All ready?' I asked.

'Yes sir. The ropes are clear and we've sharpened the grapnel.'

'Good. It's time to earn our reward. Aim well.'

They continued about their business. I looked up at the grapnel above my head. Its iron claws reached out, clasping for prey. I prayed that it would stick hard and true on the enemy's deck.

As I made my way back towards Sextus, I checked that the standard catapults were prepared. Boulder upon boulder upon boulder was stacked around them. All was ready.

It was time for a brief speech. I stood in the centre of the deck and turned slowly so that everyone could hear me.

'Comrades, the time is near when you will earn yourselves glory, riches and renown. Now is the time to earn your rewards. Now is the time to earn with your right hands the honours that you deserve. And by the gods we deserve it.'

I returned to Sextus's side, taking my spear from him.

'A bright dawn, sir,' he said.

'Indeed. A shame it is wasted on this wretched war.'

'Perhaps it's a sign of a new beginning. Maybe the omens are good.'

I never answered. A horn sounded across the bay. Its call lingered for many seconds, a numinous tone. Immediately my soldiers were on their feet, apprehensive.

'That is no horn of ours,' I called, 'Comrades, to your posts.'

The *Centaur* sailed passed, its figure head of a horse leaping over the waves.

'Captain,' Paullus, my newest recruit, called, 'They are signalling. *Put out. Engage the enemy if they do not withdraw.*'

I called down to the Oarsmen chief, 'Put out!'

There was a shout below the deck. With a rumble the great oars of our fleet began to strike the water in unison. Slowly we advanced, to the ominous rhythm of the rowers. Soon we were heading briskly towards the enemy. The din of the oars sent a surge of fear through me. I said a short prayer to Fides, my protectress.

As we closed on the enemy, I fought with my conscience. I had always struggled to come to terms with killing fellow Romans. But whether Egyptian or Roman, I had to be ruthless. They would not hesitate to exult in claiming the life of an officer and a senator. I steeled myself. Never would I be ruled from Alexandria.

We drew close enough to see that we had the greater numbers, but they had the larger ships. They loomed over us.

'Rest your oars,' I shouted.

'Rest oars,' came the muffled command through the deck.

The oars clattered and rattled. And then silence.

There was a pause.

I could feel the wind sweep across my breastplate, tugging gently at my spear. The water lapped against the side of the boat as we slowed to a complete halt.

There was still about a mile between the ships. I doubt

there had ever been two such mighty fleets drawn up against one another. There we were, the two armies of the Empire, just outside the bay of Actium, until that day little known Actium, ready to determine the rule of the world.

The faces of my men showed no fear. They pressed against the side of the ship, straining to catch a glimpse of the enemy. Some checked their armour, and the grip of their shield, others drummed their fingers on the shaft of their spear. Killing fellow Romans had become second nature to them. I envied them.

We watched. We waited.

Behind the front line of marines stood our archers. As time passed, and there was still no action, some began to restring their bows.

'Courage, comrades,' I called. 'Victory will be ours. Spoils will be ours.'

The men let out a roar of feral ferocity. The *Centaur,* still sailing beside us, took up the call and soon our entire fleet was bellowing a war cry. I felt a prickle down my back. I was ready for action. I lusted for it.

I spotted a signal from our flagship, the *Minerva.* Two wings were to encircle Antony's fleet. We formed a crescent of death around him, compelling him to engage.

'For Rome!' I shouted.

'For Rome!' the sea returned the call.

It was at that moment that I made my oath, the oath which I had to go to such great lengths to fulfil.

I turned to Sextus.

'Witness this oath. If we claim victory today, I will build a temple for Fides.'

'Fides is no goddess of mine, sir,' Sextus replied.

If only she had been.

'Why not?' I asked. 'You said that the sun may herald a new day. Maybe it heralds a new divinity for you too. You say you need a cause to fight for. If money's not enough, then fight for Fides.'

He grinned at me. Gripping his spear he roared, 'Roman Victor!'

Again the cry came back, 'Roman Victor!'

And so it began.

As I predicted in my earlier history, the poets have sung of Actium. It has been immortalised as a great battle, worthy of its great contenders. In truth, it was much less than that. The catapults were fired. The sky was filled with stones which smashed into decks or plunged into water. Arrows pierced the air on their deadly flights and many men fell, but in the end it was Cleopatra's courage that failed. She would flee, leaving the outcome of the battle certain.

We were the victors.

That is not to say that the battle was free of blood. It was the most gruesome I have witnessed. Since our ships were so small compared to the monstrous warships of Antony, we used cavalry-like tactics, charging and retreating like waves on a beach. By doing this, most evaded capture. Those that were grappled, though, were buried in rocks and arrows.

As for myself, my *Triton* sank many enemy ships, including the *Neptune*. It felt wrong to be attacking one of my own gods.

In the midst of the mayhem, a pathetic sight stopped me. In a soldier's arms lay the body of a comrade, riddled with arrows.

The soldier turned his raging eyes on me. 'Roman arrows! These are Roman arrows!'

The full horror of the civil war had dawned on him. I could find no words of comfort. I pulled him to his feet and back into the fray.

As I write this, I am filled with remorse. I admire the Marcus Rutilius Crispus I am describing; officer, soldier, leader. It is hard for me to accept the deeds I have since done, especially when I consider that Agrippa, like me, faced many challenges but never lost his nobility or principles.

My first error of judgement, a signal of the turning of the tide in my life, occurred not long afterwards. My face still bears the scar from the wound.

I commanded the helmsman to aim alongside the *Osiris* in order to snap its oars. High risk, as it was so close range, but, if we succeeded, the enemy would be stranded.

It looked as if we would make it. The rowers lost their grip as their oars shattered and splintered. I crouched behind my shield, feeling tired. Even then my age was beginning to show itself, and at a most inopportune moment.

The oarsmen were exhausted, but fear of death drove them.

Until the boulders landed.

The *Triton's* deck splintered and collapsed, crushing all who were beneath it. We were floundering.

I raged that I would be slain by a coward at a distance and condemned to a tomb of water. I called on the men to board the *Osiris*. It was on the deck of that accursed ship, that I suffered my first ever wound in battle. Too late I saw an axe swing to my left. I spun round and slashed the attacker's arm. My cheek was struck a savage blow. It was agony, but I could see that the attacker's arm was nearly severed. As my vision turned red with blood, I stabbed forward with my sword and skewered him.

Young Paullus fell on the *Osiris*. The helmsman charged at him with a grappling hook. Paullus never saw the blow. The prongs pierced his helmet and he fell. I thought we were done for, that death would come, but by the gods' grace, another of Octavian's crews boarded the *Osiris* and saved us.

We joined their ship. My men were few, thirty at the most, but I was relieved to find Sextus was still alive.

'You could tell they weren't true Romans,' he growled. 'No fight in 'em. That's what comes of being slaves to a woman.'

The battle dragged on, losing momentum. Antony's warships were floating fortresses, unbreakable. We were using pikes to hack at the turrets of an enemy ship when I heard Captain Duilius call out.

'Rutilius. The first of Cleopatra's ships have hoisted sail. They are fleeing! Look! Not one is engaging.'

I felt a rush. More relief than joy.

'Curse this wind,' I said. 'It's strong enough for them to escape.'

Duilius saw my cheek was still pouring blood. He summoned physicians. I waved them away.

'Not until the end.'

News of Cleopatra's flight spread. What would happen next? The great purple sail of Cleopatra's ship, the *Antonias* itself, was unfurled.

'Roman Victor! Roman Victor!' The cry went up.

Our enemy was thrown into confusion, even Antony himself. They were given the signal to retreat. All about us, sails were raised.

To gain speed, the turrets which we had just been working so hard to break were thrown overboard by the very soldiers who had been defending them so fiercely. It was total chaos.

'Duilius,' I called, 'Why are we letting Cleopatra escape? Let's kill her.'

Duilius shook his head. 'We have no sails, and the oarsmen are exhausted.'

I was about to protest when he held up his hand.

'Octavian's orders were to stop fighting at the earliest possible opportunity. The fighting is over.'

'But the money, Captain,' I argued. 'It's on the *Antonias.* Think of the reward if we were the men to capture her. You say the fighting is over. Look around. The fighting is far from over. We outnumber them. Let's crush their attempts on the Empire once and for all.'

Duilius held firm. 'Octavian's orders were clear.'

I watched as the faster of our ships set off to pursue Cleopatra.

'But this is our chance for glory,' I cried. 'This is our chance to earn reward for what we have lived through.'

But Duilius would not change his mind. Instead, we joined a blockade to the north, where the fighting, not at all close to finishing, continued until dusk.

I often wonder if I could have done more to persuade Duilius to change his mind. Had we set off in pursuit, even unsuccessfully, it would have changed my fate.

As the daylight failed, orange light caught my eye. I pointed across to the *Minerva.* Behind it, more warships were arriving from our base on the shore, laden with fire. We fell back to be issued with many arrows. A blaze was lit on the deck, while hundreds of javelins with flaming torches attached to them were brought on board.

Now the battle changed in appearance. Flames covered the sea. The air was filled with jars of pitch and charcoal, fireballs of death. The fire ate through Antony's fleet. Soldiers desperately threw their drinking water to douse the flames, but the fire kept spreading. Men burnt like torches. They tried to use their cloaks to smother the flames, then the bodies of the dead. Smoke rose up and a dreadful smell lingered. The breeze stiffened, fatally. It cooled my face, but fanned the flames as the fire licked with tongues of death.

We withdrew to a safe distance from the burning ships and watched our enemy die. Some fell, choking in the smoke, others were incinerated in their armour as it glowed red with heat. I walked to the archers on the ship.

'Pick them off. They are unprotected.'

With unerring accuracy, they were felled. As they realised all hope was lost, those with any wits remaining jumped overboard. It was a great fall. Too great. Many made no stroke when they landed, but drifted on the surface of the water, lifeless.

I crossed to the port side. There, on the deck of another floundering enemy vessel, in the midst of the flames, I saw soldiers killing each other, putting an end to their misery. The sight filled me with a sudden dread. How could I possibly feel pleased by what I was seeing? These men were Roman citizens. They had probably even fought for the glory of Rome in the past.

'Hold back,' Duilius called. 'Victory is assured.'

A mighty cheer went up.

'Let's get the plunder!'

Duilius shook his head. 'Our instructions are to stay away from the blaze.'

There was a clamour of dissent.

'We fight for plunder. You can't deny us,' growled a soldier.

'There'll be treasure on those ships. It's ours,' bawled another. 'We've earned it with our own blood.'

Duilius looked unnerved. I can picture his face as vividly. And the reason I can see it so well, is because this was the moment I made my mistake.

I wanted the reward as much as the angry soldiers, for having to fight the sickening war.

I uttered the words which sealed the fate of Senator Marcus Rutilius Crispus.

'They're right. Let's sail in, put out the flames and take all the plunder we want.'

As I was taller than Duilius, I stood over him, trying to intimidate him. I suspect my wound had some effect. He struggled to look me in the eye.

'You were at the meeting,' he said, his voice wavering. 'You know the instructions. Any wealth belongs to Octavian. He is the commander.'

'Are you denying these men reward for their loyal service?' I challenged. The soldiers pressed around in a group. Duilius gave in.

If only he had not.

Every soldier except Captain Duilius busied themselves gathering water to put out the flames. But as we approached, we were struck by a wall of heat. My face ached, the wound even more so. We hurled water but it made no impact on the flames. Around us, others of Octavian's fleet followed our lead and moved in on the burning vessels.

It should have been obvious to us that the flames were unquenchable, but the desire for reward urged us to maintain our futile attempts.

Unseen, a single arrow fizzed out of the burning vessel. None of us was guarded anymore. The battle was over. This was my last element of fortune. It struck yards to my right. I heard a stifled moan and a body slumped to the deck. We all turned to look. To my horror, it was Sextus. The arrow had pierced just below his cheekbone. He lay motionless and sprawled over the planks. I could see the tension in his contorted face, the agony of the blow.

A cry went up. Our ship had caught alight. The water was no longer hurled at our enemy's ship, but our own. It had no effect. We were ablaze.

'Row back. Row back.'

I have never seen anything burn as fast. The flames surrounded us. The ship was going to burn out. The first men caught alight. Their cloaks burned. They struggled to tear them off as fire consumed their flesh.

I looked in dismay as the body of Sextus began to smoke. The arrow was still lodged in his face. It is still lodged in my mind.

I jumped for my life.

Duilius survived. But many did not. Nor did our ship. And worse, the others who had followed our lead, seeking the plunder, had also sailed too close to the burning wrecks and suffered the same terrible fate. These were our greatest losses, greater even than the battle itself. All because of me.

My life was spared when I was rescued from the sea. But if you have read my previous history, you will know that when Captain Duilius reported what had happened to Octavian, that moment was the beginning of a spiral of events which cost me my lands, my command, my wife, my status, my rank, everything. Worse still, in my desperate pursuit of regaining favour with Octavian, I lost my principles. So, in reality, the good man that was Marcus Rutilius Crispus died in that sea.

Ironic really, as I was supposed to die in the sea a second time, when I tried to commit suicide. My destiny, it seems, when the moment finally comes, is to die on land.

II

Now that I have had the chance to tell my version of that tragic battle of Actium, and explain the mistake, the understandable mistake that cost me everything, this history will tell the story of what has happened since that time. I am sorry to say that I have not been a good man, but in confessing my story, I will reveal the truth about Agrippa, the most loyal man ever to have lived, and that will give me some small satisfaction.

When I left the household of Aemelia, the kind lady who rescued me from her garden path, I roamed the Empire for months, scratching together an existence. I suffered daily hunger and thirst. I grew thin and weak, but no physical pain matched the troubles of my heart. There were times when I curled up to sleep in the shade of a tree hoping never to wake. But for everyone who suffers a torment, there always comes a moment when something changes for the better.

It was another scorching morning. I remember the terrible thirst. I had walked on blistered feet for miles. On the horizon I saw woodland, and a mist amongst the trees. I prayed for a source of water and persisted with my slow progress.

On I trudged, hoping that somewhere in the depth of the woods there would be a river. I had to keep stopping to rest. Huddled against the trunk of a tree, I realised that the noise I could hear amidst the rustling of trees was exactly what I had prayed to hear, the babble of flowing water.

There was a river; clear, cool, fresh. I plunged my

shaking hands into it, and revelled in the sensation of water flowing between my fingers. The stinging of my blisters cooled. I scooped water to my broken lips and poured life into my mouth. When I leaned over to wash the dirt from my face, I saw my reflection, distorted in the surface. That was the moment.

That was the moment when something changed. The bearded man staring back at me, though gaunt, had life in his eyes. I had survived for a reason. I had not travelled this far and run away from death for so long to die a nameless body on unknown land. I looked at the scar on my cheekbone. I traced its line with my finger across my face and recalled the touch of Whisper.

"You really are stupid then, aren't you?" I heard her saying. She had held my head in her hands, and kissed me gently on the forehead.

She knew me well. How I longed for her touch again. That had been the first brush of intimacy; a hint of the love to come.

As I washed away the dirt and dust from my face, I recalled the evening we had spent making a mask, the delicate way she painted the linen to my face, the smile so often seen, and her eyes, gleaming vitality. There was a moment where we stared straight at each other. I still wonder if she felt as I did. Neither of us broke the stare, until my senses swayed and I could look no more. I have not felt anything like it before or since. It was as if my very foundations shuddered.

When Octavian ordered me to die, I had freed her and told her to head for Marseilles. If she had listened, then I had a reason to continue. She could be there. I was not going to die before I found out whether she had made it. It would only take the sound of her laughter to bring meaning back to my life. And so I held on to that thought.

There were still many dark moments, but always I had

memories of Whisper to guide me through them; the flush of her cheeks as we made love, the tears she had shed as we parted. I knew she loved me. I had to find her. Marseilles has long been one of the busiest ports in the Empire, so making my way there was easy. All I had to do was find merchants heading in that direction.

I could smell Marseilles from miles away, a city which bustles with trade. The harbour was full of ships. The air stank with rotting stores, fish, and human effluence. Birds constantly circled, hunting stray cargo. It truly was a malodorous place. People from all over the Empire inhabited the streets. As I stood at a crossroads, I lost count of the number of different languages and dialects I could hear.

Near the port, there were vast warehouses, many in a state of disrepair. The city was still recovering from the mistake of supporting Pompey in the civil wars. Marseilles had been sacked. Although its Greek origins were, and are, still visible, the re-building which had gone on since then had that Roman sense of order. That said, Marseilles was not a clean or pleasant place. The flies swarmed constantly.

The same could be said for Marseille's character. Much that is improper occurs in Marseilles, even in daylight hours. Rome's night life is suspect, but at least ill deeds are carried out under cover of darkness. Here, the blazing sun and the searing heat do nothing to prevent brawls, rapes, robberies and murders. Some are to do with race, others are personal. I have never seen wine drunk in such excess. Here, it is taken undiluted and in such quantities that violence is inevitable.

Amidst the piles of rope, and the wafts of tar, I searched for Whisper. A woman as good looking as she was would have been a prime target for rape. I hoped that she had had enough money to stay some place better than the insalubrious inns I was walking past. Assuming she had arrived at all.

She could always have come to Marseilles, and left again. It had been so many months since our parting. How could she know I was not dead? There would have been no trace of me to be found and I had not intimated in any way that I intended to survive. Had Octavian's agents discovered my sandals on the beach? Had they relayed the news to Octavian? And if they had, would it have filtered throughout Rome? I doubted it. I had become too insignificant. The more I searched without success, the more I realised that as far as Whisper was concerned, her former lover Marcus Rutilius Crispus was dead.

It nearly broke me to consider that she may have taken up with another man. This was entirely possible. In fact it was likely. She was so beautiful, despite the hideous scarring of her back. Had I been in her position then I would have sought the security of a marriage. Being a woman she would not have been able to survive in the same way that I had.

I had arrived in Marseilles with nothing, save the filthy tunic I was wearing. Within days, I learned that Marseilles was the kind of place where you needed to have a knife at the ready at all times. I swiftly acquired one for myself from between the shoulders of a murdered man. It never left my belt, asleep or awake. With this, I was able to ensure that I stayed fed and watered.

In the bustle of the marketplace I became adept at stealing. My biggest problem was my foul odour. Passers-by gave me a wide berth, and kept themselves out of the range of my light fingers. There were no fountains in Marseilles, unlike Rome. In fact there was barely any clean water at all, something I later pointed out to Agrippa. Now there stands a mighty aqueduct, the like of which has never been seen before in Gaul; it carries his name.

It was in that market place, that my fortune changed. That boiling, stinking, sweltering market sapped my strength so I lurked on the corner of the square, sprawled across a paving stone. I sat near the stalls where traders were selling jewellery and finery for women. A voice carried above the hubbub of the merchants.

'Make way. Make way for Gnaeus Scribonius Labeo. You there make way.'

I did not move. I was too stunned. Had I heard that name correctly? I was interrupted from my stupor by a firm kick.

'Get out of the way, pleb.'

Weak as I was, it took me a while to recover from the blow. But once I did, I shuffled aside.

When I could see Scribonius properly, I realised, to my astonishment, it was indeed him. He looked very different from the last time I set eyes on him. But that was understandable. The last time I had seen him, he had just been found guilty of treacherous comments against Octavian.

He was pale as death then, with his dirty clothes, unshaven face and bloodshot eyes. Now the ruddy hue and fat jowl I had seen at the dinner party where he said those critical words were restored. And more. Clearly the red mullet of Marseilles were agreeing with him. Exile had not been such a terrible punishment after all.

I bowed my head in case he should see me and recognise me. Enjoying his exile or not, he would surely not take too kindly to meeting me again.

But he did not see me, he was too busy fondling the woman who walked beside him. I could see his hand draped over her shoulder, squeezing at her breast.

He was still the lecherous man I had chosen to inform against at his dinner party.

His hand dropped off her shoulder as he approached a market stall, and dropped to her bottom, squeezing her buttocks through her long, luxurious looking dress.

It was so long since I had laid eyes on a woman, or witnessed anything sexual, that I could not help remembering Whisper.

She had long, wavy dark hair, just like the woman Scribonius was pawing all over. She had a beautiful figure, just like the woman I could see. A goddess in human form.

I was about to turn to shuffle down an alley out of the way, when the woman turned and I saw her face.

I could not believe my eyes.

There was make up. There was jewellery; pearls and emeralds. There was an unhappy expression I did not recognise, but the woman, the woman I did know. My mission had been achieved. My prayers answered. Not ten metres away stood the woman I had longed to see for all those months.

It was Whisper.

'Come Flavia,' Scribonius ordered. 'I haven't got all day.'

I resisted the urge to cry out, though I wanted nothing more than to speak to her again.

But that was not the moment. Instead, I stalked them for the day, until I followed them up the hill to a vast villa.

Had I not been so focused on meeting Whisper, I might have been enraged by the indolent luxury Scribonius was enjoying. The villa was far grander than his previous home in Rome. And, unfortunately, it was well attended at the front doors.

But, whatever happened, I was going to get inside that villa. I had stormed Cleopatra's Mausoleum. Scribonius' walls certainly were not going to stop me.

That night is so vivid in my memory. I arrived at the villa close to the middle of the night. I had hidden myself in a cloak, and tucked the knife into my belt, just in case.

It was short work to climb the garden wall. I made my way through the colonnade, slipping between the columns to avoid the night guards' looks. But they were not really on the lookout. There was not much trouble this far up the hill from the city. The fighting and robberies were all near the docks.

I searched the corridors and rooms for Whisper. At that time, I had not realised that she was more than a slave to Scribonius. Perhaps I should have known from her dress. But I searched the slaves' quarters first. I felt sure I would recognise her scent. To my disappointment, none of the snoring, thin and bedraggled bodies I saw sleeping was her.

A dreadful thought struck me. Was she sharing Scribonius' bed? I felt my face flush with anger.

It's not her fault, I reminded myself. She had to do whatever it took to survive.

I skulked into a few more rooms, before conceding defeat. What was I to do? Daylight was coming all too quickly.

I decided to hide within the villa. I found what looked like a lady's dressing room and hid myself in there.

I stared at the door and the window for what felt like hours. I was sure I could stay alert and awake. I felt as alive as when I had stood on the decks of my ship *Triton*, moments before the battle of Actium. But, perhaps the months of starvation had weakened me. I fell asleep.

I was woken with a start by the noise of shouting. It was that bloated bastard Scribonius.

'You will do what I say,' he bawled. I heard what sounded like a slap, and a woman moan.

'Get down and take it,' Scribonius growled. 'Why do you think you get a choice?'

The voices were coming from the room next to mine.

I listened in horror as I heard Scribonius strike Whisper, push his flabby body onto her, and thrust himself into her.

'Moan you bitch,' he snarled. Whisper responded. The

thrusting grew faster, till at last, Scribonius groaned in climax.

My hand gripped the handle of my knife as tight as I could. I wanted to storm the room. I wanted to cut off his wilting penis. I wanted to stab out his eyes. I wanted to slice off his tongue. I wanted to rescue my Whisper.

But I could not. She had suffered this for many weeks. One more morning would not change anything. I had to think of a way to make my presence in Marseilles known to her. Then we could run away.

Suddenly, the door of their bedroom opened and shut, then the door to the room I was hiding in swung open.

It was Whisper. In the dark, she did not see me lurking in the corner of the room, beside a statue. I could see that she was naked. She slumped onto a chair, and began to sob uncontrollably.

It was more than I could bear.

Swift as an assassin, I stepped across the room, and clamped my hand over her mouth, to muffle her scream.

'It's me, Whisper, it's me,' I hissed into her ear.

Her scream, subdued by my hand, stopped as suddenly as it had begun. Whisper's eyes widened.

I held my finger to my lips. 'Sssshhh,' I said, and slowly released my hand from her mouth. I ran it down her naked back, tracing the scars I knew so well. She had those scars because of me, because of her sacrifice to me, to give evidence on my behalf. And because she loved me, she had done it. Those scars were my conscience. I owed this woman my life.

'Rutilius?' she asked.

And I wept.

I wept because I heard my name. I wept because I heard Whisper's voice. I wept because of all the things I had suffered since I last saw her.

I wept because of all the things she had suffered since she

last saw me. I wept, tears of joy. It felt as if our troubles were over.

But they were not over.

I was standing in another man's house, with a naked woman, as he slept off his sex in the bedroom next door. Meanwhile the sun was rising. Soon the household slaves would set about their daily chores. I would be discovered.

'Come with me,' I said.

'I can't,' Whisper replied. 'He'll want me again in a moment.'

'Come on,' I demanded. 'It's time to run away.'

She shook her head. 'No Rutilius. Not now, not yet.'

I held Whisper's face. As the room grew lighter, I could see marks on her cheek, and her neck.

'Does he beat you?'

Whisper bit her lip. 'He's been good to me,' she replied. 'I came here, just as you told me. But I didn't have enough money to survive. Scribonius took me into his household.'

'Does he know who you are? What you did to him?'

Whisper nodded.

'And he still took you in?'

Whisper nodded. Then she said words which wounded me. I can still feel the pain.

'He married me,' she said.

'He what?' I replied, aghast.

'He married me. He said he would provide me everything I wanted,' she looked down at the mosaic floor, 'so long as I gave him everything he wanted. Whenever he wanted.'

'And do you?' I asked, fury consuming me.

There was a long silence.

'I try not to,' she said. Tears began to fall down her cheeks. 'But what can I do?'

I paced around the room, clenching and releasing the handle of my knife.

'I could kill him?' I said.

She shook her head.

'Don't be rash Rutilius. We need to plan.'

I almost smiled.

'By the gods it's good to hear my name. To hear your voice.'

Whisper leapt up from her chair and flung herself into me. We embraced, clinging to each other as if the waves were sinking our ship.

Our clasp was interrupted by noises from next door. Scribonius was stirring. It sounded like he was getting out of the bed.

'I must go back,' she said. 'You need to go. Meet me at the temple of Apollo.'

'When?'

'Later today. I'll find a way.' She kissed me on the lips and slipped out of the room.

I stood in shock for a moment.

'What are you doing getting up? I'm not finished yet. Get back on the bed,' she said.

'That's more like it,' Scribonius replied.

I clenched my fists in frustration, raised my hood over my face and slipped out of the house, unnoticed.

At the summit of the rocky spur which overlooked the bay, standing on the ridge stood the elegant Greek temple of Apollo.

As I approached, I had to admire the temple, comparing it as was only natural, with my temple back in Rome to the goddess Fides. There were six vast columns of white porous stone, rough to the touch. However, the frieze was carved out of a fine marble. The detail of the relief was fading, though I could certainly make out centaurs. The paint looked as if it could do with refreshing. It was clearly ancient.

I made my way into the building. There were three porches. But only one that really mattered, the one furthest from the entrance. There the cult statue would stand. Apollo. In this temple Apollo was cast in bronze, standing naked with his arms held forward. Detailed ringlets of long hair hung on either side of his face. The statue was a marvel. A new style. I envied the body which confronted me, my own weakening with age.

Apollo is the god of many things: light, truth and music. He is also the god of healing. I prayed to him; for healing of my body, for healing of Whisper's and for healing of her spirit, which Scribonius had so harmed.

But Apollo, a bit like me, has two sides to his character. As he heals with one hand, with the other he brings plague and sickness. You can imagine that I prayed to him for Scribonius to suffer.

It was nearly midday when I heard footsteps arriving. It was Whisper. I ran to her and pulled her to my body. We kissed, passionately.

'I thought you were dead,' Whisper said, plying my face with kisses, squeezing my body as if to check it was really there in front of her.

'So did I,' I replied.

'You told me you were going to die,' she said, anger in her tone.

'I know,' I said, feeling guilty. 'I thought I was going to. I was supposed to. Those were Octavian's orders.'

'You sent me away,' she said, clenching her slender hands and beating them into my chest.

At last, she grew weary, and collapsed into my arms again.

'You're so thin,' she said, feeling my bones through my tunic. 'And look at this beard,' she said, tugging at my matted, dirty hair. She sniffed.

'You need a bath Rutilius.'

I felt ashamed. I told her about my months stranded at sea. About my recovery. She listened intently.

'What about you?' I asked. 'You made it to Marseilles,' I said.

'Yes, but with no money, and suspicious eyes looking at my scars. Everyone thought I was a runaway slave. Life was difficult. I needed a man. But the men in Marseilles, well, they are not noble.'

I pictured the men I had seen in the port. Whisper was right. They were not noble.

'So when I saw Scribonius, I decided I had to approach him.'

I shook my head. 'How could you attach yourself to such a man?' I asked.

'I thought he wasn't that bad a man,' said Whisper. 'You had him prosecuted for treacherous comments when he was drunk. And I knew you actually agreed with his treachery anyway. You hated Octavian as much as Scribonius. If not more so.'

'Yes, but he was a coward,' I retorted.

Whisper touched my face in her hand. 'But a coward isn't dangerous. I needed security. You'd told me he was a man with a keen eye for ladies, so I thought it was worth taking a chance.'

'And was it?'

'At first yes. Scribonius treated me very well. He plied me with gifts and his touch was tender.'

'What did he do when he found out?'

'It was the scars that gave me away. I had to tell him everything.'

'Everything? You gave him my name.'

Whisper nodded.

For a moment I was angry, but then I realised that it did not matter. Rutilius was dead.

'After we were married, he changed.' Whisper said.

'He slept with other women?'

'Oh he always did that. No, he became violent. I didn't seem to please him any more. But he won't leave me alone either. I hoped that he would just leave me be in the house. It was still a far better life than when I was a slave girl and it would keep me safe from the men in the harbour.'

'But he didn't,' I replied, 'leave you alone I mean.'

Whisper's eyes looked to the ceiling as she recalled the constant beatings. She shook her head and wiped away a tear.

'No child at least,' I said, thinking aloud.

'What are we going to do?' Whisper asked.

I drew her close.

'We're going to go back to Rome,' I replied.

'To Rome? But isn't it dangerous?'

'How so? Rutilius is dead. The man standing before you now, is Sextus.'

'Sextus,' Whisper repeated. 'Sextus, but wasn't that the name—'

'Of my comrade at Actium. Yes.'

Whisper looked. 'Sextus is a good name,' she said.

'Better than Flavia at least,' I replied.

'That was the name Scribonius gave me. I had kept the name Whisper.'

'Well, Whisper is the name you will return to. We will return to Rome. The money is still in the temple there. We can start a new life. But first, I will kill Scribonius.'

'Kill him? But can't we just escape?' she asked, fear echoing in the temple chamber.

I shook my head. 'Not a chance. I heard what he did to you. He must pay. By the gods he must pay.' I turned and looked again at the bronze statue of Apollo. 'I swear, by Apollo, that I will punish Scribonius. He will pay with his life.'

'But how will you do it?'

'Leave that to me,' I said. She looked at me searchingly, as if considering whether I was up to the task. She embraced me again.

'You should go,' I said at last, 'or he will be suspicious.'

Then Whisper did something I will never forget. Something I had longed for. Something I had treasured in my months of destitution. She traced once again the battle scar on my cheekbone with the tip of her finger, my permanent reminder of Actium's wake. She took my head in her hands, as she had done once before, and kissed me on the forehead.

But this time, what she said brought me even more pleasure.

'I love you.'

I closed my eyes. And when I opened them again. She was gone. I looked one last time at the statue of Apollo behind me, then set off back to the market place, to steal some food and construct a plan of attack.

I have killed many men in battle. I have killed men in the street, in the heat of the fray. I had killed the men who were attacking Whisper in the street on the night that I met her. But I have never killed in cold blood.

The closest I had come to that was when I had the arrow drawn in my bow, aiming for Octavian's head. But even then, with all the hatred I had for that man coursing through me, I could not bring myself to release the arrow.

In truth, I feel guilty when I kill. Very un-Roman. Even when I killed the deer to survive or when I struck the fish, when they flapped and flailed on my hook.

I could have killed Scribonius when I heard what he was doing to Whisper. Then it would have been different. I could have killed him right where he was. But now, if I encountered him in the street? If I met him in the baths, or the theatre? Could I kill him then?

As I tore at the loaf of bread I had just acquired, I tried to think of a way to put myself in the state of mind to kill him. I concluded that I would have to do it in the dark, however much I wanted to see the look on his face.

'I bet Apollo does his dirty work in the dark,' I mused.

I felt oppressed, tortured even, by my plan. But what added to my pain all the more, was the need to do it quickly. Every day I delayed, Scribonius would harm Whisper. Every night I waited, he would sleep with her, beat her, scar her. And with each rape, there was a greater chance she could carry his child. And that I could not bear.

'I will do it tonight.'

And so that night, at about the same time as the previous night, I was scrambling over the wall into Scribonius' garden, intent on murder.

I slipped past the statues and the fountain, and wove my way through the columns into the house. I made for the room I had been in before. There I would lie in wait, until the right moment came.

I suspected it would be first thing in the morning, when he tried to take Whisper. If I could catch him, in media res, there would be far more chance of me sticking him with my knife.

Just as I had done the night before, I failed to stay awake. With the whole villa silent, I fell into a deep sleep.

I was roused by shouting and screaming.

It was Scribonius and Whisper once again.

I grabbed for my knife. But it was not there. I felt all over my belt, my tunic, in disbelief. But the knife was gone.

Where was it? It was always there. I could not believe that now, at the moment I needed it above all else, I could not lay hands on it.

'You little bitch,' I heard Scribonius shout.

I'll do it with my bare hands, I concluded, and I ran to

the door.

'Come here, you whore,' Scribonius bellowed.

Whisper screamed.

'I'll teach you a lesson you'll never forget.'

'You won't!' she cried.

I burst through the door to their bedroom, just as Whisper plunged the knife into Scribonius chest.

A stunned expression emerged from his face. He looked down at the knife wedged deep into him, blood leaking down his naked body. His erect penis, swiftly lost its strength, just as he slumped to his knees.

Whisper suddenly grabbed the knife and twisted it hard.

Agony spread over Scribonius' contorted flabby face.

'To Hades you go, you evil bastard,' She spat on his face.

He tried to speak. But could not. He slumped, face down to the floor, pressing the knife still further into his body.

'*You* took my knife,' I said, awestruck by the temerity of the woman.

'You're no killer,' replied Whisper over her shoulder. 'I knew I had to do it.'

I walked up to Whisper and clutched her shoulder.

'I would have done it. I was here, to do it,' I said, 'even without my knife.'

Whisper grabbed my hand with hers.

'I know,' she replied. 'But it's done now. And your hands are still clean. Your conscience is clear. Mine,' she paused. 'Mine is already burdened.'

I looked with delight at the corpse of Scribonius.

'Come, collect your belongings.' I nudged Whisper out of her trancelike state. 'We must go. At once.'

III

After safe passage on one of the many wine ships bound for Rome, we disembarked.

As we approached the outskirts of Rome from the west, we arrived at the low-lying Plains of Mars. It was here that I had gathered with the troops, preparing to enter the city in triumph. Now I arrived as a traveller, a foreigner in my own home.

I took in the sights. I felt sure more tall blocks of tenements now crowded the plains. The stone theatre of Pompey, where Caesar had been murdered still stood, vast and imposing. The enclosures Julius Caesar had started to build for the elections looked as if, now, they were complete.

As we walked along the Via Flaminia, travelling the last miles of our odyssey to Rome, I could see in the distance, the Circus Flaminius, the chariot racing track. Many a *denarius* I had lost at the races. But to the far north was a building I did not recognise. It was surrounded by a large park with trees and grassland. My eyes were drawn to the building. Immense circles dominating the horizon, even though, from the distance we were at, it looked incomplete.

Then I remembered.

'That must be his Mausoleum,' I said.

'Whose Mausoleum?' Whisper asked.

'Octavian's. He started it after Actium. By the gods...it's enormous.'

And it truly was, far bigger than any tomb I had seen before. The honorary tombs of former consuls Hirtius and Pansa were on the Plains of Mars. But they were as nothing compared to this.

'That must be nearly forty metres tall,' I said in amazement. 'It's incredible.'

'It certainly is impressive,' Whisper agreed.

'How big will the statue have to be?' I wondered. 'It will have to be colossal.'

'The statue?' Whisper queried.

'He will be putting a statue of himself on top of that conical roof,' I replied, 'just to make sure that everyone knows who's got all the power.'

'I see,' she replied. She looked again at the vast monument which seemed to dwarf even the river Tiber. 'Effective,' she concluded.

I tried to contain my anger.

Seeing Octavian's Mausoleum made me decide where I wanted to go next. To my wife Olivia's grave.

FRIENDS, I HAVE NOT MUCH TO SAY. STOP AND READ IT.
THIS IS THE GRAVE – NOT BEAUTIFUL BUT OF A BEAUTIFUL WOMAN.
HER PARENTS NAMED HER OLIVIA.
SHE LOVED HER HUSBAND FROM HER HEART.
HER SPEECH WAS CHARMING, HER CONDUCT FITTING.
SHE KEPT HOUSE.
SHE SPUN WOOL.
I'VE FINISHED. GO NOW.

That was the inscription on her grave. My Greek architect Argoutis had put it up to her, just before my exile. I had stood beside it, holding my dagger, SPQR inscribed on the handle, and told her I was joining her sooner than I expected.

'I'm sorry,' I said. Sorry for not joining her, sorry for all that I had done, sorry for causing her death. 'I won't be joining you.' I wept. 'Not now, at least. Not yet.'

Whisper clasped my hand.

'You know she forgives you,' she said softly. 'She loved you.'

When the tears subsided, I noticed another gravestone beside Olivia's. When I read the inscription I stared in disbelief. This was the strangest sensation of my entire life. The gravestone in front of me, was mine.

Who had put this up? It had only become a recent fashion to inscribe tombstones. Olivia had deserved the very best. I, on the other hand, did not.

The inscription was very simple.

IN THE HANDS OF THE GODS.
MARCUS RUTILIUS CRISPUS.
A LOYAL MAN.

'How peculiar,' Whisper exclaimed. 'You're dead, Rutilius. You're actually dead.'

'It would appear I am,' I garbled.

We stared again in silence.

'Well, I can tell you one thing,' I said at last. 'Death doesn't feel as bad as I thought it would!'

We had returned to Rome in the searing heat of August. It was nearly two years to the day that I had trodden the triumphal route into the Capitol as part of Octavian's triple triumph.

Now, Rome's face had changed almost as much as mine in the short time we had been away.

Octavian had made his mark.

When we arrived in the Roman Forum, home at last in the heart of my city, Octavian was not there. He was away, campaigning in Spain. Had been for some months.

But it did not feel like he was absent. Not in the least.

'Look,' I said, shaking my head. 'He's everywhere.'

All I could see reminded me of the man I hated above all others. On the east side of the main square stood the temple of Divine Julius, with its altar beside it and the veiled statue of Caesar inside.

'Caesar has much to answer for,' I muttered.

'Why's that?' Whisper asked.

'It was his will which adopted Octavian in the first place. If he had not written that line, that one sentence, who knows? Maybe Rome would have been a Republic once again.'

'Or Antony would have been king in Octavian's place,' Whisper countered.

'Perhaps,' I mused. 'Perhaps you're right. The Republic was doomed. It certainly is now. Just look.'

Mark Antony had worked with Octavian to choose the site of that temple to Divine Julius. That was in happier times between the two of them, before they inevitably fell out and embroiled us all in their civil war; war, as a senator, I had to fight.

The temple stood where Julius Caesar's body had been burned during the funeral on the same spot Antony had delivered the eulogy. There he showed the people Caesar's torn and bloodstained toga. Now, it was complete, adorned with prows I recognised. They were prows recovered from Antony's defeated ships at Actium, ships my *Triton* had faced.

To the north-west towered the new Senate House, the Curia Julia, site of my demise as senator. That building with its perfect acoustic chamber could affect me no longer.

'That was the beginning of the end,' I said to Whisper. 'Right there, in that chamber. That's where I lost my rank. In front of all the other senators. The cowards.'

I had been stripped of my rank during a census by that sly, ruthless Octavian. Shaming me so was his vengeance for failing to keep Cleopatra alive. Octavian had never forgiven me for letting her commit suicide under my guard.

Do not misunderstand. I did not permit it. She deceived

me, smuggling a poisonous asp into her chamber in a basket of figs.

That deception cost me dear. At the time it cost me Octavian's favour. He passed me over for the governorship of Egypt for that trumped up knight Gallus. How I wish that had been the only punishment. But that oversight carried a far greater price. My home, my rank and, ultimately, my life. All at the hands of Octavian.

It was Octavian who burned my house down, leaving me short of the wealth required to be a senator. It was Octavian who stripped me of my rank in the senate house. It was Octavian who ordered me to die.

Even though I was consumed with anger at Octavian, I still could not resist venturing inside the senate house. We marched up to the porch, glancing at the statues of Victory on the roof gables. On the front pediment, she carried a wreath in her right hand and raced over a globe, marking Rome's world domination.

Inside, it was just as I remembered. At the far end of the chamber, there was the low platform, the elaborate altar to Victory, almost entirely shrouded in burning incense. To one side the beautiful golden statue of winged Victory stood, brought from Tarentum on the southern coast, which Octavian installed and presented before my very eyes. In her hands were weapons from our Egyptian conquest.

'I remember when he unveiled this,' I said, walking around the statue. 'I remember how he always used to stand in front of it for his speeches.'

I pictured Octavian standing before that statue, announcing his planned census, the census that cost me my rank.

I stared with hatred at Victory, the goddess Rome now revered above all others.

'The folds of her dress seem so real,' Whisper said, with admiration, 'and the feathers, they look as if her wings could beat.'

I had to confess that the statue was magnificent, with far greater craft than the statue of Apollo I had left behind in Marseilles. But I resented her presence.

The senate house still gleamed with treasures from Egypt. Statuary and plate, cinnamon and spices whose names I did not know. I felt sure that some of the precious objects I had seen piled up in Cleopatra's half-built Mausoleum, now decorated Rome's new seat of government. I spotted a silver jug and two chalices.

'If I didn't know better,' I said, 'I'd think they were the same jug and chalices I saw lying beside Antony's body in Cleopatra's Mausoleum.'

I was about to inspect them more closely when my attention was caught by something unfamiliar, something I had not seen before. A golden shield. I walked to examine it. An inscription was engraved into the boss. It read *virtue, piety, clemency and justice.*

Surely this was not in honour of Octavian? What virtue had he other than cunning? What piety had he shown to the gods, usurping them with Victory and statues to his adoptive father, Julius Caesar, a mere mortal?

What clemency had he shown me, a man who had proven his loyalty? What justice had he meted out?

I confess, it was difficult standing inside that chamber, difficult to accept the new Rome, difficult to accept my new life.

Once, I had been important. I had had a role. I had been a senator. I had been a good man. A Rutilian. Now I stood, an onlooker, a bystander, like the foreigners standing beside me. A man with the humble name of Sextus. All because of Octavian.

I had had enough. I turned to Whisper. 'Let's go.'

We emerged into the daylight and were immediately confronted by Octavian once more. He was everywhere. By the speaker's platform stood the gilded statue of my enemy mounted on a horse. Unlike most equestrian statues, he was not in military dress. No, not for Octavian. He had to be different, even back then. His chest was naked, sculpted to show far more strength than that weakling has ever had.

'I should have seen this coming,' I muttered. 'After all, he was only nineteen when he was voted the statue.'

Now he was in his thirties. No wonder the whole Forum reeked of him.

'Look at that,' I pointed to the middle of the Forum.

A gilded column with ships' beaks protruding was topped by a golden statue of Octavian leaning on his spear and clutching a long dagger.

I stared up at the statue.

'It's a crime,' I complained to Whisper. 'The Senate voted it to Octavian. I was there. I didn't vote for it I can tell you. Do you know why they gave it to him?'

Whisper looked at the ships' prows sticking out of the central column.

'A naval victory?'

'Precisely,' I replied. 'They voted it to honour his defeat of Sextus Pompey. Pompey was beaten at long last, at long, long last at Naulochus.'

'I see,' she replied, looking slightly confused, 'so, he earned it...'

'No he did not,' I snapped. 'Pompey was defeated. But not by Octavian.

It was Agrippa. The most loyal man I know. I'll never understand why he always allows Octavian to have the glory.'

I shook my head. For the first time since setting foot back in Rome, my thoughts turned to Agrippa.

He had been a dear friend, even if, in the end, he had

been involved in my demise.

Agrippa had agonised over whether he should hand over the wax tablet with Whisper's inscriptions that would give me away. But he knew his duty. And the tablet passed to Octavian's hands. Yet I do not bear Agrippa ill will. It was the right thing to do. And he had always done right by me.

'Agrippa is a better man than Octavian,' I said, 'always has been. But whose face is it which litters the Forum?'

As if the monument to Naulochus was not affront enough, now, beside that column, four more bronze columns with ships' prows stood. More remnants of Actium. Would I ever escape that place? Would I ever escape those memories?

It would seem not. Even when I looked away to the temple of Saturn, I was greeted by Tritons blowing their horns in the pediment. Those marine creatures were supposed to have helped us win at Actium. I never saw them. It was Agrippa's grappling hooks and our flaming arrows which did the damage. And it was an arrow which had done for Sextus, my friend.

I had seen enough. Already I regretted returning to Rome. All I could think of was how much I hated Octavian, and how much I wanted him dead.

Whisper had stood by my side, listening with patience to my complaints as we took in the sights of Rome. She gently squeezed my hand.

'It's time to head to the temple of Fides,' I said, 'time to get some money.'

In comparison to the extravagant and opulent temples in the Forum, my temple of Fides seemed small and insignificant, but it was beautiful.

When I set eyes on it, I felt a surge of emotion. I had sworn an oath to Fides that I would build her a temple. And there it stood. My oath had been fulfilled in my absence.

Who by? Well, I had started it. I had bought that

garrulous Greek slave Argoutis for his skills as an architect. I had approved his plans and started the build. And I had done everything I could despite my money troubles to see the job through. But when I left Rome to die, the temple remained a building site, abandoned, agonisingly close to completion. In my absence, however, someone had clearly taken on the project and seen it through so handsomely. And that someone was Marcus Vipsanius Agrippa. Who else?

On the day that I was revealed as "The Mouth of Octavian" and ordered to die, my last words to Agrippa, as we stood in Octavian's 'little workshop', were for him to complete my temple to Fides.

He had done as I asked, loyal even to my memory. Perhaps he admired Fides, the goddess of loyalty, as much as I do. Whatever his reasons for fulfilling the request of a condemned man, all I can say is that no better man could have fulfilled my oath to Fides than Agrippa.

For all the admiration and pleasure I had at the sight of my completed temple, it was what lay inside the chamber which interested me the most. Not the silver statue of Fides, modelled on my love Whisper, but the secret chamber which Argoutis had devised with all his Greek cunning. It lay under the altar. And inside that chamber lay the wealth I had acquired as a *delator*, an informant. I am still not proud of that deed, of what I did to Gnaeus Scribonius Labeo. I had targeted him for ruin because I perceived him to be a coward. But the manner in which I brought him down, and the consequences for dear Whisper, trouble my spirit.

On the other hand, it was so exciting, thrilling even. And, though I say so myself, cunning.

As time has passed, I can console myself that Scribonius turned out to be worse a man than I thought, not only a coward for avoiding the war, but arrogant, violent and a rapist of Whisper. Rome, whether a Republic or kingdom, should have no place for men like that.

But what *I* did to Whisper. That was unforgivable.

Though she has forgiven me, I cannot.

The collection of teethed wheels and ropes which worked the entrance to the secret chamber was disguised amid flamboyant drapery.

But the ropes, concealed in folds of cloth, still dangled, awaiting knowing hands to pull them.

Would the treasure still be there? Would Argoutis not have looked in the chamber? He had built it, and must have been curious to look inside once I left him a freedman. And Agrippa. He had overseen the temple's completion. Would he not have discovered the temple's secret?

I heard the familiar grind of the floor moving to reveal the dark hole which formed the entrance to the chamber. Inside that darkness lay the key to my future. My prize for the conviction of Scribonius was a percentage of his estate. The Praetor, who judged the case, had only given me a fragment of my reward in spendable silver coins. Those I had swiftly drained. The rest I was given in expensive drapery, cups, plate and fine figurines. It was a clever act by the Praetor. He had not approved of "The Mouth of Octavian". But he never found out who was behind the mask. By giving me the reward in such items, he knew it would be difficult to enjoy the reward without revealing my identity, either by displaying Scribonius' wares in my home, or by trying to sell them.

Now, though, nearly two years later, if those ill-gotten gains were still there, I could re-build a life. I could establish myself once again in Rome.

But if the boxes lay empty, I remained nothing.

Whisper caught my eye before we made our way down the Carrara marble steps, descending into the shadow.

'Don't be afraid,' she said. Her eyes gleamed with the flame of her torch. 'We have nothing now. If we have nothing when we leave this chamber, what have we lost?'

My shoulders relaxed. Even if the treasure had gone, Whisper would come up with a plan. She always did.

We made our way slowly, steadily down into the chamber.

I lowered my torch to cast light on the boxes. They were still there. But were they full?

I closed my eyes, said a short prayer to all the gods and goddesses of Rome, and opened the first box.

Figurines.

I clenched my fist in delight. Then reached into the box and picked up a small bronze figure of Neptune. In his left hand, he held a fish, in his right he held a trident. It was an ancient Etruscan piece, without a doubt.

I kissed Neptune and thanked him for preserving me on the sea for all those agonising days. I clutched onto that figurine. This would become an item I would treasure, not only because of Neptune's protection, but because Agrippa, himself Etruscan, was acclaimed as Neptune amongst us, and he was a man I would honour and obey.

While I stood immersed in these thoughts, Whisper, impatient, opened the next box. She peered down inside it.

'Well?' I asked.

She looked back at me. Then smiled. She held up a silver cup.

The next box was also full. Drapery. And the next and the next. To my relief, every single box was full, except the one I had originally emptied of the silver coins.

With each box, we let out an exclamation of delight.

When all the boxes were checked, I rushed over to Whisper and embraced her. We kissed. Kissing led on to more, and under the altar of Fides, we had one of the most memorable love makings of my life. I was alive again. I was a man.

That evening we made our way to an inn. Ordinarily, if visiting Rome, you would arrange a stay with a friend. But I was dead, had been for two years, and, more importantly, I was supposed to be. So I could not just go marching to Agrippa's house and declare myself.

Sextus had no friends, and so we made our way to an inn, dirty and unpleasant though the experience was. As I sat down on a rickety wooden stool and balanced my watered down cheap wine in its grubby drinking cup of horn on the rotting wobbly wooden table, the fine glass cups, Campanian wine, mosaic floors and cushioned couches of my late friend Balbus' dinner parties seemed a lifetime ago.

In a funny way, I suppose it was.

There were some similarities. There were paintings on the walls of the inn, just like in the villa. Well, graffiti really. And the graffiti was a pretty simplistic representation of what additional services were on offer. It was an extensive range from the look of it. I could not help myself letting my imagination place Whisper and me in some of the activities set out before me.

There were also dwarves in this inn. I recalled the dwarves Balbus had such delight in presenting to me at our last dinner party together. The heroes Ajax, Achilles and Agamemnon if I remember rightly. They were presented to provide pleasure, a source of mockery. But that was a different kind of pleasure. Here the dwarves were also a speciality. At a premium price. To say it was a different atmosphere is an understatement.

I ordered two bowls of unspecified meat stew. Judging by the bits and pieces hung from pegs above the innkeeper's bar, it was best not to ask. But after so many months with virtually no food at all, I was grateful.

'What's your name?' asked the innkeeper.

'Sextus,' I pointed to the table. 'We're sat over there.'

'It don't matter where you're sat, Sextus,' he replied. 'You can take your own food over.'

He pushed the two bowls over to me.

He began ladling the stew into the bowls.

I rolled the coins I had ready to pay for the meal over the back of my hand.

Octavian's head caught my eye on an *as*. I tightened my lips. That man was everywhere I looked.

Then another image caught my eye on a bronze *dupondius*. It was Neptune crossing my path for the second time that day. I flipped the coin and saw a familiar portrait. Agrippa.

There he was, wearing a naval crown. In case you failed to recognise that nose, that chin, that frown I knew so well, his name was clearly written around the edge, declaring his third consulship.

The innkeeper pushed the bowls across the counter and stared expectantly at me. But I was still staring at the coin. If Agrippa was consul for the third time, that meant he had to have been consul the year I was away from Rome too. Back to back consulships. He had done well for a man of no background.

'I haven't got all day,' growled the innkeeper.

I paid up.

'You're not from Rome are you?' he asked.

I hesitated, considering my answer.

'No,' I concluded. 'Why?'

''Cos if you were, you wouldn't leave a pretty little lady like that unattended.'

I turned in horror to see two large men in raggy garments pressing themselves over Whisper's table.

It was the first time I had felt the rage which used to consume me in battle. I was ready to kill.

I grabbed the bowls and paced across the room.

'Move on lads,' I said, curtly.

They stared at me.

'You all right?' I checked on Whisper.

She nodded, but looked pale.

I placed the bowls on the table before standing up to the men and flicking my head to send them on their way.

They stared at me with malicious eyes then fixed Whisper with one last lecherous look before they made their way slowly back to the counter.

I scratched my cheek irritably with my finger, feeling my blood lust recede. I was feeling too old for a brawl. It had been a while since my soldiering. But the knife from Marseilles was with me, beside the figurine of Neptune. And if I needed to, I would use it. Without hesitation.

'It looks delicious,' said Whisper, revealing her sarcasm with a frown.

I settled myself on the splintering stool and took up my spoon. We fell silent as we both ate the food. When the bowls were scraped empty, I put the *dupondius* onto the table and slid it across.

'Look,' I said.

'What is it?' she asked. She picked the coin up. 'Oh, it's Agrippa.

Haven't they captured his likeness?'

'Yes,' I replied. 'But look...it says he's consul for the third time.'

'Consul!' she exclaimed. 'Good for him.' She hesitated. 'But hadn't he been consul before?'

'Yes, but this says consul for a third time,' I pointed at the inscription on the coin. 'See? That means he must have been consul last year as well. He'd only been consul once before my...' I realised I was speaking too loudly in my excitement, '...before Rutilius died. As you say, he was consul before then, but that was six or seven years ago, and it was only the once. That was when Octavian needed him to defeat Sextus Pompey.'

Whisper looked thoughtful. She turned the coin over and traced the figure of Neptune with her finger. 'Why does this matter?' she asked.

'It matters because Agrippa is a Republican. Deep down. I know it.' I said. 'And if he's still that close to power. It only takes justice to fall on Octavian, and Rome will be in good hands.'

'You want to watch talk like that, son.' I looked sharply to the table beside me. A grizzled man, obviously an ex-soldier, downed the wine from his grimy horn cup. 'Words like that only bring trouble.'

'Legionary?' I asked, shortly.

The man slammed his horn onto the table. He nodded. 'Used to be. My name is Aurelius. I was leading cohort standard bearer of the sixth legion. It was my honour to carry the bull. I fought under Agrippa himself at Perusia, all those years ago.'

'You served under Agrippa?'

'The greatest man I have drawn my sword for.'

'Then you fought for the Republic,' I said.

'I did.' Aurelius dragged himself up from his stool and slumped onto our table. He gazed at Whisper, admiring her, before returning to the conversation. 'Or at least I thought I did. What's your name?'

I nearly said Rutilius.

'Sextus,' I replied.

'Well Sextus, the Republic is not coming back. Rome has changed. Forever. That's why I left the army. It was the proudest thing of my life to carry that standard. But when Octavian became 'Augustus', he brought in a new standard, a metal image of himself. I wasn't carrying that.'

Aurelius' fist clenched and he looked to the floor.

'They made you leave because you refused?' I asked.

Aurelius nodded, sullen. 'Yes,' he replied, 'even though I said I wanted to carry on carrying the bull. I told them to get someone to carry Augustus' image beside me.' His eyes flashed with anger. 'But they didn't see it that way. I was discharged. Apparently I should be grateful I'm still alive and able to retire after refusing such an honour.'

Aurelius delivered the word 'honour' with utter contempt.

'Augustus?' I queried. 'You said when Octavian became Augustus?'

'Augustus is Octavian's new name. "The illustrious one". The Senate voted it to him.'

I shook my head in disbelief. I would never call him Augustus. There had been many about him who called him Caesar when he took up his adoption. The great orator and senator Cicero had made a point of still addressing him as Octavian. If such a tactic was good enough for Cicero, it was more than good enough for me.

'And,' Aurelius continued, pointing his gnarled finger at me, 'if you're relying on Agrippa to bring back the Republic, you're wrong. There's no chance of that.' He waggled his finger. 'Not after he's married Marcella the Elder.'

'Marcella,' I repeated, 'Marcella...where do I know that name?'

'She's Octavia's eldest daughter. Augustus' niece.'

'Ah,' I said, disappointment welling up inside me. Had Octavian's cunning and blandishments conquered even Agrippa? 'But Agrippa was married already,' I said, 'what happened to Attica?'

'She died.'

'Natural causes?' I asked, suspicious of Octavian.

Aurelius shrugged. 'How should I know?'

We sat in silence.

Suddenly I noticed our table was surrounded. The two men who had leered over Whisper had returned to our table. This time they had brought their friends. I looked up at them. They stared straight back at me. They meant trouble.

Thankfully, despite my hardship all those months at sea, the years of military training, strength and speed, had not yet left me. Outnumbered as I was, it was vital I struck the first blow.

So I did. Sticking one with my dagger, I punched the second square in the jaw. I felt hands grabbing at me from behind. Whisper screamed. I kicked out and flailed my elbows. I was taking punches. To my relief Aurelius joined me. There was blood, there was thudding of punches, the crunching of bones and teeth. Then I was free.

'Best you leave,' Aurelius shouted at me.

'But...' I hesitated, At that moment all three of our assailants were on the floor, the fourth was held half upright by Aurelius.

'Go!' he shouted.

Whisper took my hand, and we hurried out of the inn door. As we left, I saw Aurelius turn his attention back to the ruffian held in his hand. I saw Aurelius' other hand clench. 'You cost me a drink,' he growled and knocked him senseless with one hard punch to the face.

I wiped the blade of my dagger clean of blood. A quick glance around me made me conclude that I should keep it at the ready. It was dark, and we were in the streets of Rome, unguarded. Not a good place to be.

'Where are we going to sleep now?' I wondered out loud.

Whisper tugged my arm.

'Why don't we sleep in the temple?'

I smiled. Why had I not thought of that? Of course, the secret chamber was the perfect place to hide.

Dark shadows shifted around us. This was not the time to hesitate. Without another word, we hurried back to the temple of Fides.

Inside the chamber, we made love and slept in each other's arms.

IV

The next days were spent establishing a strange form of home inside the secret chamber. Carefully, we converted goods from Scribonius' chests into money, or into supplies and basic furniture.

The temple of Fides was not frequently visited, so our constant activity around the building went unnoticed.

But once this was achieved, tedium prevailed. I had not survived everything to hide away in a secret chamber till I died in a temple no one visited. The gods had preserved me for a purpose. I just did not know what that purpose was.

One morning, I woke early. I left the sleeping Whisper and sat on the steps of my temple in the Plains of Mars staring back towards the city.

How could I be so close to Rome, and yet feel so distant?

I even had money now, but money had not bought me information.

Then I had a thought. Perhaps money did not need to buy me information. It could tell me for itself.

I sorted through the coins we had gathered since our arrival in Rome. Any coin with Octavian or Agrippa on I lay out to inspect more closely. The first few coins I cast my eyes over told me things I knew, most of all what an unashamed claimer of others' deeds was Octavian. One *denarius* celebrated the defeat of Sextus Pompey, a victory entirely achieved by Agrippa. But it was Octavian who was portrayed as Neptune, sceptre in hand, foot on the world. On another coin he struck the same pose as Zeus in Olympia, the gall of the man.

I passed over the coins which had images of the Curia Julia, the new senate house, scene of my shaming, and home to *that* statue of Victory, and *that* shield. I knew about those developments all too well.

A silver *quinarius* captured my attention because it was so elaborate. Octavian was on one side, declaimed as conqueror. On the other side was the clear message, 'Asia Recovered'. Winged Victory, Octavian's common companion, was there, standing on top of a sacred Dionysiac basket flanked by snakes. It was the baskets which intrigued me. I had seen them on a coin before. But that was released by Antony, Octavian's archenemy. It surprised me Octavian had used the same image.

Antony's coins had been celebrating his marriage to Octavian's sister, Octavia. That was during the time Antony and Octavian had an alliance, before Antony fell into Cleopatra's arms.

Was Octavian, by using the baskets everyone would associate with Antony, mocking his fallen enemy for betraying his marriage? For betraying Octavian's sister? For betraying Octavian?

I pursed my lips. Of course he was. Octavian is a cunning, brutal man. But I have said that before.

Whisper emerged from the temple.

'You should have woken me,' she said, ruffling my thinning hair and kissing my cheek.

I clutched her hand and looked at her. She was beautiful.

'You looked so peaceful in your sleep. I didn't want to wake you,' I replied.

'What are you doing?' she asked, looking at the array of coins on the temple steps, 'counting?'

'No,' I shook my head and glanced down at the coins, 'learning.'

Whisper sat herself beside me and arranged the folds of her dress. She peered over the coins.

'What are you learning?' she asked.

'Well,' I replied, 'Octavian is a shameless thief of glory for one thing. Look.' I picked up the coins I had looked at. 'Here, Octavian is Neptune. And on this one he's bloody Zeus.'

Whisper rolled her eyes. 'He thinks a lot of himself doesn't he.'

I almost laughed. Many words will be written about Octavian, but few will sum the man up so succinctly.

'Yes he does,' I said, 'he certainly does.'

Whisper passed her hands over the coins as she looked for one which interested her.

'What's this one?' she asked, passing me a *dupondius*. 'I've never seen such a thing.'

'That's a crocodile,' I replied. 'Crocodiles are fierce creatures. That must represent our capture of Egypt. Though I can assure you, Egypt may be captured, her crocodiles are not. I'm more frightened of them than any Egyptian I can tell you.'

Whisper laughed. I looked at her. I was in love.

It turned out several coins celebrated Actium. Trophies on ships' prows or images of the column we had seen in the Forum with the beaks.

'Tell me about Actium,' Whisper said.

But I fell silent. I did my best to block the memories of that battle. I shook my head and moved on to another coin.

A *denarius* took me back to a different event. Octavian was standing in a triumphal chariot. Immediately memories flooded back of the moment I had an arrow aimed at his eye.

'You were in that triumph weren't you?' Whisper said.

'I certainly was,' I replied.

That was during Octavian's triple triumph celebrating his victories over Illyria, Actium and Egypt. Some days I regret not loosing that arrow.

Other days I feel quite the opposite. Ultimately, for all

my flaws, I do not think I am able to kill a defenceless man. Looking back it was probably that, as much as my fear of plunging Rome back into civil war, which stayed my hand.

When I turned the coin over, I was immediately thrown back to Actium once more. I could not escape Actium. I can never escape Actium, the scene of my mistake. This coin had the clearest depiction of a warship yet. I could almost see the sea, smell the salty air, hear the splash of the oars. Victory stood on the prow, holding a branch in one hand and a wreath in the other. Octavian had won that day. But, despite being on his side, I had lost.

'Come on,' I said, ill-tempered, 'I'm not learning anything from these.'

I sorted hastily through more coins, trying to escape my past. Somewhere amongst the pile there had to be more recent coins, to tell me what had happened in my absence. That had been my purpose, not to face my own past which I knew all too well, but to learn what I had missed.

Whisper examined a golden *aureus.* A young Octavian wore an oak wreath.

'Does that say he's son of a god?' she asked.

'Probably,' I replied, before examining the inscription. I nodded. 'Yes it does. He's claimed that from the moment Caesar died.'

'I thought men couldn't be gods?'

I snorted in derision. 'Mortals, like Caesar, should not be gods. You're quite right.' I stared into Whisper's captivating eyes. 'And,' I emphasised, 'let's say Caesar was a god, which I'm not saying I think he is, but let's say he was, even Octavian's claim to be his son is weak.'

Whisper frowned. 'What do you mean?' she asked. 'You don't have to claim to be a son. You either are or you aren't?'

I laughed.

'Don't forget adoption,' I said.

'Ah, yes,' Whisper replied, flushing as she felt foolish.

I touched her cheek, resisting the urge to take her back into the temple.

'In this case, the adoption is not straightforward. Normally you do it when everyone's alive. But Octavian only became Caesar's son after Caesar was murdered. The adoption was a clause in Caesar's will. How different life might have been if Antony had chosen not reveal it. But I suppose he didn't think Octavian was a threat. No one did. He was eighteen, just a boy. How things have changed.'

Even now, I am still not certain that such an adoption is legal.

Neither was Octavian, which is why he spent so much time and effort publicising his dutiful sonliness.

That I had learned to live with, though I remember bickering about it frequently with dear old Balbus. What angered me more about the coin was the reminder that Octavian had been consul for a sixth time. In the days of the Republic, a man could only be consul once. Others had breached this, of course they had; Caesar, Pompey, Crassus to name but a few. But even Caesar had only been consul five times. Octavian becoming consul six times revealed just how far from the principles of the Republic Rome had fallen.

On the other side of the coin, Octavian was sitting in his curule chair, the very chair he sat in when he stripped me of my senatorial rank. He held a scroll, just like the one he used to refer to during our confrontations. Seeing him like this, even in such miniature form, brought the horrors of my past rushing back into my present.

'I like this one,' said Whisper, distracting me from my memory.

An eagle with wings outspread gleamed from another golden *aureus*. An oak wreath was held in its talons. I turned it over. What I saw just added to my ire. There was Octavian's portrait once again. Consul for the seventh time, for saving the citizens.

'Saving the citizens?' I exclaimed in disbelief. 'Seven consulships?' I could feel my cheeks flush with the heat of my anger. 'How can this man be so acclaimed? How did anyone believe he was restoring the Republic?

Was the truth not obvious to everybody?'

We sat in awkward silence.

'Didn't you fight for Octavian?' Whisper asked.

I threw the *aureus* to the floor. It bounced and rolled down the temple steps.

'I had to,' I replied mournfully. 'We all had to choose.' I recalled the dread of civil war, the moments when every senator, every family had to choose which side to fight for.

'It was either Octavian or Antony. One or the other.'

'You must have believed him then?'

Admittedly I had put up with Octavian's claims when I made my choice against Antony and Cleopatra. You could say my decision was vindicated when I witnessed them both die in that accursed war. But sitting there, it did not feel like a victory. I fought to restore the Republic. Those coins told me I fought for the right man, that Octavian 'saved the citizens', 'restored the laws and rights of the Roman people' and was the 'recoverer of Asia'. But it was all lies. I hated that man, and the kingship he had clearly forged in all but name.

'Believed?' I shook my head. 'Hoped, maybe.'

Still at a loss as to what we should do, I found myself drawn to Octavian's home on the Palatine. That was the scene of my ultimate demise, in his 'little workshop'. Why I walked there, I do not know. It could serve no purpose, and Octavian was not even there. He was campaigning in Spain. But I had to lay eyes on the place.

Inevitably, as had so many things, the place had changed while I had been away. The approach to Octavian's home was transformed beyond recognition. The site always gave one of the most broad views over the city, but now arrival at Octavian's house felt far grander than before because the temple of Apollo was now complete. It was, we discovered, coming up to the anniversary of its dedication. A ramp connected the temple to Octavian's home, as if Octavian was that connected to the god.

Though I wanted to feel unimpressed, I could not, in all honesty, deny the temple complex was stunning. And I was not alone. The whole place was packed with people, Romans and visitors alike.

Approaching the temple, the first thing to catch the eye was the portico. It was still a work in progress, with slaves and builders wherever we looked, but already it caught the eye. Between the red and yellow columns of Numidian marble, fifty stark black basalt statues of women holding water jars faced fifty horsebacked men. In the middle, a man drew his sword, ready for battle.

'Who are they?' Whisper asked.

'These must be the daughters of Danaus,' I replied. 'Egyptian women who killed their husbands on their wedding night. Those must be the husbands,' I said pointing at the men on horseback. 'And that will be Danaus himself, I said pointing to the man drawing his sword. As punishment, the women were condemned to fulfil an impossible task; to fill a bath with leaking waterjars.'

I spoke before I thought, a habit I would never lose.

Whisper's face paled as she recalled how she had murdered her husband Scribonius.

I tried to gloss over the mistake. 'The point is these women are treacherous Egyptians, just like Cleopatra. And now we make them for our pleasure in Egyptian basalt, stone we own, just as we own Egypt.'

I slapped one of Numidian marble columns. 'Same goes for this. No marble in Italy carries this colour. Octavian's brought this all the way from Egypt, just to show who is master.'

Whisper, with tears in her eyes, mumbled.

'I suppose Cleopatra did for her husband too. In a way.'

'Who, Antony?' I replied. 'Yes, I suppose she did. Things could have been very different. But I've said that before.'

I placed my arm about Whisper.

'None of these women, nor even Cleopatra had as much justification for what you did.' I kissed her head. 'You're not a murderer. Scribonius was an evil man. You had every right to strike.'

Those words were more apt than I knew.

It was a contest as to which sight caught our attention next. The statue of Apollo in front of the temple, or the four horse chariot gleaming on the temple roof, the chariot of the sun.

We shuffled to the statue. Apollo towered above us, standing on a high platform decorated with ship's beaks. His right hand poured an imaginary libation from the offering bowl to an altar beneath. His left hand held a magnificent lyre. The god of harmony, his mouth open in song.

'Rome would be a good deal better if we all had lyres in our hands as often as we held swords,' I said. 'I've not seen too many people killed by a lyre.'

Whisper was staring at the statue's face. I followed her gaze.

'What is it?' I asked.

'Doesn't that look familiar?' she said.

I looked again. Then I saw it. That was a face Whisper would recognise. Because she had painstakingly copied it when she made me a mask. A mask I would wear to become "The Mouth of Octavian".

'They've used his face,' she said, 'I'm certain of it.'

I felt my neck tense with anger. But before I could rant, Whisper had moved on. Four life-like oxen around the altar had caught her attention.

I followed her through the crowd. At the altar, we overheard tourists being regaled with tales, and told that these breathtaking works of art were by Myron. That was a name from the days of my education, long ago. Ancient Greek was all I could tell Whisper with certainty.

'Athenian if I had to commit to an answer. Four or five hundred years old.'

Whisper loved those statues. Her favourite animal, she declared. They were outstanding. There was a reason Myron's name was known by all Roman senators' children.

Finally, we made it to the doors of the temple. I was still seething about the statue of Apollo, but I was distracted by an attack on my senses. The strong scent of incense wafted through the doors as we approached them. They were carved out of African ivory, inlaid with relief sculptures of Apollo's exploits. We shuffled our way towards the entrance, jostling and bumping into the people as they pushed their way in and out.

At last, close enough to see the doors, I could work out that the stories they depicted had been carefully selected. I could almost picture Octavian sitting in his 'little workshop' choosing each and every detail for the greatest effect.

It was working. The visitors gawped at what they saw.

I pointed to the first door. 'Do you see this Whisper?' I said. 'Apollo killing the fourteen Niobids. Vengeance against their mother Niobe.'

'What had Niobe done that was so bad to deserve that?'

I recalled Homer's 'Illiad', so deeply engrained into my memory from school.

'Niobe insulted Apollo's mother, Leto, by boasting about how many children she had had, while Leto had given birth to only two,' I said.

'Is that so bad?' Whisper asked.

'Perhaps not,' I shrugged. 'But one should take care not

to insult the mother of a god and a goddess. In fury, Apollo killed the sons and Artemis killed the daughters.'

'How terrible,' Whisper shook her head. 'So severe,' she said, struggling to keep her feet amongst the people. 'Every mother will love her children the most and believe they are the best.'

When Whisper said 'mother', for the first time I considered how she would be as a mother. How perfect she would be. How she deserved to be one.

On the other door, Apollo was defending Delphi from the invading Gauls.

'Why did he pick that scene?' I mused aloud.

'Why did who pick?' Whisper asked.

'Octavian.' I waved my hand about my head. 'All this is so carefully considered, believe me. There's not one statue, one relief, one slab of marble which will not have been put here without a purpose.'

Whisper looked about her, absorbing the surroundings. She nodded.

'He's good,' she said simply.

'Vengeance,' she said pointing at the Niobids, 'and justified killing,' she said pointing at the other door.

I nodded. 'Exactly. Just as he claims he was right to kill those who murdered Caesar, and right to defend Rome from Antony and Cleopatra That's the story he's selling.'

Whisper stared at the inscriptions. 'Very persuasively,' she said. 'Can we go inside?'

As we passed through the threshold, I had a moment of inspiration. I tapped Whisper on the shoulder and gestured back to the doors.

'Right to strike.' I said, meaningfully.

Inside should have been calm and respectful. Instead, it was crowded and had the hubbub of a theatre.

The oversized head of Medusa the Gorgon caught my eye on one of the metopes of the frieze. Perseus was handing the snake haired head to the goddess Athena. In Athena's other hand was the shield upon which she would forever place Medusa's head.

'Is the snake-haired head Cleopatra?' Whisper asked.

'Well, it's Medusa, but it certainly could represent Cleopatra. Many called her a witch. Many believed she was a witch.'

'Did you?' Whisper asked. 'You met her.'

I took a deep breath. My encounters with Cleopatra were another period of my life I did not wish to remember too clearly. At first I had helped prevent her from committing suicide, only to be the sole person responsible for allowing her to commit suicide weeks later.

And that, ultimately, was the mistake from which I would never recover with Octavian. When we won that war in Alexandria, he had wanted Cleopatra to be the ultimate trophy in his triumph back in Rome, the crucial proof to be paraded in the streets to all the people that the war had not been a civil war, but a war against an Egyptian. But I had ruined it all.

'No,' I concluded. 'She's definitely not a witch.'

Whisper followed along the frieze, until another relief caught her eye.

'What about this one?' she asked.

Two men were wrestling for control of a tripod, one on either side. The lion skin hood of the figure on the right told me it was Hercules. The club in his left hand confirmed my thinking. On the left stood Apollo, bow and arrow in hand, tussling for the tripod. The tripod of Delphi. This was Apollo defending Delphi again. But it was much more than that.

'Antony claimed he was Hercules,' I said to Whisper. 'To be fair to him, he was a mountain of man. It was not a wild claim.'

'And Octavian says he's Apollo,' Whisper continued,

pointing at the relief. 'So this represents the civil war.'

I nodded, fighting to keep my disgust at Octavian under control.

A lamp stand in the shape of an apple tree caught my eye.

We made our way over to inspect it more closely. From the branches, oil lamps shaped like apples and pears suspended. As we looked on in admiration, we were regaled by a temple attendant about how this beautiful lamp stand had been brought as an offering to Apollo by Octavian from the temple to Apollo at Cyme.

So, stealing a gift to Apollo to dedicate to Apollo. An interesting approach.

And the man who had dedicated it to Apollo the first time?

Alexander the Great. He had originally acquired it from a temple in Thebes. It was a well-travelled lampstand.

My lips twitched, involuntarily. A conversation with Octavian played out from my memory.

'Tomorrow, I am doing something I have wanted to do for a long time.' Octavian had said. *'The Alexandrians are showing me the tomb of Alexander the Great. I shall at last set eyes on the man whom I respect above all.'*

'He was a great king. The greatest,' I replied.

And then came his words which rile me even now.

'The greatest...yet.'

His intent was so clear. Even back then. And here it was, manifesting itself. In the short time I had been away from Rome, Octavian had built this monumental complex, supposedly to honour a god. But it was a god he had associated himself with so closely.

The statue in the square bore Octavian's own face, by Jupiter. That man was striving his utmost to inveigle himself into the hearts and minds of the people. Where was the Republic in this temple?

All about me was Greek art, spoils of a civil war and self-aggrandising of a selfish, brutal man. I felt so angry and frustrated, I physically ached.

A gentle touch of my arm from Whisper brought me back into the temple. There was nothing to be done but finish seeing the rest of the temple.

We made our way to the inner chamber. Three ancient greek statues received us. Apollo, clutching his lyre, stood in the centre, dressed in a long robe. His sister Diana, goddess of the hunt, stood on one side and his mother Leto on the other. Beautiful works of art I cannot deny.

'No expense spared,' I muttered bitterly. 'These are all of the highest quality. Three Greeks on the highest hill of Rome. Who won after all?'

'Look at the drapery,' Whisper said, 'Look at the muscles. Look a that lyre. It's even better than the one outside.'

Where previously I would have walked away, disregarding. Now I looked. Was it Whisper changing me? Or was it because I was having a second chance at life, at appreciating life?

'What is Apollo the god of?' Whisper asked.

'Octavian,' I said, moodily.

Whisper rolled her eyes.

'I'm not entirely joking,' I replied. 'Octavian claims that Apollo is his protector.'

'But he'll be god of something,' replied Whisper, 'like Mars is the god of war.'

I nodded. 'Apollo is the god of many things. God of the sun, god of truth and prophecy, god of music,' I said, pointing at the lyre. 'God of medicine and healing. And ironically, plague. Perhaps he is the right god to be associated with Octavian.'

Whisper glared at me. 'Careful,' she seethed. 'You don't want to die at his hands again.'

I looked about me, sheepishly, to check if anyone had overheard.

'Because of the healing, I meant,' I said loudly. 'Rome is healed from civil war.'

I felt able to say this. As it was true. Rome was healed from civil war. She was still sick, gravely ill in my view. But that much, at least, Octavian had achieved. With Agrippa's help.

We stepped out of the temple. Connected by a ramp was the original purpose of my visit. Octavian's house. The building was now totally unrecognisable as the former house of the great orator Hortensius. That was because Hortensius' house lay deep beneath this new complex, covered by the new monumental expanse.

I dared to walk up the slope towards the entrance door. It was guarded, as one would expect, even when he was absent. Evergreen laurels stood on either side of the door I had once had the status to enter. On the lintel was a civic crown of oak leaves.

Here dwelled Octavian, master of the world, Apollo beside him, Victory and the Great Mother as neighbours, and the Circus Maximus below him. Republic? I think not.

I fell into a melancholy silence. Why was I still alive? What was I here to do? What was I able to do? What could I do against this man, revered above all others? It seemed to me he had become greater than Caesar himself. The adopted son had usurped the father.

I turned to Whisper.

'He must have spotted something,' I said.

Whisper looked confused. 'Who? Spotted what?'

'Caesar,' I replied. 'He must have seen something in Octavian when he was a young man. There was a reason he adopted him, even if he did it strangely in his will.'

Whisper looked about her.

'He's done very well,' she said.

I glowered at her. I was about to rant when I remembered where I was standing.

Without another word, I turned and walked away.

Whisper hurried to catch up with me as I barged my way through the crowds. As I pushed through the portico, I spotted another building. It was a library, adorned with medallions of famous writers. On one side was Greek literature, scroll after scroll as far as I could see. On the other side was Roman literature. There was plenty of space.

'Augustus wishes Roman poets to fill these shelves now we are at peace,' said an attendant, reading my mind.

I clenched my fists.

I knew of one set of scrolls at least which should be on those shelves. 'Actium's Wake', scribed by my own hand. A personal history which revealed the true nature of Rome's king.

I have not seen those scrolls since the day I left them. I fear they may never see the light of day. Doubtless Octavian's agents would have destroyed them when they came for me and found only my sandals.

Whisper found me.

'Rutilius!' she said in a curt tone.

My eyes widened. I turned slowly to look at her.

She realised what she had done. She fell silent and grew pale.

I turned my head from side to side.

'I don't think there is anyone of that name here,' I replied. I gave the faintest of flicks of my head to signal Whisper to leave, to break our association.

A few minutes of browsing later and I stepped outside. Whisper emerged from behind a basalt Danaid.

I shook my head at her.

'I'm so sorry,' she said, tearful.

'We escaped this time, I think,' I replied, tersely. 'We may not escape again.'

'It won't happen again,' she stammered.

In the past I would have surmised that the only safe way to guarantee it would never happen again would be for Whisper to die. But I was not that rash young man anymore. And I loved her.

I smiled at her and wiped away the tear from her cheek.

'I know it won't,' I said. 'As you were just telling me, I don't want to die at Octavian's hand again.'

I looked back at the temple of Apollo, and Octavian's house. I smiled grimly.

In fact, quite the opposite.

'Follow me.'

I stared at the words on my gravestone again.

IN THE HANDS OF THE GODS.
MARCUS RUTILIUS CRISPUS.
A LOYAL MAN.

'Why have we come back here?' Whisper asked.

I did not answer. I was thinking. We had had no time to purchase a votive offering. I would have loved to have bought votive eyes. Those eyes had pierced me on so many occasions. How apt it would have been.

Or perhaps a votive ear. That would have been equally satisfying.

Instead, I fumbled in my pocket and found some of the coins I had inspected earlier in the day. I dared not bury a god, so I overlooked the *dupondius* with Neptune, and the *as* with Zeus. I settled on the *denarius* which had the Curia Julia on, the scene of my demise as Rutilius the senator.

'Perfect,' I said. I dug my hand into the ground just in front of my gravestone and made a small hole. I placed the coin into it. Whisper watched in silence. As I took up the soil, to bury the coin, I turned to her.

'Whisper, you are my witness to this vow. Over a hundred years ago, Cato the Elder's hatred of Carthage was legendary. He pronounced the famous words, "Carthage must be destroyed". And so it came about.'

I turned to the coin in the soil. I covered it once more and held my hand on the ground.

'For the sake of Marcus Rutilius Crispus, I offer this coin, as a symbol of my vow. Cato said, "Carthage must be destroyed".'

I took a deep breath.

'Now I say, Octavian must be destroyed.'

V

One thing had not changed while I had been away. I was still rash. I had no clue how I was going to destroy Octavian. I had not thought beyond the promise, beyond my desire for his destruction. All I wanted was Octavian to fall. And if we could not return to a Republic, then at least Agrippa should run the empire. Of lowly stock Agrippa may have been, but he was a worthy man. A man of virtue, courage and loyalty. A man who could inspire others and lead Rome to prosperity.

'How?' Whisper asked, exasperated at what I had done.

'I don't know,' I replied.

'Isn't he in Spain?'

I wiped my face in irritation.

'Yes.'

She shook her head and walked away.

'Agrippa is consul,' I shouted after her. 'So if Octavian did die, he would be the natural successor.'

Whisper turned. 'Does Octavian not have a son?'

I had not thought of that. As a Republic, Rome did not have bloodline successors in the manner of foreign kings. The consuls were elected. But, in my last speech as a senator in the Curia Julia, had I not accused Octavian of precisely that, of behaving like a king? Had I not dared to call him 'king' to his face, in front of all the senators, exhorting them to challenge him? It was clear that no one had taken up that challenge. The monumental temple of Apollo was evidence enough, quite apart from the repeated consulships. So, if he did have a son, would he, rather than Agrippa, be the successor?

'I need to speak to Agrippa,' I concluded.

'Again, how?' Whisper countered.

'I don't know, but we must find a way.'

It turned out that finding Agrippa was not so difficult. Not only was he the only consul in Rome, he was in the midst of a number of vast building projects, in particular on the Plains of Mars.

Just before my suicide, he had told me that his substantial wealth was tied up in contracts. It was for that reason, and I believe it was genuine, that he could not loan me the money I needed to meet the property qualification and remain a senator when Octavian set about his census and stripped me of my rank.

Agrippa's commitment to buildings was evidently continuing. On the Plains of Mars, the activity was constant. Marble, brought by barge up the Tiber from Ostia, was being unloaded near the Mausoleum of Augustus and dragged on rollers to the various sites which were all progressing at once.

One in particular had a raised pediment. I learned it was to be the Pantheon. The stairs were in place, leading to a facade of columns. At the summit of the columns were ornate capitals of Syracusan bronze.

I looked at the inscription on the facade of the building:

MARCUS AGRIPPA, SON OF LUCIUS, MADE ME WHEN CONSUL FOR THE THIRD TIME

There were a number of stunning caryatids. Their drapery and expressionful faces matched, if not surpassed, the greek masterpieces I had admired in the temple of Apollo. Agrippa's spending power seemed at least as great as Octavian's. The more I thought about it, the more I believed Agrippa was more than a natural successor to Octavian. He was a natural rival.

Behind the Pantheon, the foundations were being laid for

another Basilica, the Basilica of Neptune, an appropriate dedication given Agrippa's naval prowess. I had been there on the day Agrippa had been awarded the blue ensign for his exemplary command of the navy. When I learned that the building in front of me was to be in Neptune's name, it made me all the more adamant that it should have been Agrippa, not Octavian, shown as Neptune on that coin celebrating the demise of Sextus Pompey.

I found myself drawn to the mighty building that was the Saepta Julia, the marble voting hall with a story to tell even before it had opened. It was Caesar who made the original plan to replace the rickety wooden sheep pens of the Ovile with this vast marble structure. And when I say vast, I mean vast. Three hundred strides by one hundred strides. But Caesar was assassinated before it was complete, a death we are still feeling the effect of even now. A death which activated *that* clause in *that* will.

Then Lepidus, our Chief Priest, took it on, seeing that Caesar's death was not popular and that by taking over the completion, he could steal some reflected glory off of the man.

But Lepidus, though he is still alive, will never set eyes on the completed building. His incompetent attempt to oust Octavian, doomed to failure, brought him exile. The only reason Lepidus is still alive is because even Gaius "You must die" Octavian did not dare to kill the chief priest of Rome.

As I stood, admiring the enormity of the place, such an expense, just for a voting hall, I found myself hoping that in some way this building was cursed. An ill fate had befallen Caesar, and Lepidus. Perhaps that trend could continue. If Octavian wanted to steal Agrippa's glory, could the Saepta Julia bring about his demise too?

My eye was caught by the arrival of a group of men. An ordered line of twelve lictors, carrying their staffs of bundled rods, axe blades protruding. My heart thumped. My legs grew weak. My hands trembled.

Behind those strong, hardy men, would be a man I was desperate to see. A man I was desperate to serve. A man I wished to speak to, more than any other. Marcus Vipsanius Agrippa.

And there he was. Tall, sturdy and full of life. The dark hair may have greyed, but the dark-tanned skin I remembered so well, still shone with vitality. He wore the purple bordered toga of a magistrate and it suited him so well. As he surveyed the building sites about him, he looked every bit a ruler. If the Republic was to fall, then, seeing him like this, I became determined it should fall to him. Octavian's changes in Rome had been all about himself. But Agrippa had built roads, bridges and aqueducts ever since his younger days in earlier offices. Now, all around me, he was building voting halls, temples, basilicas and baths.

He had always been a man for the people.

Or so I thought.

I took a step, as if I could go to greet him. But then I remembered. How could I? How could I reveal myself? I was a condemned man. Agrippa had been present in the 'little workshop' when Octavian ordered me to commit suicide. That was as good as a sentence in court. If not stronger. Even then, Octavian was the leading man in Rome. If I was found alive, I would be killed.

Suddenly the axe blades sticking out of the lictors' bundles of rods took on a whole new meaning. They were there precisely because they represented the consul's power to mete out capital punishment.

I could not speak to Agrippa, though, by all the gods, there was nothing I desired to do more.

Frustrated, anguished even, all I could do was stand on the Plains of Mars, surrounded by the great works of the man, and watch him. There may only have been twelve lictors and a few feet between us, but there might as well have been oceans.

Agrippa made his way to the Saepta Julia. As his presence was spotted, a crowd gathered around him, some cheering him, others just wanting to be part of the troupe which followed his footsteps. This was a man who was adored by the people.

He came so close to me, I even heard his voice. That deep, serious tone I had heard so often before my shaming.

I could still hear the last words he had said to me.

'I am sorry, Rutilius.'

That was an apology he did not need to make. He had said it as he handed over the wax tablet to Octavian, the wax tablet which had inside it the proof Octavian needed to condemn me.

But Agrippa had no choice but to hand that tablet over. It was the right thing to do. And I cannot think of a time when Agrippa did not do the right thing.

Now he spoke about trivial matters.

'Have the marble tablets arrived?' he asked.

'Not yet sir,' an attendant replied. 'They are due tomorrow. Along with the first batch of Greek paintings.'

'Good. We're getting there at last.'

It was all I could do not to call out to him. Instead, overcome, I ran back to the temple of Fides.

I threw myself into Whisper's arms.

'I have seen Agrippa,' I exclaimed. 'I just saw him on the Plains. He's here.'

'Did he see you?' Whisper asked in horror.

I shook my head. 'No. Though I was desperate to talk to him.'

'You can't.' Whisper shrieked, breaking away from me.

'I know I can't,' I replied, 'that's why I didn't.'

'They'd kill you. They'd have to.'

I sighed, frustration welling up inside me.

'But what's the point of me being here? This is no life. Skulking in a temple. We have food and money, but this isn't living.'

Whisper looked hurt. 'We have each other.'

I hesitated. The beautiful woman in front of me was the beautiful woman who had kept me alive on that boat. Then, I would have given anything just to see her again. Now I had her, inevitably, I wanted more.

I drew Whisper in and kissed her gently on the lips, inhaling the scent of her skin, closing my eyes, and feeling the sense of calm she brought as it swept over me.

'Yes we do.'

We made love.

I stared at the flickering flame of the lamp inside our hidden chamber.

Ordinarily, after love making I would either doze or leap into action, determined to get on with something. This time, I lay staring at the flame, at a loss what to do next.

'I've had an idea,' said Whisper.

I turned and looked at those beautiful eyes.

'Am I going to like it?'

'I think so.' Whisper shifted her weight onto her hand. She lay her arm onto my chest and traced her finger through the hairs on my chest.

'You want to see Agrippa. To speak to him, I mean.'

'Yes. I don't know why, but that's the only idea I have. It's as if the gods are telling me that's what I should do.'

'But you can't reveal your identity.'

I paused, weighing up the consequences.

I shook my head. 'I don't think so. Agrippa wouldn't have any choice but to have me killed, or at least handed over to Octavian,' I shuddered at the thought, 'who would kill me.'

I recalled the tale of the demise of Praetor Quintus Gallius only a few years ago. Octavian would say he had banished Gallius for treachery.

But the taverns of Rome would tell a different story, of how Octavian tore out Gallius' eyes and tortured him as a slave, before finally putting him out of his misery. And what had Gallius done? Held folded tablets under his toga as he paid respects to Octavian.

Octavian, full of mistrust and violence, must have thought it was a knife. Looking back, I had escaped lightly in the 'little workshop' on that accursed day. I would not be so lucky twice.

'Octavian would kill me, for sure,' I repeated. 'But not before he tortured me.'

'So you need to hide your identity,' said Whisper.

'How?' I asked.

'We've done it before,' said Whisper, her eyes gleaming with excitement.

'The mask.'

Whisper nodded. '"The Mouth of Octavian". Meet him wearing the mask. I can make a new one.'

'But they knew "The Mouth of Octavian" was me.'

Whisper put a finger to my lips.

'No,' she corrected. 'They knew that "The Mouth of Octavian" was senator Marcus Rutilius Crispus. And senator Marcus Rutilius Crispus is dead. He died a couple of years ago. You can go and look at his gravestone.'

'What if they unmask me?'

Whisper tilted her head and assessed my face. 'If they unmask you, they could recognise you. It's possible. Even with the beard, that scar on your cheekbone could give you away.'

I frowned.

'But,' Whisper encouraged, 'don't lots of men have scars on their face?'

'Lots of soldiers certainly.'

'Then I suppose it depends how much you want to speak to Agrippa.'

I thought for a while. It was a risk. But had I not just argued that I had no purpose in life. Whisper was giving me a chance.

And even if Agrippa unmasked me. He may recognise me. But others may not. And then the choice would be his, as to whether I could remain Sextus, or return to Rutilius and suffer the consequences.

If my life was to be in any man's hands, then Agrippa's were the

hands I would prefer. Especially with Octavian away in Spain.

'Do it,' I said. 'Give me a new mask.'

Her hand wandered from my chest to my groin.

'I will,' she replied with a smile, 'but you need to give me something first.'

What I did not realise then, that I do now, is that she meant a child, not just the pleasure. Despite my misunderstanding, I did not hesitate.

So it was that once again I felt Whisper painting linen onto my face to create a mould.

Though it had been years since the first time Whisper had done this, as I felt the cold texture of the linen pressed to my face, it felt as if it had been only a few days ago.

Then, she had created a mask for me to wear in court, to hide my identity as the *delator*, the informant, as I brought the case against Scribonius.

Now, she would make me Octavian's face once more.

Octavian, Agrippa and Maecenas discovered that I was "The Mouth of Octavian". But I wondered how many they bothered to tell. The fall of Marcus Rutilius Crispus, unlike the fall of Caesar, would barely have made a noise in Rome.

I almost laughed out loud. For a time "The Mouth of Octavian" was the talk of the city. But Rome's memory is short. I doubted anyone cared who had been that mysterious man anymore. New stories and rumours would be tearing through the streets.

While Whisper wandered the streets to find a statue of Octavian to copy his features for her painting, I made my way to the market to buy a new loose fitting hooded cloak.

When I returned to the temple of Fides, Whisper had already finished her amazing work with the paint. Once again the mask looked as good as a death mask.

I put on the cloak. Whisper carefully placed the mask back onto my face. It fitted perfectly. I remembered the strange smell of the paint, the limits it made to my vision, even the effect it made on the sound of my voice. Whisper reached up and pulled the hood of the cloak over my head. I resisted the temptation of her breasts, even though for a moment, they were right in front of my eyes. This moment neither lust, nor even love, would spoil. I felt a deep sense of excitement. This was surely it. My purpose. I was "The Mouth of Octavian". But now, as "The Mouth of Octavian", all I needed to learn was what would I say?

In the end I decided that the most appropriate word for me to say was the name of the man I admired above all.

'Agrippa'.

Whisper and I loitered in the Plains of Mars, learning what we could of Agrippa's movements. Of course, with Whisper's looks, it was far easier for her to extract information. It was she who learned of Agrippa's next visit.

The night before Whisper and I talked through how I should approach Agrippa.

'You shouldn't be present,' I insisted. 'He may recognise you.'

'Very well,' Whisper replied, 'but how will you make sure you are not unmasked?'

'I can't,' I shrugged my shoulders. 'But something tells me Agrippa, even when he works out that it is me, will not hand me over again. I trust that man, with my life. Always have done. Always will. He will know what to do.'

'You're sure?' Whisper asked. 'Should you not at least take a blade?'

I shook my head.

'Unarmed is best.'

'What do you think he'll say?' Whisper asked.

I thought for a moment. It was not so much what he would say that worried me. It was what he might do. This could be a short foray indeed.

Agrippa was entirely within his rights to execute me on the spot. But something in my mind was certain that all would be well.

'I don't know,' I finally replied. 'I really don't know. But I suppose, that's why this is so exciting.'

Whisper grabbed my face and kissed me long and hard.

'For luck,' she said.

'The gods take more persuading than a kiss,' I replied, pulling her into me.

The next morning, I was up before dawn. Whisper placed the mask over my face and drew my hood.

'Be careful,' she said.

I walked slowly from her, holding her fingers until my arm could no longer reach.

'All will be well,' I said with feigned confidence.

I made my way the short distance from my temple in the Plains of Mars to the new building complex of Agrippa's works. The Saepta Julia was nearing completion. I loitered amongst the columns of the Pantheon's portico. Standing under the massive inscription of Agrippa's name seemed to me to be an appropriate place to unveil myself to the man. And I would be in the protection of the gods.

Whisper's information had been correct. Agrippa and his entourage emerged from the city and inspected the works once more.

I felt the same racing heartbeat as the day I intended to assassinate Octavian with an arrow. Then I had lurked behind a statue, waiting to see his face, waiting for him to come into range.

Today, I waited once more, this time behind a vast column, amidst so many other vast columns, hoping for a glimpse of Agrippa, and the chance to approach him.

How different my intent.

At first Agrippa inspected the Saepta Julia. This was so close to completion that he was inside it for a number of hours, clearly inspecting the interior. The Greek paintings and marble tablets he had been expecting, should now be installed. I could almost picture him adjusting each one by the merest movement till he was satisfied that the positioning, or the lighting, or the angle was perfect.

At last, he emerged back into the sunlight. The lictors turned towards the Pantheon. He was coming.

I was standing beside a column in front of the actual entrance. I decided to conceal myself amongst the columns at the end, and try to catch Agrippa's eye so that he would have to pull away from the group to see me.

As the lictors led Agrippa up the stairs, and into the entrance, I made a swift movement from the front of the portico to the back. Enough motion, I hoped, to be noticed.

Then I turned, and keeping my body hidden behind the column, I leaned my head back, and showed my hooded and masked face. I stared straight at Agrippa.

And he was staring back.

His footsteps halted.

His eyes widened.

His head turned and looked into the temple chamber.

He looked back at me once more. I could feel my mask

vibrate on my face, as my heart beat thumped.

With a swift gesture of both his hands, he waved his entourage into the chamber.

He stood alone. Slowly, he turned to face me and placed his hands on his hips.

I decided to step out. I shuffled to the middle of the portico and stood in plain view.

Agrippa, slowly, steadily, approached. Not once did his eyes leave my mask.

We stood in silence for a long moment, barely ten paces apart.

'Who are you?' Agrippa said in a low voice.

I cleared my throat. '"The Mouth of Octavian",'

Agrippa stared. He shifted his weight. 'But "The Mouth of Octavian" is dead.'

I opened my arms wide. 'Yet here I am.'

'Rutilius?' ask Agrippa in disbelief.

I shook my head.

'Then who?' Agrippa pointed at the mask. 'Reveal yourself.'

I shook my head again.

'Reveal yourself,' Agrippa commanded. 'At once.'

I physically trembled. The last thing I wanted to do was to take off the mask.

'Your consul has spoken. Obey me. I am Augustus' colleague. No one should represent him, but me.'

I stood still, not knowing what to do. I wanted to run away. This was not how the conversation was supposed to go. Agrippa was growing red with anger.

'Lictors!' he bellowed.

I held up my hand. 'Wait,' I called, breathless. 'Agrippa, please.'

The first of the twelve lictors stormed into the portico, rushing to their master's side, their bundles of rods gripped in such a way that they could be swung in arcs of death. I swallowed as I saw the axe blades. This really could be the end. Could I outrun them?

'Send them away,' I said, waving them back into the chamber with my raised arm. 'I mean no harm.'

Agrippa hesitated. At last, he motioned his head ever so slightly as a signal for his lictors to retreat.

Suspiciously, guardedly, they stepped back into the Pantheon chamber, never taking their eyes off me.

Agrippa walked towards me. I lowered my hand to my side as he approached, large strides from a large man. He drew up close. Close enough to smell the paint of my mask. Close enough to tear the mask off with his mighty hands.

'I say again, who are you?'

I raised my trembling hand, gripped the mask on my face, hesitated for one last moment, then I pulled the mask away, dropping the hood with my other hand.

I felt naked before Rome's consul, Rome's greatest man, Marcus Vipsanius Agrippa. I was entirely at his mercy.

His mouth opened. His dark eyes gleamed as they absorbed my features. His finger pointed hesitantly at the scar on my face.

He reached out and gripped the greying, thinning curls of my hair.

'But you're dead,' Agrippa said.

I closed my eyes, feeling the large, warm hand of Agrippa clasping at the side of my head, as if checking that I was real.

'I am,' I said.

Suddenly he pulled me into him, into an embrace, a fierce embrace which crushed me into his chest. My face was buried into the folds of his purple-bordered toga. I felt his chin press onto the top of my head.

At last, he released me.

'How?' he asked.

I puffed out my cheeks. 'The will of the gods. Nothing

more.'

'But they brought me your sandals. They told me you were dead. I've visited your grave.'

'I am dead Agrippa. I have to be. The man you see before you now is Sextus. Or better still, "The Mouth of Octavian".'

'Sextus,' Agrippa repeated, at once understanding why I had picked the name. 'He was a good comrade to you. I remember him well.' Agrippa adjusted the folds of his toga. 'Why have you come back?'

I swallowed hard.

'Always the same mission, Agrippa.'

'The Republic,' Agrippa replied.

'The Republic,' I repeated.

We stood in an awkward silence.

'You cannot return,' Agrippa concluded. '"The Mouth of Octavian" is as dead as Marcus Rutilius Crispus. For a start, Octavian is now Augustus.'

'Hmm,' I grunted. 'I had heard. Not a very republican title, to be sure.'

'If he learns you are alive...'

'He mustn't,' I replied. There was a pause. 'Are you going to tell him?'

I saw Agrippa's eyes look into the distance, into his past, reliving our final moment in the 'little workshop'.

'I have handed you over once,' he said with a furrowed brow, 'as was my duty.' He gripped my shoulder. 'But Rutilius, as you say, is dead. So is "The Mouth of Octavian". Before me now stands Sextus. Why should I hand him over to anyone?'

I felt relief consume my body. And a sense of excitement. If I had access to Agrippa, I had a life.

'But you must understand Rome has changed, Sextus.'

'I know. I have seen it.' I replied. 'I have seen the temple of Apollo, attached to our king's house.'

'Augustus is not a king,' Agrippa replied firmly. 'He is a

consul. And I am his colleague. Before he went to Spain, when we were both in Rome, he passed me the bundles of rods, just as he should to his colleague, at the end of his month, and at the end of my month, I returned them to him, just like the consuls of old.'

'Augustus—' I said with a challenging tone, my distaste for the title evident.

'...has brought peace to the empire,' Agrippa cut across me. 'While we are not fighting, look what we can do.' He gestured with his arm.

'Now, Ruti—, I mean, Sextus, I must go, but meet me at my house.'

'Do you still live here, on the Plains of Mars?'

Agrippa stroked his chin.

'Yes, but don't come to that house. Come to my new home on the Palatine.'

'New home?'

'Well, not new. When you were away, Augustus gave me a share of Antony's house on the Palatine.'

'"The House of the Rams"?'

Agrippa nodded.

'But Marcella and I were hardly going to share a house. She is determined to have a baby. So we use it very rarely. Plus all my efforts are here in the Plains of Mars, so my own house is more convenient. While Augustus is away, I spend my time there.' Agrippa waved his arm in the general direction of his home. He faced me again. 'So, go to Antony's house. We can meet there and no one will know. The password for today is "Actium".'

Actium. Always Actium. Wherever I turned.

'Do I wear the mask?' I asked.

Agrippa thought for a moment.

'I think not,' he said slowly. 'Not yet. Your adventures have weathered you my friend. And your curls have greyed. I do not think you will be recognised by the guards,

Sextus. After that...we shall see.'

And with that Agrippa turned sharply on his heel and strode back into the Pantheon.

VI

"The House of the Rams" on the Palatine was famous so it was easy to find. Years before, it had been Pompey the Great's residence. When Pompey had been killed during the civil war with Caesar, the house had been handed over to Mark Antony. And, by all accounts, Antony had wrecked it. Banquets, orgies, gambling, prostitutes, fighting, auctions, you name it, Rome believes it happened. And, since it was Antony, it probably did. I honestly believe if he had put as much effort into controlling Octavian as he did into satisfying his appetites, Rome would have a different master now.

As I looked about me on the route to the Palatine, I have to confess, I began to wonder if Octavian's victory had been such a terrible thing after all. Rome seemed cleaner, more beautiful, more stable. Water flowed across the city, pooling into the public drinking basins, and pouring out of fountains. Statues were littered all over the city, not just adorning the temples. Even the smell, always pungent, seemed less odorous.

Had Antony won, with Cleopatra's influence, his efforts would not have been so focused on Rome. Whether it was true he intended to move the capital to Egypt or not, his attention would have been far less intense on our city and its people, and far more on himself.

What was I thinking?

I cursed that for even one moment, I found myself having favourable thoughts about Octavian. In the searing heat, I headed for one of the drinking bowls. I let the cool water pour through my hands, noticing their increasing lines of age, before plunging my head into the water.

And that reminded me. The water pouring over my head, the water serving the people freely, was not provided by Octavian. This was Agrippa's work. It was Agrippa who had repaired and enlarged the sewers which cleaned the city, long ago, when he was but an aedile. Was it not Agrippa who so loved the Greek arts, that he pushed for statues and artworks to be made public in the city? Truly, it was Agrippa, not Octavian, who acted for the good of the people.

I raised my head out of the water and looked up to the sun.

It *was* a good thing Octavian had won. I had supported the correct side in the civil war, because, in supporting Octavian, I had supported Agrippa. But it was Agrippa, not Octavian, who should be Rome's leading man.

I made my way to "The House of the Rams". The password 'Actium' ensured me safe passage past the guard and into the atrium. This was the first time I had entered Pompey's famous house, so, while I waited for Agrippa to return, I dared to take a look at the rooms I could freely enter. I admired the ships' battering rams which adorned the walls. They had come from Cilician pirate ships Pompey the Great had defeated many, many years ago and they were the source of the house's name.

I scratched my head. Unfortunately, these magnificent ornaments, like the ships' beaks on the column in the Forum and the representations on the coins and the password I had just given, only served to remind me of Actium. And that was not a pleasant memory. Rutilius might be dead. But his memories lived on.

Agrippa hurried in.

'Sextus,' he said, remembering my new name, 'come, let us drink together, you and I. The finest Campanian wine for a new friend.' He gestured to a slave who scuttled off to fetch the wine.

'What do you think of my little project?' he said.

'Which one?' I smiled. 'There are so many.'

Agrippa looked proud. 'I have been busy while you are away.' He clapped his hands together. 'But there is still so much to be done.'

'When we departed, in that "little workshop", I wished you peace and prosperity.' I glanced around the house. 'Thankfully, it seems that you have had ample of both.'

'Indeed,' Agrippa replied. 'Life has been good to me.'

'Two more consulships.'

Agrippa nodded.

'Gifts.' I gestured at the house about me. 'Triumphs?' I asked.

Agrippa shook his head.

'A new wife.'

Agrippa took a sip.

'I am sorry to hear about Caecilia Attica.'

Agrippa sighed. 'Thank you.'

'How is your baby girl Vipsania Agrippina? Not so much a baby I suppose...'

'Growing up,' Agrippa replied.

'She is to marry Octavian's stepson isn't she, Tiberius?'

'She is. When she's old enough. But that is a while away yet, thankfully. Tiberius seems a sombre fellow.'

'And now you are married to Octavian's niece, Claudia Marcella.'

Agrippa nodded.

'How is she?'

'She's only a girl.' Agrippa replied firmly. 'I'm nearly three times her age. She's only just fourteen. I feel more like a father than a husband. But she will become a beautiful woman.'

'A good marriage though,' I said, 'for you I mean.'

'Of course,' Agrippa replied, not entirely enjoying my

questions.

'Something Octavian was very keen to point out.'

'I expect he was,' I said. I could almost picture the conversation when Octavian would have offered Claudia Marcella to him. It would have been not so much an offer, more of an order, but coated with his honeyed tongue. Even if Agrippa had not desired the marriage, he would have been trapped. 'Life is treating Octavian well too,' I added.

'Augustus,' Agrippa corrected me. 'Octavian was voted the title of Augustus by the Senate. He is addressed by that name or by his title "princeps".'

'The "leading citizen",' I mused. 'Why not king?'

Agrippa took a measured sip of his wine.

'We debated long and hard about the name Augustus should be given,' he said. 'Should he be Romulus? After all, some believe Augustus has founded a new age for Rome.'

I shook my head in disgust.

'But,' Agrippa continued, 'you will be pleased to hear that it was Augustus himself who rejected such a title. Romulus is the only founder of Rome. And he was a king. Something Augustus will never be.'

'Really?' I replied. 'Is that what your Pantheon tells me?'

'My Pantheon?' Agrippa repeated, confused.

'Pantheons focus worship on the ruler. At least that's how they are in Greece. So I assume Octavian will feature inside?'

Agrippa hesitated for a second.

'No,' he shook his head. 'No, his statue will be in the porch with me.'

'Why did you hesitate?' I asked.

Agrippa pursed his lips. 'When we first planned this, many years ago, it was the only time I let my devotion to Augustus overwhelm me.'

'How do you mean?'

Agrippa looked crestfallen. 'I wanted to put a statue of

Augustus in the chamber,' Agrippa shifted his weight, 'with the other gods.'

I stared at him, disbelieving.

'And I was going to give it a different name.'

I raised my eyebrows, waiting.

'The Augusteum.'

I stood, shaking my head. 'Even you, Agrippa.' I held up my hands. 'How could you?' I implored. 'A living god?'

Agrippa flushed. He slammed his cup of wine down on the table, leapt to his feet and paced the room.

'I grew up with him, remember. Everything I have. Everything I own. Everything I am is because of him.' Agrippa raised his arms. 'Of course I am loyal. Without him I am nothing.'

'Childhood was a long time ago,' I replied. I fixed my eyes on his. 'You have become a man. You have outgrown him.'

Agrippa looked stern.

'I cannot outgrow him.'

I went to challenge again but he held up a restraining hand.

'Please, Rutilius. Don't say anymore.'

We stood in an awkward silence.

I ran my hand through my thinning hair, and realised that arguing with Agrippa was not only pointless but dangerous. He was my only chance to have a role in the new empire. Who was I to disapprove of Agrippa?

I held up my hands.

'Far be it from me to criticise Rome's consul,' I said, 'or my only friend in this city, so let me just say how delighted I am with the final outcome, that the statues will be in the porch, and leave it at that.'

Agrippa clasped his hands together. We stood in silence for a moment.

'Ah,' said Agrippa suddenly, releasing his hands. 'Here's

something,' he said, reaching into the folds of his toga. 'See what you make of this.'

He held out his tanned hand to me. My pale hand reached up to pull his closer and inspect what he held. It was a beautiful pearl.

'Guess whose pearl this is?' Agrippa said.

I had not a clue.

'Marcella's?'

Agrippa shook his head. 'Perhaps I should have said, "was". Whose pearl was this?'

I shook my head.

'It was Cleopatra's.' Agrippa said with a beam. 'I will split it and each half will be a pendant for Venus's ears in the Pantheon. Tremendous, don't you think?'

I blinked.

Clearly this pearl, and particularly its former owner, was meant to provide an interesting topic of conversation, as well as a chance for Agrippa to show off. But for me, the name Cleopatra stirred up a very different reaction.

I bit my lip.

Another reminder of my past, the failings of my past. Even dead, Cleopatra could haunt me.

'Agrippa,' I finally managed to say.

Agrippa's face changed as he realised. He closed his hand shut and swiftly tucked the pearl back into the pocket in his toga.

'I'm so sorry. How tactless of me.'

Agrippa returned to his seat. He slumped down and reached for his cup. He was struggling to think of a new topic of conversation. I was pleased to see how much he cared that he had upset me.

'So tell me how Octavian became Augustus?' I offered, changing the subject.

He welcomed the bait. 'Apart from saving the state from the wars? He handed back the provinces to the people.'

'Ah yes,' I grimaced, 'the myth of January the thirteenth.'

'It was no myth,' Agrippa countered. 'Ten provinces have been returned. The people's provinces.'

'The people's indeed,' I said, scornfully. 'Not one province with an army to speak of.'

Agrippa frowned. The deep lines in his forehead had deepened even further with age. 'No. Those with problems still to solve we did indeed keep,' he replied. 'Gaul, Spain, Syria and Egypt.'

'A wealthy selection,' I muttered, 'teeming with soldiers.'

'Soldiers a plenty, yes,' Agrippa agreed, 'but problems a plenty too. That's why Augustus went to Gaul, and now on to Spain.'

'And how long was it he secured ownership of those provinces? Ten years?'

Agrippa nodded.

'And you still say you believe that he would restore the republic?'

'Everyone has a desire for grandeur,' replied Agrippa. 'You and I are no different. But whatever you think, he has restored the Republic. We were destroying ourselves. Now, Rome is reborn and we are prospering in a manner we have not enjoyed for generations. If at all.'

I shook my head in disgust.

'It's not just me who believes it.' Agrippa countered. 'Senator Munatius Plancus voted Octavian the title "Augustus". Just days after the "myth" of the thirteenth, as you call it. Evidently he was convinced by the settlement of the provinces.'

'That treacherous old fool,' I replied. 'What is he, sixty now? First Antony's, now Octavian's. No wonder he was involved in such flattery. Still needing to convince Octavian of his support. I may be dead, but I'm no fool, Agrippa. Plancus would have been lined up long before the settlement to vote Octavian the new title.'

I finished my wine and placed the cup carefully on the mosaic topped table. I traced the ornate relief of the silver cup with my finger. Agrippa had come such a long way from his humble beginnings.

'I fear you are beginning to believe the propaganda, Agrippa. Tell me you have not lost your ambition. Tell me the Republic has not lost its last ambassador.'

'It has not.' Agrippa flashed. 'Have I not given proof?' He pointed at me, the muscles in his tanned forearm becoming clearly visible. 'You have seen with your own eyes the efforts I am making to improve life for our people. While Augustus builds and restores the temples and sanctuaries, I'm delivering what the people truly need,' he said, pointing at his chest. 'Water. It is I who have built the aqueducts, sewers and baths,' he counted out each project on his fingers. 'And the voting house for the people, and the hall to count the votes. Sextus, since you have been away, my tile kilns in Bruttium have been firing day and night. There's not a day goes by where another load isn't brought up from the south. And it's never fast enough.'

I could sense Agrippa's anger, his animation. I sought a change of subject, to calm him. I selected one which always brought me calm.

'You're building baths?' I said. 'Where?'

'The Plains of Mars.'

'But they used to be a swamp.'

'Not by the time I've finished with them.' Agrippa replied. 'It will take years, but I have a vision for them you would scarcely believe.'

'With you I know that anything is possible.'

'Not anything,' said Agrippa, 'but I have learned to tame water. It will take time though. First I will build an exercise area and a Spartan Sweatbath. About two years graft. Then I have plans for an aqueduct which will turn them into real baths. But that will take many, many years.'

'Like your aqueduct Julia?' I asked, picturing Agrippa's grand work in my mind's eye.

'Precisely.' Agrippa looked wistful, 'though it will not need as grand a scale.' Agrippa had been building aqueducts long before the battles with Antony and Cleopatra. 'Julia serves seven of the regions that need water,' Agrippa continued. 'The new one will serve the remaining three. At last, I will finish something.'

I resisted the temptation to point out there was something else I would like him to finish. Or someone.

'So,' said Agrippa. 'That's what I've been up to. The question is. What are you going to do with yourself?'

'I rather hoped you would be able to help me,' I replied.

'I have a potential role.' Agrippa said. 'How does "The Mouth of Augustus" sound? But not just his mouth, his ears and eyes too.'

I stared in horror.

'Do you remember Cornelius Gallus?' Agrippa asked.

'Remember,' I replied. 'How could I forget?' Gallus was the jumped-up knight, and poet who became governor of Egypt. A post I had hoped to take up myself.

'Well, there was a revolt in Thebes, not long into his governorship. By all accounts he did well, and subdued it. But the news now is not so positive. He is overstepping the mark.'

'Are you surprised?'

Agrippa's expression remained impassive. 'It is just rumour. You could see if the rumours are true, and report back to me.'

A chance to ruin Gallus? Presented such an opportunity to gain revenge on that oily knight, I ignored the fact that I would be serving Octavian. Gallus was yet another reminder of my demise as Rutilius.

Despite being miles away in faraway Egypt, Gallus was

all too often in my mind. His sickly-sweet poems about Cytheris, the actress he so dearly loved, were all over Rome.

Cytheris. Now there was an interesting character. Gallus was the latest in a long line of her lovers. She had had Antony. After him, she moved on to the conspirator Brutus. When he died it was Octavian's star that was rising, literally. The baleful comet which appeared during the games Octavian held in Julius Caesar's memory showed us as much. Octavian himself was out of reach, so Cytheris set her sights on Gallus, as one of Octavian's intimate circle. She lured him with as much skill and expertise as Cleopatra lured Antony.

And Gallus was the wretched poet and knight who had been selected over me, a senator with a proven record as a general, to govern Egypt.

The choice was easy.

'I'll do it.'

Agrippa smiled. 'Good man.' He reached into the folds of his toga. 'Here.' He passed something to me, wrapped in cloth.

'What is it?' I asked.

'See for yourself,' he replied.

I unwrapped the cloth and gasped. There, glinting back at me was a familiar blade. A dagger, with SPQR inscribed on the handle.

'Where did you get this?' I stammered.

'I found it, by Olivia's grave,' said Agrippa. 'I took it as a token to remember you by. Now,' Agrippa smiled, 'it can return to its rightful owner.'

I wiped a tear from my eye. Agrippa was such a kindhearted man.

'You visited Olivia's grave?'

'I did,' replied Agrippa. 'With you gone, I was not going to leave it unattended.'

I gripped the dagger's handle and lifted it aloft. The last

time I had held that blade, I was crouched by Olivia's grave, with the tip pressed against my own skin, trying to commit suicide. I must have cast it aside, when I decided to flee.

I looked at the familiar inscription, SPQR, the Senate and the People of Rome. How fitting it would be if this dagger pierced the flesh of Octavian.

'Thank you.' I said, re-wrapping the blade in the cloth. 'I hope it will not be needed in Egypt.'

VII

Whisper held me tight when I returned to the temple of Fides.

'How did it go?' she asked, beaming a smile at me. 'I'm so relieved you're back.'

'I told you we had nothing to fear from Agrippa,' I replied. 'He has a mission for me.

'Oh?'

'We're going to Egypt,' I said. 'To Alexandria.'

Whisper's eyes widened.

'How exciting!' she exclaimed. 'I've always wanted to go to Egypt.'

I was surprised and delighted by this reaction. I had not expected Whisper to be happy to leave Rome. Then it struck me how little she had travelled in her life. She was born in the countryside of Italy, sold into slavery at a young age and brought to Rome. Only after my exploits did she leave Rome and journey to Marseilles, where we were re-united. Perhaps the journey to Marseilles had whetted her appetite. Little wonder the prospect of visiting Egypt with all its stories was exciting.

'It is exciting, isn't it,' I agreed. 'We need to make provision. We will sail from Ostia as soon as possible.'

'Who are we travelling as?' Whisper asked.

'Well, I am Sextus. And you,' I thought of a new name for Whisper to travel under, 'will be called Hope.' I looked longingly at her. 'For that is what you have brought me, from the moment I met you.'

Whisper smiled back at me. 'What are we going to be doing when we're there?'

'Assessing the behaviour of one Gaius Cornelius Gallus.'

'Cornelius Gallus,' repeated Whisper, 'but isn't he—'

'One of the men I hate above all others. Yes. Apparently, he has let the power of his governorship overtake him. His arrogance has finally brought him trouble. But then, he always was so full of himself, ever since he invented that sickly love poetry.'

'He's a poet?' Whisper queried.

'Quite!' I snorted. 'What kind of governor is that?'

Whisper furrowed her beautiful brow. 'So Agrippa wants you to see if there is any truth in the rumours.'

'Precisely. The irony. No longer "The Mouth of Octavian", but as Agrippa put it, his ears and eyes.'

'How long will it take to get there?' she asked.

'Depends on the winds. A couple of days from Ostia to Puteoli. Then it's a thousand miles from there to Alexandria, so nine or ten days. But it could be double that if the winds blow the wrong way. Assuming we don't wreck of course.'

Whisper hit me. 'Don't say that.'

'Don't worry. We'll make the necessary sacrifices to the gods before we depart,' I replied.

'I thought you said you didn't believe in all that,' she said.

'I don't. But we're still doing it.' I laughed. It was the first time I had laughed in a long time.

When the laughter subsided, there seemed only one logical thing to do.

So we did.

'I think I've been to Puteoli before,' Whisper said. 'I recognise the stink.'

I laughed. Puteoli was named after the sulphurous stench which emanated from the ground. Here the sand was black, and in places the ground steamed with the reek of the underworld.

'The stink is so bad, even the birds stay away. You won't see a single bird at Lake Avernus.'

'They're more sensible than us then,' she quipped. She yawned. 'I don't know why but I feel so tired today.' She stretched out her arms. 'Perhaps it's the lack of clean air.'

'We'll move on as soon as we can,' I replied.

Grain ships sailed almost daily between Puteoli and Alexandria so it was not long before we were on our journey. We sacrificed to the gods to ensure that it was a safe journey before setting sail. As we drew out of the harbour, I inhaled deeply. I remembered the last time I had sailed for Alexandria. It was just after my beloved wife Olivia had been murdered by the informant.

Then, I had sailed to Alexandria seeking death or glory. To win back my honour through valour. Now I sailed to Alexandria with a different purpose. Revenge.

It was an unfamiliar experience sailing without my leather cuirass, or troops beside me.

As Whisper sidled up to me and slipped her arms about my waist, I wondered where that informant was. I had not seen or heard from him since he murdered Olivia. Where was he now? Whose life was he ruining?

I spat over the side of the boat, remembering the curse I had written and offered to Fides. The last paragraph I could recite word for word.

MAY YOU SUFFER AN AGE OF AGONY FOR EVERY SECOND OF PAIN OLIVIA FELT. MAY YOUR WIFE SPURN YOU AND YOUR CHILDREN, IF YOU HAVE ANY, DIE YOUNG SO THAT THEY CAN NEVER BECOME AS SHAMEFUL AS THEIR FATHER.

Whisper stood and listened to me. When I finished she placed her hand on my arm and squeezed gently.

'That's a strong curse,' she said, 'wishing children dead.'

'It is a strong curse,' I nodded. 'But murder should not

go un-avenged. I hope it came true.'

Whisper puffed out her cheeks. She had grown pale.

'Are you all right?' I asked.

She shook her head. 'I feel a little sick,' she replied. 'Must be the rocking of the boat.'

'You'll get used to it,' I smiled.

Whisper was sick every day of that journey. I had hoped to enjoy her pleasures to pass the time, but she was in no fit state. Instead, I regaled her with tales of my previous visit to Alexandria.

Eleven days passed and the winds were benign.

'Soon you will see one of the wonders of the world,' I said, proud to have seen it before. 'There will be a light on the horizon.'

'A light?' Whisper said.

'Yes. It's a lighthouse. It guides ships away from the rocks so they don't run aground. The approach to the harbour is very narrow.'

'Why's that such a wonder?' Whisper asked.

'You wait till you see it,' I said.

Then it came into view. The same bright gleam which baffled me all that time ago.

'How?' Whisper asked, squinting.

'It's a mirror,' I said. 'The navigator of our ship told me the legend of that mirror.'

'The legend?'

'If an enemy ship approaches, that mirror will detect it, and burn it before it reaches the harbour.'

Whisper looked at the mirror.

'Let's hope it's not on Gallus' side,' she concluded.

Thankfully, it was not. In scorching sunshine, we sailed peacefully into the Great Harbour, surrounded by the white, marble buildings I knew so well.

'That's the palace,' I said pointing out the buildings on

the east side of the harbour to Whisper.

I fought to control the emerging feelings of the horror of my past.

Whisper looked. 'So that's where it happened. That's where you kept Cleopatra?' Whisper's beautiful eyes widened. 'The most famous queen in the world, in your power, in that building. That's incredible.'

I clenched my hands together. I could feel Octavian's fingers around my throat again, squeezing hard. And all those threats and curses; all because Cleopatra had managed to kill herself in my care.

'*You failed me,*' he hissed, his spittle hitting my face.

I thought he was going to kill me there and then. I could not pull his hands from my throat.

But he had let go.

'Sextus?' Whisper asked, concern on her face.

I shook the memory from my head.

'Yep,' I said, shakily, and pointing back to the Great Harbour, I said, 'That's the great library of Alexandria. Another landmark in this wonderful city.'

'It's beautiful,' Whisper said. 'You can see where Octavian and Agrippa got their ideas from.'

'Their ideas?'

'The buildings. They are magnificent and make such an impression. Soon Rome will have majestic buildings of its own, but more of them, and grander.'

I did not correct Whisper. She was right, partially. But I knew for a fact that Agrippa had always known the power of buildings, ever since he was inspired by the Greeks. And doubtless, given they had been brought up together, Octavian held a similar view. The difference between the two of them Agrippa himself had distilled for me. Agrippa's efforts were for the people. Octavian's were for himself. There was a certain irony that I was seeking evidence that Gallus had committed the same crime as Octavian. Hubris.

'Come,' I concluded. 'Let us see what there is to see.'

When we disembarked, we were immediately in the hustle and bustle and stink of a harbour.

There was a statue of a man on horseback, in Roman military garb.

I nodded to Whisper to head over to it.

'He's handsome,' said Whisper, 'apart from the big nose.'

'Yes, but who is it?' I asked, trying to force our way through the crowd to see the inscription.

My eyes settled on the words. 'It's him.' I pointed at the inscription. 'Gaius Cornelius Gallus, see? Our first piece of evidence.'

Whisper peered at the letters.

'So this is the man who invented love poetry?' Whisper asked.

'Not quite invented. There's been love poetry since time began. But this effeminate wastrel did create a new kind.' I shook my head. 'And now he owns this province. It's unbelievable.'

'He doesn't look effeminate. He looks Gaulish,' said Whisper.

After her time in Marseilles, Whisper knew Gauls. I looked at the statue again, considering what she had said. He did have a strong jaw and broad lips.

'He was born in Gaul,' I replied. 'I don't know his lineage, other than he doesn't have any. But that's the point.'

'Neither does Agrippa,' Whisper countered.

I recalled Gallus' appearance when I last saw him. He had tanned skin and deep, dark eyes. He even had a deep frown. In more ways than I first thought, he was not that dissimilar to Agrippa. But, in so many more, he was so different.

'This man is no Agrippa.' I muttered. 'Let's find out what

else he has been up to.'

It turned out Gallus had been a busy man. We spent over a month gathering evidence for the case against him. It was not hard to point out follies, though, in my heart, I knew there was no treason.

The man was an artist, and the glory and power had gone to his head. Perhaps it was inevitable that the governor of this province would end up behaving like a Pharaoh. The Egyptians wanted one. It was how they understood the world.

Of course, the true Pharaoh was dead. The line died when we executed Cleopatra's children. To my horror, I realised who that meant was the new Pharaoh.

Octavian.

They may never have crowned him, but that was what he had become.

Alexandria had not changed a great deal since I was last there, apart from the fact the Forum Julium had been completed. Caesar had started the construction. When he died, Cleopatra carried on the project until we had so rudely interrupted with our war. And now Gallus had seen it through. The Forum was central in the city, facing the harbour. Covered walkways enclosed a public square, a very Roman set up, pointedly positioned right in the middle of this Egyptian city. In the middle of the square towered a vast obelisk, visible from miles around. It must have been eighty feet high. A monolith of red rock.

We made our way to inspect it, and in bronze letters the inscription read;

> AT THE BIDDING OF IMPERATOR CAESAR, SON OF THE DIVINE, GAIUS CORNELIUS GALLUS, SON OF GNAEUS, CHIEF ENGINEER OF CAESAR, SON OF THE DIVINE, BUILT THE FORUM JULIUM

'Caesar?' Whisper queried.

'Not Julius,' I replied. 'Remember that Octavian is Julius Caesar's adopted son. And the name of Caesar has power here. When this was put up, Octavian wouldn't have had the title Augustus yet. The sycophants hadn't given it to him by then.'

Whisper ignored my rant. 'So that Caesar means Octavian,' she said, pointing at the letters.

'It does,' I nodded. 'Son of the divine. So, Julius Caesar is the god, apparently,' I said, bitterly.

I could sense Whisper was becoming irritated by my complaints.

'What does that say?' she asked.

I had forgotten that she had only learned to read and write when she had come into my household.

'*Imperator*.'

'*Im-per-a-tor*,' she repeated back to me. 'And that means?'

I thought for a moment.

'You know, I'm not sure anymore. In the Republic, *imperator* simply meant commander. In recent times it became more of an honorific title all good Roman commanders sought; to win a battle and be acclaimed *imperator* and gain a triumph in your name. And after your triumph, you should relinquish the title.' I pointed at the letters. 'But Octavian has had his triumph, a triple triumph at that, yet still he keeps the title.'

Whisper considered for a moment. 'This isn't the Republic anymore,' she said.

I sighed.

'No. No it's not.'

Later, we learned that that mighty obelisk had originally stood at the temple of the sun god Ra in Heliopolis, the city of the sun in the South. It had been brought up to Alexandria, intended for Mark Antony. But Antony had died. Gallus had not missed the opportunity to take over such a striking monument.

'I can't see that there is anything wrong with the obelisk,' Whisper said.

I could not disagree. The inscription was humble to Gallus' master, and appropriate given the efforts Gallus had gone to in founding the new Forum.

'I agree. Perhaps we could attack the scale of the monument. But I don't doubt that Gallus consulted Octavian all about it.'

'So this doesn't provide us any case against Gallus.'

'No. So far, the only thing I could accuse him of is doing his job properly.'

Whisper looked thoughtful. 'There are an awful lot of statues of him, though. I can't help noticing them with that nose. If it wasn't for that, he'd be a handsome man.'

I playfully slapped Whisper on the shoulder.

'You shouldn't be noticing other men,' I said.

'Don't worry, I don't.' Whisper beamed her broad, beautiful smile at me. 'I don't know why, but even in the last couple of weeks, I've felt stronger...closer to you than ever.'

That timescale coincided with my new mission, my new life.

'Perhaps it's because Agrippa gave me purpose. I'm a man worth loving again.'

'That you are,' she replied, moving in to kiss me. 'That you are.'

I learned very quickly that Whisper was an extraordinary asset to acquire information. She had men selling their souls to her in no time. Combining Whisper's skills with the fact there were plenty of men dissatisfied with Gallus' rule and it did not take long to gather a picture of Gaius Cornelius Gallus.

A breakthrough occurred in the docks, always a seat of rumour and gossip.

'If you want to get the true picture,' one surly Egyptian sailor said, 'seek out Valerius Largus. He's on Gallus' staff. They used to be friends. But something's happened. Although he still works for Gallus. It's obvious the two despise each other.'

'Valerius Largus,' I repeated, noting the name and trying hard to recall whether I knew it. That was a Roman name. I did not want to meet anyone who knew me. There was a slim chance I would be recognised.

'Excuse me,' Whisper suddenly said and she dashed from the table and stepped outside the shop.

A moment later, she returned, wiping her mouth.

'You alright?' I asked.

'Yes,' she said. 'Just needed some air. It's so hot in here.'

I returned my attention to the sailor. 'Where will I find Largus?' I asked.

'For the right price, Largus will be at Caesar's statue in the Forum Julium tomorrow.'

'What is the right price?'

'A few drachma. Nothing too dear.'

The following day we stood before the statue of Caesar, trying to hide in his shadow from the blazing heat. We were early. The plan had been to meet at the eleventh hour. I was stifling. I was stifling because the closer I got to Gallus' court, the more important it was that no one knew who I was, and so I had donned my mask and become "The Mouth of Augustus". There was also a chance that as "The Mouth of Augustus", Largus might speak more freely.

As we waited, I recalled the grim tale of the statue which overshadowed us.

'This was the statue young Antyllus clung onto,' I said.

'Antyllus?' Whisper asked.

'Antony's son. When we took this city, Octavian ordered us to find and kill him. Antyllus ran to this statue, hoping that Caesar would protect him.'

'And did it?'

'Protect him from Gaius "You must die" Octavian?' I shook my head with a sarcastic smile. 'I think not.'

'That's awful,' Whisper said. She frowned and looked about her. 'To think the poor boy was dragged from this very spot...' She fell silent.

I refrained from telling Whisper that the person who had overseen his execution, his decapitation, was me.

'How old was he?'

'Seventeen maybe?'

'Just a boy,' Whisper said.

'Not just a boy,' I countered, 'By seventeen you are a man. Antony had named him his heir. That's why he was killed. None of Antony's other children were. But as Antony's heir, Antyllus was a threat to Octavian. His fate was sealed the moment Antony named him heir. From Octavian's point of view, Antyllus had to die.'

Valerius Largus approached. He was alone. Another Roman knight, with oily dark hair, dark eyes and tanned skin. As soon as I laid eyes on him, I knew I would not like him. But that day was not about liking the man, that day was about gaining information.

When he spotted my mask, he stared with patent suspicion. He stopped a distance away from us. 'Who are you?' he asked. 'And why are you wearing a mask?'

'I am "The Mouth of Augustus",' I replied. 'My name is not important. Why I am here, is. I am led to understand that you are a close associate of Gaius Cornelius Gallus. That means you can help me. Tell me all that you know about him.'

Largus tucked a straggling hair behind his ear nervously.

He had not expected to meet a masked man.

'You were sent by the *princeps*? By Augustus?' he asked.

'Who sent me is none of your concern...yet. All you have to do is talk.'

Largus dallied a little longer. He was clearly seeking an opportunity to attack Gallus. It was only a short delay before he made up his mind.

He talked.

And we learned. A great deal. Largus had been Gallus' trusted friend. But that was the key fact. Had been. From close friend to bitter enemy, that was the journey Largus had taken. Now, he simply worked for Gallus administering the province, as was his role. You could feel the enmity flowing from him as he tore into Gallus.

By all accounts it had started well. When Gallus had gained office, he had immediately been confronted with a revolt, in the Thebaid district. He suppressed it. All well and good. Then the first signs of his ambition were revealed. Gallus pushed on, crossing the first cataract into northern Nubia, where he laid claim to the temple of Isis at Philae.

'What's a cataract?' Whisper asked, a question I too was thinking.

Largus turned and took in Whisper. As he replied to her, he had eyes only for her. He ran his hand through his slick hair. 'It's a part of the river Nile you can cross,' he said. 'The water becomes shallow and there are boulders and stones so you can actually reach the bank on the other side.' He drank in Whisper for a little longer, before turning back to me. 'If you want to learn about Gallus,' he said gruffly, 'Philae is a place to go. You need to visit that temple.'

'Why?' I asked.

'You'll see.'

I considered for a moment. Philae was hundreds of miles away. But I had not gained any evidence of poor conduct as yet.

'What about Gallus the man?' I asked, 'still writing poetry?'

'Of course,' Largus sneered. 'Everyone seems to rate it highly, but I think it's dreadful. That said, nowadays he doesn't write as much as he used to. Too drunk.'

'Fond of the wine then,' I said.

'Understatement,' Largus replied, 'he drinks it by the amphora not the cup.'

Wine Loosens Tongues drifted into my head. A phrase from my past. A phrase an informant needs, as I had learned when I brought down Scribonius.

'Octavian is the Pharaoh,' Largus said, 'of course he is, but Gallus acts as if he is. He can't help himself.'

'How do you mean?'

'Everything about him,' Largus vented. 'His dress. He doesn't wear a toga anymore as the prefect of Egypt should, but Greek dress. And Athenian shoes.'

'By the gods,' I replied.

Whisper looked non-plussed. 'What's wrong with that?' she asked.

'Antony used to dress like that. Octavian braided him for it in Rome. He used to call him the "little Greek",' I said.

'What's wrong with Greek?' asked Whisper.

'Effeminate, excess,' Largus replied. 'Weak,' he concluded.

I scratched my face. 'Republicans would say Rome was built on dignity, gravitas and traditional, rustic values. Rome is strong.'

Whisper looked about her. She resisted saying out loud what I believe she was thinking. Alexandria looked just as strong a city, if not stronger.

'Come,' I said to Whisper, 'we need to go to Philae. At once. Largus, I thank you. When we return, we will meet again.'

'What do I get for this information?'

I looked at Largus, assessing him. 'For now. Nothing but the gratitude of Rome.'

Largus looked about to protest. I held up my hand.

'I may have need of you in the future, though. Need which will bring potential rewards.'

'Do you wish to meet Gallus?' Largus asked.

My hand moved involuntarily to my scar, hidden behind the mask. Gallus could well recognise me. We had seen each other at close quarters many times. Not least, only a few hundred yards away from where I was standing, in Cleopatra's Mausoleum which we had scaled together.

'Not yet,' I said. 'Not before Philae at least.'

The journey to Philae was hot and slow. My skin baked in the manner it had when I was stranded at sea. This time, however, I had ample supplies of water. And a companion.

Philae was a small island emerging, as if from nowhere, from the Nile. Steep walls of strange, dusky brown rock appeared. Within them, vast summits of temples towered high, white sandstone shining out from the dark, surrounding walls.

I blinked furiously, trying to focus. That view is still imprinted in my memory if I close my eyes.

'They say the light is strange here. Different somehow,' I said.

Whisper looked.

'It's just as intense a sun as in Alexandria,' she said.

'But the shadows, flowing over the walls. They look alive.'

Whisper looked again, unimpressed.

'It's smaller than I imagined,' she said.

'That's because you're used to Rome and Alexandria.'

'So what's at Philae?' she asked.

'It is one of their sacred places. The temple of Isis we're going to see. It's over three hundred years old. The

Egyptians believe Osiris, god of the afterlife, was buried here. Only priests can live here now. They say that no bird flies over this island, and fish swim by.'

'Incredible,' Whisper replied. 'But what about that one?' She pointed at a large bird, soaring high in the sky.

I chuckled. 'Never let the truth get in the way of a story.'

We disembarked. From the riverbank we approached the temple through a double colonnade.

'This is as impressive as the temple of Apollo,' Whisper said. 'Completely different though.'

She was right. The temples here were massive, solid and square forms. Very different to what I was accustomed to. Somehow, these were more dominating.

Whisper wiped her sweating forehead with her hand, suddenly flustered by the heat.

I caught her round her slender waist. 'What's wrong?' I asked.

'I don't know,' she replied. 'I feel giddy and can barely breathe. Must be the heat.'

I poured water over her hair and face to cool her.

'Come, we are nearly at the temple. It should be cooler in there.'

In front of the portico there were two colossal statues of lions, behind which two obelisks towered. We loitered in their shadow. As I waited for Whisper to recover, I looked around. This place was truly awe inspiring.

Everywhere I looked there was something to admire. All about me were inscriptions, characters I did not understand. The entire portico was covered with hieroglyphs in two layers. Six figures, divinities and priests as far as I could make out, all far bigger than a man, were on the upper layer of the two towers which loomed above me. Beneath them, larger figures. And two more on either side of the entrance. I did not know who they were. I did not need to know. I was already suitably impressed.

'Exciting huh?' I said. I felt a strange sense of privilege. After all, I should not have even been alive to witness this place.

'It's incredible,' Whisper said.

When Whisper felt able to move on, we climbed the few steps there were and passed through the entrance. As we passed under its shadow, I gave Whisper a little kiss on the neck.

We stood and absorbed our surroundings, assaulted by so many things to see. Sculptures, paintings. So many colours, and so vivid. I had been inside Cleopatra's palace, and that was stunning. But this was even more so. It left us speechless.

Forgetting our purpose, we entered the temple. We shuffled our way through three large chambers before reaching the sanctuary, where a hole, like a small cave, was carved out of the rock.

'In there is the cage of the Sacred Hawk,' I whispered. 'That's Osiris' space.'

There were other, smaller temples in that court. We spent the afternoon admiring them. One in particular honoured childbirth. Perhaps, in the enchantment of that place, I should have seen a sign. But I was never a seer.

Dusk was drawing in.

I nudged Whisper. 'We should find what we came for,' I said. 'Gallus' inscription.'

It did not take long to find. It was the one object which no passers-by were showing interest in. A slab of red rock, a little taller than myself, forming a *stela*.

'Well, I don't see what's so terrible about this?' said Whisper.

'Other than being unsightly,' I said, 'I agree, but let's read the inscription. There must have been a reason Largus sent us here. Look,' I said pointing at the writing. 'This is

Greek at the bottom. At least I can read that, and here look, there's Latin, and then Egyptian.'

'Do they all say the same?' asked Whisper.

I read aloud the inscription in Latin first.

'"Gaius Cornelius Gallus, son of Gnaeus, Roman knight, appointed the first governor of Alexandria and Egypt after the kings had been defeated by Caesar, son of a god."'

'Julius?' Whisper asked.

I shook my head. 'No, Octavian again. Remember the monolith in Alexandria? This is the same. Octavian used to called himself Caesar after his adoption. Then, he needed it to give himself authority. In those days, everyone thought he was so young and insignificant.' I sighed. 'How the world has changed.

'"He, Gallus, was twice victor in pitched battles during the Theban revolt in which he defeated the enemy within fifteen days. He took five cities, Boresos, Coptus, Ceramice, Diospolis Magna and Opheium." Well, I've never heard of any of those. "And captured the leaders of their revolts. Afterwards he led an army beyond the cataract," that word again, "of the Nile, into the region where arms had not previously been taken either by the Roman people or by the kings of Egypt".'

I paused for a moment and looked at Whisper.

She pulled a face at me. 'There's not much to criticise is there...'

'No,' I said, deflated. I turned back and continued. '"Afterwards he took Thebes, the shared fear of all the kings. After that he received ambassadors of the Ethiopian king at Philae and received that king into his protection. After that he appointed a ruler over the Ethiopian region of..." some place I can't even pronounce. It looks like Triacontaschoenus. I've never heard of it, but anyway, after all that, "he gave and dedicated this monument to the ancestral gods and the Nile, his helper."'

'That's it?' queried Whisper.

'That's it,' I replied, forlorn.

'What a waste of time this has been,' said Whisper, 'although we have seen this amazing place.'

I frowned. There had to be a reason Largus sent me here. Perhaps he thought that such a monument by a knight was inappropriate. But Octavian would surely have known Gallus was going to erect this stone, and in the environment it was in, it was pretty feeble. A pebble amongst mountains.

I looked at the depiction of a man on horseback, about to kill what looked like an enemy soldier.

'I suppose that's him,' said Whisper.

I shrugged my shoulders. 'Probably.' I was reeling. How was I going to build a case against Gallus? This was no evidence at all.

The Latin version and the Greek version were basically the same. 'There's a different tone occasionally,' I said. 'The Greek is softer, the Latin more triumphant. Probably because no one can read Latin around here. But there's nothing too self-glorifying in this. It's just like any other Roman monument. I suppose Largus' point is that this is a knight putting up a monument to himself. Not a Caesar or a Pompey. But I don't think it's enough. Not what I was hoping for at all.'

I looked again at the *stela*. Amongst the hieroglyphs there was a cartouche, an oblong frame. My limited knowledge of this language told me that this was used to show that the name inside was royal.

'Unless...' I said, exciting welling up inside me. 'Perhaps I could have Gallus after all.'

If it was his name inside the cartouche, proclaiming himself Pharaoh in Octavian's stead, I would have my evidence.

I inspected closely.

The name inside the cartouche was Octavian's.

'Damn,' I shouted and beat the *stela* with my fist.

'What?' said Whisper, startled.

'It even acknowledges Octavian as Pharaoh.'

'Pharaoh?'

'Octavian may never have been crowned as the new Pharaoh of Egypt, but that's what he is. Egypt has to have one. It's how their society works. Just as we need our consuls, well, we used to, Egyptians need their Pharaoh, their living god ruler. These priests need someone to worship, otherwise their whole society would break.'

'I see,' replied Whisper. 'So,' she pointed at the cartouche, 'that says Octavian.'

I nodded. 'It does.'

'And if Gallus had put his name as the Pharaoh, rather than Octavian's, you would have had something against him worth taking back to Rome.'

I sucked in my cheeks, trying to check my anger.

At last, I nodded, 'I would have indeed.'

I stared at the cartouche. Octavian's name seemed to sear my eyes. I blazed with anger. How could he be Pharaoh? I seized my dagger and began hacking at the stone. I stabbed wildly, again and again. I imagined the blade was actually cutting Octavian.

When at last Whisper managed to stop me, I was pouring with sweat.

'He's no Pharaoh,' I spat.

Whisper looked at the rock.

'Not any more,' she said. 'No one will ever be able to read that again.'

She looked about us, worried about witnesses. But the area around us was deserted. No one cared for Gallus' monument.

VIII

We returned to Alexandria. There again, we were confronted left, right and centre with statues of Gallus. It reassured me that I was making the right decision. Although he had not usurped Octavian outright, nor had he plotted against him, he had behaved in a way that the *princeps* would disapprove of. From what I knew of Octavian, there would be little patience with anyone trying to seek too much glory for themselves. All glory was reserved for the leading citizen, for Augustus.

I gathered further evidence. Inscriptions on the pyramids. Some would argue that these showed how Gallus had embedded himself into the Egyptian culture, how he was ensuring that the message of Roman dominance would be received loud and clear by the natives. But for the purposes of my case against him, this was clear evidence of hubris.

The final element of my plan involved Valerius Largus. With appropriate encouragement, it was clear that here was a man who would happily attend a dinner party with Gallus, ensure that sufficient wine was drunk, not a tricky task, and listen to Gallus' drunken comments.

Wine Loosens Tongues would surely come into its own once more.

Largus was a true businessman. He would only carry out the task once we had agreed a lucrative reward. A professional *delator* in the making.

Sure enough, Gallus, drunk, gorging on his glory, on the luxury of his palace and his kingdom, let slip a few coarse words about our *princeps*, Augustus.

Largus reported the careless words Gallus uttered to

"The Mouth of Augustus".

'There was the usual kind of comment about Augustus' frailty, and how it always seemed to occur before the battle. "How many times was he laid up in his tent, safely behind the battle lines?"'

'I bet he meant the battle against Sextus Pompey,' I laughed, before I realised how utterly inappropriate it would be for me to show any sign of agreement with negative comments about Octavian.

Largus was taken aback by my reaction. 'He mentioned that one, amongst others,' he replied hesitantly. 'He basically said what Antony always used to say, that Octavian was on his back in some fear ridden stupor, until Agrippa had put the enemy ships to flight.'

I knew this was true. Proof, if ever I needed it, that Agrippa should be the *princeps,* but that day, I had to play my role as "The Mouth of Augustus".

'That is a callous lie,' I said, firmly. 'You cannot trust a word Antony said. They were at war. What an insult this is to our *princeps.*' Then I remembered the one and only thing that had impressed me about that loathsome man. 'Who can doubt Augustus' mettle? Remember his efforts to join Caesar in Hispania?'

Largus evidently did not know of them. 'Fine efforts, I'm sure,' he said, with an oily tone to match his oily hair.

Years ago, when Octavian was perhaps only seventeen years old, he missed the departure of Caesar's campaign to Hispania because he was ill. It was Octavian's first military experience with Caesar, an opportunity not to be missed. So as soon as he was well, he set sail with Agrippa by his side, of course.

They were shipwrecked. Agrippa often told me that was the closest to death he had ever been. But they survived and made their way across hostile land, enemy troops surrounding them. Somehow they made it safely to

Caesar's camp.

I do not doubt for one moment that Agrippa was the driving force behind this effort, impressive as it was. Alas, Caesar credited Octavian. By the time they returned to Rome, they shared the same carriage.

Doubtless Caesar's trip to the Vestal Virgins to deposit his new will, with that wretched extra clause, followed soon after. So it would be that from his ashes in the Forum a new Caesar would be born after all.

And where was Agrippa in all of this? A loyal servant, winning the wars, fixing the roads, cleaning the city, giving water to the people. I will forever wonder what it was that Octavian did for Agrippa in those early years that made him so loyal?

I was disturbed from my thoughts by Largus.

'He said worse,' Largus smiled. 'Much worse.'

'Go on,' I said, listening eagerly once more.

'Conversation moved onto Caesarion. As you can imagine, here in Alexandria, there is still so much ill feeling about his death.'

'Not to be unexpected,' I replied. 'Caesarion, Cleopatra's son by Caesar, had escaped us when we took Alexandria. But there was no escape for that boy. Octavian's orders were simple and familiar. Find and kill.'

'Exactly,' said Largus, 'I'm sure the Alexandrians can voice their views. But I'm also sure Augustus would not be pleased to hear what his governor said.'

'Did he not defend the *princeps?*' I asked, refusing to use the name Augustus.

'He most certainly did not. Do you know what he said?'

I shook my head.

'He said, "That was murder. Plain and simple. He needed to do it, to secure his position. That boy had Caesar's blood flowing through his veins. Caesarion was the true successor in the making. Why else call him little Caesar?"'

Largus smiled. 'Does that sound like treason to you?'

It did not. But it was enough. Behind the mask, I smiled.

I turned to Whisper, 'We've got him.' I turned back to Largus. 'Largus, you are to return to Rome, at once. Seek an audience with the *princeps*. There you will report these accusations: that Gallus has betrayed his Roman roots, that he is boastful and behaves like the Pharaoh and that he is putting up monuments to himself.'

'It's a shame the *stela* identifies Octavian as Pharaoh,' said Largus, running his hand through his long hair.

I spotted an opportunity. If only I could claim it had been the plan all along.

'When we just visited, we could not read who was Pharaoh,' I replied.

'I was involved in that contract,' said Largus. 'It definitely says Octavian.'

'It has been defaced,' I said.

Largus frowned, thoughtful.

'Completely illegible?' he asked.

'Completely.'

'Very well,' he said. 'That damage must have been at Gallus' request.'

'Perhaps,' I replied. 'But there is no proof.'

'Who needs proof? When they hear the other accusations, no one will believe anything else.'

I smiled. The Fates must have guided me to deface that monument.

'Be sure to save the greatest accusation till last,' I said. 'That beyond usurping him in Egypt, he undermines the *princeps*, challenging his claim to be Caesar's rightful heir. That,' I pointed at Largus, 'is unforgivable.'

Largus grinned.

'So Gallus will fall?' he asked.

'That's for others to decide,' I said. 'But he will not be governor of Egypt for much longer I'm sure.'

Largus rubbed his hands together. 'Excellent,' he beamed.

I looked at the man in front of me. He disgusted me, so gleeful, so unrepentant.

'What happened between you two?' I asked.

Largus thought for a moment, considering whether to tell me or not.

'It doesn't matter,' he said, at last. 'Suffice it to say, I doubt there's anyone alive who hates anyone as much as I hate Gallus.'

I was fairly certain that I hated Octavian as much as he hated Gallus. And I was fairly certain that I hated Gallus as well. But I did not challenge his assertion, nor did I press him on the matter. Ultimately, it did not matter why Largus was doing this, so long as he saw it through.

'When you report back to Rome, it's vital you make no mention of me,' I said. 'If Rome hears that "The Mouth of Augustus" is involved, they will think that the whole affair has been engineered by the *princeps*. And we wouldn't want anyone to distrust our *princeps* now would we?'

I could not believe those words were emitting from my mouth. It is amazing what self-preservation does to a man.

Largus nodded.

'Do you understand me?' I said forcefully. 'It's vital that no mention of me occurs in Rome. If it does, you know how unforgiving Gaius "You must die" Octavian used to be...'

'I understand,' Largus said, holding up his hands. 'Anyway, why would I want to give anyone else share of the reward?'

Driven by money. The despicable man in front of me was precisely what I needed.

'Was Caesarion the rightful heir?' Whisper asked when we were alone.

I shook my head. 'That depends on your point of view,'

I said. 'In the eyes of some he has Caesar's blood in him, so he has more right than Octavian to be Caesar's heir. Others would say he's the illegitimate son of an Egyptian witch, who seduced Caesar and when he was dead, corrupted Antony.'

'What did most people think?' asked Whisper.

'It didn't matter,' I replied. 'If there was anyone who could try to challenge Octavian, there was only one solution.'

'So Octavian had Caesarion killed,' said Whisper.

'Yes,' I replied shortly. 'Seventeen years old and strangled to death. It was murder, plain and simple. Gallus is right.'

Whisper shook her head. I thought she was disapproving of Octavian's actions. She was, but she was also disapproving of something else.

'And we're going to ruin Gallus because of this?' she said. 'It doesn't feel right.'

I took Whisper's slender shoulders in my hands and turned her to face me. I looked into her beautiful eyes.

'Those are merely the words we'll use to bring about his demise, a demise he deserves, remember? You've seen the statues, and the *stela*, and the inscriptions on the pyramids with your own eyes. Hubris has overcome him. If we were able to see him, you would not feel that guilt.'

Whisper's eyes filled with tears.

'It's the same as Scribonius,' I continued. Until I met him again in Marseilles, and learned of the true beast of a man that he was, I had been racked with guilt about what I had done to him, and what it had caused for Whisper. 'I brought him down because he was a coward. A coward who dared to insult those who risked their lives during the civil wars.

The words he spoke against Octavian that I used to prosecute him were just the means. It was the outcome that mattered. And the outcome was just.'

Whisper's tears were flowing now. I had taken her back to the trial. And if she was recalling the trial, there was no way she was not remembering her torture.

I had nearly killed her.

I wiped the tears from her face.

'Here, the outcome is just,' I insisted. 'Gallus has done wrong. He has overreached himself. Such inscriptions, and Athenian dress, and too much wine, this is not conduct becoming of a Roman knight.'

Whisper just looked at me. 'Enough to bring him down?' she repeated.

'The governor of Egypt should be a senator, not merely a favourite of Octavian's,' I ranted. 'Certainly not a knight,' my voice was rising, out of control. 'It should have been me.' I paused, trying to calm myself. 'I am serving Agrippa, and he promised to restore the Republic.' I grabbed Whisper's arm. 'If bringing Gallus down hurts Octavian, even one tiny little bit, and restores a fragment of the Republic, then it's the right thing to do. He should be stripped of his governorship.'

She pulled away from me and wiped her face, taking a deep breath to compose herself again. As I watched her, I realised just how much I loved her. More even than my first wife, Olivia.

'What do we do now?' Whisper asked.

I thought for a moment. Gallus was doomed. It was just a matter of time. I felt I should confront him, face to face. If I did not, then it would feel like knifing someone in the back.

'I want to see him. To face him,' I said.

'Who?' asked Whisper alarmed, 'Gallus? You can't.'

'It doesn't feel right not to.'

'But he'll recognise you,' she said.

'Perhaps,' I shrugged.

Whisper looked exasperated. 'Don't you understand?' she exclaimed.

'No one must even begin to believe you could still be alive. No one must see that scar. With a scarred man, and a masked man wandering around the Empire calling himself "The Mouth of Augustus", you'd be dead in no time. And I can't live with that. I've lost you once already.' She pulled me into a tight embrace. 'I'm not losing you again, as Fides is my witness.'

I sighed. Whisper was right. There could be no final showdown between myself and Gallus. She took my head in her hands and kissed me gently.

'I knew you had a heart too. It's because you feel guilty as well.'

Despite my hatred of Gallus, and Octavian, there was something about bringing destruction in the shadows which did not sit well with me.

'But,' Whisper tucked her hair behind her ear, 'as you said. We are doing the right thing. Gallus should be punished. He's not committed treason, but you're not accusing him of that. You're getting the truth reported back into Rome.'

'Apart from the cartouche?' I mumbled.

'The truth with a few exaggerations,' she conceded. 'But when you look around the province, we're in the right. It is fair if he's stripped of the governorship. He's another who thinks an awful lot of himself. And, as you always say, he's only a knight. Even in Octavian's Rome, knights should know how to behave, no?'

'That, I can't argue with,' I said. 'So,' I sighed, 'we press on.'

'Are we returning to Rome with Largus?' Whisper asked.

I shook my head. 'No. I think it best we stay away from it all. Looking Largus in the eye, I am certain that he will carry out his orders. The combined lures of revenge and money are far too great for him to do anything else. We will make our way to Rome in our own time. I would like to return via Greece, to set eyes on Actium once more.'

'Do you send word to Agrippa?' Whisper asked.

'I think not. Keep him clear of the whole affair. He sent me to find out the truth of a rumour. Largus will bring the report back to Rome. There need be no link to say I am behind it, and definitely no link to Agrippa. His character must never be tainted.'

That evening was to be our last in Alexandria. We strolled the beautiful city. The Greek and Roman quarter was laid out in a very structured way, with straight streets from north to south meeting more straight streets from east to west at crossroads. We ambled down the colonnade of the main route through the city, enjoying the cool of the north wind.

I looked about me. I had probably run through this broad road, so much more spacious than any street in Rome, with bloodied sword in hand on the day we took Alexandria. The city fell on the first day of the month of Sextilis. Since that time Sextilis has been renamed August, after our *princeps* Augustus. But, in defiance, I still say Sextilis, just as I will always call that man by his true name, Octavian.

As we reached the centre of Alexandria, we entered a vast precinct. We saw the Mausoleum of Alexander the Great, enclosed within high walls. It was surrounded with people. I pointed it out to Whisper.

'That's the *soma,*' I said, directing her to look at the small edifice. '*Soma* is greek for "body". Hundreds of years ago, they brought Alexander the Great's body to this city from his original burial place in the south, in the former capital of Memphis.'

'What did Alexander do? Why are there so many people?'

'He was king of Macedon, from an early age, and a warmonger. He expanded their empire to one of the greatest and biggest in the world.'

'Lots of people have done that,' replied Whisper.

'Ah, but Alexander never lost a battle, even winning when he should have lost. Given he fought so many, that's all the more remarkable. In the end, guess what killed him?'

'His wife?' replied Whisper with more wisdom that I realised.

'No,' I said. 'Fever. Simple fever.'

'So many people want to see it,' said Whisper, admiring the queues.

'Indeed. Octavian visited, when we here.' I felt a flicker of anger when I remembered his veneration of a king. 'Do you know what he said to me, when I said Alexander was the greatest king ever?'

'"The greatest yet..."' Whisper replied with a roll of her eyes.

She had heard that rant before, many times.

'Octavian laid flowers on the tomb and put a golden diadem on Alexander's head, you know. And still the Romans were blind to his pursuit of kingship.'

Whisper patted my arm.

'There was a story going round that he knocked Alexander's nose off, but I doubt it was true.' I said. 'He would have been far too worshipful to damage it.'

Whisper turned and looked at me. 'Shall we see for ourselves?' she asked, with excited eyes.

'Oh, very well,' I replied, staring reluctantly at the crowd. 'Caesar and Pompey visited the tomb as well as that reprobate. Even if I don't agree with kings I suppose it must be worth seeing.'

It was. We queued for a long time and when at last we entered the chamber we were shuffled along, hurrying to let as many people in as possible, all of them paying their way.

There were several bodies in there, family of one or other

of the Ptolemies. But no one cared about them. Everyone had a sole interest.

At last, deep in the inner sanctum, by the flickering light of our guide's flaming torch, we saw him. It was eerie and awe inspiring all at once. The peculiar smell of the chamber adding to the sense of strangeness. It truly felt as if we had left the land of the living.

There was no damage I could see, so the story about Octavian had been false, but, to my further displeasure, the diadem Octavian had given was still there.

When I stood in front of that diadem, I pictured Octavian standing in my exact position. I shuddered.

'He was here,' I muttered, 'standing right on this spot.'

Whisper did not reply. She knew who I was talking about.

'How do I hurt him?' I implored Alexander. 'How do I get revenge? He's not a king worthy of you.'

'What did you think?' asked Whisper as we emerged back into the evening sunlight.

'I'm glad we saw it,' I replied. 'Though it wasn't as impressive as it would have been originally. They buried him in a sarcophagus of pure gold at first, filled with honey. And they put the golden sarcophagus in a casket made of gold too. That would have been worth seeing. But one of the Ptolemies saw the worth in it too. He melted it all down for coins.'

'So we don't get to see it. That's so unfair,' Whisper complained, 'and disrespectful.'

I considered the glass replacement we had just seen. It was not nearly as impressive.

'Once you're dead, there are no rules,' I mused, 'no matter how great you were. Perhaps Octavian should think on that.'

We continued our tour of the city. Somehow as we trod the streets, I knew this would be the last time I set eyes on Alexandria. It was a beautiful city. We made our way slowly towards the shipyards.

'There are so many,' Whisper said.

'More here than any other port in the empire, they say,' I looked on at the hustle and bustle of the docks.

Above the harbour stood the great theatre, rival to any I had seen in the empire.

'Caesar withstood a siege in there,' I said, 'when he took Alexandria.'

'What about when you took Alexandria?' Whisper asked.

I shook my head.

'There was no siege then,' I replied. 'They knew they were beaten.'

We looked across to the small island connected by the mole, emerging from the murky waters of the harbour. On one end stood the vast lighthouse, which would soon guide us back out to sea. At the other end, on a promontory, stood the Temple of Poseidon, and behind that was a building worth contemplating. It was at the far tip of the promontory. The last refuge of Antony, a magnificent temple.

'What's that?' asked Whisper.

'That was built by Antony. After we defeated him at Actium.'

'That quickly?' Whisper queried. 'I thought you followed him here and killed him.'

'We did. So you're probably right. He was already building a temple. But he definitely named it after the battle.' I scratched my chin thoughtfully. 'He called it the *Timonium.*'

'*Timonium,*' Whisper repeated slowly. 'What does that mean?'

'Timon is a man. An Athenian, famous for his generosity. But he was so quick to spend, he ran out of money and his friends abandoned him.'

'Bit like you,' Whisper laughed.

I scraped my sandal on the floor. 'Yes I suppose so,' I said. 'Timon was reduced to working in the fields. One day, like me, he found money again and suddenly, unlike me, the friends were back. He literally threw mud at them.'

'So Antony was comparing himself to Timon?' asked Whisper.

'Presumably he felt deserted by his friends,' I replied. 'They say after Actium, he boarded Cleopatra's ship and ignored her for three days. He sat at the prow, alone, and refused to speak to anyone. Perhaps it continued when they finally returned to Alexandria? Perhaps he sat isolated in the wilderness in that temple.'

'He had everything,' Whisper mused. 'And lost it all. That is something to grieve.'

'But he lost it to Octavian,' I said. 'I fear there is no one who can withstand that man.' I folded my arms. 'I don't blame Antony for losing. I don't fall for all the ill comments about his love of this place, and of Cleopatra. Look about us. This is a great city, a great people. All Antony did wrong was underestimate Octavian.

'He missed the only chance we ever had to stop Octavian. That clause in the will. If Octavian could never have claimed to be Caesar's son, he would never have become the *princeps.* But once he had the name, with the loyalty and prowess of Agrippa, he's been unstoppable, and relentless, and all the things I hate.'

We gazed out to sea.

'Come, it's time for us to go. Say farewell to Alexandria.'

We set sail but not for Rome. I wanted to return to Actium, to face my past. I had to lay eyes on the scene of my demise one last time. It all happened so fast, in the furore of the battle. Before that moment, my life had been a success. After, it had spiralled so quickly out of control I had behaved in ways I cannot believe.

So we sailed to western Greece and, like Antony before me, I stared at the waves of the Ionian sea, picturing the horror of the battle of Actium, the flicker of the flames, the arrow in Sextus' cheekbone.

I wept with Whisper's arms gently holding me.

'How could I have known?' I sobbed.

'You couldn't,' Whisper said quietly and kissed my shoulder.

'One mistake,' I said, 'one mistake.'

'I know,' said Whisper, 'I know.'

We headed a short while north to Nicopolis, the City of Victory which Octavian had founded in celebration of Actium.

It was not the new walls which linger in the memory, nor the theatre, the gymnasium, nor even the aqueduct being constructed at such a remarkable speed. No, I will always remember Nicopolis because it was there that I took up my conflict with Octavian once more, and there that I had the moment when my life changed forever.

The site of the new city was founded where we had pitched camp in the build up to the battle of Actium. From the city's northern gate, we could see on the summit of a hill the very spot where Octavian's tent was pitched. Now, as we looked up on the hillside, there was a new monument. From a distance it looked like an open-air sanctuary.

We traipsed up the track to inspect more closely. In the heat, and with the slope, Whisper struggled for breath.

The monument was built on two terraces. Standing on the concrete of the lower terrace we were confronted with a wall perhaps five times my height with an incredible sight.

A striking line of monstrous bronze rams from the enemy galleys taken at Actium. Thirty-six of them were mounted in a line on the wall in front of us. They were placed side by side in size order, from smallest to largest. All of them had been taken from Antony and Cleopatra's fleet. Above these were vast white blocks, monumental foundations of the upper terrace. They bore an inscription.

We walked in wonder along the full length of the wall. The ram display nearly rendered me speechless. This monument's purpose was to command attention. It had it, completely and utterly.

I read the inscription to Whisper.

'Imperator Caesar, son of the divine Julius, following the victory in the war which he waged,' I hesitated, gall gathering inside me, 'on behalf of the Republic,' I snarled. I shook my head in contempt before continuing. 'In this region when he was consul for the fifth time and imperator for the seventh time, after peace had been secured on land and sea, consecrated to Mars and Neptune the camp from which he set forth to attack the enemy, which is now ornamented with naval spoils.'

'No mention of Agrippa then,' said Whisper.

I stared in dismay as yet again, another reminder of that battle was in front of me.

'Neptune and Mars?' I raged. 'Where's the gratitude for Agrippa?

'Yesterday, I felt as if I had at last left Actium behind,' I moaned. 'But today, I face these rams from the ships. Will I never escape?'

I marched away from the inscription, heading up the slope of the hill on the east side to a gate.

There, at the summit, was a portico with covered colonnades on three sides. When I entered the gate, I saw a collection of items in the courtyard: coils of line, anchors, oars, a couple of figureheads from Egyptian galleys, all trophies of the victory, but my focus was brought to two statues on pedestals in the centre and a monumental altar.

'Octavian I bet,' I said and strode over to look.

But it was not Octavian. That much was immediately evident for one of the statues, because it was an ass, a bronze ass. The other was a man, but it was not a face I recognised.

'Who is it?' asked Whisper who clutched at her stomach as she made her way over.

'I'm not sure,' I replied, thinking hard who these could be. 'This must be the man driving the ass whom Octavian was supposed to have met the day before the battle. He had a strange name, Eutychos, and the ass was called Nikon. Octavian took it as a positive omen because their names meant "lucky" and "victorious". Perhaps he was right.'

I glared at the monumental altar.

'That's where his tent was pitched,' I nodded. 'Right on that spot. Now what is it? An altar to Apollo?' I sneered.

As I stood looking at the altar, I realised that my eyeline could see Actium in the background and the shore where the temple of Apollo Actius stood. I gazed wistfully to sea, before looking around and admiring the mountains in the background.

I looked more closely at the altar. The relief was covered with ships, and soldiers, weapons and trophies. There was a frieze with a sacrificial procession, a young face which looked too much like the many representations of Octavian to have been anyone else. The whole piece was covered with floral decoration. I had not seen such scale and quality before. Then my eye was drawn to another procession.

A man, inevitably Octavian, stood behind a four horse chariot. The chariot was heavily decorated with acanthus leaf vines.

'This represents his triple triumph,' I whispered. My finger traced his face on the marble. I could recollect the moment I had an arrow trained on him, aiming just under his eye, where Sextus had been struck.

I was there at the triumph, hiding on the rooftop behind a statue. I could have loosed the arrow and Octavian would be dead. There would be no *princeps,* no 'Augustus'.

It was a peculiar experience, as strange as seeing my own grave.

There I was, stood on a hill in Greece, but I felt as if I was on that rooftop in Rome, on the triumphal route.

Whisper tugged at my arm.

'What is it?' she asked.

'Nothing,' I said. 'More regrets,' I added.

We stood in silence for a moment, the sun blazing onto the altar.

'Apollo is the god of the sun, isn't he?' Whisper asked.

'He is,' I replied. 'Amongst many other things.'

'You came here to heal Actium, didn't you?' said Whisper.

I nodded. 'But I have not healed.'

'Perhaps, if you were to remember Actium for a different reason, that would help?'

I raised my eyebrows.

'What different reason?' I said, shortly.

Whisper smiled at me.

'I'm carrying your child,' she said.

I stared in utter disbelief.

Whisper smiled at me, a tear in her eye.

'You're going to be a father,' she said.

I slumped to my knees and buried my face into Whisper's stomach, clutching at the folds of her dress.

She pulled me to my feet.

'Now, when you think of this hill, of this sanctuary, of that sea,' she pointed at the glistening waters in the bay of Actium, 'you can think of this moment.'

I wept with joy.

'And because it's a sunny day,' she continued with a

beaming smile, 'you can take me to that other temple of Apollo.'

The temple of Apollo Actius, an ancient shrine, stood close to the site of the battle. Octavian had enlarged and renovated this temple partly in thanks but just as much to ingratiate himself with the locals.

We gave thanks in that temple of Apollo for the unborn child.

As I left the temple I felt a new strength, a new purpose and a feeling that I could achieve anything brewing inside me. To my amazement, nearby we discovered ten beached warships, complete warships.

'Those must be the ones Agrippa told him to dedicate,' I said in wonder.

'What?' asked Whisper.

'I overheard Octavian and Agrippa talking in Octavian's tent just after the battle.'

'You were destined to be an informant!' taunted Whisper. She looked at her stomach, 'Don't you go listening in the shadows,' she said.

I smiled at Whisper, still disbelieving that inside her beautiful body was a son or daughter of mine. My firstborn.

I looked back at the ships. 'Look, there is one of every size that was involved in the battle, from the smallest to the biggest.'

'What size was yours?' Whisper asked.

'My *Triton?*' I said, 'certainly not as big as these. These monsters were definitely Antony's. But mine wasn't as small as the smallest over there. It was probably like this one.' I patted the wood of the hull.

When my hand touched the hull, something inside me ignited. It was the wrath I felt for Octavian. Somehow, where it had been seething like embers in a fire, now, seeing this offering, the flames erupted. Octavian had done so much to make Actium stand out as the moment the gods chose him. And yet the admiral of his fleet, the man who won it for him, was Agrippa.

This gift to Octavian's protector god, to Apollo, was simply wrong. I had to do something about it. Imbued with new confidence, with the manliness of being a father, I did.

That night under cover of darkness, I turned the flames of my anger into real flames. I set fire to those ships and burned them, all ten of them, to ashes. The flames leapt to the sky and lit up the hills. I stood wild-eyed and furious, watching the blaze eat the ships as they had done so horrifically in front of me in Actium.

But this time, the warmth of the fire on my face was a source of comfort, of joy even. This was a small attack on Octavian, but it would be one of many. This was the revenge of Marcus Rutilius Crispus.

I looked about me, wary of the city folk who would surely come to save the ships. But no one came.

No one cared.

IX

Whisper and I made safe passage back to Rome. I began to notice changes in her. Her stomach grew. Her breasts began to swell, but I swiftly learned that as they grew, they became sensitive too.

I was going to become a father. Was it a son or a daughter? Romans always want a son, a man to carry on the family name. But I had lost my family name, so as I stared out to sea on the return journey, I realised that I did not care. Girl or boy, all I wanted was a healthy baby and, more importantly, a healthy Whisper.

'What will we call him if he's a boy?' Whisper asked.

'I'm not sure,' I replied, 'A name will come to us. Perhaps, in some way, we can honour Agrippa by it.'

'And if it's a girl?'

I hesitated. If it was a girl, I had no idea.

'If I was still Marcus Rutilius Crispus, she would be Rutilia.'

'I'm not sure that's such a good name,'

'Neither am I,' I agreed. 'Inspiration will come,' I said caressing the back of Whisper's head. 'We still have time.'

As we drew into the port of Ostia at the mouth of the Tiber, twenty miles west of Rome, I felt a rush of nerves. Soon we would learn what had befallen Gallus. Soon we would learn whether Valerius Largus had kept his word. Had he mentioned "The Mouth of Augustus"?

Ostia had developed into a flourishing harbour town because of the multitude of grain ships flowing to Rome. As a result, there were plenty of shops to choose from for food and drink to nourish ourselves. The most notable difference compared with Alexandria, apart from size, was the absence of marble in this town. The temples, four small and handsome ones that I saw, were all made of stone. Only one, the temple of Hercules, stood out.

'We should go in there,' I said, beginning to climb the eight stone steps to the temple entrance.

'Why?' asked Whisper. 'It's not particularly impressive.'

'No,' I said, 'but it's to Hercules. And he is a god of children, and childbirth.' I turned and smiled at my blossoming Whisper. 'I wouldn't want to upset him now would I.'

Whisper shook her head.

'What has Hercules got to do with children?' she asked as she carefully made her way up the stairs. 'I thought he was all about strength. Juno Lucina is the goddess of labour. I have already prayed to her.'

'A good plan. And there are the goddesses of childbirth. Their altar is in the Plains of Mars, not too far from our temple to Fides. We will pray to them too. But now I am determined we need to buy a proper home.

We cannot hide in the temple of Fides forever.

'And when the time comes, whatever home we are in we will offer a bed to Juno, and a table set for Hercules. There are countless other deities who will get involved, but we can worry about them later.'

'But why Hercules?' Whisper persisted.

'I'm not sure. Perhaps it's because he was such a strong child. He strangled a snake sent to kill him in his cradle.' I had another, less venerable thought. 'Or because he fathered so many children. Who knows? I'm not particularly superstitious, but in this case, I'm not taking any chances.'

I looked at Whisper. 'Babies die, Whisper. So do their mothers. And it doesn't matter how important the person is. Remember Julia, Caesar's daughter, wife of Pompey the

Great? Few ladies in Rome could have been more important than her and she was taken in childbirth.'

Whisper grew pale. 'And the child?'

'Died a few days later,' I said, 'which is why, delighted though I am by our news, I am also afraid. Come, let us pray to Hercules.'

The temple was small. Inside we found the first trace of marble in the city. It was a statue of Hercules. The base told me a freedman had dedicated it, Publius Livius. Beside Hercules, in the temple chamber, another naked statue caught Whisper's eye because it was entirely nude.

'Who's that?' she said, almost blushing.

I read the inscription.

'It's Gaius Cartilius Poplicola, *duovir* of the city.'

'*Duovir?*' Whisper asked.

'Leader,' I explained, 'like a consul of the town. It says here for the third time, but I'm sure he's been elected more times than that. He is a supporter of Octavian. His name has been around the senate a long time, ever since he warded Sextus Pompey off of this port.'

'Well,' she concluded, 'I've seen more of him than I needed too.'

We made an offering at the altar and stepped back into the light.

Perhaps instigated by our visit to Hercules, as we descended the steps, hand in hand, I thought of the knot of Hercules, tied around a bride's waist. It became clear to me that I should marry Whisper. Her mother may not be there to tie the knot, and, technically, I had more than untied it on several occasions, but Whisper had done more than enough to become my wife. Whether I was worthy to be her husband was less certain.

At the foot of the steps, I gripped her shoulders.

'Whisper,' I said, 'you have brought love and laughter

into my world which was filled with darkness and hatred.' Whisper looked at the ground, almost embarrassed. 'Now, you will bring life. By Hercules, by

Jupiter, by all the gods of goddesses in all of the world,' I said looking to the skies, 'I love you, more than I can put into words, and I would be honoured if you would become my wife.'

Whisper bit her lip as tears of joy welled up in her eyes. I will forever remember her expression. Genuine happiness. Even after all the things I had done.

'Of course,' she said. 'Of course.'

We kissed and embraced, loving and long.

'We must buy you a betrothal ring,' I said and we headed back to the town.

There were so many shops in Ostia and so much choice. There were just as many taverns, but with so many merchants and seaman, that was to be expected.

It was a squalid, smelly town. I looked about me.

'You know what this place needs?' I concluded.

'What?' asked Whisper.

'A dose of Agrippa. He'd soon sort this.'

'He's too busy in Rome, surely?' said Whisper.

'Rome,' I repeated. 'Half of me can't wait to return. The other half,' I clasped my hands, 'dreads it.'

'Well, you don't have to think about it yet,' smiled Whisper. 'You need to buy me a ring.'

Several hours later and with very sore feet with all the walking, I bought Whisper a plain, slim, iron ring.

'Simply beautiful,' I said as I handed the money over, 'just like you.'

'Which finger do I put it on?' Whisper asked.

'The third of your left hand, because a vein runs straight from there,' I traced from her finger up her arm to her chest, 'all the way to your heart.'

She slipped the ring on. I kissed her hand. 'I pledge that our marriage will be as strong as this iron. The Fates brought us together. They will not tear us apart, no matter what threads they have in store for us.'

'I am yours forever,' said Whisper.

It was the happiest I had felt in my life. I knew then that if there was any way I could engineer it, I wanted Agrippa to marry us, but I did not tell Whisper, in case I was dreaming the impossible.

We acquired passage on a small boat which sailed up the Tiber and returned us at last to Rome.

'Now we discover what Largus has achieved,' I said. 'And what next for us?'

I had no idea whether Octavian and Agrippa still used the code I had discovered to communicate, but it seemed a sensible way for me to request an audience with Agrippa.

J IBWF SFUVSOFE. NFFU NF JO UIF IPVTF PG UIF SBNT. UPNPSSPX.

'What if he's busy?' asked Whisper.

'Then he can send word. I will go there as "The Mouth of Augustus", just in case.'

Whisper took the letter to "The House of the Rams" and ensured that the message would reach Rome's consul. Then we hid away in the temple of Fides and made love, relieved to be back in Rome.

'This place feels like home now,' Whisper said.

The following day, I dressed as "The Mouth of Augustus" and loitered in the vicinity of "The House of the Rams". When I saw a large entourage arrive, I knew that Agrippa had received the message and made himself available. Before he would even have settled himself into the house, I knocked on the door. I was eyed warily by the guard at the door before Agrippa's consent was given.

Even in the months we had been away, Agrippa had aged visibly. His hair was almost entirely grey now, with only surviving traces of the jet black it used to be.

'Hail consul Agrippa,' I said, saluting.

Agrippa stared at me.

'I am no longer consul,' he replied.

'Who is?'

'Augustus,'

'That goes without saying. What's this his eighth consulship? Ninth?'

Agrippa ignored me. 'Statilius Taurus is his colleague.'

I knew Statilius Taurus. I had described him before as Octavian's most loyal commander after Agrippa and this consulship proved me right. Consul despite the fact he was a new man, rising from southern Italy to the pinnacle of Rome.

'Ah,' I replied, 'Taurus. He is a worthy man.'

But I had seen Octavian's hands round his throat, just as they had been around mine. Since that day in Alexandria, Taurus had been at the forefront of Octavian's wars. He must have performed so well that Octavian had rewarded him with the consulship.

'Enough of the formalities,' Agrippa said, reaching for the wine. 'It's good to see you. Honestly it is.' He poured wine into two silver cups. 'I wondered if you'd return at all, or whether I had, in fact, seen the last of you.'

'Seen the last of me?' I asked, 'that sounds a little hostile.'

'Does it?' Agrippa sighed. 'It doesn't mean to be. I am weary Rutili—' he checked himself, 'Sextus. It has been a difficult time.'

'Why's that?' I asked. 'Is Octavian back in Rome?'

Agrippa glared at me. 'Augustus,' he corrected me. 'No, no he's not. He's ill. Heading to Tarraco in Spain to recover.'

Agrippa took a sip. 'But you didn't come here to talk about Augustus.'

'No, I did not,' I picked up the silver cup. 'I came to report on Gallus.'

Agrippa's thick eyebrows rose and his brow furrowed with deep grooves. He looked at me.

'Gallus?'

'Yes, as was my mission,' I said hesitantly.

'Gallus is dead.' Agrippa replied.

I gaped.

'Dead?'

Agrippa nodded. 'He committed suicide.'

'Suicide?' I repeated in disbelief. 'Why?'

'Because he had been ruined. I thought you'd know,' Agrippa said staring at me intently.

'No I didn't,' I replied honestly. 'I don't understand.'

'It was a sorry affair,' said Agrippa. He took a draught of wine. 'Betrayed by his friend, one Valerius Largus.'

'I see,' I said trying not to reveal recognition of Largus' name. 'What did Largus do?'

Agrippa sighed. 'Accused Gallus of a number of things. Some we suspected,' he pointed the cup in my direction, 'which is why I sent you there. Others were new.'

'What did Largus find?'

Agrippa paused.

'What did you find?' he asked.

I swallowed, took a shaky sip of wine and thought furiously. What should I say? How much should I reveal? Then I remembered. Gallus was dead. He had obviously been found guilty of whatever he had been accused of.

'I found evidence of what you feared.'

'What evidence?'

'Surely the same as Largus,' I replied hoping that might be sufficient.

It was not.

'What evidence?' Agrippa said testily.

'Besides too much drink? And arrogance equalled only by Antony?'

Agrippa took a long sip of his wine. He wiped his mouth. 'People should not lose their lives over drink,' he said.

'There were inscriptions,' I countered. 'On the pyramids, statues everywhere. An enormous obelisk.'

'I know about the obelisk. I was involved in the contracts and the wording was personally agreed by Augustus.'

'And a *stela*.'

'Ah yes, the *stela*,' Agrippa replied, leaning forward. 'What did that say?'

I stared at Agrippa. Had he been involved in the contracts and creation of that monument too? If he had he would know what it was supposed to say.

'I don't know entirely,' I said. 'I read the Latin and the Greek, but could not understand the hieroglyphics. The Latin inscription was boastful, more so than the Greek.'

'Sensible,' replied Agrippa. 'The people subjected to his rule were Greek speaking. He wouldn't want to instigate hatred.' He began to pour himself another wine. 'I find it strange, you see. Most inscriptions are worded strongly. That's the thing about conquering people. You've defeated them.'

'So you would not have punished Gallus with the evidence I bring?' I asked.

'What does it matter?' Agrippa replied. 'He's dead.' He stopped pouring and set down the wine jug beside his cup. He gripped the table and bent over it wearily. 'I'm sorry Rutilius, I don't mean to be short with you.

'Largus accused Gallus of treasonable comments at banquets when he had drunk too much. He also mentioned that Gallus had proclaimed himself Pharaoh rather than Augustus.'

'How so?'

'In a cartouche, on that *stela.*'

'I'm afraid I wouldn't know,' I lied. 'I couldn't read it.'

Agrippa eyed me for a moment. 'It appears no one can anymore. I am certain it used to read Augustus, but now, it appears, no one in Egypt can read it.'

There was an awkward silence.

'But if you would not have punished him for the evidence I have brought back, how is it that he is dead?'

Agrippa took up his wine cup.

'*I* might not have punished him. But Augustus saw fit to. Perhaps, sitting in Spain, he is more afraid of rebellion, I don't know. Whatever the reason, Augustus decided to renounce his friendship, formally. He stripped Gallus of his governorship, of all his honours and even forbade him entry to any of the imperial provinces.'

'Banned him from the provinces?'

'To restrict his business,' Agrippa replied.

'Vindictive,' I said, failing to restrain myself.

Agrippa took a sip. It seemed to me that he agreed, the first sign of disapproval I had witnessed.

'So Gallus committed suicide?' I asked.

Agrippa shook his head.

'That renunciation was only the beginning. The senate set on Gallus like a pack of dogs. Accusations of this, that and the other. It was a bloodbath, metaphorically speaking. All this, when from what I can see, indiscretion of the amphora was his only true vice. But amongst the senate, suddenly he was accused of embezzlement, of plotting against Augustus. You name it, he'd done it. The senate decreed that Gallus should be brought to trial at the jury courts. Without Augustus' support, Gallus clearly only saw one option.'

I was a whirlpool of emotions. I confess the strongest was guilt. I had, for years, wanted revenge against Gaius Cornelius Gallus. But now I was confronted with his death, his suicide, and I had blood on my hands, I did not feel any satisfaction. Perhaps it was my impending marriage and fatherhood, or perhaps the gods had finally granted me wisdom, but I felt sorrow for Gallus.

In the Rome we returned to, it appeared there was not a Roman in the city who did not believe that in a cartouche on a *stela* in Philae, Gaius Cornelius Gallus had proclaimed himself Pharaoh. Largus had more than achieved what was intended.

'The senate voted unanimously to exile him, strip him of his lands and hand them over to Augustus.'

That punishment felt all too familiar.

'They even voted a solemn thanksgiving to the gods for the discovery and suppression of a conspiracy.'

'So he really was treated as a public enemy.'

Agrippa nodded. 'He was. Scant reward for years of service. Augustus wept at his death.'

'Wept?' I said bemused, 'but he caused it?'

'Precisely. But he didn't mean to. All he wanted was to secure his own position. Gallus was supposed to retire and write poetry to his heart's content.'

I huffed scornfully.

'Augustus let it be known in Rome how unhappy he was that he could not be as angry as he wanted with his own friends.'

'How was that received?' I asked.

'I fear the point was missed,' Agrippa replied, 'Augustus masked it with some phrase or other praising the 'loyal devotion' of those who were so greatly indignant on his behalf at Gallus' conduct.'

I laughed. 'People hear what they want to hear,' I reflected on the news. Gallus, despite my hatred of him, had caused me to feel guilt and even admiration for him. After all, when his world had fallen apart, he had achieved what I could not, even under instruction; he had fallen on his sword.

A sudden thought struck me. 'Who is governor of Egypt now?'

Agrippa hesitated. 'Aelius Gallus,' he said, 'another knight.'

I could not help the smile that crossed my lips. It was not genuine. It was rueful, disbelieving, an alternative to screaming.

One knight for another. Even worse, albeit unrelated, one Gallus for another.

'Little change then,' I concluded. I looked about me, wondering what next. 'What happened to Largus?'

'It did not end well for him either,' said Agrippa. 'Initially the weak-minded flocked to his side, expecting him to be in favour. But Largus is not a likeable man. Have you met him?'

Thankfully, Agrippa did not wait for me to answer.

'Proculeius soon saw to that,' he continued, 'on Augustus' instruction of course.'

'Saw to what?' I replied. 'What does that mean?'

'A story flew about Rome that when Proculeius met Largus in the street, he clapped his hand over his own mouth and nose, claiming it was not safe even to breathe in Largus' presence, or he will falsely accuse you. He then arranged for another man, someone Largus had never met before, to come across him in the street, and ask in front of witnesses whether they knew each other.'

'What happened?'

'Largus said no, they had not met before. So the man told the witnesses to write it down, so there was no way Largus could inform against him.'

'Informing is a sordid business,' I replied cagily.

'It is,' Agrippa replied. 'There's a fine line between informing and reporting though. Your venture to Egypt was to provide a report. Largus, and "The Mouth of

Octavian", that was different.'

'I don't imagine "The Mouth of Octavian" will return.' I said.

Agrippa fixed me with a strong gaze.

'"The Mouth of Octavian" must never return, you understand?'

I took a sip, choosing to remain silent.

'What next?' I asked.

Agrippa put down his cup and traced his finger around the edge, as if deciding whether to talk more.

'You know Augustus' nephew, Marcellus?' he said at last.

'I know of him.'

'He is to marry Augustus' daughter Julia. Later this year.'

Now I understood the reason for Agrippa's foul mood.

'I see. He must be what, sixteen, seventeen years old by now.'

Agrippa nodded.

'A successor in the making, no doubt,' I added.

I noticed Agrippa grip the top of his cup so firmly the muscles of his forearm bulged.

I waited a while. Agrippa said nothing.

'You know my views, Agrippa, I would follow you into the very depths of Hades. If there is anything you command, I will do it. You are the man to restore the Republic.'

'I am, and I have.' Agrippa stared at the mosaic floor. 'But there is nothing to be done.'

'There is—'

'There is nothing to be done,' Agrippa bawled. 'Do you hear?'

I stood and watched my mighty general breathing heavily as he regained his composure. There was plenty to be done, but there was nothing to be gained by pushing further that day. So I changed tack.

'There is another wedding to celebrate next year,' I said.

'Oh?' replied Agrippa. 'Whose?'

'Mine,' I smiled. 'To Whisper. I was hoping that by some wonder of the gods you might officiate over it.'

Agrippa hesitated only for a moment. 'Of course I will, but I insist that it is traditional and it will need to be discreet.'

I nodded. 'Tradition is fine with me,' I said.

'And I will need to know who I am marrying,' Agrippa said with a smile.

'Just don't say Rutilius, and we'll be fine,' I laughed.

Agrippa laughed with me, a deep booming laugh.

'It's good to hear you laugh,' I said.

'It's good to laugh,' Agrippa replied. 'It's been a long time.'

That was the night I learned that vengeance was not satisfying. At least, personal vengeance was not. Gaius Cornelius Gallus was a name which had provoked such strong emotions within me. Jealousy, anger, injustice.

His rise to power challenged the very principles I had been brought up with. He took my commands. He took the province I had hoped for.

And just because he was Octavian's friend, with his dark, gallic looks, his erudite poetry, and his litany of achievements, he had overreached a senator who had been striving just as hard.

But that night, the night I had learned of his suicide, I did not feel satisfied. I even felt sadness and respect for the man. But this did not mean I had transformed into a good man. Faced with my guilt, I remember what I said aloud to the shining moon. Words I cannot believe I uttered. How callous a man can be!

'Whatever anyone else says, I thought his poems were

rubbish.'

From that moment, I no longer pursued personal vengeance. I cared not that another knight, Aelius Gallus became the governor of Egypt. I chose only to pursue Octavian, because when I pursued him, I fought for the Republic. That was a different matter, for how was it different to war?

Rome was under attack. The people of Rome would soon learn the truth about Octavian. The moment Octavian would announce Marcellus' marriage to his daughter, the reality would, at last, be in plain sight. Octavian was establishing a dynasty. Where was the reward to Agrippa, or even Taurus, men who had served the people better than Octavian?

Where indeed.

But it was clear that I had to bide my time, and so for once, I did. As Marcus Rutilius Crispus, I was often accused of being rash, of acting without thinking things through. Now, as Sextus, I had changed. I had learned. I would wait. I had a marriage and a child to prepare for.

We bought a house in the slums of the Subura. This was a necessary purchase, not just because we were beginning to go mad, trapped in the depths of the temple of Fides, but because I had to carry Whisper over a threshold in the marriage ceremony.

When it came to picking the day of the marriage, I struggled to remember all the rules. It had been a long time since my marriage to Olivia.

My first marriage had ended so tragically. I would not take any chances by picking a day of bad omens.

'It's not as simple as picking a day,' I told Whisper. 'Nearly all of them are unlucky. May is entirely forbidden.

'We can't get married on the Kalends, Nones or Ides of any month, nor the day after any of those.'

'What does that leave?' replied a bemused Whisper.

'Not much,' I agreed. 'Whenever it is,' I continued, 'it can't come soon enough. I remember something about the second half of June being the most propitious time for marriage.'

'The second half of June it is then.'

At last we settled on a suitable date.

During the weeks leading up to the day, we wandered the streets of Rome hand in hand, showing all that we were to be married. A few people made a kind comment, or looked knowingly at us, but the vast majority jostled past, ignoring us completely. It was so easy to be anonymous in Rome, even openly walking the streets.

Whisper did not have a father. Or if she did, she did not know who he was, or where he was. So there was no dowry to arrange, nor could we hold the ceremony in her father's house as we should.

I had an idea. I asked Agrippa if we could hold the ceremony in his house.

'We'll hold it in "The House of the Rams",' he replied.

'"The House of the Rams?"' I repeated. 'I was thinking more of one of your country estates. Perhaps in Campania?'

'I cannot afford to leave Rome, Ruti–, I mean Sextus,' he said with a frustrated wave of his hand. 'There is too much going on, with the wedding preparations, Octavian being ill in Spain. It feels as if all the burdens are on me at the moment.'

I thought for a moment. The only reason I baulked at "The House of the Rams" was the fact that it was in Rome. But no one knew me. And no one would have access to that mighty home, heavily guarded as it would be with Agrippa present.

'It would be an honour to be married there,' I said.

'"The House of the Rams!"' Whisper exclaimed. 'That's

incredible. I'm getting married in Pompey the Great's home. And Antony. He lived there too, didn't he?'

'He did,' I replied, smiling. 'And certainly celebrated in there...'

'We can decorate the rams on the walls?'

'I'm sure Agrippa will let you do as you wish,' I replied. 'He is such a kind man.'

Whisper looked tearful. 'I still can't believe that we are to be married by Agrippa. A former consul.'

'This all does feel beyond belief,' I said, embracing Whisper. 'But the most unbelievable part of the whole story, is that you will become my wife. I am a lucky man.'

That was the first love making where I noticed the swelling of Whisper's stomach getting in the way. It did not put me off, but filled me with excitement. I would soon be a father. And I had so many stories to tell.

X

As we finalised preparations for our wedding, it was Agrippa who thought of everything.

'I will consider you a citizen,' he said, 'so whatever Whisper's status, this is a regular marriage. Your children, will therefore have all civil rights.'

'Thank you, Agrippa,' I replied.

We needed ten witnesses. And between Whisper and I, we did not have ten friends. In fact we had none, bar Agrippa. He solved that too.

'My lictors can be the witnesses,' he said. 'There's twelve of them. What about a bridesmaid? He asked.

I looked bemused.

'I'll arrange for one of Marcella's maids to be bridesmaid. Pretty, but not beautiful like your Whisper.'

I wanted to embrace him.

'Whisper needs a mother?' he asked.

I nodded.

'Then I shall ask my wife Marcella. She enjoys this sort of thing.'

'Is there any chance she will recognise us?' I asked, fearful of Octavian's niece.

'Marcella?' Agrippa replied. 'Not a chance. She's far more interested in the newest face paint and the newest way to tie her hair.' Agrippa shook his head. 'I'm too old for her really. She should have married Iullus.'

'Antony's son?' I asked.

'That's the one,' Agrippa replied. 'They were playmates, you know. Octavia brought Antony's orphans up in her household, along with her own children. So Marcella knows him well and loves him dearly.'

Iullus was Antony's second son by Fulvia. No doubt he would be cultured and handsome, with a father like Antony, but so was Agrippa, in his own earthy way.

'I feel more like Marcella's father than her husband,' Agrippa continued. 'Her real father died when she was three.' He looked wistful.

'Too young for such a tragedy.' There was a silence. 'Marcella should help prepare Whisper on the day,' Agrippa concluded. 'And she can play mother for the ceremony. Send Whisper to "The House of the Rams" the night before. And leave the decorating to us. We'll make sure it's a ceremony Whisper will never forget.'

At last, the day of our wedding came.

I would have liked to have worn a purple bordered toga. But I was no longer a senator. In fact, I was posing as a freedman, not even worthy of wearing gold rings. So a clean, simple tunic was all that I had.

Whisper was already in "The House of the Rams". She would already be in her one piece tunic, falling all the way to her pretty feet. Marcella would have dressed her in it the night before, as was custom. I wondered how Whisper was finding Marcella.

She told me how playful Marcella was, lively and full of laughter. A little more open in her talk of sex than Whisper was prepared for, but a sweet young lady. Although Whisper was older, they were closer in age than Agrippa and his young wife.

Whisper was dressed in a beautiful white dress and covered in a flame coloured veil. The veil was oblong, transparent and matched the colour of her shoes. Marcella carefully tied a woollen girdle with the knot of Hercules around Whisper's swollen stomach. Only I, her husband, could untie the knot.

She had tied bands in Whisper's hair, and gently placed

a wreath of amaracus, such a sweet-smelling herb, with sprigs of purple verbena on Whisper's head. She had, by Whisper's account, been as sweet, excitable and tender as a mother.

I too had a wreath of flowers and herbs. I was certain it was coming apart. I had woken before the sun rose that morning and dressed all too quickly.

Despite preparing it the night before, I re-piled wood on the hearth, adjusting it fastidiously to make sure that it would catch light easily. As I walked to the entrance, I adjusted the symbolic marital bed, a bed in miniature form which would be part of the ceremony later that night.

Even with all this fuss and preparation, before the sun had risen, I found myself anxiously waiting outside "The House of the Rams", long before I was needed.

At last, I was called to enter. The ships' rams on the wall had indeed been decorated with beautiful and strong smelling flowers. Incense was burning, torches flickered. It was beautiful beyond my dreams.

I made my way into the chamber which had been prepared for the ceremony. Two stools were positioned by a small altar. They were covered in the sheepskin from the morning's sacrifice. I processed to the altar and waited. Agrippa entered first. As priest, his hood was over his head.

'Good day, Sextus,' he said with a broad smile.

'Hail Agrippa,' I replied, bowing my head.

'The auspices are good this morning,' said Agrippa.

I was relieved. The ceremony could go ahead. Whisper was soon to be mine. I had always been sceptical of the religions, often scorning pompous old Cicero decrying our neglect of omen taking. But today, I was glad Agrippa had carried them out. I was glad it was part of his and Octavian's plans to re-invigorate religion. I had lost one wife. I was desperate not to lose another. And any help the gods and goddesses would give me was a blessing.

'Thank you.' I said to Agrippa. I looked about me. 'For all of this.'

Agrippa checked over the cake of spelt which was on the altar, ready for the offering.

'Life is full of tragedy and death,' he said. When he had confirmed he was happy that all was ready. He looked me in the eye. 'When there is something to celebrate, we must make sure we seize it with both hands. And Hope,' Agrippa smiled knowingly at me as he had correctly named Whisper, 'is someone to celebrate.'

If I close my eyes, I can still picture Whisper. When she entered the room with her bridesmaid, I was stunned.

She was unrecognisable from the slave-girl I had rescued in the streets of Rome, or the pitiful state I had found her in after the torture during the trial. Behind that flaming veil, she was as beautiful as any goddess. My own personal Venus.

She stood opposite me and the bridesmaid gathered my trembling right hand and placed it on Whisper's. I could see the work that had gone into her hair. It was just like Olivia's had been all those years ago.

Whisper told me that Marcella herself split the six locks out with the special spearhead. They were curled and coiled on top of her head, with seductive tendrils draping down her face and neck.

'You look beautiful,' I mouthed.

Whisper smiled. 'So do you,' she said.

Agrippa positioned himself between us.

'When you're ready,' he said to Whisper.

She began the chant, her voice faltering through the tears of joy.

'When and where you are Gaius, I, then and there, am Gaia.'

Agrippa carried out the rites, calling those present to witness our marriage. He carried out the nuptial prayers and announced our wedding pact. The dotal tablets were read aloud and signed. Agrippa even fixed his own seal to the marriage contract as a witness, along with his lictors.

A young boy appeared by Agrippa's side, carrying a covered basket. Agrippa extracted the necessary implements to carry out the sacrifice to the gods. He crumbled the sacred cake onto a small plate, and poured wine over the offering to Jupiter.

Whisper and I, with shaking hands, each took a piece and ate. I remember the salty taste of the spelt cake so well.

Agrippa recited a prayer to Juno, the goddess of marriage. Prayers to Tellus, Picumnus and Pilumnus followed. Long enough that my bottom was numb and sore all at the same time, sitting on that stool. At last, Agrippa dropped his hood.

The guests all called out, 'Happily, Happily.'

Whisper smiled. We kissed.

The ceremony was over, and the feast could begin.

And what a feast it was. Agrippa had seen to it that we would be dine in a manner we would never forget.

Whisper reclined on a couch beside me, a great honour she was blissfully unaware of. Few women reclined. At best they sat on chairs by the couches. But today she was to be treated like a queen.

Agrippa reclined on my other side. This is one of my proudest memories, that I can claim that man dined with me on our wedding day.

The music was playing before we had even entered the dining room. Fine players they were, and fine, lilting music they played. After we had all washed our hands and feet, the food began to arrive.

So much of it I can still taste, if I think back. It started with salads, and oysters and eggs. How quickly the mosaic floor was scattered with shells. How fast the slaves had to work to sweep them away. And the olives, white and black, which seemed to taste better than any I had ever had before. And pickled vegetables. All served to an accompaniment of honeyed wine. Wonderful.

Then the main course. And what a main course. Mullet.

'I have treated you,' Agrippa said. 'This,' he passed me the jug of fish sauce, 'is the best fish sauce money can buy. "Fish sauce of the allies".'

'Not from New Carthage?' I said in disbelief.

Agrippa smiled.

'But that's hideously expensive.' I replied.

He took a deep draught of wine, trying to hide his pride.

'I think it's rude to bandy about figures,' he said. 'The important thing, is that we enjoy it.'

So we did. Heartily.

And finally, the dessert came. Not that I needed it. All I wanted was to take Whisper to bed. But the fruits came, grapes and dates which tasted succulent and sweet, and then I noticed something which for the briefest moment, took away my unadulterated joy. Figs.

I remember wondering if I would ever escape my memories, my mistakes. I gulped down another wine.

On the walls in the corridor, the ships' rams reminded me of Actium. In front of me lay figs, reminding me of Cleopatra. The snake she had had smuggled in must have been in that basket of figs I had allowed in. And beside me sat Agrippa, a man of humble origins, far humbler than mine. Now he had been consul of Rome, three times, and held power beyond measure, while I? I was nobody. Wherever I turned, my failures confronted me. Except from beside me. Beside me the beautiful Whisper reclined. She was anything but a failure. She was my redemption, and in her belly, our future grew.

'Well,' I said aloud as I picked up a fig, refusing to let the memories it caused spoil my day, 'I am alive.'

I bit into its succulent flesh. It tasted divine.

At last, drunk and content, it was time for the wedding feast to end. The wedding cake was distributed amongst the guests. It was truly delicious; meal steeped in must and mixed with anise, cumin and cheese baked on bay leaves. A perfect ending to a perfect meal.

It was time to begin the procession to our new home in the Subura. I took one last look around the luxurious dining room in "The House of the Rams", before making our way to the entrance.

Three boys were waiting for us at the gate of the house.

'This is where we say goodbye,' Agrippa said.

I embraced him heartily.

'I cannot thank you enough,' I said, 'for everything.'

'Perhaps one day, I will need you,' Agrippa said. 'But for now, go, be married. Enjoy your life. And,' he smiled, 'by all the gods, enjoy your wife.' He kissed Whisper on the cheek. She embraced him long and hard, nearly enough for me to feel jealous. But not quite. How could I be jealous of Agrippa? He had been as good to me as any father could hope to be to their son.

'Oh,' said Agrippa, and pointed at Whisper's stomach. 'And when the time comes. Let me know. I have a mid-wife, Imerita. She will help you, as long as she isn't busy with us.'

As he walked away, I felt a strange feeling, a depth of gratitude I had never felt before. It was nearly overwhelming, certainly all consuming.

Whisper nudged me. We were ready to process. She smiled a broad smile at me. I kissed her.

'What a perfect day,' I said.

Two of the boys stayed near Whisper, ready to take her hands during the procession. The third was waiting for a lit torch to be handed to him.

Needless to say, it was Agrippa who handed it to him.

He picked up the white thorn, lit it from the hearth of the fire in "The House of the Rams" and handed it over carefully to the young boy.

'My final duty,' he said. The boy smiled and prepared to lead us on our route.

We gathered outside. Flute players were at the head of the procession, with torch bearers to guide us through the dusky streets. Marcella took her place as 'mother' beside Whisper. All was ready, so the marriage hymn began.

I stumbled over to Whisper and her mother, Marcella, swaying from too much wine.

I grabbed clumsily for Whisper imitating the rape of the Sabine women. She coiled herself into Marcella's arms, feigning horror at my advances.

At last, my flailing hand locked onto her arm, and I pulled her roughly to me.

'You're mine,' I said and planted a kiss on her beautiful cheek. 'It's time for you to come to my home.'

The two boys took each of Whisper's hands, and the young bearer of the wedding torch led Whisper as the procession set off from "The House of the Rams" to our house in the Subura. Behind us, a distaff and spindle were carried, emblems of home life. The last procession I had been a part of was a triumph. That had been a great day, but this, this felt so much more exciting.

I do not know if Agrippa had paid for the streets to be lined, or if the presence of any wedding procession would gather such a crowd, but we seemed to collect an almighty throng as we passed through the streets. The wedding songs filled the streets and passers-by cried out the wedding cry. 'Talasse, Talasse.'

No one knows why. No one cares. A wedding procession is simply an excuse to have fun.

And fun we had. Whisper's smile never dropped from her face. I threw nuts at the crowd, symbols of fruitfulness.

But as I looked at Whisper's belly. It was clear, no luck was required on that front.

On the route, Whisper took one of the three coins she had for the ceremony.

'I've picked these carefully,' she said.

'How do you mean?' I asked.

'You'll see,' she said. I was to be given one of those coins. One would be offered to our household gods. The first would be dropped on the route, an offering to the gods of the crossroads. 'This one is Agrippa.' She held it out to me, and I saw Agrippa's profile, wearing his naval crown, declaiming his third consulship.

Whisper turned the coin to reveal Neptune holding a dolphin in his right hand and a trident in his left.

'I thought it was fitting,' she said. 'Agrippa who we both owe so much, and Neptune who gave you back to me.'

She cast the coin onto the paving stone below.

'I thank both of them, as I offer this to the gods of the crossroads,' she said.

I bit my lip, holding back tears.

As we approached the Subura, I took my leave of the procession and hurried home to be ready to receive her over the threshold. I checked that the offering of the marital bed was still in place, exactly as I had positioned it earlier that morning.

I could hear the procession long before it arrived, the customary cheering and naughty taunts, the hangers-on hoping for a meal. I could not stand still but paced in circles, desperate to receive Whisper into my arms.

I heard scrabbling at the threshold. Whisper had arrived. She was binding the door posts with strands of wool and smearing the threshold with lard and oil.

'Who goes there?' I called. 'What is your name?'

'Where you are Gaius, there shall I be Gaia,' came

Whisper's reply.

I opened the door, tears of joy in my eyes, and Whisper was swept off her feet and carried over my threshold.

In the hallway, I offered Whisper fire and water. In return, Whisper handed me her coin.

I looked at it. It was a silver coin. On one side was the head of Fides wearing a crown of laurels. On the other, the she-wolf, suckling Romulus and Remus. The inscription read, ROMANO, 'of the Romans'.

'I realised this coin represented everything about you,' she said.

I tugged her into an embrace.

'I love you so much,' I said.

'I love you too,' Whisper replied smiling.

She walked to the hearth I had carefully prepared. She took the wedding torch from the young boy who had carried it in the procession and lowered it to my carefully tended pile of wood. To my relief, the fire caught.

We broke up the remnants of the burnt-out white thorn torch and distributed them amongst the followers who scrabbled for a piece of the lucky charred wood.

In the confines of our new home, I said the customary prayers.

Whisper offered her third and final coin to the household gods.

It was only days after that I looked at it. On one side, the personification of piety's face stared back at me, wearing an earring and necklace. On the other, there was a pair of clasped hands, just like our marriage ceremony. Most suitable Whisper will have thought. The staff of Mercury was in the background, the patron god of monetary gain. I had proven in my past that I needed his support, so all in all, this was a very appropriate choice by Whisper. This coin could be a plea for protection for merchants, shepherds, gamblers, liars, and thieves. Unfortunately, the last three professions were particularly apt.

I told Whisper of the history of that *denarius.*

'This was minted by one of the conspirators who murdered Caesar,' I said. 'Republican to the core.'

'More suitable than I thought,' she replied. 'I had chosen it because of the clasping hands. It's just like our marriage. But if it's Republican too, so much the better.'

'It is.' I smiled. I looked at the inscription. Albinus Brutus. I hesitated, then decided not to tell her what else I knew of this coin. Albinus Brutus, along with all the other conspirators had fallen to Octavian.

And Octavian, always the master of evil, had this coin reissued. It had the same clasping hands and Hermes' staff, but this time, Concordia, peace, was on the other side.

Octavian knew how to exploit every opportunity. No one would have missed the reference to Albinus' destruction.

Thankfully, on the wedding night, I was far too intent on getting a hold of my wife to look at the coin she offered to the household gods, so Octavian did not remain in my thoughts.

The bridesmaid guided Whisper to the elaborately decorated miniature marital bed in the hall.

Songs encouraging consummation were sung.

'I can wait no longer,' I told the bridesmaid. 'Take her through to the real marital bed.'

The bridesmaid led Whisper through. I followed close behind.

'She won't need any help,' I said, dismissing the bridesmaid.

'Aren't I supposed to say some prayers?' Whisper said.

'I can't wait for that,' I replied, gesturing the bridesmaid to leave. 'I've been waiting long enough.'

Whisper was also supposed to resist me, to pretend reluctance. But she had been waiting long enough too.

So it was that Whisper and I were married, a day full of happiness and joy, and I owe so much of that to Agrippa. My debts to that man were ever increasing.

A few months later, Whisper suddenly clutched at her belly and fell to the floor in agony.

'By the gods,' she screamed. 'The pain!'

I stared in horror, dumbstruck. I knew childbirth was supposed to be painful, but surely not this bad.

Whisper was writhing on the floor, moaning, unable even to answer me.

'This can't be right,' I said, trying to keep myself calm.

I carried Whisper to the bed.

'Unbind your hair,' I said, loosening off her dress. 'Pray to Juno Lucina. To bring our child to the light.'

I sent a messenger to Agrippa's house on the Plains of Mars.

'Whisper is in labour. Please send your midwife.'

Within an hour, a stern-looking woman, Imerita, arrived at our door. She was the midwife within Agrippa's household, a midwife with years of experience, he had assured me, taught in Alexandria before coming to Rome. She had pleasingly long fingers but short fingernails. A good start, that much at least I knew.

Imerita clutched a bag, a bag which I would soon learn had all the devices of her craft. She bustled past me and hurried to Whisper in the bedchamber.

I tried to follow, but Imerita's scowl deterred me.

'Not yet,' she said. 'I must assess your wife.'

After a short while that felt like an eternity, Imerita emerged.

'That bed is no use,' she said. 'We must send for a harder one for the labour.'

I gaped, bemused.

'I thought it was comfortable,' I retorted.

'It is,' Imerita replied tersely. 'Far too comfortable. It will be perfect for her recovery, but the best part of useless for the labour. Come.'

I traipsed behind Imerita like an obedient dog, no longer the master of my household. She paced to the front door and sent one of her attendants back to Agrippa's house. Her others she bade carry her midwife's chair into the house. When I saw the crescent-shaped hole my baby would pass through, the precarious nature of the situation struck me.

Imerita saw my concern.

'Don't worry, my man,' she said. 'I've lost very few babies in my time.'

I swallowed.

'What about mothers?' I asked.

Imerita hesitated.

'None,' she said. I could not tell if she was lying.

I immediately prayed to all the gods.

Spare me Whisper and I will serve you loyally for the rest of my life.

'This is a good chair,' Imerita said. She gripped the pi-shaped arms.

'Strong, sturdy arms for your wife to grip.' She knocked the back of the chair. 'Strong wood,' she said. 'No treacherous slipping against the attendant.' I looked at the burly woman Imerita had pointed at. She looked as strong as a goth.

'Your wife can press her beautiful buttocks and hips against this as hard as she likes.' Imerita concluded.

It was those beautiful buttocks and hips which put her in this situation in the first place, I thought.

'Come,' Imerita summoned me to the bedchamber. 'Usually, I wouldn't let the man in the room.' I shuffled towards her. 'But usually, there are friends and mothers and sisters around.'

I shook my head. 'No mothers here,' I replied. 'In fact, no one here at all.'

'Then she should have company. Come.'

I entered the bedchamber. Whisper was lying on her back. Imerita had already propped blankets underneath her hips. Whisper's feet were drawn up and her thighs parted.

Whisper was pale. Her eyes shut. Her mouth formed into a fierce pout as she was breathing out hard.

'Dignity left the room some time ago I see.' I said, trying to be humorous as I gently caressed Whisper's forehead.

She opened an eye to focus on me all too briefly, before shutting it again as another wave of pain coursed through her.

'Can we not do something for the pain?' I asked.

But Imerita was already rummaging in her bag.

'We can do many things,' she replied.

'You're not one of these mad women who will put a dog placenta on my wife,' I said in horror.

Imerita scowled at me. An expression I became all too familiar with.

'What do you take me for?' she snorted.

Imerita brought out soft sea sponges, a cloth and olive oil.

'We start with massage,' she added.

She ordered an attendant to bring fire. She warmed the olive oil a little before soaking the cloth in it and laying it over Whisper's heaving stomach. It covered her swollen privates.

'At least, now I know where to look,' I said. Again I failed to raise a smile.

'Stroke your wife,' Imerita commanded me.

I began to rub her.

'Not like that,' Imerita interrupted. 'She's about to have a child. Put some effort into it.'

I pressed harder.

While my arms grew weary with the effort of massaging Whisper, Imerita filled bladders with the warm olive oil, tied them shut and placed them against Whisper's sides.

'Keep at it,' she said to Whisper.

Occasionally, Imerita would remove the cloth, dip her left forefinger in olive oil and place it inside Whisper.

'What are you doing?' I asked, fighting back a wave of nausea.

'Gently rubbing,' she replied brusquely. 'It helps,' she added.

I did not know what to say.

'When the hole is the size of an egg, then we move her to the chair,' she said.

I shuddered.

'We will summon my attendants then,' she said.

'Then,' I replied, 'why not now?'

'Because it could be a long wait,' she said.

I looked at Whisper who had not once stopped the heavy breathing or moaning in pain. It did not look as if she could bear this for a long time. But then I remembered, she had suffered horrific torture on my account. She was strong enough for child-birth surely.

'The size of an egg,' I said, 'That's not too big. It won't take long,' I said to Whisper.

Out of the corner of my eye, I saw Imerita roll hers.

But it did take long. The sun set. And so began the longest night of my life. Whisper never spoke. She did not need to. I could tell from looking at her just how much pain she was in.

'Is this normal?' I kept asking Imerita.

'This is normal,' she would reply flatly.

Throughout the evening, Imerita delved into her bag. Each time, something new emerged.

At first, it was herbs, which she made into drinks and gently gave to Whisper.

Leaves of dittany mixed in water.

'This is from Crete,' Imerita said. 'It's the best dittany there is for bringing on childbirth.'

But it did not seem to sooth Whisper at all, nor bring out our child.

Next, Imerita tried scordotis mixed in honeyed water.

'Different herbs work differently for different people,' she said.

But, the scordotis had no effect, other than a little later, Whisper was sick.

'So,' Imerita said, wiping up Whisper's vomit, 'we will try the root of the sacred herb, vervain.'

Whisper, for all these efforts, seemed to struggle to take the drink. I was watching her fade before my very eyes.

I remember rubbing my face frantically. I wanted to be able to pause everything, re-gather our thoughts and start again. But there was no stopping the fates.

Don't you dare, I thought. I've been devout to you all. Whisper must survive this.

The gods were not listening.

Whisper, exhausted, seemed to pass out.

Imerita tried many things to rouse her.

'Have no fear,' she said to the panic-stricken me. 'This is tiring work. She can rest through it.'

Those were the words Imerita uttered, but she worked frantically to rouse Whisper all the same. Numerous items wafted under Whisper's nose, trying to revive her. The mint smelling pennyroyal seemed to work. But as the hours passed, Whisper reacted less and less.

Imerita unleashed everything her bag had to offer; apples, quinces, lemons and melons. I raised an eyebrow when she pulled a cucumber from the bag. Imerita hoped Whisper would nibble at it. But she barely opened an eyelid. Finally, Imerita gathered a handful of pungent dirt from her bag.

'How much have you got stuffed in there?' I asked in wonder.

Imerita ignored me. By now, her entire focus was on Whisper.

'Come on my child,' she said softly, dabbing Whisper with a sea sponge, and waving the soil under her nose. 'You must keep going.'

'Must?' I questioned.

Imerita looked me in the eye. It was the first indication of a problem.

'We should be preparing for delivery by now,' she said. 'But there is little change. I can feel the baby kicking, so all is well at the moment, but...' She checked herself.

There was a silence. A silence filled with my increasing fear.

'Labour is supposed to be hard,' said Imerita.

Daybreak came, and I had not slept for one moment, or eaten.

'You must eat,' Imerita commanded. 'I don't need two patients.'

But I could not eat. I could not bring myself to leave Whisper's side.

Suddenly, she let out an almighty howl of pain. She sat up, eyes wide open and screamed. I took a backward step in horror. Imerita and her attendants rushed to Whisper's side and guided her to lie back down.

'Summon Musa,' Imerita shouted. 'At once.'

The attendant ran from the room.

'Who's Musa?' I asked.

Imerita was pinning Whisper's shoulders down on the bed.

'He's the best physician in Rome. And he's the best chance these two have. Thank the gods, he is Agrippa's guest.'

It seemed an age, that wait for Musa.

I whispered in Whisper's ear.

'I love you, Whisper. Please, if you can hear me, I love you. Help is coming. You must survive. I cannot live without you.'

At last, Antonius Musa arrived. It is hard to put into words what I felt when he entered the room. Certain people demand attention, command respect and emanate warmth. Certain people you meet in your life inspire you. Musa was one such man.

As soon as Musa entered the room, I was awe struck by his presence, and not just because I was desperate for someone to help Whisper. He was a handsome man, in a peculiar way. There were deep lines in his face, a prominent greek nose, and dark eyes to match his dark, smooth skin, eyes which sung of wisdom. He was calm, even in the face of this crisis.

'Hail,' he said. 'You must be Sextus.' He patted me on the shoulder. 'I will do whatever can be done,' he said. 'Now, let us see how your wife is.'

He arranged his robes as he peered over the stricken Whisper.

He gathered all the bladders of warm oil and placed them to one side.

'Heat is not our friend,' he said. 'We will try a cold bath of herbs.'

'Cold?' Imerita questioned.

'Yes cold. You must do as I say,' Musa said, fixing Imerita with his mesmerising eyes, 'or this woman will die.'

Of all things, given what was happening, I was surprised that he tried to feed Whisper lettuce. But I was no longer in control. All I was doing was praying. Praying that Whisper would live. I confess. I cared nothing for the child. One person had to leave the room alive. Two would bring double joy.

Musa gestured for me to leave the room.

'I'm afraid you will be nothing but a distraction. There is nothing you can do,' he said. 'Trust me. I will do everything I can to save your wife and child.'

I went to protest, but something in his look made me believe him. I should leave.

So I did.

I wandered the streets of Rome in a haze, gripped by a dreadful, sickening feeling. Even now, years later, when I recall that walk, I feel the strength leave my legs, my stomach tightens and I feel nauseous.

I made my way unsteadily westward, the short journey towards the Capitoline Hill. I grew increasingly frustrated as everyone else went about their daily lives, while back in my home, my life teetered on the brink of disaster.

I made for the Capitoline Hill, not for the temples, though by this point I was calling on all the gods and goddess of Rome to help, but to pray to the statuary group of the birth deities, the three Nixae. The statue had been seized more than a hundred years ago from Antiochus the Great, the defeated ruler of Syria and set up in front of the temple of Minerva by Manius Acilius Glabrio. Since that day, many a woman and many a man had prayed at their feet. The birth deities were squatting or kneeling, in the throes of childbirth. I beseeched them for their divine aid. As they were on their knees, so I too fell to my knees and bowed my head. I closed my eyes, and pictured Whisper in the agonies of her labour.

'Help her,' I mouthed. 'Please, help her.'

I reached out and touched the feet of one of the Nixae. I turned, wiped a tear from my eye, and concluded I could be apart from Whisper no longer.

When I returned to our home in the Subura, I heard

Whisper breathing in a peculiar forced, rhythmical way, and then periods of intense screaming.

After four or five hours I could bear it no longer. I dared to enter the chamber.

Imerita had donned an apron. It was covered in blood. Musa was buried in between my wife's legs. Imerita's attendants were holding Whisper in the delivery chair, while another held a cloth firmly to her bottom.

Imerita was wrapping her hands in thin papyrus.

'What's happening?' I asked.

'For grip,' Imerita replied. 'So I don't drop your baby.'

'Please don't,' I said, meekly.

Musa emerged from between my wife's legs. He held a bloodied pair of forceps. My eyes widened with horror.

Musa smiled. 'My herb infusions and cold baths worked. Your wife is now trying to deliver. Your baby, on the other hand, decided to be awkward. I had to re-align it.'

It was nearly more than I could bear. The smell of blood. The tools which looked like instruments of torture. It was the horrendous moment I had recovered Whisper after the trial, all over again.

'Trust me,' said Musa. 'We will look after your wife.'

Whisper howled, 'You,' she screamed. 'You bastard!'

I laughed.

How was it, when I tried to raise a smile, I failed miserably, yet Whisper, in the midst of delivering a baby, made me laugh. I laughed all the more.

'Well, Imerita,' Musa said, 'I think my work here is done. It's back over to you now.'

He placed the forceps carefully down on the table, adjusted his sleeves, patted me reassuringly on the shoulder once more, and walked calmly out of the room.

I stared in awe. That man had the power of the gods pouring from him.

Imerita took over and calmly instructed the screaming

Whisper through the final stages.

Whisper was clinging to the arms of the midwife's chair. I took Whisper's wrist in my hand.

'Come on Whisper,' I said. 'You're nearly there.'

'I can't do it,' she said, weakly.

'You can,' I said. 'For me, you can.'

With a tremendous lunge she pushed. The attendants pushed down on her stomach, and Imerita reached into Whisper to pull our child into the light.

In one swift motion, our baby emerged. I saw its bloodied body slither out, lifeless and limp.

The papyrus worked. Imerita did not drop it, but placed it down on a small mat.

'Hmm,' she grunted. 'No cry.'

She poked and pulled the child, examining its nose, ears, its bottom and its privates.

'Clear,' she said.

She pulled and stretched the baby's arms and legs. She counted its fingers and toes.

'Normal enough,' she said.

She put the baby down again and poked it with her finger.

At last, a cry.

Imerita stood back, her blood-stained apron causing me to avert my eyes.

'I believe this child to be healthy to rear,' she said.

I stepped forward, peered at Whisper who was slumped, barely conscious, in the midwife's chair.

'What is it?' I asked.

'It's a girl,' Imerita replied.

Whisper roused. Both Imerita and Whisper stared at me. I suppose, if I were traditional, I should have hoped for a son. They were watching me, fearful that I might leave the child to be exposed.

But I had nothing to bequeath. I had no family traditions

or lore to pass onto a son any more. What was the point of tradition here?

Cicero once wrote how some people think that, if a small child dies, it should be borne with equanimity; that if it is still in its cradle there should not even be a lament. When I stared down at our nameless daughter, I could not countenance it. That girl had to live, just as her mother had to. Had to, or my life would no longer be worth living.

I stooped and took the tiny baby girl in my hands. I scooped her up.

'Welcome little one,' I said. 'You better survive now. You nearly killed your mother. She'll be wanting words with you.'

The cord which attached the baby to Whisper was still attached. Imerita smiled and gently took the baby from me. She scrubbed it down with a woollen cloth.

She drew a knife from her bag and cut the cord, then squeezed the blood out of the part which was still attached to the baby's stomach. She tied the end with a strong piece of woollen thread and pressed it into its navel. She sprinkled a fine powder over the baby's skin.

'What is that?' I asked, fascinated.

'Salt,' Imerita replied. 'Stops rashes.'

Imerita then mixed more salt with olive oil and wiped the baby all over with it, before washing it off again with warm water.

As I watched, I realised that I wanted to learn about medicine. Not about childbirth. That had been disgusting. Best left to midwives. But becoming a physician, like Musa, that could be my future.

Imerita cleansed the baby's nose and ears, before dropping olive oil into its eyes. Finally she swaddled the baby in bandages and handed her to the attendant. She turned to Whisper.

'It's time for the afterbirth,' she said. 'Now, do you want

earthworms mixed in raisin wine?'

Whisper frowned.

'No?' Imerita bustled into her bag once more. 'I wouldn't either. More Cretan dittany for you my dear. Let's get this over with.'

XI

So it was, thanks to Musa and Imerita, I had a daughter. And a wife.

'I will care for the mother, until she is safe,' Imerita declared.

'Safe?' I asked, afraid. 'Has she not survived?'

'How naive you are,' Imerita replied. 'But Whisper is in safe hands, I can assure you of that.'

However safe Imerita's hands were, they were not working. Whisper was complaining of pain in her breasts. At first, Imerita tried sponging them with diluted vinegar. Here, at last, I could play a role.

At least now Whisper was talking. I tried to soothe her too.

Imerita took the baby away. Presumably wet nurses fed her because it was obvious that Whisper would not be able to suckle the child. At this stage, I cared little for the child. The Fates would decide whether she would make it to her naming day. My concern was focused only on Whisper, who was fading fast.

When the diluted vinegar did not work, Imerita tried wrapping a tight bandage around Whisper's chest. Suddenly, her beautiful breasts had gone from objects of attraction, to functional parts of Whisper's body. And, most importantly, at that moment, they were malfunctioning. Whisper wept with the pain as Imerita bandaged her. Given the pains of birth, it must have been excruciating for her barely to be able to tolerate it.

Whisper grew incoherent. Only the pain stirred her from our soft, marital bed.

Imerita began to mutter to herself. She prepared a

poultice and gently applied it to Whisper's swollen chest.

'Bread, honey and olive oil,' she said. 'If this doesn't work, we will try linseed and water.'

'I thought you said you had never lost a mother,' I replied, testily.

'I haven't,' Imerita said, flustered. 'And I'm not about to start.'

But the poultices did not work.

Whisper ran a fever and began to whimper in her sleep.

'Should we not try the cold bath?' I asked, thinking back to Musa's treatment. 'Or some lettuce?'

But Imerita carried on with her poultices. 'This ought to work,' she muttered. 'Why isn't it working?'

Days later, when Imerita removed the bandages from Whisper, there was a foul stench, and pus oozed from her breasts.

I saw Imerita's face was horrified.

'Fetch Musa,' she mouthed. 'At once.'

Musa breezed into the room once again, his very presence immediately bringing reassurance.

'Sorry to see you again so soon,' he said. 'Now, let us see how your wife is.'

He arranged the sleeves of his gown in that particular way, and peered over Whisper once more.

'What treatments have you been applying Imerita?' he asked.

'Poultices,' she replied, nervously.

'Very good,' Musa said. 'I'm relieved to hear that you haven't been laying earthworms on her.'

'Earthworms?' I repeated.

'Yes,' said Musa. 'It is a common treatment amongst the ignorant. They believe it draws out the pus. Trust me, it doesn't.' Musa inspected the suppurating skin more closely.

'How do you know all this?' I asked in wonder.

'I have studied medicine for many years,' he replied,

'ever since my father fell ill.'

'You saved him?' I replied.

Musa hesitated.

The gleam in his eyes briefly dulled.

'No,' he said.

I felt crestfallen. Not for his father, but, selfishly, for Whisper's hopes.

'I'm afraid I will have to perform surgery,' Musa continued. 'But have no fear. We can solve this, and cold poultices and baths will cure the fever.'

'Will she survive?'

Musa stared at me.

'This is a strong woman. I have seen her scars.'

I swallowed, sensing a surge of guilt.

'For someone to survive such a wounding, this should not be insurmountable. But I must act swiftly. This pus and fluid must be removed.'

I could not watch the surgery. The tools of Musa's craft were too similar to those of torture. The comment about the scars, inadvertent though it was, had already sapped my strength as I recalled the horrors Whisper had suffered on my account.

After many hours, Musa emerged, looking entirely unruffled.

'Well?' I asked, leaping to my feet.

'The surgery went well,' Musa replied. 'Imerita now knows the treatments I think will bring your wife back to us. She is strong. I believe she will survive.'

I stepped forward and embraced Musa. He seemed a little taken aback.

'Thank you,' I said.

That evening, I was surprised by a visitor under cover of darkness. It was Agrippa.

'How are you?' he asked.

'As well as can be expected, thank you.'

'And how is Whisper?'

'She is recovering,' I replied. 'Thanks to Musa.'

'He is a brilliant man,' agreed Agrippa. He gestured to one of his slaves. 'I thought you might need this,' he said.

It was an amphora of the finest Campanian wine.

'Thank you,' I replied.

Agrippa spotted the miniature wedding bed in the hallway. His hand reached out for it. 'Not quite the start to the marriage we had hoped for,' he mused.

'No,' I replied. 'But honestly, if it wasn't for Musa, there wouldn't be a marriage at all. How do you know the man?'

'He has a growing reputation. He's one of those people who's brilliant at everything. Quick to learn and adept at whatever he turns his hand to: Soldiery, divination, poetry, an excellent player of the cithara by all accounts. In the end he has chosen to put his talents into medicine, just like his brother, Euphorbus. They were trying to prolong the life of their aging father.'

'Is his brother here too?' I asked.

Agrippa shook his head. 'No, he's the physician to King Juba of Mauretania. That's how I learned of Musa who learned his craft in Alexandria. Euphorbus is a very different man to Musa. Fat and arrogant. Musa, on the other hand, I have found to be nothing but delightful company.'

'He knows a great deal,' I said. 'I admire him very much. It was inspiring to watch him at work.'

'Let's hope he's done the job,' Agrippa replied.

I hesitated, wondering if I should ask what I wanted to ask.

'I would like to learn medicine. I would like to learn from Musa. Do you think he would have me? Do you think it would be possible?'

Agrippa paused. I awaited his answer nervously. I could tell Agrippa was assessing my appearance. His eyes dwelt on my scar. Was that scar under my eye recognisable?

'It's difficult, Sextus.' Agrippa's hand patted the miniature wedding bed. 'Augustus will return to Rome shortly. And Musa is now part of my entourage. What if Augustus recognised you? That would be the end of both of us.'

'But if I'm Musa's attendant, why would the great man ever see me?'

I countered. 'And,' I held out my thinning, frail, tanned arms. 'Look at me. I am half the man I used to be. Literally. My hair is thinning and grey. My skin is wrinkled from the sun. And my scar has faded.'

Agrippa let out a deep sigh.

'Very well,' he said at last. 'Learn alongside him. But when the time comes, you are to avoid Augustus' presence.'

I embraced him.

To our great relief, our baby girl survived the eight days to her day of purification and naming. Just as importantly to me, Whisper's health improved dramatically. Musa was literally a man who performed magic.

Whisper and I sought to agree on a name.

'She should be called Rutilia,' I said, 'but I fear we cannot.'

Whisper clicked her tongue. 'I don't want to do anything which puts our baby in danger.'

If I could not call her Rutilia, carrying on the family name, I wanted to pick a name which represented my love of the Republic. Porcia would have been an obvious choice. She was the wife of Brutus, the man most people blamed for assassinating Julius Caesar in the name of the Republic.

'Too obvious,' Whisper said. 'You don't want to get the little girl killed do you? I told you. I don't want to put her in any danger.'

So I told Whisper the story of Lucretia, the famous lady who, when she was raped by the son of the king, killed herself because of the dishonour. 'It is a name which stands for virtue,' I said.

'Not a chance,' Whisper scoffed. 'What a horrible story.'

Then the name came to me. 'I have it,' I exclaimed. 'Are you able to walk?'

Whisper considered for a moment. She had not, as yet, regained her usual vibrant colour. 'Fresh air will do me good.'

'Fresh air in the streets of Rome?'

We laughed.

I led Whisper, hand in hand, through the streets of Rome, from our house in the Subura to the Portico of Metullus. This stood in the district immediately to the west of the Capitoline hill, an area thickly covered with public buildings. The portico surrounded two temples, Jupiter's and Juno's. Metullus had built them all. They were the first to be made entirely of marble. Nearby towered the vast Circus Flaminius, bustling as always with the activity of the markets.

To recuperate from the heat and the exertion, Whisper took a drink of water by the equestrian statues of Alexander's generals.

'These are by a man called Lysippus.' I patted the sculpture. 'Another Greek at the top of his trade, like Musa,' I said admiringly. 'Can you believe these are over three hundred years old?'

Whisper was suffering in the heat. She glanced up and smiled a feigned interest. But I could see she was unwell.

I touched her gently on the arm. 'Come. I was going to show you the many works of art in this portico. But let's head straight to the important one.'

'This name had better be good,' was all Whisper could say.

'It is,' I replied.

As we made our way towards the statue in question, I glanced at the temple of Jupiter, with the six imposing columns across its front. There was no inscription, but curiosities like a lizard and a frog as decorations.

'It's a shame,' I said. 'They say that there was a mix up and all the statues were set up by the workers in the wrong temples. So, in there,' I said pointing at the temple of Jupiter, 'the decorations are clearly to Jupiter, but the statue in the chamber is Juno. And then,' I pointed at the other temple, 'in there it's the other way around.'

'Sounds like the kind of thing you would do,' Whisper said.

We arrived at the statue I sought.

'Here she is,' I said.

We stood before a beautiful marble statue of a seated woman. She was dressed plainly and wore simple, strapless sandals.

'This woman is the symbol of fertility, loyalty, chastity. Basically everything good.' I said. 'You won't find many statues of women around this city. It's a rare honour. So I think we should name our baby girl after this lady. How does Cornelia sound?'

'Cornelia,' said Whisper. She paused, considering it. 'Cornelia,' she repeated. 'That is a good name.' She read the inscription. '"Mother of the Gracchi". The Gracchi. Who are they?'

'Cornelia was the mother of twelve children,'

'Twelve,' replied Whisper. 'Don't you get any ideas.'

'Never fear,' I replied at once. 'I don't want to go through that again.'

'Cornelia outlived all of her children. The most famous were the Gracchi brothers, Tiberius and Gaius. They stood up for the people, and were assassinated for their efforts. But Cornelia had the dignity and strength of character to bear the losses.'

Whisper reached out and touched the foot of Cornelia. 'Let us hope that her spirit passes to our daughter.'

'As long as she has your spirit, she will be fine.' I replied. 'Cornelia it is.'

On the morning of the naming ceremony, I went to the temple of Fides. There, in the secret chamber, lay the remnants of my strongbox. It was no longer secure. Before my 'suicide', I had to have it broken into by a blacksmith after it was damaged in the fire that burnt down my home, Octavian's last cunning act to remove me from the senate. I flipped the lid and looked inside. The ring with the seal of the sphinx had only just survived the heat. Today, I needed another item, my *bulla,* the amulet which protected me through childhood. I wore it every day from my naming day until I gave it up on the day I became a man. That was when I was sixteen years old. Since then, it came out only on important occasions.

I picked up the *bulla.* It was damaged, but in one piece. The gold foil had peeled in places revealing the lead centre. It looked somewhat misshapen, but it was my *bulla,* and I would not replace it. The damage represented the challenges of life only too well. Clearly it was hard and dangerous work warding off evil spirits.

As I held the medallion before my eyes, I raised a smile. It was in such a sorry state. How apt. That *bulla* had protected me through my childhood and protected me when father died. But even the *bulla* could not protect me from the cunning of Octavian.

I placed it over my neck. Today, Cornelia would receive her *lunula,* an amulet in the shape of a crescent moon. It would protect her until the eve of her marriage, when she would give it up.

For my daughter I had spared no expense. Her *lunula,* unlike my *bulla,* was solid gold.

We were honoured that Agrippa and his wife Marcella attended the naming ceremony.

'What will you name her?' asked Agrippa.

'I presumed I could not call her Rutilia,' I replied. 'Though, in my heart, I would wish to.'

Agrippa shook his head. 'As you have decided to join Musa, and my entourage, I fear you cannot. It would not be safe. That's not fair on the little one.' Agrippa pinched the cheek of my baby girl. 'What a beautiful baby,' he said. She opened her eyes, just briefly. 'She has her mother's eyes,' Agrippa exclaimed.

'And her father's curls,' I replied, ruffling her hair. 'Not that I have many of mine left.'

Agrippa kissed Whisper on the cheek. 'You look well,' he said. 'I'm delighted to see. May I?'

He outstretched his arms to take the baby.

Whisper handed over our daughter, swaddled and letting out the occasional gentle gurgle.

Agrippa's vast, dark-tanned hands enveloped her.

'Welcome, young lady,' he said. 'What a beautiful girl you are.'

And that was when my daughter demonstrated her first good judgement of character. For, despite her eyes being tight shut and her awareness of the world being so limited, she smiled, a broad, beaming smile of gums.

Agrippa smiled back. 'So what have you decided to call her?'

'Cornelia,' I replied.

'Cornelia. That is a good name. Come,' he said to Whisper and I. 'Let us protect this little one. She has your spirits and deserves a good life.'

Marcella caught Whisper's arm.

'I know I should wait for the ceremony,' she said, 'but I had to show you this.' She held up a necklace which would be put around Cornelia's neck to ward of the evil spirits. It was a string of tiny metal trinkets.

'It's wonderful,' said Whisper. 'Thank you.'

'Couldn't resist,' said Marcella. 'Each of my slaves, and everyone who helped with the wedding has given one of those trinkets. We need to protect this little one.' She kissed the baby and rattled the necklace in front of her. The jingling prompted Cornelia to open her eyes.

'With eyes like that,' said Marcella, 'and those curls, she'll have men falling over for her.'

I felt the first paternal pang of protection. No one was touching her. Not while I was alive.

The threshold of the house was decorated with laurel, and all the floors were swept to purify the home.

Agrippa took on the role of priest once again. He uttered prayers beseeching protection. He performed the rites which included clapping his hands together, and suddenly making loud noises, a trial for Cornelia before she was allowed to enter the family.

When Agrippa shouted, Cornelia raised her arms and kicked out her legs. Mercifully, though, she did not cry. Instead, she opened her eyes and stared at Agrippa. It seemed as if she was listening to his deep, booming voice. He poked and prodded her. She let him, without a moan.

We stood around her, in silence, mesmerised.

Agrippa washed Cornelia, purifying her. Then the gift of the necklace was given. Marcella placed it carefully over Cornelia's head. Cornelia barely noticed it, but throughout her early days, she was always playing with it, enjoying the jangle.

Finally, the *lunula* was handed over. With trembling hands I passed it to Agrippa. He examined it with an admiring look before placing it around Cornelia's neck.

Agrippa kissed Cornelia on the forehead, and the

purification ceremony was complete.

It was time for the naming. Agrippa smiled broadly as he announced her name to be Cornelia.

All those present welcomed Cornelia to my family.

'Now,' said Agrippa, 'you can announce her formally to the public registers.'

He handed the swaddled Cornelia back to Whisper. Cornelia, to her credit, had not cried. Her mother and father, however, were both streaming with tears of happiness and pride.

'You have a beautiful daughter,' said Agrippa. 'I pray that she has a long and happy life.'

So it seemed that my new life had established itself. And a good life it was too.

At first, all seemed well with the empire. Octavian was still on campaign in Spain. While he was away, Agrippa continued to flourish. He completed and dedicated the Saepta Julia, decorated beautifully with the marble tablets and Greek paintings I had seen him organising. As I looked about me, I could see Agrippa's love of all things Greek was having its mark on the city. The baths and the public park and gardens on the Plains of Mars, and the Pantheon, all continued their progress.

I was delighted when, just as Agrippa had said it would, the statue of Octavian, clutching a spear, did not go into the main chamber of the Pantheon, but was set up in the porch. There was a statue opposite. The two of them flanked the bronze doors to the scared space. And who was the statue opposite? A man more than Octavian's equal, Marcus Vipsanius Agrippa.

My joy was tempered somewhat by the presence of Julius Caesar's statue inside the temple alongside all the other gods and goddesses. After all, Octavian was his adopted son. The presence of Caesar's thin face staring at me would bolster Octavian's claims that he had the favour of the gods.

But as the teeth emerged from little Cornelia's gums, and she began to crawl, I was distracted from my distaste.

I saw less and less of Agrippa as he became more and more involved in the running of the empire. People from all parts of the empire fawned at his feet; embassies from India, Parthia and the Scythians came, followed by ambassadors from Greek cities, one after another. Whatever they wanted, be it help with a legal case, or assistance following an earthquake, Agrippa was the man they sought. Never mind that Statilius Taurus was the consul in Rome, Agrippa was the only man they wanted to see.

In my brief conversations with Agrippa from time to time, it was clear that there was a new party to contend with in Rome. I am sure that from the moment this woman had married Octavian, she had had some part to play. But now she was beginning to exert her influence. And who was this woman? Livia.

Livia and Octavian were married eight years before the battle of Actium. Their union was a surprise to many. Both Livia's father and husband had fought against Octavian. An unwise move. When Octavian rose to power, Livia and her family fled to Greece. Only when the amnesty was finally announced did Livia return to Rome. There she met Octavian.

But how had that meeting turned into marriage? Livia is a beautiful woman, for which she is renowned. But looks alone could not have influenced a man such as Octavian. In his position, he could have any beautiful woman he wanted.

Livia must have said or done something remarkable in that meeting.

And I mean truly remarkable. She already had a child, the surly Tiberius and she was pregnant with another, Drusus. Meanwhile, Octavian was already married to

Scribonia and she was carrying their child.

Despite this, on the very day Scribonia gave birth to Julia, Octavian divorced her. Further evidence, if it were needed, that Rome has a cruel father.

True, Octavian's marriage to Scribonia had been a political alliance to tie him closer to Sextus Pompey and the rumours were consistently telling of an unhappy marriage. Scribonia had an impressive ability to nag.

Free to marry again, Octavian hunted down Livia's husband, Tiberius Claudius Nero. Needless to say, in short order Livia and Tiberius Claudius Nero were divorced. Their son Drusus was born.

Three days later, Octavian and Livia were married.

And who gave Livia away at the marriage? Her former husband Tiberius Claudius Nero. Precisely the sort of cruel act which epitomises Octavian. I can picture all too clearly Octavian's spiteful face and smug expression as he took Livia from her former husband's grasp.

I recalled the eye I could have pierced with an arrow. Octavian's eye. I should have loosed the arrow, on behalf of Tiberius Claudius Nero, as well as so many others.

Octavian and Livia's marriage had been successful and long lasting, albeit barren. Yet Octavian clearly honoured her. He commissioned a beautiful statue in Rome. Any statue of a woman in Rome is rare, for the woman still to be alive, even rarer.

But Livia was a powerful woman, wife of the most powerful man in the empire. Octavian had granted her authority over her own accounts. Throughout the years Livia had not wasted time in gathering her own clients and promoting people she deemed worthy. While Antony had lived and the empire was being contested, I never saw how influential this woman had become. But now, as the water calmed, all became clear.

'She's been interfering ever since the settlement and

Augustus' departure to Spain,' Agrippa complained. 'I don't mind her promoting her boys. They are good generals, the gods know they are, but she is interfering in everything. It feels as if she is checking on me. Me, as if they are challenging my loyalty?'

It took a lot to rile Agrippa, but Livia was managing it. The perfect match for Octavian after all.

It was not Livia's growing presence or her uncanny ability to interfere that caused Agrippa his next strife. It was the marriage of Octavian's nephew Marcellus to his daughter, Julia.

Marcus Junius Silanus was the new consul in Rome. His consular colleague was Octavian, of course, his ninth consulship in a row.

'Restoring the Republic'? I think not.

Silanus was a man whose career was on the rise. As I was stripped of my senatorial rank, he passed me going the other way. Now Silanus held Rome's highest office. I consoled myself that the consulship had not the gravitas it once had. If anyone was asked who was more important, consul Silanus or Agrippa, there would be only one answer.

But still, it was remarkable that Silanus was in the position of consul given his background. I suppose he relied on the fact that long years ago, he was a legate to Caesar. He would have to because, after Caesar's assassination, he supported a succession of Octavian's enemies. First Lepidus. Then Sextus Pompey. Then Mark Antony. Only at the last minute, just before the battle of Actium, did he turn again, at last joining Octavian.

And yet, here he was as consul to Octavian, while here I am, loyal from the moment I made my choice, a nobody.

My desire for revenge continued to burn. But I would have to wait a long time. I still had not even set eyes on Octavian since my return from the dead. Octavian was still campaigning in Spain. Rumours told of him being ill. I hoped they were true. I hoped that he was suffering. I prayed that the Fates would solve Rome's crisis for me.

Agrippa in the meantime continued his transformation of the city. The Pantheon was completed and opened to an awestruck public. A stunning portico with paintings depicting the tale of Jason and the Argonauts was finished. It became known as the portico of the Argonauts for the simple reason that those paintings were astounding.

Many an hour I stood admiring them and talking through the stories with Whisper and baby Cornelia. It became one of our favourite places to visit in the city, apart from the occasions when the traders brought in their temporary canvas stalls and blocked the path in their fervour to sell their luxury goods; books, plates, dishes, vases, jewellery, ivories, precious cups, you name it. The traders were expanding from their traditional haunts beside the Forum. But it was not just a buyer's market. It was seller's market too. I saw countless people pawning their rings and cups, as I had been forced to do, not so long ago.

I smiled ruefully as I recalled my own desperate attempts to keep up the pretence of my wealth, of my rank, selling off my late wife's jewellery in desperation.

But, as I watched on, I realised we had discovered another place to trade the goods smuggled inside the temple of Fides.

So at last, Agrippa's ambitious plans were coming to fruition. He was transforming the city as he had set out to do. The Plains of Mars were barely recognisable. The sheer number of people always present there was proof of the great man's success. The portico of the Argonauts seemed, in an instant, to be the most popular in Rome.

Beside the Basilica of Neptune whose foundations I had seen when first I returned to Rome was the Spartan Sweatbath.

'I call it Spartan,' said Agrippa proudly, 'because the Spartans have the greatest reputation for stripping, anointing themselves with oil and exercising. That is how I want the Roman people to behave.'

I, being fond of baths, immediately tried out this new style of bathing. The slaves worked hard to keep the furnaces outside burning, and filled the floor and flues in the walls with hot air. It was a large room to fill. At least fifteen paces across. I stripped, covered myself in olive oil and sat in the heat. I sweated. By the gods I sweated. More so than in any other baths I had visited. When I could take no more, and thought I would pass out, I took up my bronze scraper and carefully removed the sweat, pressing lightly to avoid a rash.

Finally, I plunged into the cold pool. As I hit the cold water, I could not breathe. As I emerged, I felt a new man. I felt as if, at last, I had washed away the traumas of my suicide attempt, of those countless hours baking in the sun, parched, starved, alone. Now I was part of the new city of Rome. All about me were excited people, admiring the efforts of our great benefactor Agrippa.

The Basilica of Neptune itself was also finished. I marvelled at the building, of course I did. What a difference it would make to the traders during those cold, bleak winter months, but I could not avoid the pangs of my bitter memories of Actium. This whole construct was donated to Neptune in gratitude for our victory at that sea-battle. All about me there were intricate decorations with dolphins, tridents and shells. But instead of beauty, they just took me back to the moment that I lost everything.

Actium had not just brought about my destruction. The wake of Actium was still being felt by so many. The people were being duped, duped unintentionally, by Agrippa's honesty. He really was striving for the good of the people. But the man he served. Well, he served only himself.

The next time I saw Agrippa in "The House of the Rams", he was looking grey and drawn.

'We are the wrong way round,' he said, 'Augustus and I.'

'How do you mean?' I replied.

'He is commanding troops in Spain. I am trying to keep the politics under control here in the city.' Agrippa took a deep draught of wine. 'He is losing the war, and I...I despise the politics.'

'Losing the war?'

Agrippa hesitated, fearing he had said too much.

'He has fallen ill,' Agrippa said. 'He's retired from his base at Segisama and headed east to Tarraco. At least now, the legates Vetus and Carusius will take charge of the war. They are good men, able generals. In their hands, I am sure victory will be ours.'

'More able than our king?' I said.

Agrippa shook his head. He was speaking too openly. 'We have no king,' he countered. 'The legates are more experienced perhaps,' he added. 'Seven legions we had out there, and a naval command. That was before Augustus came with the re-enforcements. We now have eight legions, and auxiliaries in great numbers. There must be over fifty thousand troops out there.

'We owned so much of Spain already. Just the north-west to conquer. The Asturians and the Cantabrians.' Agrippa scratched his forehead. 'This was supposed to be an easy victory to bolster his authority.'

I felt smug at Octavian's failure. 'So why has he failed?' I asked, mischievously.

Agrippa's hesitation revealed the truth. He clearly believed the failure was down to Augustus' leadership. What followed sounded like the excuses from despatches.

'The Asturians and Catabrians won't engage,' Agrippa

replied. 'They stay, cowering behind their walls, or throwing their javelins from afar. They have expert cavalry. Apparently, we could learn a thing or two from them.' Agrippa traced his finger around his cup. 'I would like to see it with my own eyes.'

He gazed into the distance. I could see just how much he wanted to be at the front.

'With Augustus retired from the fray,' Agrippa continued, 'perhaps they will engage properly. Over-confidence is the downfall of many.' He drained his cup.

'So Octavian is ill again,' I said, trying to hide my smile. 'He's always ill when it matters, or when a battle is about to start,' I said.

I recalled the time when Antony had mocked Octavian for missing the critical battle of Naulochus against Sextus Pompey through 'illness'.

What was it Antony said. *When ready for battle, he could not even look with steady eyes at the fleet, but lay in a stupor on his back, looking up at the sky. And he did not rise or appear before the soldiers until the enemy's ships had been put to flight by Agrippa.*

Agrippa once again. Even one of Rome's greatest generals praised him. This, despite their fighting on opposite sides.

'Worst of all,' said Agrippa, rousing me from my thoughts, 'Because he's too ill to return to Rome, I'm left in charge of the wedding.'

'You?' I questioned. 'But why not Silanus? He is consul.'

Agrippa grimaced. He ran his hand through his hair and scratched the back of his head with vigour. 'I suppose I should be flattered,' he concluded.

I could sense Agrippa was unsettled by the whole Marcellus business. I had no doubt Octavian had very deliberately and cruelly selected Agrippa to oversee the ceremony.

How galling would it be, to wed the young stripling who could be usurping all that hard earned power and respect Agrippa had achieved. And yet, still Agrippa was prepared to do it. Without hesitation. Such nobility.

'How is the boy?' I asked.

'Bright enough,' said Agrippa. 'Cheerful. A promising prospect for sure.'

'But not worthy to be Octavian's successor?' I tested.

Agrippa pursed his lips and shook his head.

'Marcellus may be for the next generation, but, for now, it is vital to the peace of the empire that Octavian survives.'

I resisted the temptation to tell Agrippa that not everyone shared his view. In my opinion, it was far more vital for Rome that Agrippa survived.

The day of the wedding came. I remember the ceremony and festivities well. At first it made me ever prouder that Agrippa had overseen our wedding, given he was now leading this most prominent of public occasions. The whole of Rome came out to celebrate. It was as big a crowd as the throng which turned out a few years previously at the triple triumph. Young and old alike. Men and women. Boys and girls. All strained their necks and pushed onto tiptoe, just for a glimpse of the boy Marcellus.

I looked about me, bemused. Marcellus had achieved nothing. But, because he was Octavian's nephew, this was his reward. Octavian had no son of his own, so he clearly doted on the boy. Not that this meant Marcellus was immune to Octavian's self-serving schemes. At the age of three Marcellus had been engaged to the daughter of Sextus Pompey by Octavian, to try to broker a peace. When Agrippa crushed Sextus Pompey, that engagement was promptly forgotten.

As I watched the cheering crowd, almost delirious all about me, I could not believe how quickly the people had abandoned the Republic. No wonder the assassins of Julius Caesar had failed in their attempts to restore the Republic. They had believed these people wanted the Republic. But they did not. The people around me cared only for bread, circuses and money in their pockets. Octavian was giving them all this and more.

I despaired.

The contrast between the man who should be praised and the boy who was being worshiped was made all the more apparent when Agrippa, imposing and authoritative, stood before that young boy, all long nose and top lip. There was no comparison, nor could there be, however bright a boy Marcellus was, however much support he had.

As Marcellus' hand was joined to young Julia's, I swore to Fides that loyalty should be rewarded, that I would do everything in my power to ensure when Octavian died, Agrippa would be the leading man of Rome.

That vow was never going to be easy to fulfil. After the wedding, all of Rome spoke of Marcellus as the natural successor to Octavian. It must have been galling in the extreme for Agrippa to hear this seventeen year old nobody being bandied round as the potential king of Rome. If Agrippa did not feel it, I certainly did on his behalf. After all, Agrippa was married to Marcella, Octavian's niece. He had just as strong an alliance and far more justification to be the natural successor. But the favour of Rome has no logic.

Rome threw out its king years ago, and swore never to return to the days of tyranny. Now, it seemed those days were knocking on our door once more.

I had to stop it. As I held my fast growing daughter Cornelia above my head and let a thin line of her dribble fall onto my face, I felt inspired that that was my purpose. This was why the gods had spared me. I had to act where Agrippa, through his loyalty, could not. My vengeance might be a long time in coming, but I had, at last, learned patience.

My time would come.

XII

While I waited for an opportunity, I spent as much time as I could with Antonius Musa, a man I owe so much. Not only did he save both Whisper's and Cornelia's life, but he also imparted his wisdom on me.

I learned from him, not just about medicine, but about the healing powers of herbs, the way to treat wounds, to cauterise, to stitch, and bind. He taught me the ways of the leech, the secrets of cold baths, the many different compositions of poultices. He also taught me philosophy and music. Any time I was privileged to spend in his company, I came away a better man.

And slowly, I gained his trust. This would prove vital.

'He is coming,' said Agrippa. 'He is returning to Rome.'

I felt my pulse quicken.

'When?' I asked.

'As soon as he is able.' Agrippa stretched his arms. 'But judging by how the rest of the campaign has gone, that could be a while.'

'So he has achieved his ambition has he? His military authority is bolstered?' I challenged.

'Augustus' original purpose when he left Rome was not to fight in Spain,' Agrippa said defensively. 'He went to re-organise the provinces of Gaul after we claimed Aquitania. But news came of uprisings in Hispania.'

'And once he heard of the uprising, he was never going to pass up the opportunity was he?' I said with a challenging tone.

Agrippa looked wistful. 'I could have crushed them. I could have got out of this city and felt the joy of battle once more.'

'Why didn't you go?'

'I was never offered the chance.' Agrippa's brow furrowed. 'You are right I suppose. There wasn't even a hint of it in Augustus' letters. He needed the military glory for himself this time. I suppose I have to accept that the people of Rome credit me with military successes.'

'As the people of Rome should,' I replied. 'Because it was you.'

'That's as may be,' said Agrippa, 'but my position relies on Augustus''

'It doesn't,' I said. 'You were consul in your own right. By the gods, you were consul three times. Why can't I make you see that you could stand alone? The people of Rome adore you.'

Agrippa scratched his head irritably.

I looked at Rome's greatest living man. He was trapped by his own principles. Unable to take what could be his, what should be his. Unable to betray his loyalty.

'The gods presented the opportunity to Augustus, not to me,' Agrippa said at last. 'Conquering Spain is good for Rome. There are mines there, rich not just with copper, lead and tin, but gold and silver.'

'That's not the only reason,' I scoffed. 'A military success over foreigners as opposed to the civil wars he won—'

'—is particularly helpful to him, yes.' Agrippa cut across me. 'So even before he'd taken up his eighth consulship they were across the Spanish border to Tarraco.'

'They?' I asked.

'He took his stepson Tiberius and nephew Marcellus with him.'

I shook my head in disgust.

'In just the manner Caesar took him to the very same province,' I said. 'Can you not see what Octavian's doing? He's grooming successors.'

'I see it,' replied Agrippa, his eyes flashing with anger. 'I see it.'

There was a pause.

'But we must develop the next generation,' he concluded. 'I am the same age as Augustus. I should not be his heir.'

The tone in Agrippa's voice told me not to argue. I rubbed the scar on my cheek, remembering the sensation of battle.

'Has he been a good general?' I asked.

'I have advised him as much as I can from this distance. In time for Spring, he set up headquarters just south of the Cantabrian mountains, in Segisama. There's a broad plain there, with the river Brulles flowing through it, perfect for supplies. From there we unleashed three divisions to overrun Cantabria. The campaign started well. The first division marched north. The town of Vellica was the first to fall. Taking Vellica opened up the pass to the north, so the other legions landing on the north coast could join forces. The enemy retreated to the lofty peak of Mons Vindius, just as I had planned.'

I smiled. I could see the excitement in Agrippa. What a general he was.

'But once they were in Mons Vindius,' Agrippa grimaced, 'in that terrain, battles were difficult.' He scratched his forehead. 'I don't like advising it, but it was clear that the best approach was a siege. Starve them out.' Agrippa clasped his hands together.

'Sometimes, such tactics are necessary,' I said.

'It saved Roman lives for certain,' said Agrippa, 'but it's not as honourable...they held out for so long. It was about that time I got the first messages that Augustus' health was failing. Before long, he withdrew himself from the front and headed back to Tarraco. I considered sending Musa to him there.'

My eyes widened. An opportunity for an audience with Octavian had appeared. A gift from the gods. I tried to hide my interest.

'You told me he was ill,' I said, 'but that the legates were more than capable replacements.'

Agrippa nodded. 'They performed admirably,' he replied. 'At last, Mons Vindius surrendered. So all in all, I'd say yes, the first campaign was a success.'

'And the other two?'

'The second division proceeded almost without losses all the way to the walled town of Aracelium, some hundred, hundred and thirty miles from Segisema. But there they were fighting high in the mountains. They were short of breath and easily tired. And the walls were strong. We lost many men. Aracelium would not fall for months.'

'But we claimed it in the end?'

Agrippa nodded. 'And because it had put up so great a resistance, we razed it to the ground.'

'Your choice?' I asked.

Agrippa shook his head.

Gaius 'You must die' Octavian was at his old tricks again.

'Winter came, faster than we had hoped. The third division had further to march than the other two. As they headed west into the mountainous country, the attacks began. Sudden strikes which retreated almost as quickly as they started. Arrows of death from unseen archers. The enemy would never engage properly.'

'I remember you telling me. And that we could learn a thing or two from their cavalry.'

Agrippa nodded. 'I would hate to fall to an arrow I never saw released.'

I shuddered, remembering the death of my dear friend Sextus, the man whose name I had taken. He had not seen the arrow.

I had.

Lodged in his face.

Lodged in my mind.

'Slowly, we pushed the Spaniards back,' said Agrippa. 'They retreated to the summit of Mons Medullus, a rampart of rocks on high, baked in the sun.'

'Rome talked of the great siege works we built around that mountain top. The town was surrounded for eighteen miles around.'

Agrippa smiled. 'It was. What an earthwork. That must have been something to behold.'

'In the face of that,' I replied. 'I'm surprised the Cantabrians didn't yield at once. They must have been very determined.'

'They were. Even more so than at Mons Vindius,' Agrippa said. 'Months they held out. Months and months. With no food. No respite. And an army waiting for them.'

'How did it end?'

Agrippa sucked his teeth. 'Grimly,' he replied. 'They committed suicide. Some threw themselves on fires, others stabbed themselves and some even took poison of the yew tree.'

I flinched. I had seen men burn at Actium, a horrendous way to die.

I had pressed my dagger to my stomach, and failed to cut the skin, too afraid to do it. And as for poison of the yew tree, Musa had taught me all about poisons. A concoction of yew tree seeds could form a potion of death. But it was not an easy death.

'They feared the wrath of Octavian,' I said. 'Suicide rather submission.'

'Perhaps,' replied Agrippa. 'We have seen it before amongst these barbarian tribes. They prefer to die than become our slaves.'

'Have we taken many prisoners?' I asked.

Agrippa shook his head. 'Not this time.' I watched him clasp his hands together once again. 'I have heard stories that they sang hymns as they were crucified.'

'You've heard me say this before. Rome has a cruel father.'

Agrippa said nothing.

'Did any survive?' I asked, breaking the awkward silence.

'Yes,' replied Agrippa. 'The few that remained surrendered. About the time that Augustus was becoming consul for the ninth time with Silanus, he received the good news in Tarraco. When he felt well enough, he set out to receive their formal surrender on the mountain.'

'I bet it was a speedy recovery.'

'Victory is quite a tonic,' said Agrippa.

We sat in silence. I looked at Agrippa. He looked weary. All the talk of battles had excited him. But only temporarily. For here he was, stuck in Rome.

'You should introduce Musa to him,' I said, trying to mask my interest, 'when he returns.'

Agrippa studied me, assessing my intent. I had been too hasty. It was too obvious. He did not say anything. But he knew what I was hoping for, an audience as Musa's attendant.

I cursed myself. Too hasty. Again. When would I learn?

'I should go,' Agrippa said. 'There is much to be done.' He got up to leave. 'Rutilius,' he said. 'When Octavian returns, I fear I cannot see you again.'

I gaped, regretting the reaction I had caused.

'But Agrippa—'

He held out his hand to stop me. 'I'm sorry, my friend. I have enjoyed seeing you again. Enjoyed sharing my burdens from time to time. Enjoyed watching you, Whisper and little Cornelia blossom, but I cannot see a way, a safe way for this to continue.'

I stood up and embraced him.

'You are a greater man than you know,' I said.

'Farewell Rutilius,' he said. 'I am sorry that it has come to this once again.'

I recalled Agrippa's apology in Octavian's 'little workshop'.

I smiled at him. Older and greyer he might have been but he was still the strongest man I knew, not just pure strength, but strength of character.

'You still have nothing to be sorry for.' I said. 'You are Rome's saviour and protector. I wish you all peace and prosperity. Go. Protect. Rome needs you. More than ever.'

XIII

You should introduce Musa to him, when he returns.

Those few words, spoken in haste, had cost me dearly, not only Agrippa's trust, but months, years even, before I would have the opportunity to meet Octavian again, face to face.

I held my head in my hands. Why did I not bide my time?

Months passed. Still Octavian did not return. All I could do was wait. Once I found myself wandering the streets of Rome, enjoying the evening sunshine. My footsteps led me to the Argiletum, to the site of my old home. A new building stood there now. Someone else's home. I could hear people inside, slaves hurrying about their tasks. It was a strange and sad feeling, a memory of a life lost.

I walked on and came to the temple of Janus. There, I hesitated. The bronze double doors were both open, front and back. Years ago, I had attended the closing ceremony of these doors, one of the most fulfilling moments of my life celebrating the end of the civil wars. Back from Alexandria, I had celebrated with the whole city that Rome was no longer at war. Agrippa himself led the ceremony.

Now, the two heads of the bronze statue were staring back at me once again. The god of new beginnings. Octavian must have re-opened the doors when he declared war on Spain. A new beginning for Rome. The empire of Octavian.

I sighed. Even the peace I thought I had been a part of bringing about was not real. Now, just as many Roman soldiers were dying in Spain at the whim of Octavian, our tyrant, as had fallen during the civil wars.

With the new year came a new consulship. Octavian again. His tenth. Unbelievable, but a sign of the future. A distribution of four hundred sesterces per plebeian, the same sum he had given out with his triple triumph, ensured that no one cared.

His colleague was Norbanus Flaccus, one of 'The Fifteen', the members of the college with priestly duties. Flaccus was the son of a former consul, a friend of Octavian. And being in Octavian's circle of friends, I knew only too well, was vital for advancement.

I resented seeing the consulship handed around like a condiment at a dinner party.

In Spain, the surrender at Mons Medullus had not signalled the end of the campaign. The barbarians rose again. Had it not been for Octavian's legate, Carisius, they may have succeeded. But barbarians are not to be trusted. It was fellow Spaniards who betrayed the uprising's plans. The rebellion was slaughtered and the city of Lancea, until then a stronghold, was finally taken.

So Octavian announced his long awaited return. The war was over. He would close the doors of Janus. After so many months and years the moment was coming. I would set eyes on my nemesis. How I had longed to see him, to cut his flesh with a blade, to take revenge for all he had done to me.

Rome prepared for his return. Streets were cleaned. Garlands went up wherever I looked. The temples were filled with incense to burn when he set foot in the city. Stands were erected by the gates of the city for the crowds to gather and celebrate his arrival.

As I watched with gathering anger, I decided I would not go to the gates. What was the point? There was no way I could get close to him there and the joy and celebration that would be all around me from the sycophants would be unbearable.

My intention was not just to set eye on the man, but to set hand to him. Somehow, some way, I had to bring about his demise so the power of the state would fall to Agrippa.

No, the moment I would lay eyes on Octavian once more would be at the Temple of Janus. As the doors closed, so too would Octavian's empire.

'Before the god of beginnings.' I lifted little Cornelia. 'I will bring about a new beginning. Then what will your future hold?' I asked her, as I held her high above my head.

'A father who is alive I hope,' said Whisper behind me.

I turned to her. 'How do you mean?'

She tucked her hair behind her ear. 'Don't do anything rash now Octavian is back,' she said. 'He will be guarded more closely than ever. Cornelia needs her father,' Whisper took my arm, 'and I need my husband.'

I stared at the two women who meant everything in my world. And nodded.

I knew that nod was false. I could not let Octavian become Rome's king. But I would achieve my ambition without losing Whisper and Cornelia.

'I haven't planned anything,' I said with truth.

Whisper looked at me, considering. 'That's what I'm afraid of.'

They came out in their tens of thousands to greet Octavian. To hear their cheering nearly drove me to madness. I sat in silence in our home in the Subura, trying to ignore the noise. But the celebrations went long into the night and all over the city.

Whisper entered the room, clutching Cornelia to her hip.

'Perhaps we should have escaped to the countryside,' she said.

I looked up at her.

She could see the anger growing in me.

'Can you hear them?' I shouted. Cornelia's hands flew up in shock. Whisper soothed her gently. 'They are eating out of his hand,' I said. 'He has bought their love. Four hundred sesterces? Is that all it takes? By the gods, how weak are the plebs?'

Whisper frowned. 'That kind of sum means a lot to many people,' she replied. 'You of all people should know what it's like to be poor.'

I scowled at her.

'And he has stopped the wars,' she continued. 'People like it when they are not dying. I can't say I blame them. Imagine Cornelia was a boy. Imagine, if she was a Cornelius, that she was off to fight a war...'

'I survived many wars,' I replied. 'If you're good enough, war brings honour.'

'Survived?' Whisper looked almost tearful. 'Are you sure, Rutilius?

Are you sure that war didn't wound you more than that mark on your face?'

My hand went to touch the scar from Actium. Whisper was right, the wounds of Actium cut deep; my face, my friend, my status, all had fallen in that war, and its wake had reached further. The wound on my face had healed, but the wound to my spirit had turned septic, poisoning my morals, my conduct, my principles. I had become a shameful man.

And that shame was burning, burning like the incense in the temples around the city. The only way to douse the fire was to eliminate the cause. And the only cause I could see was Octavian.

Whisper read my mind.

'Nothing rash,' she said again.

I clenched my fist.

'Nothing rash,' I agreed.

It was a bright spring morning on the day of ceremony of the closing of the doors of Janus. I rose early, kissed both Whisper and Cornelia in their sleep, placed the dagger Agrippa had given me in the folds of my tunic and made my way to the temple of Janus. I needed to be at the front of the crowd, to set eye on Octavian.

But when I arrived, already the plebs had come. Scores had slept overnight in the street to gain prime position.

All about us were Praetorian cohorts, Octavian's bodyguard. Antony formed these cohorts to protect himself when Julius Caesar was assassinated. It was clear, that such a guard would never be released by Octavian. A tyrant needed protection despite swords inside the sacred city boundary being against the very traditions of the Republic.

Agrippa had no need of such a guard. The traditional lictors with their axes wrapped in bundles of rods were sufficient for him because the people genuinely loved him. The love for Octavian was bought.

I looked about me. Were there others amongst the crowd who wished Octavian harm? If there were, they, like me, would have no chance of reaching him past the praetorians. They were huge men, toughened by war.

I felt a surge of disappointment and cursed my naivety. Of course, it was never going to be that simple.

I chose to remain amongst that crowd. Not for the ceremony but because I had to lay eyes on Octavian, to see what he looked like after all this time, and to look him in the eye when I swore to the gods that I would have my vengeance.

As the morning passed, the crowd grew and grew. Cheers rippled throughout the streets celebrating Augustus. 'Io triumphe!' they cried, as if it was a triumph.

At last, I could tell by another raucous cheer, longer and louder than the rest, that Octavian was coming.

I strained on my tiptoes, desperate to set eyes on the man. I was shoved forward. The man next to me trod on my foot, as the whole mass of people pressed in, frantic to see him.

My heartbeat was quickening with every passing moment.

Where was he?

I scanned the crowd, trying to spot him.

Guards were carving a path through the people.

Where was he?

'Can you see him? Can you see the *princeps*?' the man next to me asked.

'No.'

My mind was filled with hate. I could taste the salt of the sea, feel the burn of the sun, smell the decay of my flesh from my months adrift. This man had destroyed me, taking my life apart piece by piece before casting me aside.

'Where are you?' I mouthed. 'Where are you?'

Then, at last, I saw him.

He was still a lean, hungry looking man. He had aged a great deal. There were lines in his face. Perhaps the illness in Spain had taken some of his life from him. His hair was thinning. I could detect grey hairs at his temples, but the eyes, the eyes had not changed.

They were still piercing, wide, malevolent. Those eyes are unmistakable, the kind which haunt your dreams.

He wore a purple cloak just like the one he wore in his commander's tent. On his head was the civic crown of oak leaves. My father had taught me to dream of achieving an oak crown. In the days of the Republic, it was given to men who saved the life of another citizen. Only the grass crown brought greater glory, awarded for saving the lives of an entire army. But as I looked at the oak crown on Octavian's head, I wondered whose life was he supposed to have saved?

The Senate had voted it to him because he had ended the civil wars, and so spared thousands of lives, more of the sycophancy that gave him the ludicrous title of Augustus.

Octavian made his way slowly forward, ever closer to the temple of Janus. The people applauded him, cheered him, raised their fists in celebration.

I bit my lip in anger. What about the thousands of deaths on his hands? The fact that he had caused the civil war in the first place? The fact he had forced men like me to choose which side to take? I had drawn my sword against fellow Romans, all because Octavian usurped Mark Antony. He left us no place to be neutral. You were either for him, or against him. We were all tainted with the same sin. And now there he was, wearing that crown, one of the greatest honours in Rome.

I looked at the statue of Janus and prayed.

'Let Janus, god of new beginnings, witness this oath. I shall bring about a new beginning for Rome, a new beginning for peace, a new blessing to the people of Rome; I shall deliver Agrippa as ruler. But this time, by the gods, I will show patience.'

I took one last look at our smiling king, with the gap in between his front teeth. I delighted in the slightness of his frame. Agrippa was the better man. It would be clear for all to see, now the two would stand side by side in Rome.

I turned my back on Octavian and walked calmly away.

'Your time will come,' I said aloud.

And while I waited for that time to come, I became Musa's dedicated assistant. He was barely able to scratch a living. I was tempted to offer him some of my wealth, but doing so would reveal too much of my background. Instead, I did my best to solicit custom for him.

'What I need is to treat one of the elite,' Musa said. 'Just one treatment of them, and I am sure I can persuade them of my ways.'

'I don't doubt it,' I replied, remembering the attempt I had made with Agrippa to get Musa in front of Octavian. To date, promotion of Musa was my best and perhaps only hope of getting close to him.

The end of Octavian's tenth consulship came.

And so began his eleventh.

Who was to be his consular colleague was the topic of much debate. Just weeks before taking office, the consul elect, Aulus Terentius Varro Murena, died of a sudden illness. I did not grieve the loss of Murena. His appointment had blatantly been because his sister was married to that smug, self-centred, self-important knight, Maecenas, the man who, before my very eyes in Octavian's 'little workshop', advised Octavian to establish his sole rule in the constitution. I remember that day so clearly. Agrippa had argued passionately to restore the Republic. But Maecenas won. I despised Maecenas almost as much as I hated Octavian.

Since that time, Maecenas had made a name for himself across the city, not just for his fondness of luxury, but as patron of the arts. The poets Horace and Virgil were under his patronage, writing their fawning works to celebrate Octavian. I reserved particular dislike for Horace. He described Agrippa in his satires as a cunning fox imitating a noble lion, a misnomer if ever I heard one.

So Maecenas' reputation was forged in the city. A man of greater contrast to Agrippa you could not find. Poems versus aqueducts, I knew which I thought were more use to society.

Being Maecenas' friend clearly could bring great rewards, but, just as clearly, it could not protect one from death as Murena had found out.

So the whole city debated who would join Octavian as consul. A simple choice for me, of course. Agrippa.

It was at this time Agrippa caught a fever. He summoned Musa. Despite Agrippa's previous orders, as Musa's assistant, I dared to enter his home.

Agrippa did not look ill. He just looked grumpy.

'I feel weak,' he complained.

Musa set about his prescription of lettuce, a bout of cold baths and cold poultices.

Agrippa spotted me straight away.

'A new career, Sextus?' he asked.

'Yes indeed sir,' I replied. 'I am privileged to learn from such a master.'

'He is good isn't he,' said Agrippa, 'but then the Greeks are good at most things.'

Agrippa waved away the slaves from his bedchamber so that we were alone.

'You should not have come,' he said.

'I heard that you were ill,' I replied. 'Nothing would have kept me from helping you.'

Agrippa smiled. Then he grimaced and rubbed at his temples. 'My head,' he said, 'it throbs so much.'

'It will pass,' I said. 'Such an illness cannot last long against a man of your strength.'

'How are Whisper and little Cornelia?' he asked.

'Both beautiful,' I replied. 'They both send their love, to you and to Marcella.'

We stood in silence for a little while.

'I hear there is a vacancy for consul,' I said at last.

'Yes,' Agrippa replied, 'unlucky Murena, so close to his year.'

'Is a successor lined up? You perhaps?'

Agrippa almost laughed.

'Not you then,' I said, disappointed. 'We should have a vote.'

Agrippa laughed aloud.

'The good old days,' he said. 'You are amusing, Rutilius, sometimes. Still hanging on to those dreams.'

'Still?' I replied. 'Always.'

Agrippa shook his head slightly.

'If not you,' I persisted, 'then who?'

'That,' said Agrippa slapping his thigh wearily, 'has been the subject of quite some debate.'

'Not Marcellus, please,' I said. 'Even Octavian wouldn't dare promote that boy so far above his station, surely?'

'Livia dismissed that idea, even before it reached me,' Agrippa replied.

'So he had dared to consider it,' I said in disgust.

'More Maecenas than him. You know how keen he is for Augustus to establish a dynasty, and one formalised in the constitution at that.'

'And what do you think?' I asked, wondering if even Agrippa's loyalty to the Republic had finally crumbled.

Agrippa closed his eyes and I saw his eyelids flicker with fatigue. He looked worn out.

'My views hardly seem to matter,' he said at last.

'How can that be?' I protested. 'You are the saviour of Rome.'

'I am just its builder.'

'What a ridiculous thing to say.'

'Is it?' Agrippa scowled at me.

'Your time will come,' I said.

'My time has already been,' countered Agrippa.

'The people love you,' I said. 'Genuine love.'

'Yes,' replied Agrippa, 'but I feel I'm not able to earn it anymore. All I do is build.'

'You are building a peaceful future. More than that, you are controlling a vengeful and violent king.'

'That's where you're wrong,' said Agrippa. 'I may have been, once. But there are others now, who have greater control than I ever had.'

'Maecenas?' I said.

'Maecenas. Livia. That morose son of hers Tiberius. That oily young Marcellus. Even Julia his daughter seems to hold greater sway with him. And she's only fifteen.'

I shook my head.

'Don't believe that, for one moment. Rome needs you, more than ever.'

Agrippa gripped my arm.

'You're a loyal man, Rutilius. I'm sorry for how things turned out for you. You made mistakes, but at least they were honest ones.'

Not all of them, I thought, recalling my false charges against Scribonius.

In fact, some were downright terrible. I cursed myself as I recalled Whisper's torture.

I composed myself. 'I have Whisper, Cornelia, and you,' I said aloud, 'what more could I want?'

When the man selected to become Octavian's colleague as consul was finally announced, it was a surprise to everyone. Calpurnius Piso.

'Why are you so surprised?' asked Whisper.

'Piso's an enemy of Octavian. He fought with Brutus and Cassius. And before that, he fought against Julius Caesar. Anti-Caesarian to his core. After all that, I could scarcely believe it when Gaius 'You must die' Octavian pardoned him. As you can imagine, when he was pardoned, Piso retired from politics altogether and has barely been seen since.'

'I see,' said Whisper, working this through. 'So why would Octavian make him consul now?'

'Or more importantly, why would Piso do it?' I said. 'What's Octavian bought him with? I hope it was more than four hundred *sesterces*.'

'He always was a cunning man,' said Whisper to

Cornelia. 'Nasty Octavian,'

'Nasty,' repeated Cornelia.

'That's right,' I said with a smile, stroking Cornelia's head.

'Although I can see what's in it for Octavian,' I continued. 'By picking a known Republican, it looks as if Octavian is not a king, as if the old Republic can still prosper. Bringing Piso in must be an attempt to quell the discontent about Marcellus, the obvious truth that Octavian is trying to establish a dynasty. But what's in it for Piso?'

'Well,' Whisper replied. 'You wanted to be consul. Or so you kept telling me before you said that the consulship wasn't worth anything anymore.'

'I did,' I replied.

'Then can't Piso have just wanted it for the same reason?'

'Personal dignity?' I said. 'Don't be silly. He'll think the consulship is worth even less than I do. He's as staunch a Republican as they come.'

Whisper looked at Cornelia. 'Pater is in a mood. He was rude to mater,' she said. Then she lit up. She had had an idea. 'Does Piso have any children?' she asked.

'Yes,' I replied. 'Two sons.'

'Then it's obvious, isn't it?' she replied. 'It's for them.'

'How do you mean?'

'You would do anything for Cornelia wouldn't you?'

'Of course.'

'That's it then. If Piso becomes consul, he's brought his family back into politics, at the very top. If he does what Octavian tells him too, perhaps his sons can have a career too. How many times have you gone on about the fact it's more important to be Octavian's friend than to be a good man?'

'Sounds like me,' I said.

I stared at little Cornelia, with her beautiful curls. Would I sell my principles to protect Cornelia?

I would.

And it would be that much easier at the price of the consulship.

'You're a clever, clever lady. That's why I love you.'

XIV

Several months later, we were woken by a frantic knocking on the door.

It was a messenger from Agrippa.

'Agrippa,' I replied, 'what does he want?'

'You to come to Augustus' house.'

'To Augustus' house?' I replied in total shock.

'Yes. You must come at once, with Musa. Augustus is gravely ill.'

I was in front of the door of the palace before I could even gather my thoughts. I had barely wiped the grit out of my sleeping eyes before the laurels on the doorposts and the civic crown of oak leaves on the lintel confronted them.

I stared at that crown, barely believing that such an opportunity was being presented to me.

I looked to the skies and thanked the gods. Storm clouds were gathering. I hoped it was a portent.

Musa arrived. I could see his smile from the other side of the Palatine.

'This is it Sextus, my friend. If I can cure Augustus, I will be a rich man. We will both be rich men. Think of it.'

I feigned a smile.

I almost felt sorry for my friend Musa. He had saved Whisper's life and given me Cornelia, and here I was, about to do everything in my power to ensure Octavian was not going to survive this illness. So Musa could not as he hoped become famous as the man who cured Rome's king.

It was only as I crossed the threshold when Agrippa ushered us in, that I was struck by a dreadful thought, a dreadful, but obvious thought.

What if Octavian recognised me?

It was as if Agrippa could read my mind.

'Augustus is delirious,' he said. 'He keeps drifting in and out of consciousness.'

Agrippa led us through the atrium towards the bedchamber where Octavian lay stricken.

'It is another bout of fever, which is what he suffered in Spain. His physician was prescribing all manner of treatments, but he says this is far worse than Spain.'

'Have no fear,' said Musa. 'I will examine him. I am sure my remedies will assist.'

My throat was pulsing as much as it ever did before a battle as I passed through the doorway into Octavian's bedchamber.

The room smelt of sickness, a stale, sweaty, unwholesome smell. But it was not the stench of death. Not yet.

A man stood beside Octavian's bed. 'I am Augustus' physician,' he declared.

Musa disregarded the physician with a peremptory wave of his hand.

'Let me see the patient.'

'This is no patient,' said a lady sternly. 'This is Augustus.' From her tone, and her dress, I presumed this must be Livia. I had never seen her in the flesh. She was not a beautiful woman, but she had presence and something else. She had an air of severity.

'Is he ill?' Musa countered.

'What do you think?' she retorted.

'He's very ill,' Musa replied. 'So, he is my patient.' He turned to me. 'Come, Sextus, some lettuce at once.'

'I have banned him from eating lettuce,' said Augustus' physician.

'Why, by Asclepius, would you do that?' replied Musa. 'In fact, why are you still here? I am now in charge of this man's care.'

The man looked as if to protest but caught Agrippa's stern eye.

'Very well,' he said, and withdrew crestfallen from the room, his position and reputation as physician of the *princeps* gone.

Octavian's eyes did not open once in that first consultation. A relief. No chance of recognition. Musa planned his usual treatment of cold baths and cold poultices.

While he was busy gauging Octavian's health, I was busy gauging how I could kill him. If I were to murder him there and then, it would be the last thing I did. The guards were ever present and there were more than enough of them to exact an instant punishment.

I needed time alone with the *princeps* and then enough time to escape.

With each visit to his house, I observed the patterns of the people. Livia was a loyal wife. She was always present. Quite often I would see her son Tiberius with her. To my surprise, the one person I never saw was Marcellus.

Inevitably, one day, Maecenas turned up when we were there. I scurried to the corner of the room, avoiding eye contact. Maecaenas was as likely to recognise me as Octavian.

Several times I witnessed Maecenas and Livia having impassioned conversations. One day I was close enough to overhear.

'This is why I want him to sort out his succession,' said Maecenas. 'Life is fragile, even for great men. I pressed him after Tarraco. Why didn't he learn? That was a clear warning if ever there was one. If he dies now, everything could be for nothing.'

'You think Rome would be safe in the hands of Marcellus?' replied Livia, tartly. 'He's barely able to strap his own sandals.'

'That's patently not the case,' said Maecenas. 'He's taken to the office of aedile like Antony to Cleopatra.'

'He's doing the right things because Augustus and I are telling him exactly what to do,' said Livia. 'The only thing he's good at is being obedient. And handsome.'

Maecenas pulled his hand through his long hair. 'Well, whatever you think of Marcellus, your boy Tiberius isn't ready either.'

Livia gaped at the open affront from Maecenas.

'I know your true intentions. Who doesn't?' Maecenas said. 'They are understandable from a woman of such ambition, and such,' Maecenas considered the word carefully, 'calibre. But if Augustus dies now, neither Marcellus nor Tiberius will succeed him. So what next? That's what we need to worry about. Both of us, together.'

As I mixed yet another poultice, an idea dawned.

Why was I always imagining stabbing Octavian? I had in my hands the means to kill him. Had I not learned of the poison of the yew tree? All I had to do was make a lethal potion and no one could be certain it was me.

I checked my excitement. If Octavian died from poison, his physicians would certainly be killed without question. Not such a good plan after all.

But then I thought again. It would not be instant, so it would buy me the time to escape. I could administer the poison and depart Rome forever, never to look back, but safe in the knowledge that Agrippa would have his opportunity once again.

Musa left Octavian's side.

'I must speak with Livia,' he said.

And so I was left with Octavian, alone at last.

I made my way slowly over to the prostrate *princeps*. He was white as death, with beads of sweat emanating from his forehead. His skin, blotchy at the best of times, was covered in spots and rashes. The cold baths and cold poultices were not working.

Suddenly, lightening flashed and almost at the same moment, a clap of thunder tore through the palace. It was so loud I leapt away from Octavian through pure reflex.

His eyes flicked open. They were filled with terror.

A second flash of lightning. Another thunderous clap. The palace shook. It sounded as if the gates to Hades were opening beneath us. Octavian's eye's roved the ceiling. I could see his fear. And I loved it.

His eyes rested on me. I watched his pupils shrink as he focused. He looked at me. Then I saw his eyes move to the scar on my face.

Suddenly, I was afraid. As a third peel of thunder tore through the palace, I saw, to my horror, recognition in his eyes.

'You,' he mouthed, faintly.

His arm shot out from the bed and grabbed me by the throat. I dropped the bowl of poultice. His hand was squeezing the life out of me, as it had done once before.

Livia and Musa ran across the room to pull him off.

'You cost me Cleopatra,' he said, wild eyed and trembling.

'He's raving,' said Livia. 'Musa, do something. He's delirious?'

Musa bowed to Livia. 'I will, I will.'

Octavian's eyes refused to leave me as I stood, pale as death, watching. A series of lightning flashes in the window broke his gaze. He stared, fear-stricken outside. Then, his eyes rolled and he passed out. As his head fell to the bed, another ear-splitting clap of thunder shook the palace.

'What, by the gods, was that about?' said Maecenas striding across the bedchamber.

'I have no idea,' said Livia. 'Raving about Cleopatra.'

'That's not a good sign,' said Maecenas. 'We must plan

quickly.'

Livia looked at her husband. She looked genuinely mournful. She kissed him on the forehead, then guided Maecenas out of the room.

'I think we should begin by his resigning the consulship,' Livia said. 'It's wearing him out too much. If he survives, we'll worry about how he keeps the real power.'

'If he gives up the consulship and survives, he'll need something constitutional,' replied Maecenas.

'I know, Maecenas,' replied an exasperated Livia, 'I know. But we need him alive. That's the only thing we need to worry about for now...'

That night, I told Whisper what had happened. I could still feel his fingers around my throat. I still can. Sometimes I even dream of them. And those eyes.

Whisper looked terrified.

'He recognised you?' she exclaimed.

'Yes,' I replied. 'It must have been the scar.'

'But he'll have you killed.' Whisper's lips started to tremble. 'We'll have to leave.' Tears of panic filled her eyes. 'You idiot,' she screamed. 'We have to leave at once.'

'Calm down,' I said grabbing her arms and trying to still her. 'He's delirious. In a high fever. Musa says he doesn't know what he's saying or doing. In fact, Musa's saying he's terribly afraid we can't save him.'

'Good,' replied Whisper, her voice cracking. 'We need him to die.'

When she said that, I stopped dead.

I nodded.

'Of course. You're right. We need him to die, so he can't reveal my identity.'

'All we can do is pray to the gods to take him,' said Whisper.

I shook my head.

'That's not all we can do,' I said. 'There is another way.'

That night, I carefully prepared a potion of the yew tree poison and slipped it into the bag of items I would bring with me to the palace.

But when I entered the bedchamber, it was as if a senate meeting was occurring. Agrippa was there. He did his best not to acknowledge my presence. Livia was there. Tiberius was there. Even Marcellus was there. Maecenas stood beside Octavian's head and finally there was an older man I did not recognise. His purple bordered toga told me it was a senator. Could this be Piso? He looked old enough, and submissive enough.

I placed my bag on the floor and noticed, to my utter disbelief, that Octavian was sitting upright, conscious and alert.

'I fear,' he said, with a weak voice, 'that I will not survive this.'

'Come now,' said Agrippa, 'I was ill only a few months ago, and now I feel hale and hearty once again. You'll defeat this. I'm sure of it.'

'I wish,' said Octavian, his voice fading, 'that I shared your confidence. I have gathered you here today,' Octavian nearly collapsed forward. Livia's hand pulled him back upright. He looked up at her and gave a little smile.

'I have gathered you here today,' he began again, 'to set my affairs in order.' His head lolled towards the senator. 'Piso,' he said, 'take this.' His trembling hand lifted a book.

Piso bowed and took it from Octavian.

'In it you will find the details of every soldier in every legion in every country of the empire,' Octavian said. 'And,' he handed over a second book. 'In this, you will find the record of the public revenues.'

Piso looked gravely at Octavian.

'If,' Octavian coughed. It wracked his whole body.

Livia's hand gripped his shoulder. Octavian corrected himself, 'When I die, you will be the sole remaining consul in Rome. Your task is to maintain peace and good order. See to it with every ounce of your strength and abundant experience.'

'I will Augustus, of course I will,' said Piso.

No one spoke of Octavian surviving any more. The faces of the people around the bed spoke only of impending death.

You could see Livia's mind was torn in two. She was a scheming woman. But what I was witnessing was a woman who loved her husband.

That clasp of his shoulder was genuine.

I even felt a flicker of compassion. I had seen death many times, but as a soldier and commander it had come quickly. This long, slow demise was tragic, even when it was claiming my bitterest enemy.

I glanced at my bag on the mosaic floor.

There was the solution, a potion to ease his passage into Hades.

It would be almost merciful.

Octavian's bloodshot eyes settled on Agrippa.

'Agrippa,' he called out, beckoning the great man closer to him. 'Come, my brother. Come closer.'

Agrippa instantly came and sat on Octavian's bed.

'Agrippa,' Octavian said, holding Agrippa's gaze, 'you have been the greatest friend I could have ever hoped to have. Loyal to the last.'

Agrippa looked at the floor. Even his steadfast loyalty had been tested in recent months.

Octavian reached out and grabbed Agrippa's forearm. 'Don't let it all go to waste,' he mouthed. 'Don't let it all be for nothing.'

Octavian fumbled at his hand. On his third finger was his signet ring. The ring which sealed his letters. The ring that ruled the empire.

He tugged and pulled at the ring, until at last it slipped passed his knuckle.

Everyone watched intently.

Octavian stared at the ring for a moment. He turned it slowly in his fingers. Was this the symbol of his inheritance?

I saw Marcellus noticeably shift his weight.

Maecenas shot him a look which would have killed a stag in full flight.

Octavian held up the ring.

'Take it,' he said, clearing his throat to say it again so that everyone could hear. 'Take it,' he repeated. 'Agrippa. You of all people have earned this right.'

Agrippa stared.

My heart surged with joy. Agrippa was to succeed Octavian. The gods and goddesses of Rome were fulfilling my prayers.

Agrippa reached out. His hand trembled as much as Octavian's. Carefully, slowly, he took the ring from Octavian's grip.

'Don't let it all go to waste,' said Octavian as he slumped back. 'Don't let it all go to waste,' he stammered. 'I am sorry for how I treated you these last months. Forgive me.' And he drifted in and out of consciousness repeating the line 'Forgive me'.

Agrippa stood over the frail man, his master for so many years. Here, at last, he was to take up the mantle. He held the ring aloft. There were tears in his eyes.

'I forgive you,' he said loudly. 'Of course I forgive you.'

He looked round the people in the room. His eyes rested on Livia and Marcellus for a while. Their expressions were sullen, bitter, venomous even. Agrippa stared at Maecenas, who rubbed his oily hair.

At last, Agrippa slipped the ring onto his finger. It would fit only his little finger, another indication of the might of the man.

Piso might have been holding the records of the troops' whereabouts, and the money of the state, but there was only one ruler. The man with that ring. And that man was Agrippa.

Without another word Agrippa spun on his heel and marched out of the room.

There was a stunned silence in the room. Octavian's mumblings finally ceased as he lapsed into unconsciousness.

'Come,' said Musa, waving me forward. 'We must put him in another cold bath. It is our only hope.'

I looked one last time at my bag. The potion had been unnecessary. I had not become a callous murderer after all. I had been spared.

Almost with joy and pleasure, I helped Musa lift Octavian's frail, stinking body and place it once more in the futile cold baths.

Octavian did not regain consciousness.

Musa stood over him under torchlight until the early hours. We watched Octavian's chest barely rise and fall. With each breath, I expected it to be his last. But the chest kept moving. At last, I could watch no more. I was too weary. Musa dismissed me.

'I will watch over him,' said Musa, stroking Octavian's forehead with further cold poultices. 'Perhaps the gods will send a miracle.'

'If he deserves it,' I replied, 'I am sure they will. The Fates have a habit of meting out what is deserved.'

I returned home to the warm embrace of Whisper and the sleeping bundle of Cornelia.

'There's no need to run,' I said with a smile. 'He's died of natural causes. Agrippa is our new ruler, and best of all, my conscience is clear.'

That night, I learnt why Octavian had wept all those years ago in Alexandria when the news was brought to him that Antony had been killed. It was not tears of friendship. It was tears of relief. When you have wanted something for so long and with every part of your being, if it is finally given to you, it is almost too much to accept. Tears flowed, but rest assured, there was no pity in my tears for Octavian, as I now believe there was no pity in Octavian's tears for Antony.

After the tears came the time for celebration. Whisper and I made passionate love. Rome was to be re-born and we would be there to see it.

Perhaps I might even have a role, a status.

As I lay, recovering, a sudden thought struck me. My bag was still in Octavian's bedchamber. And inside the bag...

'By the gods,' I said in a panic, 'the bag.'

'What bag?' replied Whisper.

'My bag,' I shouted. 'My bag, with the poison.'

'Where is it?' asked Whisper.

'In Octavian's room,' I replied.

Whisper struck me. 'Rutilius,' she screamed. 'How could you...Why are you so stupid?'

I clapped my hand to my mouth, horrified by what I had done, but realising it could not be undone. 'I can't go back to get it now,' I said. 'I will have to recover it in the morning.'

We lay, side by side, neither of us able to sleep, but not another word was spoken between us, the magic of our love making destroyed.

There are days in your life which you remember as vividly as if they had happened yesterday. As I have written my adventures, I feel that perhaps I have had more than my fair share of such days. My life has been full of tumultuous events and dramas. Few, however, will match the feelings of that next morning.

I returned to Octavian's house, and was let in. To my surprise, no signs of mourning were evident. Where were the weeping slaves, the black dresses? Where even a look of sorrow? If anything, the home seemed more full of life than on any of my previous visits. The storm clouds had passed. Bright sunshine poured through the windows.

I walked to the bedchamber. I had eyes only for my bag. It was not where I had left it. In fact, I could not see it at all. I scanned the room, and all the horror I felt regarding the bag was immediately forgotten. It was forgotten because it was replaced with a new horror, far greater.

Musa was there, and beside him was Octavian, sitting upright, and talking.

'What did you do?' he was saying.

'Well, sir,' Musa replied. 'A series of cold baths and poultices. It is a treatment I have been administering after many years of study, sir.'

'You are blessed by the gods, my man,' replied Octavian. 'I am recovered.'

I stood, gaping.

How had there been such a turnaround in fortune?

Musa spotted me. 'I have cured Augustus,' he cried. 'See, he is well.'

I could not reply. My leg began to tremble. If Octavian was cured, he would recognise me and I would never leave the palace.

I was a dead man.

'And you will be rewarded,' said Octavian, 'handsomely. You and your entourage. Tell me, what is your status?'

'I am a freedman, sir,' replied Musa. 'I have, by the grace of Agrippa, been brought to Rome to practice my craft.'

'And what a craft it is,' replied Octavian. 'Well, Musa, you will be my physician from now on, and I will make you rich. Piles of gold, for you and your friend,' he said, pointing at me. 'And for you personally,' he said returning to Musa, 'I will grant you the right to wear gold rings despite your status. Rome will know your name, my friend. You have saved the state,' Octavian beamed, 'because you have saved me.'

'Thank you, sir,' replied Musa with an ingratiating bow. 'Thank you.'

I watched in terror, unable even to attempt to run.

'Speaking of rings,' continued Octavian, 'I must summon Agrippa back at once. I need my ring back.'

Beyond the tragedy of my dream of Agrippa's succession crumbling before me, I was concerned with my very life.

Musa came over to me. 'Sextus,' he said. 'What was that potion you had made? I was so weary last night, I took a look in your bag in case you had prepared some potion for Augustus already.'

I was dumbstruck.

'I found one potion in there. But when I opened the bottle to put it to his lips, I just had a sniff to make sure it was what I had told you to prepare. It smelt very different.'

'Did you give it to him?' I asked.

'No,' replied Musa.

I closed my eyes in disappointment.

'Did you recognise the potion?'

Musa looked thoughtful for a moment. 'I don't think I did,' he concluded.

I sighed with relief.

'Have you still got the potion?'

'No,' replied Musa, 'I threw it away.'

I embraced Musa. He patted my back, uncomprehending.

'It is wonderful is it not,' he said, referring to Octavian's healing.

'Yes, it is,' I replied truthfully, referring only to my

narrow escape.

Now, all I had to do was disappear.

'You,' commanded Octavian. 'Come here, let me shake you by the hand,' he said.

I turned. Was now the moment? Should I charge him, try to throttle him in his bedchamber? I would be killed. Of course I would, but Agrippa would keep the ring. Rome would be saved.

I looked at Octavian's smile.

But I could not run. I could barely walk. I made my way across the room and took Octavian's hand.

He gripped firmly.

'Thank you,' he said. 'Thank you. For whatever you did to assist that wonderful man in curing me. You have served Rome more than you could imagine.'

He suddenly hesitated, catching sight of my scar.

His grip of my hand tightened.

I could see he was thinking, struggling to recollect.

'You look like somebody,' he said thoughtfully.

'Really,' I said, trying to sound disinterested.

'Yes, you have a striking resemblance to a face I know.' He scratched his head irritably.

I was desperate to let go of his hand, but I had no choice. I was literally in his grip.

'Ah,' Octavian exclaimed. 'I have it. This sickness must have addled my memory. Yes, I once knew a man with a scar similar to yours. But he is dead. He was a worthless man. Marcus Rutilius Crispus was his name. Not someone you would want to be compared to,' he laughed. 'Tell me, how did you come by your scar?'

I took a moment to realise that he had not worked out that the man holding his hand, the man whose sweat was oozing into his palm, was the very man he maligned.

'My scar?' I stammered, buying a moment to think, 'it was in a fight I should not have been in,' I said, speaking the truth.

'How so?' replied Octavian.

'The man I fought for was not worth defending.'

'I see,' Octavian replied. 'You are rash, then. That's just like Rutilius. Let's hope the similarities end there. His life did not end well.'

Octavian smiled. At last, he let go of my hand.

To this day, I can still feel his grip.

All I wanted to do was leave the palace, but Musa was enjoying being the centre of attention. The slaves of the household were at his beck and call. I was virtually bereft of tasks.

I was busy preparing another poultice when Maecenas arrived.

'Augustus, gods be praised, it's a miracle,' he said as he strode into

the room.

'Maecenas, my man. I thought I'd been claimed this time.'

'So did we,' said Maecenas, running his hand through his hair. 'So did we.'

Octavian looked him up and down. 'You were as concerned for yourselves as you were for me,' he said.

'Not at all,' replied Maecenas airily. 'Of course, we were concerned for ourselves, but our primary concern was your welfare. The state could not live without you.'

'But could you?' Octavian challenged.

'Me?' Maecenas hesitated. 'Well, I have no position, so I suppose I could disappear from political life tomorrow.'

'You certainly could,' replied Octavian.

'But it would be rather less fun,' said Maecenas. 'It would have been such a shame at this late stage. You are so close to establishing a dynasty.'

'I thought that would come up,' replied Octavian. 'There

is no dynasty.'

'That's why it was such a concern when you were on your death bed,' replied Maecenas. 'You need an heir, to carry on your good work for Rome. If not, we will just fall into yet another civil war. And that's not good, for business, for poetry, for any of us.'

'Who would you have me choose?' asked Octavian.

'That,' replied Maecenas wagging his finger, 'is most definitely your choice. But for now, I think you have created yourself a problem.'

'How do you mean?' asked Octavian.

'Agrippa,' said Maecenas, almost with a sneer in his tone.

'Ah,' replied Octavian, 'the ring.' He rubbed his nose with his finger. 'I had to pick someone,' he said. 'Agrippa was the only option. There was no way I was actually giving Piso any power.'

'But can you unmake him?' asked Maecenas.

'Of course,' said Octavian, 'I retrieve the ring. Simple.'

'If only it were,' said Maecenas. 'You have given him a taste.'

'Maecenas,' Octavian replied, 'Agrippa has had more than a taste of power. If he was ever to threaten me, he could have done it years ago. Why now?'

'Because yesterday he was Rome's sole ruler,' replied Maecenas. 'But today, he is...well, that's the point, what is he?'

'What would you do?'

'You have two choices. Either you send him from Rome, or you bind him closer.'

'How do I bind him closer?'

Maecenas looked at Octavian.

'Marriage?' said Octavian with scorn. 'Julia is married to Marcellus. I'm not forcing a divorce there. Marcellus is the future.'

'Indeed he is,' said Maecenas with a long, knowing stare. 'Indeed he is. The future.'

'You think I've made it so that Marcellus and Agrippa cannot both remain in Rome?'

Maecenas said nothing.

'This is ridiculous,' bawled Octavian. 'Agrippa has served me for over twenty years. Perusia, Naulochus, Actium. Every time, my greatest general. He crushed the revolts in Gaul, the rebels in Dalmatia. He's been consul three times. He was censor with me, holding the power and lives of the senators in our very hands. He even bloody well presided over Marcellus' marriage, by Hercules. The boy's only nineteen. I've only made him an aedile. Don't tell me Agrippa feels jealous of him. It's ridiculous.'

Still Maecenas said nothing.

Octavian stood, shaking his head. He sighed. 'Leave it with me.'

Maecenas turned and walked from the room. I was certain I could see a broad smile on his face.

In my mind, I added his name to my list. Octavian had to fall, but so did Maecenas; he was not even half the man Agrippa was.

Musa was applying my latest poultice when Agrippa arrived.

Given the circumstances, he walked with pride, and his face was full of colour, quite the opposite of Octavian's, half covered in paste.

'Augustus,' Agrippa said. 'When I received your summons I was delighted.'

'Really?' replied Octavian.

'Yes,' said Agrippa firmly. 'For if I was receiving a summons from you, then you were still alive, and that meant my prayers were answered.'

I looked at Agrippa's hand. To my surprise, Octavian's

ring was still on his little finger. Was he trying to keep it?

'Dear friend,' said Octavian, 'dearest, most loyal friend. I thank you for your prayers. Perhaps it was the prayers of the noble Agrippa which persuaded the gods for mercy.'

'You are fully recovered?' Agrippa asked.

Octavian hesitated only for a moment. 'Nearly,' he replied. I could not help but flinch with frustration. 'It's really quite remarkable.'

Agrippa was not going to suffer the embarrassment of being asked. He pulled the ring from his finger in one tug and held it out to Octavian.

'Then this is yours,' he said.

Octavian reached out, almost casually, and took the ring from Agrippa.

The rule of Rome, changing hands once again. I could have wept.

Octavian did not put the ring on straight away, but played with it amongst his fingers.

'Thank you, Agrippa. I hope you realise I was honouring you by giving you this ring.'

Agrippa nodded.

'The legions would have followed you.'

Agrippa nodded. 'I had hoped so,' he said.

Silence.

'I am not dishonouring you by taking this back,' said Octavian.

Agrippa shook his head.

Another awkward silence.

'We must settle on a new mission for you Agrippa,' said Octavian. 'I feel as if I have been wasting your talents.'

'I am ready to serve. You know that.'

'Perhaps the east,' said Octavian. 'I will think on it.'

'Wherever you think best,' said Agrippa.

There was another short silence. Agrippa, holding his poise as best he could, was masking all the pain of ceding the power. How he could bring himself to let that feeble-framed Octavian take command once again, I will never know.

I was filled with rage. I wanted to attack Octavian and seize the ring for Agrippa. But that evidently was not what Agrippa wanted, and my duty was to serve Agrippa.

'It is good to have you restored to good health,' Agrippa said at last. 'Rome still needs her father.'

And with that, he left the room.

To my surprise, Octavian slumped forward and held his head in his hands. I watched on, fascinated. It seemed as if his shoulders were heaving. Was he crying?

Musa came to Octavian's side.

Octavian looked up.

'That man,' he said, pointing at the doorway Agrippa had just departed through, 'is greater than I deserve.'

I could not have agreed more.

'And what's worse,' Octavian shook his head. 'He doesn't deserve what I'm about to do to him,' Octavian scraped some of the paste off of his face and cast it onto the mosaic floor. 'But, Musa,' he pointed at Musa, who was taken aback, 'it was you who kept me alive, so now I have no choice.'

He sat with his hand covering his mouth, deep in thought. 'There must be something I can do with him,' he said.

It was not Musa's fault. It was Maecenas'. And Livia's. Neither of them wanted Agrippa to be Octavian's successor, that much at least was clear. Maecenas wanted Marcellus, and Livia, well, she clearly wanted her own wretched son, Tiberius.

Against those two conniving, cunning and relentless forces, what chance did years of loyal service have?

XV

From this tragedy came one moment of redemption, personal redemption. I now knew I could not kill Octavian by poison. It was the coward's way of killing. I had to find another way, especially now all Rome knew that if Octavian died, Agrippa would succeed him.

But I had to be swift. It would not be many years before Marcellus was ready. Then, Rome would be in the hands of a dynasty, and her greatest servant would fade into the past.

I did not wish to remain in Octavian's palace. But I did not know how I could withdraw from Musa's service.

Fortunately, the whim of Octavian provided me with the escape. He ordered Musa to release me because I reminded him of a complete fool called Rutilius.

'And I don't want any ill luck in this household,' he said.

So I was removed from Musa's service. Musa did not care. He was too busy gorging on his success. He had more wealthy clients than he could count on his ring clad fingers, more money than he could spend, and more fame than many a gladiator. It was better for business if I stayed away.

Not long after, Agrippa's future was laid out for him. He would head east. When the rumours in Rome first spoke of Agrippa's departure, it was not a happy tale. Agrippa was leaving in rage, anger and disappointment after Octavian's survival. This I knew was not true. Closer to the mark were the stories that he had fallen out with Marcellus and that he was being sent on a false errand to the east to keep the two apart and smooth the path for Marcellus' succession. This I believed. No doubt such a mean-spirited plan had been drawn up after careful consideration with Maecenas, Livia and maybe even Marcellus himself.

But the hurtful gossip did not entirely make sense when I learned that Agrippa was granted an extraordinary new power. The senate voted him the power of a proconsul for a five-year term. This made him, constitutionally, all but Octavian's equal. He was to go to Syria with his own legates and maintain the empire on the eastern front.

'Perhaps Octavian has a genuine mission for him,' said Whisper.

But what could that be?

One night we were rudely awakened in the early hours.

It was Agrippa.

'Rutilius,' he said, 'I am sorry to disturb your family,'

I yawned. 'I am always pleased to see you,' I said. 'Why have you come? How can I help?'

'You've heard I must go east?' said Agrippa.

'Who hasn't?' I replied.

'I am pressed for time, so I will come straight to my purpose. Do you want to come with me?'

'Come with you? What, leave Rome?'

Agrippa nodded.

'I have a mission, Rutilius. One I could benefit from your experiences as an informant.'

I flushed with guilt at the mention of my short, albeit successful career in the murky world of informing.

'I will not go to Syria as Octavian commanded,' said Agrippa. 'Instead, I will set up headquarters in Lesbos and govern from there through my legates. I could do with loyal friends in my entourage.'

'What is your mission?' I asked.

Agrippa smiled.

'Parthia.'

'Parthia,' I repeated. I could not believe he was smiling. Parthia had brought about the destruction of every Roman who had attempted to conquer them. Cassius' three eagles were still there, to the shame and ignominy of Rome. Even Antony had failed to recover them. Even Antony could not defeat the Parthians. Not one but two of his own standards had fallen to them. To take on Parthia was dangerous in the extreme.

'You're going to war?' I asked.

'We can't afford to, Rutilius. Literally. The money is running out. Spain has not worked out as we had hoped. The Spaniards are up in arms once again. And Gallus has failed in the east so the money is not flowing in. To keep paying the common people the sums Augustus chooses to, it must.' Agrippa stared into the distance. 'I am over forty, Rutilius. I may not look it, but I am beginning to weaken. Maybe my campaign days are behind me. But he's named me successor, you know.'

I brightened. 'Octavian's successor?'

'Successor to Caesar beyond the Ionian sea.'

Typical, a clause attached.

'Congratulations,' I replied, masking my disappointment. 'You know my views though.'

'I do,' said Agrippa. 'But I am here to seek your company.'

'You want me to conquer Parthia?' I replied, bemused.

Agrippa laughed.

'Not exactly. This is going to take some explaining. Shall we sit down?'

We sat, and what wine I had in the house was served. I am sure that in comparison to the fare Agrippa was used to, my wine was undrinkable.

But ever the polite man, he drank it and complimented me for its fine taste.

'Now,' he said, clapping his hands together. 'Have you heard of a man called Tiridates?'

I shook my head.

'Nearly two years ago now, he came to Rome seeking the

help of Augustus.'

'That was when I returned to Rome,' I said. 'Octavian was away on campaign in Spain.'

'Indeed he was, so I received this Tiridates. It turned out he had been king of Parthia for a time. He seized the throne after a revolution.'

'I see,' I said, plainly not seeing at all.

'The rightful king, Phraates, then recovered and ousted Tiridates, forcing him to flee. But when Tiridates escaped, he abducted Phraates' youngest son, bringing him to Rome as hostage.'

'As leverage,' I said stating the obvious.

'Yes,' replied Agrippa. 'But we have done nothing with this boy. We have been more than occupied with our own troubles. However, now is the time to find out whether Phraates values his son greater than those eagles.'

I pictured little Cornelia, sleeping in her bed. She was worth more than any amount of eagles in the empire.

'So you're not leaving Rome in anger?' I said.

Agrippa smiled. 'No, Rutilius, I am not.'

'Nor are you being exiled?'

'No, I am definitely not being exiled.'

'But this mission does get you out of Rome, away from Marcellus.'

'It does,' conceded Agrippa. 'But this is one of the most important missions I have had. Let the gossips talk. It will hide my true purpose.'

One of the most important missions.

For that moment, it felt as if Octavian himself was in the room, speaking through Agrippa. Clearly he had persuaded Agrippa of the truth of that statement, but Agrippa had not overheard Maecenas. I chose not to tell him. He had been named as heir. No matter that it was only of certain parts of the empire, there would surely be no doubt in Rome's mind who the rightful successor was.

'Why do you want me to come with you?'

'To negotiate,' replied Agrippa. 'I will make for Mytilene, on the island of Lesbos. It's a very pleasant town, a far cry from Rome to be sure. From there my legates will continue to Parthia, and I will start negotiations. You could assist me.'

'Why Mytilene?'

'Oh come now Rutilius. As a man familiar with subterfuge, Mytilene is where many before me have retired from politics. Those in Rome who don't already believe that I've retired, will believe it all the more when they learn I am there.'

I shook my head. 'Syria would be far more convenient a place for communications with Phraates,' I said.

'Yes it would, but it would also be far more obvious,' replied Agrippa.

'No, if I stay in Mytilene, Rome will never guess what I am up to. And if I succeed, we will have at last recovered the worst shame of our age.'

To my mind, that honour was reserved entirely for Octavian.

I considered Agrippa's offer. Mytilene was a beautiful place, with a hot climate and an assurance of Agrippa's good company. It should have been an irresistible proposal.

But something in me could not accept it.

My mission was to stay in Rome and bring about Octavian's demise.

Agrippa was lined up as heir, but to succeed, the *princeps* had to fall. I could not achieve that from Mytilene.

'Thank you, Agrippa, but I will stay in Rome. You must not jeopardise yourself by associating with me. I wish you good health and every success, though, truly, I will wish you every day to return to Rome.'

Agrippa considered whether to try again but could tell that I was adamant.

'This is a new skill for me, Rutilius, but I hope to do it quickly.'

'I think you will find that negotiating with someone's child as leverage will bring about a far quicker result than any of your contract negotiations for your building works.'

We laughed.

Agrippa stood up and gripped my shoulder. 'It's good to see you, Rutilius. Look after your family while I'm away.'

When Agrippa left Rome, I was hopeful. Octavian was no longer consul. Although he had taken his ring back from Agrippa, he had not bothered to take up his office again. When he attended the Latin games that summer, on the Alban Mount, he announced to the people that he was giving up the consulship.

Instead, during that plague ridden summer he summoned the senate and passed through a new settlement, more than replacing the powers of his ceded consulship. I could picture Octavian's careful plotting with that oily snake Maecenas. How they will have sniggered when they worked out that getting the senate to grant Octavian the tribunician power, without the need of the actual office, would be more than sufficient for their iniquitous purposes.

This power gave Octavian the right to veto any action of any magistrate, senate or assembly. In essence, nothing could happen in Rome without Octavian's approval.

I could almost hear Maecenas.

'Rome will be completely in your hands at last, and they, not you, will have put her there.'

Or something of that nature.

But Octavian's power was not limited to Rome. In his provinces he retained the control of his armies. That was to be expected but he was also given the power to intervene in anyone else's province as and when he deemed necessary.

Republic Restored? I think not. Republic destroyed. Kings had less power.

There were other rights, symbolic compared with the total control the tribunician power gave him, but no less sickening. He retained a seat on the consuls' platform at the front of the senate house despite no longer being consul. He retained the right to speak first at the senate meetings.

He could even summon the senate. And, funnily enough, he kept the care of Rome's grain supply, with all the accompanying adoration of the plebs that brought.

Apart from when the famine struck.

Octavian was as good as his word to Musa, who swaggered around the city, gold rings on his fingers, clients begging for his services. On the Tiber Island, the colossal statue of the healer Asclepius, with his crown of laurel and his serpent entwined staff, was given a new companion amongst the temples and porticoes. A statue of bronze. Antonius Musa. I could scarcely believe it.

With Agrippa gone, Whisper and I watched Marcellus begin to build his reputation, backed by his uncle's money of course.

His first act had all the traits of Agrippa, a monumental building project. Marcellus broke ground by the river Tiber for a new, extravagantly grand theatre. It would be an imposing hemi-cycle of tiers and arches with a capacity of over eleven thousand people.

But that was just the beginning. Like so many before him, he exploited games. To the full. Rome lived and breathed the games of Marcellus. They still do. Marcellus paid for a knight and a woman of equally high status to participate as dancers, a deed sure to capture the audience's attention.

'Is there nothing people won't do for money?' I asked Whisper.

Marcellus installed a vast awning to protect the spectators from the blazing sun. It was the first time such a thing had been done. The people stared in wonder. As soon as Marcellus realised how popular the awning was, the Forum was filled with them too, shading the crowds as they parted with their sesterces.

With Agrippa out of the city, his name was soon forgotten. All the talk of the city was of the nineteen-year-old handsome youth Marcellus. A successor in the making.

'We should have gone with Agrippa,' I muttered to Whisper. 'I can't bear to see this.'

Rome's mighty senate and people were falling into the hands of Octavian's dynasty.

I had to do something. But what?

The Fates answered for me.

News broke across the city which brought joy to my heart.

'Marcellus has fallen ill,' Whisper babbled. 'It's the gossip all over the Forum. Some say it's plague. Others swear it's Livia's doing. He has gone to Baiae.'

Baiae was a holiday resort with a reputation. In years gone by, the reputation was for healing. Now it was for drinking parties and revelry on the beach.

'He'll have gone there for the hot springs,' I said. 'Musa wouldn't approve. He's all cold baths and cold poultices, not hot springs and boiling water.' I scratched my beard. 'As for Livia, if only she wasn't Octavian's wife, I might have an ally in her.'

'Don't be silly, Rutilius,' Whisper admonished me. 'Livia's twice as dangerous as she is beautiful. Meddle with her and Cornelia will be an orphan in no time.'

Within days Musa was sent down to Baiae to treat Marcellus.

'He'll have an army of statues at this rate,' I said bitterly. 'If only he wasn't so good at his craft.'

But instead, to our surprise, a messenger arrived at my door. The scroll he bore was from Musa.

> SEXTUS,
> COME TO BAIAE AT ONCE.
> MARCELLUS IS GRAVELY ILL. MY POTIONS AND POULTICES ARE NOT WORKING. I NEED YOUR HELP. WE MUST SAVE THIS YOUNG MAN. FOR THE GOOD OF THE EMPIRE.
> COME AT ONCE.
> MUSA

For the good of the empire? Or for the good of Musa's career?

It did not matter. I was never going to refuse. Here was another chance to get close to Octavian's household and who knew what opportunity that might bring?

When I was confronted with young Marcellus's ailing body, all joy at the news of his illness faded. Here was a youth losing his life before my eyes.

Musa tended to him, desperation in his eyes.

'He is burning,' Musa muttered, 'burning whatever I do. Muscle aches, headaches, stomach pain, sickness and now, whenever he stirs, he is totally confused.'

Musa dabbed constantly at Marcellus' sweating brow.

Marcellus' noble face was pale and clammy. He took only shallow breaths. I peered into the bed pan which lay beside Musa's foot. The stool was dark and rich with blood. A foul stench reached my nostrils. The bedchamber was as touched with death as the battle fields I had stood on. It was obvious there was nothing to be done.

I looked again at Marcellus and felt an overwhelming pity. I had travelled to Baiae intent on making sure Marcellus did not survive. Thank the gods, the Fates spared me from becoming a murderer. Though, in truth, I know I would not have had the stomach to kill him. His young, fair face did not deserve such punishment merely because he was nephew of Octavian.

Instead, while Musa desperately concocted yet another potion, I dabbed that poor boy's forehead with a cloth as his life slipped away from us and he joined Pluto in the underworld.

When Octavian heard of Marcellus' death, he dismissed Musa at once. I felt sorry for Musa. It was not his fault. Not even the god of healing himself could have saved Marcellus. Not from the state he was in. I was sorry too that with Musa's departure, I lost an opportunity to be close to Octavian. But I would find another way.

When Octavia learned of her son's death, she fainted. The whole of Rome was grief-stricken. It felt as if the entire city mourned Marcellus' loss more than Julius Caesar's.

Marcellus was immortalised in a gilded statue wearing a golden crown. Octavian would have cared far more deeply about that commission than the forgotten bronze of Musa, which, to my surprise, still stood on Tiber Island.

Octavian decreed that an empty curule chair be carried to the theatre hosting the September Roman Games. It would sit amongst the games' sponsors in a position of honour. Everyone would know whose seat it was.

Meanwhile the monumental theatre that Marcellus had broken the ground for, all hale and hearty at the beginning of the year, was named in his honour. The city lamented that he would never see his gift to the people.

As for the funeral. I doubt there was such a vast public occasion since the famous funeral of Julius Caesar, with Antony's famous speech.

The whole of Rome turned out.

At the beginning of the procession, there was nothing out of the ordinary; the usual musicians led the singers through the streets singing their dirges. But then came the death masks. Famous ancestors. One, after another, after another. Six hundred, they say. True or not, they were beyond count and they were talk of the city for months.

Octavian himself delivered the eulogy with Marcellus laid before him on the funeral couch. Normally, a funeral speech was held in the Forum. But today, the ceremony was held outside Octavian's Mausoleum in the Plains of Mars.

Was it because Octavian feared a eulogy in the Forum would stir up memories of Antony's famous speech?

Or was it because the Mausoleum was now complete, and standing in the shadow of the vast bronze status on the building's summit, commanding all those it could see was the perfect backdrop?

The Plains of Mars were full of the grieving.

I was too far away to hear what Octavian said in that speech.

Instead I looked at the greying man. His shoulders were slumped. His head bowed. The grief appeared genuine. But was the pain real? Was the emotion true? Or was it horror at the demise of his dynasty.

Whatever the truth, that day, while his statue seemed all conquering, for once, Octavian looked a broken man.

As I watched the eulogy, it occurred to me that, many years ago, Octavian announced his arrival in Rome delivering a eulogy. He was only twelve years old when he mounted the speaker's platform in the Forum and spoke, in the high voice of a young boy, of his grandmother. Then, Rome loved and admired that young boy's courage.

'Now look at him,' I muttered.

XVI

The moment to strike Octavian had come. Marcellus' death had made Agrippa the natural successor once more. While poets worked at ten thousand sesterces a verse to immortalise Marcellus, I dwelt on how I might prove that Octavian was very much a mortal.

Opportunity rises in the most unexpected of places. For the second time in my life, I found mine amongst the law courts. Ever since, as "The Mouth of Octavian", I brought prosecution of Labeo at the trial which enthralled Rome, I have found myself drawn to the dramas of the law courts. It's trivial affairs most of the time; personal attacks, grievances and the like. But occasionally, as with my trial, the whole of Rome is gripped.

Such was also the case in the trial of Marcus Primus, governor of Macedonia. He was charged with treason for making war without permission on the Odrysae, allies of Rome.

I was at court on the day Lucius Licinius Varro Murena, the legate representing Primus, opened the defence of his client. Murena's words reverberated across the empire.

'You accuse Marcus Primus of treason,' Murena began. He eyed the jurors. Suddenly he raised his finger. 'But he informs me that he acted with the full support of Augustus himself. How can that possibly be treason?'

The court erupted. The claim spread from the Basilica to the Forum and from the Forum to the empire. It also reached the ears of Octavian. The claim must have alarmed him. If Murena's statement was true, he had breached the settlement he had worked so hard to agree with the senate. The province of Macedonia was under the control of the senate, so if Octavian was bandying about instructions without so much as a word to the senate, it proved him a fraud. His attempts to deceive Rome that we had a Republic would be exposed for all to see.

Primus, inevitably, was summoned to attend the trial. Nothing would have prevented my attendance on the day he presented himself. For a man accused of treason, he looked very self-assured. No unshaven, unkempt look, unlike Scribonius when I was prosecuting him. Primus was altogether very confident.

His testimony, however, differed from what Murena had said.

'You say you received instructions to attack,' said the prosecutor.

'I did,' replied Primus.

'And that these instructions were from Augustus himself?'

'No,' said Primus.

There was an audible gasp within the court. This had been the great defence. Why, by the gods, had he changed his story?

'They were from Marcellus,' Primus continued.

'Marcellus?' repeated the prosecutor with a surprised tone.

Primus nodded.

'But Murena, in representing you, declared that the instructions were from Augustus,' said the prosecutor with a disparaging tone.

'Surely I am not the only one to believe that the directives from Marcellus came with the same weight as a direct order from Augustus?' replied Primus. 'Marcellus was to be Augustus' successor. I treated his instructions with the respect they deserved.'

This declaration caused a murmur throughout the courtroom. In addition to the accusation that Octavian was meddling in provinces without authority, now Primus had brought about open talk of the succession. Octavian had always vehemently denied Marcellus would be successor, even offering to show his will to prove it.

But if Marcellus was giving orders within provinces that were supposed to be the senate's to control...

I smiled. Could this be the beginning of the end for Octavian? At last, he was being exposed as just as much of a dictator as his adopted father, Caesar. And everyone in the empire knew of Caesar's fate.

Primus was a brave man. I wondered how he could look so assured. Did he have documents which proved his claims?

The following day, the courtroom filled with people long before the session began. The trial had become the talk of Rome. There was not a tavern or drinking hole in the city which did not mention Octavian's troubles. Speculation was rife about what evidence Primus had. Everyone wanted to see it. And today, they hoped the truth would be revealed. Scrolls perhaps? Wax tablets?

The Praetor arrived and prepared to open the session. All eyes were fixed on him. He was directing a couple of attendants in final preparations for the day before he would soon bring the crowd to order.

Primus shuffled in his seat. He still looked remarkably calm given the magnitude of the event.

Murena was more restless. He kept rubbing his face. His eyes had the distant look of a man rehearsing his lines in his head, ready for the day's speeches.

Suddenly the great bronze doors clanged open.

Everyone's head turned.

Everyone's eyes widened.

There, framed by the grand doorway, stood Octavian.

He was flanked by his lictors.

As the people realised who it was standing there, they gaped in stunned silence. Why was Octavian there?

He had not been called upon as a witness.

He had no right to attend.

But his very presence, standing in that doorway, had already changed everything.

Murena looked furious. Octavian's arrival would jeopardise the honest voting of the jurors.

It was clear to everyone that Octavian would have something to say. I seethed in silence as Octavian strode across the room. A brief word in the Praetor's ear, and within moments Octavian was taking an oath, swearing by the gods to tell the truth.

'Did you instruct Primus to attack the Odrysae?' asked the presiding Praetor.

'I did not,' replied Octavian, fixing Murena with his piercing glare.

'Did you instruct Marcellus to give the order to attack the Odrysae?' asked the Praetor.

'I did not,' said Octavian.

'You're certain Marcellus did not give orders to attack the Odrysae?'

'I am. Why would an aedile be giving orders? The whole thing is absurd. Especially in a province the senate commands.'

'So, you admit that Marcellus could give orders in a province under your command.'

Octavian blinked. He looked frustrated. In the courtroom, he could not have his scroll with him, with its pre-planned words and phrases. Here, he was having to answer the Praetor at once, without the careful preparation he craved.

'Marcellus was an aedile,' said Octavian. 'He conducted himself as such and in an exemplary manner.' Suddenly Octavian snapped. He wagged his finger at Primus. 'You dare to speak ill of the dead? You dare to besmirch that youth. He was a boy of such promise.' Octavian looked tearful. He turned his gaze to the jurors. 'This is ridiculous. A trumped up charge to bring about disorder in Rome. I never gave those orders. Marcellus never gave those orders. Have either Primus, or Murena provided any evidence of these orders? No, because they never happened.'

Murena shifted his weight. He was growing increasingly agitated. His cheeks flushed red with anger.

'You swear you did not give those orders?' asked the Praetor.

'I am already under oath,' growled Octavian, fixing the Praetor with his eyes. There was a pause. Grudgingly, Octavian felt he had to continue. 'By all the gods and goddesses, I swear, I did not give Primus orders to attack the Odrysae.'

My eyes narrowed. Something in the precision of the denial made me suspicious.

I did not give Primus orders to attack the Odrysae.

Perhaps it had been Marcellus who gave the orders? Or perhaps the orders were different. Perhaps they were to attack the king? Or perhaps Primus had asked Octavian whether he should wage war, and a simple, positive response was all Octavian gave.

Suddenly, Murena could tolerate no more. He leapt to his feet.

'Why are you even here?' he said, contempt dripping from his voice. 'Were you called as a witness?'

Octavian stared at him, his eyes full of wrath.

'I came here in the public interest,' he replied.

Murena shook his head. The trial had been subverted by Octavian. That was obvious to everyone, but was Murena brave enough, or foolish enough to say it in front of all these witnesses?

Clearly Murena did not want to die.

He huffed, slapped his legs with his hands in frustration, and turned his back on Octavian.

Octavian's gaze never left him.

The key fact remained. No evidence had been provided.

So, faced with Octavian himself, his purple gown, his oak crown, the tyrant of Rome standing amongst them, which fool would be brave enough to scrawl an A for acquittal on their ballot?

The jurors cast their votes. The three urns rattled as the ballots were dropped in. It felt as if the whole court room held its breath.

To everyone's astonishment, some were brave enough.

But too few.

Primus was found guilty. Octavian walked from the court without another word.

Primus looked pale as death, all self-assurance gone.

When I looked at Murena, his face was filled with such contempt and fury, I realised there was a man I could work with. He was staring after Octavian, his hatred of him visibly as strong as mine.

The trial had shaken Rome, damaging Octavian.

The fact that jurors had bravely voted against Octavian hurt him all the more.

It felt as if embers were smouldering.

With Murena, could I stoke up a fire, and bring Octavian down?

It was time to delve into the corrupt world of plots. I had seen how to disguise myself, the power of a hood and cloak. I stopped shaving and allowed an unkempt beard to appear.

Whisper stared at my straggly beard.

'Why have you stopped shaving?' she asked. 'You look terrible.'

Should I tell her the truth? I could say that little Cornelia loved how my beard tickled her face when I nuzzled her. But I could not lie to those beautiful eyes.

'I have a plan,' I declared.

'Ye gods,' Whisper replied. 'Another one?'

'Yes,' I said. I explained what I had seen in the courtroom, the festering hatred of Murena. 'Murena has a reputation. Occasionally intemperate, and certainly forthright in his views.'

'Well,' replied Whisper, 'to speak out in public about Octavian like that, you'd have to be courageous.' She tucked her hair behind her ears.

'Or mad,' she concluded.

'Do you think I am mad?' I asked.

'Trying to kill Octavian?' Whisper looked at me. 'Yes, absolutely. Completely mad. Why jeopardise all this? Why jeopardise all our lives? Rome is safe place. What more do you want?'

'Agrippa to rule us as a Republic once more. Only Octavian stands in our way.'

'But why is it *your* mission to kill Octavian?'

'Why is it anyone's?' I replied. 'Someone always has to do something. Otherwise, nothing would ever happen.'

Whisper sighed.

'I know I'm going to regret telling you this,' she said, 'but if you are really set on this, if you have to do it, then you should meet a man called Fannius Caepio.'

'Fannius Caepio, who's he?' I asked.

'I have no idea,' said Whisper. 'All I know is he is a dreadful man, and he hates Augustus.'

'How do you know this?' I asked.

'It's the talk of the Basilicas when I go shopping. His graffiti covers the city. And he's always spouting abuse about Augustus.'

I laughed. 'And I used to say shopping was pointless.' I kissed Whisper on the cheek. 'I will bring these two men together and see what we can concoct.'

'Don't get yourself killed,' she said with wide eyes of worry.

'How can I?' I grinned. 'I'm already dead!'

It was the height of the summer when I sought an encounter with Caepio. Most wealthy Romans had retreated from the city to escape the sweltering heat. But that year, respite and recuperation was not the only reason to leave the city. Famine had struck again. The grain supply was failing and the people of Rome were beginning to starve.

Coastal villas and rural retreats were receiving their wealthy owners until the temperature cooled again, literally and metaphorically.

Somehow I suspected that Caepio was not such a man. I had always known the area behind the temple of Castor in the Forum to be where men of ill-repute loitered.

I walked through the area in my plain tunic and weighed up those present. There was a bull of a man: strong frame, furrowed brow, thick, dark hair and eyes which spoke of violence. I hoped that he was Caepio. He was just the sort of murderous man I was after.

Sure enough, after a few moments, his name was revealed to me. Fannius Caepio.

He was a very different proposition to Murena, the polished orator. Ordinarily, I doubted they would have even a moment for each other. But they shared a common purpose. I slipped away to don my hooded cloak.

I returned and tugged at the sleeve of his tunic.

'What do you want?' he growled.

'The same as you,' I replied.

Caepio frowned. 'And what's that?' he asked, turning to face me square on. I was dwarfed by him.

I leaned into his ear. 'To wound Augustus with more than words,' I whispered.

Caepio's head jerked back as he took in what I had said.

'Who are you?' he asked.

'I hardly think that is important,' I replied. These were the words the accursed informer had used to me in my past. They had been sufficient for me. Not pursuing that man's identity cost me the life of my dear wife Olivia, or at the very least, vengeance once he had murdered her.

It galled me that somewhere in the empire, that informer was probably still alive, ruining other people's lives.

However, his line worked with Caepio too.

'What are you suggesting?' he asked.

'An audience with interested parties,' I said.

'Who?'

'A senator.'

'Which one?'

'You'll find out if you agree to meet.'

'I agree,' Caepio said. 'Where?'

'The temple of Fides, on the Plains of Mars.'

Caepio smiled. 'No witnesses there, that's for sure. Loyalty is overrated. When shall we meet?'

'In three days' time, at sunrise,' I said, hoping that I could convince Murena to meet in that time.

'Done,' said Caepio and he turned his back and continued with what he had been doing.

I slipped away, walking the opposite direction from home in case someone followed me.

Next I sought an audience with Murena. As a senator it was possible to get a message sent to him. I suggested a meeting at the festival of Portunalia on the 17th August. My message read the 17th Sextilis. August was the new name for the month which the senate had granted in their sycophancy. Just like July for Julius Caesar. I remember predicting that Octavian would have a month named after him. I remember also hoping that the fate which befell Caesar would befall

Octavian. Perhaps both my predictions would come true.

By writing Sextilis, it gave a clue as to the purpose of the meeting. In the stubborn manner I refer to Augustus as Octavian, I called the month its proper name. The disapproval should have been apparent, especially to an educated man such as Murena.

The message read.

TO VARRO MURENA, GREETINGS
A MEETING ON THE 17TH SEXTILIS AT THE PORTUNALIA MIGHT PROVIDE YOU WITH THE KEY TO SATISFYING YOUR ANGER FROM THE COURTROOM
COME TO THE PORTUNALIA. I WILL FIND YOU.

The 17th Sextilis came, and I made my way to the ancient temple of Portunus in the ancient cattle market, the Forum Boarium. This temple was at the head of the oldest stone bridge in Rome, the Pons Aemelius. Portunus was a god with many purposes. The god of ports and harbours, the god of gates and gateways, and most importantly, in this year, the guardian of the port store houses.

That year, the ceremony, usually such a minor affair, was extremely well attended. The famished people of Rome were desperate for grain. Portunus must have been angered for the grain supply to stop so entirely. His wrath must be appeased. Such crowds were ideal for my purpose.

I carried a key to offer into the fire with the rest of the congregation. But in my mind, the key I carried represented the key to the gates of Rome. Today was the day I hoped to set in motion events which would wrestle the keys of the city from Octavian and give them to a far worthier man, Agrippa.

I recognised Murena. Flicking my hood over my head, I eased my way through the sweating crowds.

I tugged at the purple bordered sleeve of his toga.

'Murena,' I said.

He turned with a start. 'Who are you?'

'My name is not important,' I replied. 'What I have to say is.'

'And what is that?'

'If you believe, as I do, that Augustus has gone too far, that he is a tyrant, then there are others who think the same.'

'Others?'

I nodded.

'Others. Men who would risk their lives.'

'Such as?'

I assessed Murena. Could I trust him with a name? Ultimately, it was no risk to me. So I gave Caepio up.

'Fannius Caepio.'

'That thug,' replied Murena dismissively.

'Indeed,' I replied, 'but there will be others. And every revolution needs its measure of brute force.'

Murena stared at the columns of the temple of Portunus.

'This conspiracy needs a leader,' I said, 'a leader like you.'

Murena shuffled forward, towards the fire where people were throwing in their keys.

'Murena,' I persisted, grabbing at his arm, 'I saw your face in the court. I saw the contempt. You hate Augustus as much as I do. That man claims to be restoring the Republic, but there is only one word for him. King. There are many throughout Rome who know the truth. They want action. They just need a leader.'

Murena stepped forward. He cast his key into the fire.

He paused.

'And they shall have one,' he said.

I clenched my fist in celebration.

'The temple of Fides, sunrise tomorrow,' I said, casting my key into the fire.

That night, Whisper was terrified. She clutched little Cornelia into her waist.

'The temple of Fides,' she said, 'are you mad?'

'Why?' I replied.

'Why would you bring any attention to that building?'

'I'm not going to reveal the secret chamber,' I countered.

'That's not the point,' she said, exasperated. 'Why would you do anything which connects the plot to your past?'

'Octavian believes I'm dead,' I said, instinctively reaching for my throat. I could feel his cold fingers squeezing the life from me. 'Even if this conspiracy was discovered, no one would leap to the conclusion that I am still alive.'

Whisper stroked Cornelia's curls.

'But don't worry,' I continued. 'No one is going to discover us.'

'I do worry,' Whisper replied. 'I honestly wish you would stop. Life has changed. For all of us. You have so much to lose.'

She walked out, leading Cornelia by the hand. Cornelia glanced over her shoulder. She waved at me.

'Bye,' she said.

She was growing up fast, faster than I had expected. It felt as if I was missing it.

'It won't be long,' I said to an empty room.

The sun rose on another sweltering day.

I made my way to the temple of Fides. Caepio was already waiting.

'Aren't you going to reveal yourself?' he said.

'This hood is staying firmly where it is,' I replied.

Caepio grunted, clearly irritated.

'Is the senator coming?'

'Without a doubt,' I replied.

'So you can tell me who he is?'

'He can reveal himself,' I replied.

We did not have long to wait. Murena came with no

entourage. The two shook hands.

'Fannius Caepio,' Murena said. 'I'm glad it's you. We need a man of your,' Murena paused, seeking the right word, 'willingness to act,' he concluded.

'Murena,' Caepio replied. 'I must say I'm surprised. I thought your career was on the rise.'

'It was,' said Murena, 'until Augustus crushed opportunity for everyone except his friends.'

'I heard of your outburst in the court,' said Caepio. 'Impressive.'

'Perhaps,' replied Murena. 'I couldn't help myself. Like you, I have difficulty controlling my temper.'

Caepio smiled.

'So,' he said. 'What's to be done?'

The two men looked at me. I held my hands up and shook my head. 'Don't look to me. You know precisely what needs to be done.'

It reminded me of my school days when I used to start fights with the other boys, but somehow never ended up at the bottom of the pile.

'He's right,' said Caepio. 'We know our purpose. All we need to do is work out the means.'

'I have a freedman,' said Murena, 'Castricius. He has access to Augustus who buys his chitaras and lyres for his dinner parties.'

'Does he indeed? That will be useful.'

'If we use him to ascertain Augustus' movements, we can be poised and ready to strike.'

'Daggers, like Caesar?' Caepio asked.

'That would be fitting for Caesar's adopted son,' Murena nodded.

'Fitting indeed,' I replied, gleeful.

'Let's meet here tomorrow,' said Murena, 'at sunrise.'

We departed. I ran back home.

'It went better than I could possibly have hoped,' I shouted at Whisper as I crossed the threshold. 'They're going to do it. They're going to kill him. And I don't even have to bloody my hands. All I did was introduce them.'

'Do they know who you are?' she asked.

I shook my head. 'No. It's time to shave.'

Whisper cut the beard from my face tenderly. That close to me, I could not resist her. I grabbed her hand and pulled her into me. She stroked my clean-shaven cheek and smiled.

'You want to celebrate?' she asked.

'Very much so,' I replied. 'When Octavian is dead, Agrippa will be back in Rome in no time,' I said. 'Then,' I kissed her, 'it's over. I'm all yours.'

'Mine and little Cornelia's,' she smiled.

Each day more men gathered at the temple of Fides, a steady stream of disgruntled senators, knights and others with cause for complaint.

I remained a passive observer, hooded and cloaked. Murena was precisely the leader I hoped he would be, inspiring the new attendees with his words, luring and securing their loyalty to the cause. Caepio was exactly how I had imagined he would be too, always trying to bring violence and bloodshed.

'Should we not drink each other's blood?' he said, 'to prove our loyalty, as they did during the Catiline conspiracy,'

Murena looked aghast, as did many others, though notably not everyone.

'I don't think there's a need for that, do you?' Murena said. 'We have all sworn an oath. And,' he added, 'I'm not sure I believe that story anyway.'

I did. Catiline was a murderous rogue. Drinking human blood was probably the least he was capable of.

Further days brought more men, more money, more

weapons to the conspiracy.

Coded messages filtered through the city streets. Letters with a distinct pattern of folds to reveal they were from the conspirators. It was clear to me that the plans had become grander than just the stabbing of Octavian.

'We must learn from the failure of Brutus and Cassius,' said Murena. 'We can bring uprising to the whole of Italy. The whole country must rise up as one.'

Caepio roared his approval. A bestial cry.

He waited till the echo in my temple chamber subsided.

'We must bring death to them all,' he bawled. 'No one must be spared. Not this time. That was their mistake.'

No one must be spared? I gulped. I had literally observed the ever increasing flock of people crowding into my temple each day, occasionally listened to Murena's opening and closing remarks but ultimately sat outside for much of the time keeping a wary eye on passers-by.

When had the plans moved beyond Octavian? When had they developed into uprisings across the whole of Italy?

Who else did they intend to murder?

Did they intend to kill Agrippa?

What had I done?

'It's out of control,' I said.

'What is?' asked Whisper.

'The conspiracy. What they are plotting now will bring death and destruction to many. I think they might even be trying to kill Agrippa!'

Whisper looked horrified. She rolled her eyes.

'You have stoked the fire,' she said. 'What did you expect to happen?'

'Not this,' I replied, forlorn. 'Not this.'

The next morning, I woke up early.

'What am I to do?' I asked.

'Find out if there is a list,' Whisper said. 'Who do they intend to kill?'

'And if Agrippa's on their list?'

'Try to talk them out of it.'

'What if I can't?' I said despairingly.

'Then you will have to reveal the conspiracy to him.'

I jumped to my feet.

'Why is my life never straightforward? Others don't seem to get themselves into such strife.'

'I warned you,' said Whisper. 'You caused this. You must remedy it.'

As I entered the temple of Fides, I was consumed with fear. The code word for safe passage into the chamber was 'Cicero'. It was the name the Liberators had called out after they assassinated Julius Caesar and so it was a fitting watch word for the day the uprising would begin.

'Cicero,' I said as I approached the two guards of the chamber.

They let me through. 'Today is the day,' said one.

'Together we rise,' said the other.

I bit my lip. Who was to die this day? I had to find out. And quickly.

The list of targets had grown so long, that there was an official list. Copies were passed amongst the conspirators. I grabbed the scroll and read frantically.

Octavian, Livia, Tiberius, Drusus, Gaius, Lucius, Maecenas and Julia were all there.

Then every consul who had been colleague to Octavian; Statilius Taurus. Norbanus Flaccus, even Piso, the staunch Republican.

But there was another name.

A name I was desperate not to have read.

Agrippa.

I felt my mouth go dry.

How had I caused this? How could I have brought about the downfall of the man I loved above all others? And most importantly, how could I save him?

At that moment, a woman burst into the temple. There was a scuffle as the guards held her back.

'I don't know the watch word,' she shouted, 'but I am Terentia and I must see my brother,'

Murena's head whipped round to the direction of the disturbance.

'Murena,' cried the lady. 'I must speak with you.'

Terentia was a wealthy woman. That much was obvious from her striking dress, her fashionable hair-style and her jewellery. But she was also a beautiful woman. The entire chamber gawped at her. Even in distress, she was eye-catching.

Murena stared. He recognised her at once.

'That's my sister,' he called. 'Let her through.'

The guards released her.

Terentia ran across the chamber.

Caepio stared aghast. 'How does she know we're here?' he asked.

Terentia flung her arms about her brother. Murena, baffled, patted Terentia's back.

'What is it?' he asked.

Terentia peeled herself from her brother's body. There were tears in her eyes.

'You are betrayed,' she said, breathless. 'You have to flee. Run for your lives...'

Murena looked horrified. The chamber fell silent. Everyone was listening.

'How do you know?' Murena asked.

'Through my husband,' Terentia replied. 'I teased it out of him,' she added, suggestively.

'Your husband?' Caepio interrupted. 'How does he

know?

Murena's eyes narrowed. 'Because her husband is Maecenas,' he said clawing at his cheek in agitation. 'He knows everything.'

'Your sister's married to Maecenas?' exclaimed Caepio. 'Why didn't I know this?'

Murena threw his hands in the air.

'We're dead men,' a voice said. Consternation filled the temple.

'How?' growled Caepio. 'How did this happen?

'It was Castricius,' said Terentia.

'Who?' snapped Caepio, looking murderous.

Murena turned pale. 'Castricius is my freedman,' he mumbled.

'What?' bawled Caepio, turning on Murena, fist clenched.

Murena pinched the top of his nose. His hand was trembling. Fear and panic were disseminating through the temple chamber as swiftly as the flooding Tiber.

I felt nauseous. We were undone. Were the soldiers marching on the temple as we stood there?

Many turned to the doors. Some reached for daggers and swords hidden in their cloaks and togas. Others looked as if they wanted to run away at once.

Murena turned to Terentia. 'You must leave,' he said, 'at once. You have risked your life coming here. Go.'

Terentia made as if to protest. 'Go,' insisted Murena, almost pushing Terentia towards the door. 'You have saved us. But now save yourself.'

Terentia wiped the tears from her face, but did not move.

'Please,' said Murena with beseeching eyes.

Terentia took one last look at her brother, turned and hurried out of the temple with everyone following her every step.

There was a shocked, agonising silence.

I tried desperately to calm my thoughts. Was I personally implicated?

Could Castricius have betrayed me? I concluded he could not. No one knew my name to give it away. If I could only manage to escape the temple, I could melt into the cauldron that was Rome. I could survive.

Caepio broke the silence. 'We should go ahead anyway,' he growled.

I shook my head. 'Octavian will have doubled his guard. We wouldn't get near him. It's time to flee. Now.'

'But we can bring the fire to the whole of Italy,' Caepio fumed. 'The armies are ready. They await our command.'

Murena shook his head. 'We have lost the element of surprise. We would spill blood and bring anguish to so many, but never win.'

'We can win,' Caepio seethed. 'Or we should die trying,' he exclaimed.

There were shouts of agreement throughout the temple.

Murena shook his head. He would not be moved, no matter how much Caepio protested.

Murena and Caepio stared at me. It was obvious they wanted to know who I was. I could not help but take a step backwards.

Murena pointed at me.

I swallowed.

'You must escape,' Murena said. 'If we don't give you up, you can carry on this fight.'

Caepio clenched his fist. It was clear he was desperate to know my identity. After all, I had brought about his downfall.

Murena turned to Caepio. 'But for you and me my friend, it's flight or suicide. We cannot give up the names of all these men,' Murena gestured to the room. 'They must live to fight another day.'

Caepio grimaced. 'Why will you not fight?'

'Because we will lose,' said Murena firmly. He looked Caepio directly in the eye. 'Flight or suicide; that is our choice.'

I could hear Caepio's breathing. I could see his body rise and fall. Fury emanated from him. He paced. To him there was a third choice. To fight.

His fists clenched. He brought them slowly to his mouth. The muscles in his forearms pulsed. He looked through Murena. Would the violence start here? Now? In my own temple?

Caepio closed his eyes. His eyelids twitched with his anger.

At last, his eyes flicked open.

'Flight it is then,' he declared. He strode towards the temple exit. 'I will live to fight another day,' he sneered.

His broad shoulders knocked into me. Struck by such a force, I fell to the floor. To my horror, the hood dropped from my face. I was revealed.

My shaven face. My scar.

Mercifully, Caepio did not look back.

Murena and the other conspirators watched as I frantically grabbed at the hood to cover my face once more.

'Fear not,' Murena said. 'We won't betray you. But you must swear you will make another attempt on Octavian.'

I regained my feet.

I re-arranged my cloak. 'I swear it,' I said, 'by all the gods.'

Murena nodded. 'Good,' he said. He looked about the chamber. 'Who knows, with Maecenas as brother-in-law, perhaps I will survive.'

I shook my head, forlorn. 'There's a reason he was called Gaius "You must die" Octavian.'

Murena pursed his lips. He stared at the floor. There was no chance of clemency.

'But believe me,' I continued. 'I have been waiting for

years to kill Octavian. I will never stop fighting for the Republic. Never.'

Murena shook my hand. His grip was firm, still in control. 'How quickly it unravels,' he said. He marched out of the temple without so much as a backward glance.

So there I stood, a band of murderous men deprived of their leaders all about me. What was I to do? When I had left the house that morning, this was not the outcome I had expected.

'Gentlemen,' I began, 'Comrades,' I added, learning from Octavian. 'Today our conspiracy may have been revealed, but as silently as we gathered, we will slip away into the shadows.'

I stared at the men's eyes. Some were wide-eyed with fear, ready to run; others were slit-eyed with rage and blood-lust.

'You heard our leader. Murena spoke the truth. If we fight today, we will die with honour, but without success. Better to fight another day.' I looked about the chamber. 'Today we must flee. And we must lie low, remember our oaths to one other, but be ready for the call to come again. Because, gentlemen, the call will come. In Murena's name. In Caepio's name. You will hear it and you will know the time has come for Octavian's downfall.

'And when you hear that call, gentlemen, you will remember your loyalty, you will remember Fides, and you will gather in this temple and you will bring justice to our empire.

'Today, Octavian survives. Today he lives, but he will know in his heart that we are coming. And one day, by all the gods, one day soon, we will kill him.'

The temple chamber filled with a roar. Such approval I had not felt since I had been a commander delivering my pre-battle speech. For a moment I felt deeply proud. But unlike a battle, the next action of the men in front of me was to slope out of the temple and disperse. A bizarre blend of anti-climax and delighted relief flowed through me.

The conspiracy against Octavian may have collapsed, but with it the threat to Agrippa's life had passed. I held my head in my hands and took a deep breath.

In truth, this had been a narrow escape.

I stepped into the sunshine. What had I learned?

That Octavian's death was for me to achieve, and me alone.

'Best not to rely on others,' I said aloud.

Murena and Caepio fled the city. In their absence, Octavian used the conspiracy as a chance to promote his stepson Tiberius to Praetor, no doubt at Livia's prompting. Tiberius, as Praetor, became their prosecutor.

He found both of them guilty in their absence. They were convicted of treason and sentenced to death.

I prayed to Fides that they would escape.

But within days, the news reached Rome that they had been captured. A few days later, their heads arrived.

I am certain they would have been tortured first, to extract more names. But I was safe because they did not know who I was. The worst that could happen was that the torturers could walk away with a description of a frail, thin, man with a scar on his cheekbone.

Thankfully, as Whisper said, there were plenty of those in Rome.

XVII

So I failed again. Another in a long list of failures. Octavian celebrated the plot's suppression as if it was a victory. We had, all too briefly, been a serious enemy.

The informer, Castricius, was given unique favour. When embroiled in personal troubles in the courts, Octavian himself turned out and entreated the jurors to acquit. Unsurprisingly, they did.

There was one consolation. The demise of the plot also brought about the demise of Maecenas. His influence with Octavian waned. His inability to withhold the conspiracy's discovery from the blandishments of Terentia was not good enough for Octavian. The fall from grace of that supercilious, oily man, long-time opponent of Agrippa, was a great satisfaction to me.

Over a cup of wine, I reflected that of my list of enemies, Gallus had fallen, Marcellus had come and gone, and now Maecenas had fallen from favour. All that remained was Octavian himself. Octavian was very much alive.

And so was I.

The gods delivered their verdict on Octavian's survival. Within days of the celebrations, the Tiber flooded. Homes were swept away. People drowned. The shortage of grain had gone on for months and now the city was polluted with filthy water.

When Octavian was out of the city, escaping the terrible stench, the people rioted. They shut the senators in the Senate House and threatened to burn it down over their heads. They demanded Augustus be made dictator.

Octavian, when he heard the news, rushed back to the

city. I made my way to the Forum, in the hope of getting an opportunity to attack him. But the whole of Rome made its way to the Forum too.

His bodyguard carved a path through the mass of people. When the people spotted his arrival, they began to chant.

'Dictator, Dictator, Dictator.'

All about me punched their fists in the air.

I shook my head in horror. Days ago, we were plotting his assassination. Now the people were begging him, imploring him to become dictator.

Why had I not taken any of the opportunities I had had to kill him?

I cursed the gods for my weakness.

When Octavian reached the middle of the Forum he tore his toga from his shoulders and fell to his knees.

'Rome shall not have a dictator,' he cried. 'I will never be a dictator.'

'Consul for life?'

Octavian shook his head.

'Rome is a Republic,' he called out. 'I have had the honour of serving as consul. Let other leading men have it.'

'We need food!'

Octavian carefully pulled his toga back up and slowly got to his feet. He held his arms outstretched. 'People of Rome,' he said, 'I will take care of the grain supply. I will restore food to you all. I promise, by all the gods and goddesses, I will feed my people.'

And he left the Forum with the cheers of the people ringing in his ears.

Within three days, the grain supply was restored, securing safe passage for supplies from Egypt. Octavian was a hero once again.

I was in total despair. Even Cornelia's toothy grin failed

to raise a smile.

On 1st September, Octavian dedicated a temple of solid marble to Jupiter the Thunderer. Inside stood a tremendous cult statue by the famous Athenian sculptor Leochares. It was Jupiter, holding a sceptre in one hand and a lightning bolt in the other. The lightning bolt looked as if it was crackling with fire.

Octavian was afraid of thunder and lightning. It is the only time I have seen that man show fear. Years ago, he had nearly been killed by a lightning strike whilst on campaign in Spain. The lightning grazed his litter and killed the slave lighting the road in front of him. He had been afraid ever since.

I began to wonder if Octavian was descended from a god after all. How different Rome would have been if he had never returned from Spain.

The following day was the ninth anniversary of the Battle of Actium. It was a public holiday, but I did not celebrate. Nine years ago it may have been but I could remember Actium as if it were only yesterday. I could smell the sea, feel my breastplate pinch into my skin, remember the blow to my face which scarred me, and most clearly of all, remember the moment I pressured Captain Duilius into approaching that burning wreck.

I can still make my heart race with those memories. But I had made a mistake I believe any man would have made, an honest mistake. I wanted the just rewards for myself and my men. We had earned them.

While the public celebrated, I stayed at home. Whisper took Cornelia into the street parties. She returned excitedly.

'Rutilius,' she called, 'you won't believe it.'

'What is it?' I asked.

'Agrippa's coming back to Rome.'

'Back to Rome?' I said excitedly. 'Why? How do you

know?'

'I met his wife Marcella today, shopping for jewellery.'

'What did she say?'

'She looked very happy, so I asked why?'

'And?' I asked, willing Whisper to come to the point.

'She is to marry Iullus Antony.'

'Marry Antony,' I said, surprised. 'But she's married to Agrippa.'

'They are being divorced. Agrippa is to marry Julia.'

I gasped.

'Julia, as in Octavian's only daughter Julia?'

Whisper nodded.

I tipped my head back in despair.

'By the gods, Agrippa why have you done that?'

'Apparently Octavian was told he had to make Agrippa his son-in-law or he had to have him killed.'

'What?' I exclaimed. 'Why?'

'It was something to do with being dangerous to keep Agrippa as a rival.'

'A rival?' I shouted. 'How dare they? That man is more loyal than any I have ever seen. This sounds like bloody Maecenas' counsel,' I fumed. 'Octavian doesn't realise how lucky he is.'

Whisper ran her hand through her flowing hair.

'Perhaps he does,' she concluded. 'He has chosen to make him son-in-law rather than kill him.'

I reflected on the news. Agrippa had always said he was too old for Marcella, and that she should have married Iullus Antony. Now, Marcella could do as she wished. But Julia was only just eighteen years old. Agrippa was over twenty years older than her, more than enough to be her father. It seemed a strange match. On the other hand, Julia was the daughter of the *princeps*. However great a man Agrippa had become, he hailed from lowly stock. This marriage was the ultimate political statement. There was even a glimmer of hope that, were Livia never to carry Octavian's child, perhaps Agrippa and Julia would produce a successor. I held onto this hope.

Julia was rumoured to have a voracious appetite.

I considered how staid Agrippa could be.

'How will you cope?' I muttered.

It was at this time that Octavian left the city, heading east. His destination was Parthia to recover our standards. Parthia had brought about the downfall of so many of our leaders, there had to be some chance this journey would be Octavian's last. Such was my hope.

Agrippa, meanwhile, returned to Rome for his new wedding to an incredible reception. Crowds met him at the gates and followed him to his home.

I was highly surprised and deeply honoured that in the darkness of night, a knock came at the door of our house and Agrippa entered.

'Rutilius, it's good to see you,' he said. 'How is Whisper, and little Cornelia?' He embraced me. 'Not so little now I suppose.'

Cornelia had been woken by the noise. When Whisper realised who it was, she let Cornelia run into the atrium.

Agrippa's eyes lit up.

'Cornelia.' He crouched onto his haunches. His knees let out an almighty crack. 'My how you've grown,' he said. He patted her hair. His vast hand dwarfing her entire head.

'You are as beautiful as your mother,' he said. He slowly hauled himself back to his feet. He looked older, stiffer than before. 'Age is finally catching up with me,' he said.

'That's not good,' I said. 'By all accounts, you are going to need to be in fine fettle for your new wife.'

'Now, now Rutilius. I thought you might disapprove, but I came to see a dear friend, not get into heated debates.

Not tonight. I've only just returned.'

I was blazing with fury, but he was right. In his place, would I not have done the same thing? Would I not have married the daughter of that man?

Of course I would. No man alive would have decided otherwise.

'How was your mission?' I asked.

Agrippa beamed. 'Entirely successful,' he replied. 'The path is clear. Augustus set out east to return with the standards from Parthia.'

'All of them?'

'All of them.'

I imagined how Octavian had received the news. Reclaiming those eagles would seal Octavian's reputation as a god amongst men. Rome had never learned to live with the shame of those Parthian defeats. Now Octavian would steal all the glory for himself. Agrippa had paved the way, but once again, he had allowed Octavian to take the glory.

'Why do you do it?' I asked. 'How can you do it?'

'Do what?'

'Let Octavian steal all the glory.'

'He's not stealing anything,' said Agrippa. 'You cannot steal something which is given to you.'

'But why do you give it to him? You earned the rights. You fought the wars. You won the battles. You risked your life, time and again, not just for Rome but for him.'

Agrippa rubbed the back of his head.

'I love him, I suppose,' he concluded. 'I met him as a boy, and despite my lack of status, he liked me. And when you've grown up together, known each other from so long, there's a bond.'

'But he has treated you so badly.'

Agrippa considered this for a moment.

'At times, perhaps, but what family never has arguments? True friends can argue and remain loyal.'

'If you weren't so genuine, I'd call you sanctimonious,' I said.

'Rutilius,' he said, gripping my shoulder, 'I've told you before. I owe that man everything. Without him, I am nothing. But more importantly, without him peace would fail. Rome would never follow me as they do him. I know my place.' His hand released my shoulder. 'And I have been rewarded beyond measure. I have the chance to be co-ruler of Rome.'

'Co-ruler?'

Agrippa smiled.

'Yes. Co-ruler. Does that not satisfy you? Is that not enough?'

How could Agrippa be co-ruler if he was Octavian's son-in-law? It suggested a distinction in rank, a distance between the two.

'Why would you care what I think?' I said at last. 'I'm nobody.'

'A nobody?' Agrippa admonished me. 'You're a friend. And I care what my friends think. When I die, I want my friends to think well of me.'

'Don't talk of dying, please,' I said. 'If Octavian is about to steal the glory of Parthia, Rome has never needed you more.'

'It will be a shared glory,' replied Agrippa.

'You're sure?' I asked, scepticism flowing through me.

'The honour of marrying his only daughter is prestigious is it not?'

Agrippa replied.

'I suppose it is.'

'And she is a beautiful girl.'

I hesitated. Surely he had heard of her reputation.

'She is,' I replied, 'full of zest.'

'And a wonderful sense of humour,' Agrippa added. 'Meanwhile, Marcella is free to marry the love of her life,'

Agrippa smiled. 'So all's well that ends well.'

So Agrippa married young Julia. Even without the presence of the *princeps,* it was a momentous occasion in Rome, with banquets in the streets, incense in the temples and wine flowing into the early hours of the night.

That night, celebrating the wedding, I realised that soon I would be considering who Cornelia should marry. And that led to a new feeling, a hope for another child; a son or a daughter, I cared not which, just company for Cornelia.

Julia and Agrippa began their wedded life in Rome. They moved into a villa on the west side of the Tiber, and at first, despite the differences in their age, it seemed that all was well. Rome prospered too. While Octavian moved slowly through the east, establishing colonies and sealing allegiance to Rome, Agrippa oversaw a buoyant city. The plague had gone. The floods had stopped. The grain flowed into the city. The building works and improvements to roads, aqueducts carried on apace.

Agrippa's baths were expanding. It was a good year. Even the elections for the next consuls were positively tranquil.

But official duties called, and the summer of the following year, Agrippa was despatched by Octavian to Gaul. Well, officially it was Gaul. The Cantabrians in Spain who Octavian was supposed to have defeated were in uprising too.

Julia, to her credit, travelled with Agrippa. She became pregnant with their first child. It was a boy. Young Gaius. The whole of Rome celebrated the news.

A year later, a second child followed, a little girl, Julia the younger. Whisper was delighted at the news.

'Perhaps one day Cornelia can meet her?' she said.

I smiled. It would have been lovely, but I did not hold

out much hope.

One day, I was delighted to receive a letter from Agrippa, a letter which I feel shows the humility of the great man.

FROM M. V. AGRIPPA TO SEXTUS, GREETINGS
FIRST, I HOPE THAT YOU, YOUR LOVELY WIFE AND LITTLE CORNELIA ARE WELL.
I AM DELIGHTED TO TELL YOU THAT I NOW HAVE A SON AND A DAUGHTER. LITTLE GAIUS, AND LITTLE JULIA. THEY ALONG WITH THEIR MOTHER ARE A SOURCE OF DEEP JOY TO ME. I HOPE THEIR BIRTHS WERE AS WELL RECEIVED IN ROME AS THEY WERE BY ME.
I WRITE THIS EVENING, AFTER DINNER, AS THIS CAMPAIGN FINALLY DRAWS TO A CONCLUSION. I BEGIN TO CONSIDER THE COLONIES AND FUTURE PROSPECTS HERE AND I THOUGHT OF YOU.
THIS CAMPAIGN HAS BEEN ONE OF THE MOST DIFFICULT OF MY LIFE. IT IS MY FIRST TRUE CAMPAIGN SINCE ACTIUM. THERE WE FOUGHT TOGETHER, IN UNITY, WITH SINGLE PURPOSE. HERE, I HAVE FACED A DIFFERENT ENEMY. AN ENEMY WITHIN.
COMMANDER FURNIUS IS A GOOD MAN. BUT WHEN HE INFORMED ME OF THE PROBLEMS HERE IN SPAIN, HE DID NOT TELL THE WHOLE TRUTH. I SET OUT FROM GAUL AT ONCE. A MONTH OR SO LATER,
WHEN I ARRIVED, I FOUND, TO MY DISMAY, AN ARMY IN TATTERS. THIS WAR IN SPAIN WAS WON SOME TIME AGO OF COURSE, UNDER AUGUSTUS, BUT IT WAS IMMEDIATELY OBVIOUS TO ME, MORE NEEDED TO BE DONE. THE PROBLEM WAS THE SOLDIERS. THEY WERE DEMORALISED AND TIRED. THE WORST I HAVE EVER WITNESSED.
FOR THE FIRST TIME IN MY COMMAND, SOLDIERS DISOBEYED ME. THEY ARE TOO OLD SEXTUS. AND THEY FEAR THEIR ENEMY. YOU WILL REMEMBER HOW I FACED SUCH TROUBLES BEFORE, WHEN WE FOUGHT SEXTUS POMPEY. BUT THAT WAS INEXPERIENCED SOLDIERS. AT LEAST THEY HAD ENTHUSIASM, AND SPIRIT, AND I COULD LEAD THEM.
THESE MEN. THESE MEN HAVE NEARLY BEEN THE DEATH OF ME. SOME I HAD TO PUNISH, OTHERS I HAVE CONVINCED

WITH THE LURE OF REWARDS, BUT I HAVE NOT ENJOYED ANY MOMENT OF THIS.
THE CAMPAIGN HAS FARED BADLY. MY EARLY DECISIONS SEEMED TO GO AWRY. WE SUFFERED MANY REVERSES. NOW, AT LAST, I BELIEVE WE HAVE THEM.
I FEEL UNABLE TO OFFER CLEMENCY, SEXTUS. WITH TROUBLED HEART, I WILL DESTROY ALL THE CANTABRIANS OF FIGHTING AGE AND MAKE SURE THEIR SUPPLY OF ARMS IS CUT OFF COMPLETELY. BEFORE I LEAVE THIS PLACE, I WILL DRIVE THEM OUT OF THE HILLS AND MAKE THEM LIVE IN PLAIN SIGHT, IF YOU WILL EXCUSE THE PUN, ON THE PLAINS.
AUGUSTUS HAS VOTED ME A TRIUMPH FOR THIS WAR. I HAVE, OF COURSE, REFUSED IT. I CAN HEAR YOU PROTESTING! BELIEVE ME WHEN I SAY IT IS NOT BECAUSE I AM UNWILLING TO DETRACT ANY GLORY FROM OUR LONG TIME LEADER. IN THIS CASE I GENUINELY FEEL I HAVE NOT EARNED A TRIUMPH FOR THIS CAMPAIGN.
I HAVE, HOWEVER, ACCEPTED THE HONOUR OF THE MURAL CROWN. GIVEN THE COUNTLESS POUNDS OF GOLD ROME WILL SOON BE ABLE TO MINE FROM HERE, A GOLDEN CROWN SEEMED APT.
BUT I DIGRESS FROM THE PURPOSE OF THIS LETTER. I WRITE IN CASE THE OPPORTUNITY OF COMING TO ONE OF MY NEW COLONIES WOULD BE OF INTEREST. YOU COULD ASSIST IN THE GOLD EXTRACTION AND THE SHORING UP OF ROME'S POSITION HERE. I CAN THINK OF FEW MORE SUITABLE MEN.
I hope to return to Rome by next Spring, so you need to make a swift decision. Consider it, Sextus. A fresh start in a prospering land.
AGRIPPA

The last lines were in his own handwriting. I have kept the letter. It was brave of Agrippa to write to me. In Octavian's regime, letters were often read before they reached their intended recipient. Even amidst the chaos of a campaign, Agrippa still sought to help me.

'Well,' I said to Whisper, 'Agrippa will shortly be coming home.'

'Agrippa?' replied Whisper. 'How is he?'

'The same as ever. Achieving great things. But refusing to step out of Augustus' shadow.'

'What do you mean?'

'He's refused a triumph for his victories in Spain, even though it was Octavian offering it to him.'

'Ah,' said Whisper. 'But Agrippa's always been this way. I'm surprised you think he would do any different.'

'I suppose you're right,' I said. 'At least he's accepted a golden mural crown. A suitable addition to his naval crown.'

'He needs more heads for all the honours he has,' said Whisper brightly.

I held out the letter. 'He's asked us to move to Spain,' I blurted out.

'What?' Whisper exclaimed, taking the letter.

'He's offered us the chance to move to one of his new colonies.'

'Do you want to go?' asked Whisper.

It did not take me long to make a decision. I shook my head.

'No. My mission is here.'

That scorching summer saw many of Agrippa's projects come to fruition in his absence. The Aqua Virgo was completed, an aqueduct over fourteen thousand paces in length. I ignored the fact it was formally named after Augustus. Throughout the city it is known as Virgo.

Agrippa would have been thrilled by the astonishment of the people as the cold water flowed so clearly, so cleanly to them. No grit, no sand. Purity as if from the heavens. Shortly afterwards, the expanded baths and gardens were also finished, further developments in the Plains of Mars beside the Spartan baths he had already established.

So, while Agrippa fought his bloody campaign against the Cantabrians, I bathed idly in his bathhouse in Rome.

Without a doubt, these were the greatest and most lavish Rome had ever seen. And, in the traditional manner of Agrippa, they were for the public. Even before you set foot in the baths, raised on a plinth outside was *The Body Scraper*; a beautiful, naked statue by that great Greek sculptor of the past, Lysippos of Sikyon, court artist to Alexander the Great, no less.

The people gathered around it, admiring it, wondering at it. It set the tone for the whole complex.

Inside, there were a series of massive rooms of increasing heat, from warm to exceptionally hot. Sandals were a necessity. All were fitted with pools and raised basins. The floors were so warm. I wondered just how many slaves were needed to keep the furnaces going.

And, of course, there was the cold room and the plunge pool to finish. None of this was out of the ordinary. But it was the sheer size. High vaulted ceilings, decorated from top to bottom with the most brilliant, coloured tiles and artwork.

During my visit, I had one of those reflective moments. I recognised and felt my age when I looked at the naked bathers in the exercise area. I sat in the colonnade and watched for a while. In my youth I had exercised as hard as any of the men in front of me. Now, my waist had expanded a little, my skin had aged and looked almost scaly. And compared to those shining, lithe bodies, I had hair, greying hair, all over me, even sprouting from my back.

As I sat with the summer sun shining through the columns, I did not, however, mourn my youth. I missed the energy and strength I once had. But I remember smiling. Somehow, I was still alive. I had a child. I had a wife and no one was trying to kill me.

I considered the man who had built these baths. He had a child and a wife too. Two children in fact. But wherever Agrippa was, despite being in his mid-forties, with years of success and achievements beyond any Roman, still he was at war. There were countless men out to kill him.

It did not seem just.

I recalled the conversation with him, when he told me of his vision for these baths, for the Plains of Mars. Now it had come to reality. And it was a triumph.

Outside the baths he had utterly transformed the place. To the west he had created an artificial lake, and between the canal and the lake, the most stunning gardens I have ever seen. I have never been much of a gardener, though in the rural estates I once owned, there had been some efforts. But nothing of this scale, or beauty. When I walked the gardens Agrippa had created on the Plains of Mars, suddenly I understood their power. They bring peace, and happiness and contentment and calm. The gravel paths thronged with people, elated to escape the squalid streets of Rome.

The lawns were exquisitely tended, every blade of grass, and there were ponds full of fish of all colours and sizes. Agrippa had placed artworks and statues throughout the gardens. The gods only knew how much Agrippa had spent. To me, this was the greatest achievement of any Roman; a gift to the people, not to the gods.

It saddened me that he was not there to see it.

An announcement permeated the city. Octavian was coming. And he had conquered the Parthians.

This was far from the truth. The truth was Agrippa had negotiated the return of the standards and the surviving prisoners. But, the heralds announced that the king of the Parthians handed them over to Augustus on the 12th May on the banks of the Euphrates. Not a sword was drawn.

Rome did not care much for the truth. The city was almost beside itself with joy at the conquest of the Parthians. The arch enemy, the creatures of nightmares and terrible tales, the defeaters of so many of Rome's greatest generals had at last fallen to the might of Rome.

As parties in the street broke out all over the city, I strode home.

'This is the moment,' I growled. 'Now I can do what I should have done years ago.'

Whisper looked startled. She pulled Cornelia into her.

'What's going on?' she asked.

'Octavian is coming to Rome. He's recovered the eagles. That man is...' I trailed off, lost for words. So many great commanders had fallen in Parthia. How had that weakling survived? 'Indestructible,' I concluded.

'That's good news isn't it?' Whisper asked, confused. 'Rome despised the fact Parthia had those eagles.'

'Yes, we did. They are the one enemy we cannot destroy. First Crassus, then Saxa, then Antony. Three eagles in the hands of our enemy. And now Octavian has got them back without drawing a sword.'

'That's Agrippa's doing isn't it?'

I stared at Whisper. She was right. Of course it was. He had even told me as much. He had paved the way, and now Octavian would steal the glory.

I shook my head.

'Not this time,' I said.

'What are you planning?' said Whisper, concerned. Cornelia was fidgeting in the folds of her dress. Whisper tried to calm her, whilst listening intently to me.

'I may be older, and weaker, but I can still shoot an arrow.'

'No,' exclaimed Whisper.

My mood darkened. I could feel my eyes narrow. 'This was why I built the temple of Fides on the triumphal route all those years ago. To prick the conscience of the king. It was not ready last time, but now, now the fates are aligned.'

'No,' exclaimed Whisper again. 'Why would you do it?'

There was not so much tears in her eyes, as rage.

'Because Octavian is about to steal all the glory for Rome's greatest achievement. No one will know it was Agrippa. He's not even here for the celebration. That cunning bastard has planned it all to perfection once again.'

'You're wrong,' said Whisper. 'He married Julia to Agrippa. They will share the glory. I don't doubt it.'

'Don't you believe it,' I snarled. 'Go out in the streets. Listen to the celebrations. You will not hear Agrippa's name.'

Whisper fell silent.

'But you'll die. We'll all be killed.'

I tapped my forehead with my finger and pointed at Whisper. 'No I won't. I will release the arrow and disappear.'

'How?'

I smiled.

'The secret chamber of course.'

'But they will know where the arrow came from,' said Whisper.

'Perhaps, or perhaps not. And even if they do work it out, will they discover the entrance? Argoutis did so well. The whole conspiracy of Caepio and Murena met in that chamber countless times and they never found it.'

'They weren't looking,' said Whisper.

I held up my hand. 'Enough talking,' I said. 'This is my destiny.

Octavian will fall in his moment of triumph and Rome's true leading man will take his place. As he gorges on his false Parthian success, I will make him bleed.'

Whisper was deep in thought.

'If you must do this, we will stand by your side and hide in the chamber with you,' she concluded.

'No,' I retorted.

'You either believe you will survive this or you don't,'

Whisper snapped. 'We die together or we live together. If you must do this, you must jeopardise Cornelia's life as much as your own.'

I stared wide-eyed at Whisper. Why would I do that? But Whisper's eyes were adamant.

Did I believe I would survive?

Actually I did. They would never find us.

'Very well,' I said, 'but Cornelia stays in the chamber at all times.'

Whisper shook her head and walked out of the room without another word. She dragged Cornelia behind her. She looked back at me with her innocent eyes.

'There is no risk,' I said to the empty room.

The hood and cloak were made ready. I purchased a new bow and set off for the countryside to practise. I noticed how much effort pulling the bowstring taut was now that I was so much older and weaker. But I was still accurate enough, and the arrows' sharp points still hit their targets with enough vigour.

Everything seemed to be falling into place at last. The triumphal route would, as always, start in the Plains of Mars to the west of the city. Octavian would gather in the shadow of his mighty mausoleum, and Agrippa's grand designs. The contrast all too clear, a monument to himself against the vast complex Agrippa had provided to the people.

Doubtless Octavian had planned a speech for the assembly just before the triumphal procession began where he would hand out rewards. The public slaves would light the incense and open the temples.

But Octavian would not lay his famous eyes on any of it. He would pass my temple before he even reached the Gate of Triumph. And he would reach no further. That was my moment. Technically, he would not set foot in the city.

So it is I planned to ensure that Octavian's destiny was for the Parthian campaign to be the death of him, as it had been for so many true heroes before him.

We placed ourselves in the temple a few days before Octavian's arrival, and listened and watched the preparations all about us. The city was humming. You could hear it, even from the Plains of Mars. Souvenir trade was booming. All about us were miniatures of the standards Octavian was returning. Eagles everywhere.

At last, the day of his return arrived.

The celebrations began as soon as the sun rose. Acrobats, dancers and mimes took their places. The people from inside the city came out, but also hundreds and thousands from outside the city. It felt as if the whole of Italy had gathered to witness this celebration.

This was a momentous occasion for Rome. And I planned to make it a day which would be remembered for generations. The day Rome was handed back to the people. Handed to Agrippa. That was worth celebrating as much as the recovery of these eagles.

'He's the man who got them back for us anyway,' I muttered.

I turned to Whisper. She was holding Cornelia, but watching me. I felt as if she was expecting me at any moment to abandon my plan.

I touched Cornelia's cheek.

'We're perfectly safe here,' I said. 'No one will find us.'

It was time for Whisper and Cornelia to go into the chamber. Being on the triumphal route, the temple of Fides would be well filled that day.

The crowds would soon be coming. The public slaves came to light the incense.

I took one last look at my temple. It looked beautiful with

all the decoration and garlands. I walked inside to the silver statue of Fides and touched her foot.

'Bless my actions this day,' I prayed. 'I do it through loyalty to the Republic and to Agrippa. May his loyalty and benevolence bring peace and prosperity to Rome.'

I scrambled up the temporary seating which had been put up all through the Plains of Mars and from there was able to leap onto the temple roof.

Today I was not alone to be clambering onto the roofs of buildings. All about me, people were waving and cheering as they reached a summit and gained a view.

My bow was concealed in my tunic, and the hood of my cloak aided its disguise. I only had two arrows. Both strapped to my body. I was confident I would need only one. But just in case, I had brought a second.

I knew if I had to release a second arrow, it would be the death of me.

I would not escape.

As time passed, the numbers continued to increase, and so did the noise. Next came the chants. Slowly, surely, the excitement grew until the noise of the crowd became a part of the spectacle, a part of the excitement in itself.

Then I heard it. The blast of the trumpets. This was not supposed to be an official triumph, but it felt exactly like one.

A large mass of people appeared on the horizon. Here he came. The hero of the hour. With every step of his four horses, he was drawn to his death.

There were no senators or magistrates leading this procession. The trumpeters were at its head. Behind them came the Parthians. No shackles. No ill treatment. They were not enslaved. They wore distinctive tunics and baggy trousers. They had the short beards common to their race.

But it was not what they looked like which drew the

attention. It was what they carried.

Two of them carried Roman Standards. Golden eagles gleaming in the sunshine. The eagle of Naxa, lost twenty years ago. Not far behind, the eagle of Antony lost four years later in his failed expedition.

But who had the eagle of Crassus? The eagle of the tenth legion, lost over thirty years ago; the most famous, or rather infamous, of all.

Before we would find out, a gathering of Roman soldiers marched past. These must have been the soldiers who had been rescued. They did not sing triumphal songs. That would have been inappropriate after all those years of captivity in Parthia. Now, at last, they returned to their country, to their city. Despite the shame of their defeat all those years ago, the crowd's cheers would have reached the gods.

Women and children threw flowers. Men raised their fists in delight. The whole route was quickly covered in flowers. The heralds had given strict instructions to the city not to pelt the Parthians with rotten fruit and vegetables. This was only to be a celebration.

Some of the soldiers were weeping with joy. Others looked bewildered by the whole occasion.

There was the customary parade of weapons, shields and valuables demonstrating just how wealthy and powerful an enemy Parthia had been. They had been our archenemy for all these years for a reason.

Flute players filed passed, their tunes utterly inaudible. The white bulls traipsed after them on their final march to the summit of the capitol.

I smiled. They will have a narrow escape today, I thought.

Then I saw it, the triumphal chariot drawn by four beautiful white horses. Behind them, in that lavish chariot of gold, the man himself. Octavian.

And there was the final standard, in Octavian's right hand, the eagle of Crassus. He had kept the best for himself.

How typical, I thought.

I ground my teeth as I watched Octavian waving with his free arm to the crowds. He waved from side to side. He never stopped smiling. He clenched his fist in celebration. Pointed at individuals. Beat his chest.

I braced myself. I needed the blood lust of battle.

Where was the wrath? Where was the anger at this man parading as if military strength and bloodshed had led to this victory?

There was no paint on Octavian's face. He was not entering the city as Jupiter for the day. Today, he was evidently an immortal in his own right. He was entering as himself. He wore a golden crown of laurel leaves, glinting in the sunshine. No slave stood behind him, reminding him that he was mortal.

As he drew within range, he raised his fists to the sky again. I inspected closely. The shaft of the military standard was nearly covering his heart. But there was enough room. It would have to be an accurate shot.

I shook out my hands, tried to relax the tension in my neck and shoulders, exhaled deeply, closed my eyes and prayed.

I raised the bow and aimed the arrow. I looked down the shaft of the arrow and sought my target. There were those eyes, that famous, piercing glare, taking in the crowds. He was basking in the sunshine and the praise of the people. I lowered my aim to his heart.

'This time, you're mine,' I said.

I drew back the arrow.

Then, I felt a tug on my sleeve.

It was Whisper.

'How did you get here?' I snapped.

She was biting her lip.

'Don't do it,' she pleaded.

I brushed her away and raised the bow once again.

'You'll never make it to the chamber unseen. There are people everywhere,' she said.

'I can,' I replied. 'It will be chaos.'

But Whisper just shook her head. 'Have you seen how many people there are in your temple? They're everywhere,' Whisper looked terrified. 'How do you think you will even make it to the chamber entrance?'

'Then I'll have to die.'

'You're prepared to die for this?

I was not.

'Your daughter is crying inside that chamber.'

I pictured little Cornelia. Tears streaming down her face.

'You would abandon her?' Whisper pressed.

I looked at Octavian again.

'Agrippa may share this glory,' said Whisper.

Octavian's waving told me otherwise as he lapped up the praise of the people. Sanctimonious, cunning, selfish...no word could capture the vitriol I felt.

'Please,' begged Whisper, tears now streaming down her beautiful face.

I was filled with frustration, blood lust, fury.

All those years I had been waiting for this opportunity. It felt as if, that day at last, the fates had presented me with my prey.

I looked once more at the face of my enemy.

Then the face of the love of my life.

Then pictured my darling daughter Cornelia.

I laid down my bow.

I thumped the roof in fury. Thwarted again. That man was indestructible.

We slumped down together on the roof and waited for the procession to move on. Once the cheering had dissipated, we climbed down and recovered Cornelia.

She was utterly distraught.

It took a long time to calm her. When at last the sobbing subsided, Cornelia was mortified that she had missed the procession.

'Take her,' I said to Whisper. 'Take her to the street parties. Take her to see the eagles. He will put them in the temple of Jupiter on the Capitol.'

I stayed inside the chamber. I would look upon those eagles another day. They would be worth my time and reflection because Agrippa had been the man who recovered them. Ultimately, it was a great outcome that Rome had recovered those standards and brought our soldiers home.

No one should be left behind.

So it was that although Octavian had not officially celebrated a triumph, or even an ovation, the celebration had been as grand, if not grander. The people still talk of it. The return of the eagles. It has become a legend, a legend with one hero.

Agrippa was out of Rome, out of the public eye, out of the public memory.

The celebrations did not stop. As the weeks went by, poets wrote reams of verses celebrating Augustus' military victory over the Parthians.

Military! Can you believe it? Not a sword was drawn.

Meanwhile, yet more statues of Octavian went up all over the city, and on their breastplates a barbarian handed over standards to a Roman officer. It did not take a genius to work out who that Roman officer was supposed to be.

And just in case anyone missed the statues, copies of them appeared on the coins.

Where was the mention of Agrippa?

Where was the co-rule?

Whisper could not have been more wrong. To me it felt as if Agrippa had been obliterated. While he was loyally risking his life in Spain, defeating the Cantabrians Octavian had failed to defeat, here in Rome, Octavian was stealing all the glory.

I felt physically twisted with rage.

'The moment Agrippa left the city, we were in trouble.' I raged. 'Now look, if this isn't a tyrant, I don't know what is.'

Whisper looked worried. 'You're not going to do anything rash are you?'

I looked at my wife. I considered my daughter, babbling in the other room with her tutor.

I shook my head.

'Of course not,' I said.

'Promise?'

I nodded.

'At last.'

XVIII

When Agrippa finally returned to Rome, the time period for the powers that Octavian and Agrippa had been granted was running out.

'Now we'll see what Octavian really thinks of Agrippa,' I said to Whisper.

'Agrippa is Octavian's son-in-law, and father of his grandchildren. I'm sure he will be looked after,' replied Whisper.

'We'll see,' I replied. 'But the key questions remain. What powers will Octavian keep for himself? And what powers, if any, will Agrippa have?'

The answer to the first question was inevitable. Octavian ceded virtually nothing. His powers were extended for a further five years. His provinces were reduced slightly, Cyprus and Gallia Narbonensis were clearly no longer of use to him, but he kept his power of the tribune without the need for office, and the power of the Censor for five years.

Tiberius and Drusus, Livia's sons, were promoted and allowed to stand for promotion five years earlier than regulations allowed. Most galling of all, Octavian was granted a seat between the two consuls in the Senate House. To my mind, it was simple. He was a ratified tyrant for five years, hidden in the dress of the Republic.

Agrippa's powers, on the other hand, shocked and delighted me. He was given power greater than the proconsuls, and the same power of the tribune which Octavian had been granted, for the same five years.

'That's incredible,' I exclaimed. 'That's wonderful. He is acknowledged. He is the heir!'

Whisper smiled. 'I told you,' she said.

Octavian and Agrippa, for once in Rome together, set about reforming the city again. They used an all too familiar technique. A census. Rumours tore through the city that they would reduce the senate down to a mere three hundred senators.

When I had been dismissed from the senate, the reduction had been just shy of two hundred senators. That was from a starting position of over a thousand. So to reduce the senate to just three hundred? You can imagine the alarm which beset many of the senators of Rome.

Octavian upped the property qualification. No longer the four hundred thousand sesterces I fell short of in those days, but one million sesterces. You could almost hear the hearts wrapped in purple-bordered togas striking the floor as the realisation dawned that Octavian was on the rampage once more.

Octavian tried to pretend he was not hand-picking the senators who would survive this cull. An elaborate process was invented, supposedly a fair process. In truth, few in Rome understood what was happening.

It mattered not. The moment names were put forward which Octavian did not want to read, the process fell apart. Senator Marcus Antistius Labeo put forward the exiled former triumvir and chief priest Lepidus.

Labeo was summoned to Octavian's home, no doubt brought to the 'little workshop' where I had my confrontation all those years ago. Once again, Octavian would have been waving a wax tablet in fury.

'What is the meaning of this?' Octavian raged. 'The instructions were clear. Your selections are only supposed to be of the best men. How is it that I read Lepidus' name?'

'I understood the task,' replied Labeo, bravely. 'I swore the oath just like everyone else. Why are you so perplexed, Augustus? I have proposed to keep a man in the senate, who you are content to keep in the role of chief priest.'

How I would have loved to have seen Octavian's face.

Predictably enough, Lepidus did not return from his exile in Circeii.

After this altercation, Octavian took over the entire process. So it was, for the second time, a large number of wealthy, honourable, noble men were stripped of their powers, leaving only sycophants and subservient weaklings.

A familiar concession was granted. Octavian allowed those senators who were stripped of their rank the 'privilege' of retaining their dress and their reserved seats in the theatre. Scant consolation, to be sure.

During these dramas, Whisper became pregnant again. Alas, a few weeks later, she began to bleed, slowly at first, then faster and faster.

I felt powerless and angry. Angry that it took so long, protracted over days. On a battlefield a man dies in a second. Here a boy or a girl drips away over days. On a battlefield you can raise your shield or strike with your sword. Here, you can do nothing.

At least little Cornelia was still fit and healthy. Her smile was as important to Whisper and me then, as it had ever been.

At the start of the following year, an announcement gripped Rome. The fifteen men of the college of priestly duties, or 'The Fifteen' as they were known, had consulted the Sibylline books they guarded. These were scriptures which they would consult at the request of the Senate. I do not remember the senate requesting this consultation. But Octavian had clearly orchestrated the event. He had plans.

To everyone's surprise, the Secular games were announced. They were to be held from May 31st. These games were historic, barely known, barely remembered in tales of old. They only happened once in a lifetime, every hundred years or so, the oldest a man could live to. They celebrated the beginning of a new generation.

And that was Octavian's purpose. He was claiming the beginning of a new age, under his rule.

For months the city was gripped by preparations for the event. The talk was of nothing else. Games and festivals are our staple diet, but I have never seen so many people, so much money and so much effort dedicated to one festival. It made Octavian's triple triumph seem insignificant. Octavian was intent on making this talked about all over the empire.

Agrippa was deeply involved in the preparations, not just pouring his money into the festival, but his ideas and his practical skills. Edicts from 'The Fifteen' announced the celebration to the people, informing us of the arrangements. We were to receive everything necessary to purify the city and the first fruits to offer to the gods. Announcement by announcement, more details were released about the games, the festivals and the sacred banquets.

'He's whetting our appetite,' I said as I read the latest edict.

I confess, when I watched all the people preparing the food, cleaning the temples and carrying the construction materials to the various sites around the city, I could not help but feel a sense of excitement and curiosity.

Every effort was being made to make these games available to all. The senate debated relaxing the rule that unmarried people could not attend the games. Consul Gaius Silanus, Octavian's mouthpiece, argued that as many people as possible should see the games out of a sense of religious duty. It was nothing to do with religious duty and everything to do with Octavian's wish to induce as many people as possible to adore him.

'See,' I said, as I learned of the next senatorial decree. 'His true purpose is revealed.'

'What's happened?' asked Whisper.

'Silanus again,' I replied. 'Today, in the senate, he suggested it was "appropriate" for a record of the Secular games to be inscribed on a bronze and a marble column. Unsurprisingly, the senate agreed, for the future remembrance of the event. The contracts are out.'

As the date of the games approached, heralds in vibrant scarlet tunics filled the streets all over the city with their summons.

'Come to the games,' they cried. 'Witness something you have never seen before, and will never see again.'

When Cornelia first saw a herald, she just stood and stared at him. Then she pointed at his helmet.

I crouched onto my haunches and gripped her little shoulder. 'I know, my dear,' I said. 'It looks strange doesn't it? Can you see the feathers? Like a bird? And those are swords sticking out. Do you know what a sword is?'

Cornelia shook her head.

I stood up straight. 'You will,' I said. 'Life will not be knitting needles and spinning wool for you.'

'What's on his shield?' asked Whisper, pointing at the herald's round shield on his arm.

'That's the star of Julius,' the herald replied.

'The star of Julius?' queried Whisper.

'You remember,' I said, trying to hide my disdain. 'The comet which appeared at Octavian's games to mark the death of Julius Caesar. Somehow, when this one appeared, Octavian celebrated. In days gone by, comets were bad omens. But apparently that one marked Julius Caesar's passage to the immortals. A remarkable interpretation.

'Rome believed him and Octavian's used it ever since. On statues, on coins, and now here.'

I thought I had done well to conceal my distaste, but could not resist a barbed comment. 'Just in case anyone forgets who's putting on these ancient games.'

Preparations for the Secular games accelerated, if that were possible, all over the city. The Tarentum in the Plains of Mars was shut off to the public while Octavian's agents constructed what was to be one of the greatest shows in the history of Rome.

On May 25th, the handouts began, along with an edict telling women in mourning to put their grief on hold. It was no good having miserable people about the city. They would spoil the atmosphere.

First, the people of Rome could visit 'The Fifteen' sitting on their platforms around the city. Some were on the Capitol, others outside the temple of Diana, but outside the temple of Apollo on the Palatine would be Octavian himself. He was one of 'The Fifteen'. He would be handing out the bitumen, sulphur and torches for the people to use in the purifying ceremonies.

I did not want to see Octavian. I wanted to receive my donatives from Agrippa. He too was a member of 'The Fifteen' and I could not think of a better man to purify the city.

This was an occasion for all the family. Whisper and little Cornelia came out with me and queued with the rest of the city. Inevitably the queues to the temple of Apollo were far greater than the others because Octavian and Agrippa had by far the most prestige.

Slowly we progressed to the front. Before us, on a podium, side by side, sat Augustus and Agrippa. The people were partitioned. One line would approach Augustus, the other Agrippa. I pushed over to be in Agrippa's line.

To my horror, just as we reached the front, a herald shoved me across into Octavian's line.

'Come on you, keep moving,' he said. 'We haven't got all day.'

I went to protest, but a familiar voice called me.

'Come along my man, what are you waiting for?'

I turned slowly, terrified that Octavian may once again recognise me. That scar under my eye was still so distinctive.

Whisper gripped my hand to rouse me from my stupor.

I stepped forward.

'Hail,' I said. I bowed my head.

'You have a familiar face,' Octavian said. 'Do I know you?'

I shook my head, staring at his sandals. They looked like the sandals I had left on the beach. 'No *princeps*,' I said. 'You do not know me.'

Octavian furrowed his brow. Now in his mid-forties, his forehead and brow had dropped with age. His cheeks looked sunken. There were lines everywhere. Of course, compared to my thin, weather-beaten face, he looked a picture of health. But looking closer told a different story.

Beneath his eyes were dark patches, like bruises. His hair was receding and greying and he looked as if he was grinding his teeth. Clearly, ruling Rome was an effort.

At last I dared to look him in the eye. The face had aged, but the eyes had not. They were the same piercing gaze as ever. The look of terror at the thunder and lightning all those years ago was a distant memory.

Those eyes told me clearer than any words that Octavian was full of purpose. Before me sat a man as intense as ever.

Suddenly, he clicked his fingers.

'I have it,' he said. 'I do know you.'

I shook my head.

'You were Musa's attendant,' Octavian replied. 'Don't be shy. Just because I released him for failing to save Marcellus, doesn't mean I'm not grateful for what you did for me.' He clasped my hand with both of his. They felt cold, and clammy.

'Is this your family?' he asked.

'Yes,' I replied. 'Whisper,' I said without thinking, 'and little Cornelia.'

'Whisper,' repeated Octavian.

I realised my mistake. How could I have been so stupid?

Octavian studied Whisper.

'Come here,' he said, beckoning Whisper to him.

He studied her carefully.

'You're that brave slave girl,' he said at last.

'I'm a freed woman now,' Whisper replied, looking straight at Octavian in defiance.

Octavian looked again at me, at my scar. He folded his arms and placed his finger over his lips. Was he remembering the incident when he was ill? Perhaps he had not been completely addled by the fever. It felt as if time had stopped.

Agrippa, on the other podium, detected something was happening.

He looked over. I caught his eye. Agrippa froze in disbelief.

Octavian drummed his fingers on his chin.

'Well,' he said at last, 'what a beautiful little girl you have. Cornelia wasn't it?'

'Yes sir,' replied Whisper.

Octavian pulled little Cornelia onto his lap. 'What a pretty little girl you are.' He ruffled her hair. 'What lovely curls,' he said. 'I have a daughter too. Do you know what her name is?'

Cornelia shook her head.

'Her name is Julia,' said Octavian. 'She's a beautiful girl. Unlike her father. It's amazing how often that happens. How a little girl miraculously doesn't inherit any of her father's flaws. And do you know, it's the father's task to make sure their children, their beautiful daughters, like you and Julia, don't develop any,' he said.

He reached into the pots beside his seat and handed over

some yellow sulphur and bitumen to Whisper. To me he handed a torch.

'This is for the purification ceremony,' he said. 'A chance to wash away the sins and pollution of the past.' He fixed me with those eyes.

'Be sure to take it.'

Be sure to take it.

He knew exactly who I was. He had said those very words to me all that time ago at Actium. Those words commanded me to seize my chance to regain his favour. A chance I utterly failed to seize. Time and time again.

Now, despite everything, despite the fact he had ordered my death, he had just offered me clemency.

I did not understand it. I did not believe it. Clemency had killed Julius Caesar. If Octavian had known how close and how many times I had tried to kill him, perhaps he would not have spared me.

But many years had passed.

Did Octavian believe I would be converted by his action?

I refused to return home. That night we would hide out as a family in the temple of Fides. We barely spoke a word but waited impatiently for Cornelia to go to sleep. As soon as she shut her eyes, we began.

'He recognised me,' I said. 'We're dead.'

'I was afraid of that too, but why hasn't he killed us already?'

'Perhaps the agents are around our house tonight,' I said panic-stricken.

'He won't let me live, not with our history. It would have caused too much of a scene to have me arrested in public today.'

'You're wrong,' replied Whisper. 'If he wanted to kill you, he would have done it straight away.'

I bit my lip. Whisper was right. Gaius "You must die"

Octavian would not have hesitated. He had chosen to spare me.

'Perhaps,' said Whisper, 'these games mark a new beginning for us all.'

The following day the people were back at the podiums. They handed over the first fruits before the harvest, wheat, barley and beans for the gods. After the scare of the previous day, we did not attend the Palatine Hill. Instead, we made our way to the temple of Diana and gave our offering there.

'There,' I said, once we filtered out of the queue. 'Much less dramatic.'

At last, the opening night of the Secular games came. It was the most excitement I had ever witnessed in Rome. The games would last for three nights and three days. I was used to the fervour for chariot races, the passion for gladiator shows, the wonder at wild beast hunts, but this was an even greater level of excitement. Even triumphs, even that famous triple triumph of Octavian, did not match the atmosphere in the city for these games. There was not a house in Rome which had not been purified. The sulphurous smell lingered in the streets. It was not only something to behold, but something to smell, almost to taste.

'Come to the games,' the heralds continued to cry, as they had done every day for the last week. 'Witness something you have never seen before, and will never see again.'

No one could wait for darkness to fall that night, me least of all. But it was summer, so the sun took its time in sinking. When, at last, the sun began to set, the people could hold back no longer.

The people made their way to Tarentum, in the

northwest of the Plains of Mars, beyond the equestrian training ground. As a family, we filtered into the crowd. No charioteers were practising there now. No horses grazed the fields. All was prepared for the festival.

Even before we reached the gate of the city to head to the Plains of Mars, the wonders began. Vast three-footed candelabra lined the way, lighting the path for the people to follow. The shafts were decorated with rams' heads, while perched on the top was a shallow libation bowl. In some, incense burned. In others, sulphur with its peculiar putrid smell and eerie blue flame.

To see that line of mystical blue flames lighting up the pathway to the ceremony still fills me with a sense of wonder. You could hear the people gasp in amazement. I can still picture Cornelia's wide eyes as she took in the scene. I gripped her little hand, keeping her close to me amongst the throng. All too easily, she could slip from my grasp, never to be seen again in this crowd.

We made our way as far as we could to the river side, but already people had beaten us to it. They must have taken their places in the morning to be as close as they were to the three altars.

'Three of each on each of three,' I uttered.

'What's that?' Whisper asked.

'They will sacrifice three ewes and three she-goats on each of those altars. I don't know what it is about the number three...doubtless the Sybilline books would tell me.'

All about us, the candelabra burned, and heralds held burning torches. But it was not the usual flame of a torch. All of them were glistening with the mystical blue light.

'What's that smell?' asked Whisper. Cornelia was clutching at her nose and pulling a face.

'That's the sulphur,' I said. 'That's what Octavian gave us.'

'But that was yellow,' Whisper countered.

'Yes,' I replied. 'But when it burns, it turns blood red while the flames are that amazing blue.'

Whisper sniffed. Her face contorted.

'Smells like rotten eggs to me,' she said. 'Can't see how that purifies anything.'

I was inclined to agree, but the strange mist which filled the summer evening sky, the peculiar smell, and the intense blue colour, flickering on the river Tiber was an awe-inspiring scene.

Beside the river a temporary wooden theatre had been built in readiness for the plays, the songs and choruses. Despite the dark, it was fully lit by flaming torches, a warm and increasingly bright colour as the sky grew darker. As we approached, an altogether different music reached our ears, something I had never heard before. There were drums, like the drums used to inspire oarsmen. But a line of them. Each had a muscular drummer, anointed like wrestlers. They shone in the flicker of the flames, catching our eyes. When the first hour of darkness fell, and the crowd really began to assemble, there was that audible hubbub of excitement and chatter which precedes an event people are almost frantic to see.

Suddenly the first drummer beat his drum. Three strikes. Left, right, left. Dramatic strikes with his arm lifting high above his head before each beat. A pause. Three more strikes. Slow, steady, in rhythm. After a few minutes, the second drummer joined him. It was mesmerizing.

As time passed, another drummer joined, and another and another, until it felt as if the entire Plains of Mars were filled with the pounding of their drums. A heartbeat, with an extra pulse, an extra pulse which inspired a sense of excitement, a sense of wonder.

As the second hour of darkness approached, the chorus began to hum. Long notes, droning into the night sky, defined only by the incessant, pulsing beating of the drums. The spectators looked about, at each other, at the star lit sky, absorbing everything they could see, trying to fix the moment in their memories.

Suddenly, the procession appeared. A cloud of misty vapour, lit in a way which seemed unearthly by blue flaming torches, hissing into the starry sky. In the midst of the cloud walked Octavian and Agrippa, followed by the remainder of 'The Fifteen' men of the college of priestly duties. They were all hooded and cloaked. Slowly, they made their way to the altar by the river.

The heralds who had been calling the people of Rome to attend surrounded them on all sides. And how we had answered their call. The Plains were full to overflowing. I lifted little Cornelia over my head and sat her on my shoulders. She was startled by the presence of so many people; heads as far as she could see, on all sides. There was barely space for us to stand. Whisper was pressed into my side, occasionally shoved all the closer by the sections of the crowd pushing, desperate for a better view.

We could only just make out the scarlet of the heralds' tunics, but their bronze belts gleamed in the blue flame and their helmets with the feathers and swords were distinguishable through the blue, stinking haze. They carried short spears and round shields as they carved their way through the people.

If they were supposed to be dancing, or singing, I could not hear them. But there was no room for them to move. They were barely able to create the path for Octavian and Agrippa to the three altars. To my delight, Octavian and Agrippa processed side by side, the rest of 'The Fifteen' filed in line behind them.

It was enough for Agrippa to be Octavian's equal, as he clearly was. I felt a tearful sense of relief. Perhaps, at last, the burden of my mission was leaving me. This ceremony could indeed mark a new beginning.

The humming of the chorus turned into enchanting long notes, 'ahs' in chords which took me into the very depths of Hades. Still the drums pounded. One, two, three. You could feel the people in the crowd pulse in rhythm. The Plains of Mars in unison. I felt exhilarated. Thrilled to be alive. Thrilled to be a witness.

'Soon the city will be purified,' Whisper said, 'and you can start again.'

I squeezed Cornelia's leg, enjoying the sensation of a daughter on her father's shoulders. I held out my other hand to Whisper.

At last, Octavian and Agrippa reached the altars. The drumming changed at last. Now it was a pulse. Two beats, a pause, two more beats. A procession of sheep and goats were brought into the light. 'The Fifteen' positioned themselves for the sacrifice. Octavian stood before the first altar. Behind it, a fire was blazing, so that his silhouette was clearly visible for all of us to see.

I stared. There was the outline of the man I had hated for so many years. But tonight, tonight could I feel proud that I had held his hand? Could I be proud that once upon a time, I had served as a commander under him, proud that I, like him, was a Roman?

Octavian held up the sacrificial blade to the heavens in one hand, and the hammer in the other. The crowd cheered. The chorus began to sing a hymn. Words I could not recognise, an old Etruscan chant.

Octavian placed the knife beneath the first ewe's throat, the drummers burst into a frantic, syncopated beating.

Octavian brought the hammer down. The crowd went into what seemed like ecstasy. Two of 'The Fifteen' lifted the dead ewe's body and held it over the altar. Blood poured from the ewe's throat, splattering over the altar.

Octavian gestured to the fire. The ewe was carried the

few paces to the fire's edge, and cast in. The body erupted into flame. Octavian made his way to the second altar. He was to carry out all the sacrifices this night. This was his opening night.

Octavian began to pray.

'Oh Fates,' he called, 'as it is written for you in those Sybilline books, to you I sacrifice nine ewe lambs and nine she-goats. I beg of you that our citizens, in war and peace, will be increased by you; that you will give everlasting safety, victory and good health to our citizens and that you will look with favour upon them and their legions; that you will keep safe the Republic.'

I was surprised to hear that word. To keep safe the Republic had always been my aim.

Octavian continued. 'That you will be favourable and propitious not only to the citizens, but to "The Fifteen", to me, to my house and to my household.'

Octavian paused, accepting the glory. Technically, he had asked for the gods' favour for himself five times. Just in case they were not listening.

'Receive this sacrifice of nine ewe-lambs and nine she-goats, the proper kind for sacrifice.' Octavian gestured to the burning carcass. 'Be honoured by this ewe-lamb,' he cried. 'Be favourable to my people. To "The Fifteen". To me. To my house. To my household!'

The crowd's cheers were deafening.

The second ewe died to a cheer as raucous as the first. Its blood covered the second altar before it was burned in the second fire. After the third, Octavian held his bloody knife and hammer aloft. The crowd cheered his name. 'Augustus, Augustus, Augustus.'

I looked at Whisper. She had transferred Cornelia onto her shoulders. Cornelia was chanting Augustus' name. I stared at her, and at that moment, seeing the joy and excitement in her eyes, I realised that the Fates had stopped me all those times for all those years for a reason.

Perhaps it had been better that Octavian had survived.

I could not, however, bring myself to chant his name. That would have been too much.

I could enjoy the festival because it was steeped in tradition. Its roots were deeply in the Republic. Octavian should be admired for putting on such a spectacular show, but that was all. The adulation was for the gods and goddesses to preserve us for another generation.

Not for him.

When the sacrifice was finished, one hundred and ten matrons processed through the crowds to the Capitol. They were making their way to the banquet set up for Juno and Diana. The images of the goddesses were already positioned on the couches, ready to share the feast.

'Aren't they pretty,' said Cornelia from Whisper's shoulders, pointing at the matrons.

'I'm sure they have been carefully chosen,' I replied.

Whisper jabbed me in the ribs.

'You could have been amongst them of course,' I added hastily. 'There's one for each of the one hundred and ten years since these games were last celebrated,' I said.

The plays began on the temporary stage in front of us. There were no seats, but the people of Rome stood as one throughout the night enjoying the show.

The next morning, the sun rose early. It was a warm start to the celebrations. Today was an exciting day because the sacrifices would not only be carried out by Octavian. Today Agrippa would sacrifice too. White bulls would die today, on the Capitol. Sacrifices for Jupiter.

I felt immense pride to see Agrippa standing side by side with Octavian in front of the temple.

'Just look at those bulls, said Whisper. 'I've never seen

anything like them before.'

I glared at Whisper. 'I hope you're admiring the size of their bodies,' I said with a smile.

'I was. But now you mention it,' Whisper inspected the bulls even more closely. She shook her head in amazement. 'Carefully chosen,' she concluded.

'Makes you envious doesn't it,' an old man beside us chuckled.

I could not help but laugh.

Of course Octavian went first, but the bull Agrippa sacrificed was just as mighty, just as honourable. Perhaps I am biased, but Agrippa's voice seemed to carry further, and have more authority as he uttered the prayer.

'Jupiter, greatest and best, as it is written for you in those Sybilline books, to you I sacrifice this bull. I beg of you that our citizens, in war and peace, will be increased by you; that you will give everlasting safety, victory and good health to our citizens and that you will look with favour upon them and their legions; that you will keep safe the Republic.'

From Agrippa's mouth, the word 'Republic' felt entirely natural and heartfelt. I remembered the final words of Octavian's prayer. He had asked for the gods' safekeeping for himself, for his household. I hoped Agrippa would do the same, for himself of course. Not for Octavian.

Agrippa continued. 'That you will be favourable and propitious not only to the citizens, but to 'The Fifteen',' Agrippa gestured at the men from the priestly college standing by the sacrificial vessel. He paused and turned to face Octavian directly. 'To Augustus,' he bellowed, 'to the house of Augustus and to the household of Augustus.'

I stared in horror. The crowd cheered.

I shook my head. 'You give it to him,' I muttered. 'All the power. You just hand it over.'

'Receive this bull I have sacrificed. Be honoured by it,' he cried. 'Be favourable to our people. To 'The Fifteen'. To

Augustus. To the house of Augustus. To the household of Augustus.'

Whisper tugged at my arm.

'He is part of Augustus' household,' she said. 'Don't think badly of him. He's your hero.'

My hero. I considered the word. As was so often the case with Whisper, she was exactly right. Agrippa was my hero. But he was not just my hero. He was the hero of Rome. And here he was, from nowhere, taking his rightful place side by side with Rome's other leading man. If only he would stop his deference to Octavian, he would be the perfect man.

Latin plays followed in the open theatre on the Plains of Mars by the Tiber. The plays throughout the night had been so popular, that the crowds were almost too great for that night. The matrons held their feast with the goddesses once again.

I could not be bothered with the crowds, especially in the heat. The night-time sacrifice was the next event I was looking forward to. Entirely for personal reasons.

That night's sacrifice by Octavian, I felt all too keenly. We all traipsed back to the same part of the Plains of Mars. This time, Octavian did not spill blood. Nine each of three types of cake were offered. They were completely burned as a sacrifice to Ilithyia, the Greek goddess of childbirth.

Of course, as he made the sacrifice, he was thinking of an entire population. After the civil wars, the proscription lists, the plagues and famines he wanted the numbers to grow once more.

But for me, the sacrifice was so much more personal. I stared at Whisper as the sacrifice was made, hoping, for once, that Octavian's wish would come true. I wiped the tears from her face and held Cornelia close.

We did not stay to enjoy the plays that night, but made our way home to see if we could make Octavian's prayer come true.

The following day, Octavian and Agrippa led the procession of the one hundred and ten matrons through the streets of Rome to the Capitol.

There, two heifers were sacrificed to Juno.

'They are beautiful,' Whisper exclaimed.

'Still impressed?' I asked, 'even when they don't have…'

Whisper slapped my arm playfully. 'Yes,' she admonished. 'Look at their eyes.'

I looked. To me, they looked half asleep, no doubt dosed with herbs to keep them calm through the raucous procession.

'They are beautiful eyes,' I agreed, 'but not as beautiful as yours.'

The heifers were sacrificed. Agrippa led the one hundred and ten matrons in a prayer to the gods. What a moment it was to see one hundred and ten beautiful women, all dressed in exactly the same way, kneel in unison at Agrippa's signal, to hear them utter the same prayer as one, as Agrippa led them through it.

'Oh Queen Juno,' they cried, 'we married mothers of families on bended knee beseech and pray…'

They prayed for the same things Octavian and Agrippa had asked for. But somehow, from their mouths, if I was Juno, I would have taken note. Everlasting safety, victory and health to the Roman people seemed a reasonable request for these efforts.

Time would tell whether the gods had listened.

I looked upon Agrippa, standing above the matrons. This had been his chance to receive the honour of the people.

At last.

And how he took it.

Whisper embraced me and pulled Cornelia in. It was at

that moment that I realised something.

I realised I was happy.

XIX

The final night of the festival came. A pregnant black sow fell to Octavian's blade, a sacrifice for Mother Earth. A closing series of plays were put on until the sun began to rise. Though this was a tremendous spectacle too, nothing could touch the atmosphere of the opening night.

The following and final day of the festival, we moved from the Capitol to the Palatine to sacrifice to Apollo and Diana. Of course, it was stage managed this way, to finish beside the mighty palace of Octavian with sacrifices to Apollo, the god he virtually shared a home with. He had not missed any opportunity to extract maximum impact from the festival. A master tactician on the battlefield Octavian may not have been, but no one could touch him in terms of conducting Rome.

The sacrifice was performed in the temple of the Palatine Apollo. Cakes of cheese, honey and parsley were given to Apollo and Diana, before a procession brought the festival to a close. Horace had composed a hymn especially for this moment. At the third hour, a choir of twenty seven boys and twenty seven girls took their places on the steps of the temple of Apollo looking out towards the circus maximus, towards the Aventine Hill.

It was undeniably beautiful.

We made our way back to the Plains of Mars. Where the final plays were being acted out, turning posts would be soon be erected and four horse chariot races were to be run.

I bet on the whites. And, perhaps because the whole festival was a purification ceremony, it had been engineered that the whites would win. An exciting result, but the highlight was the extraordinary acrobatic horse riders Potitus Messalla put on display. The manoeuvres those men performed at such high speeds were barely believable. As one horse thundered by, I turned in amazement to see that Whisper had tears in her eyes.

'There's something about the union of man and beast,' she said.

'Well,' I said as the last race was run. 'I can't deny, the whole festival has been spectacular.'

'It is as if Rome is starting again,' Whisper said.

'It is.' I embraced her. 'I wonder what the future holds.'

But it was not the end of the festival.

A herald declared an edict from 'The Fifteen'.

'The board of fifteen,' cried the herald, 'declare the following. They have supplemented these customary games with seven mores days of games.'

The cheer of the crowd could have been heard from anywhere in Italy.

'They will begin the day after tomorrow. Latin plays at the wooden theatre by the Tiber at the second hour.'

Another huge cheer.

'Greek musicians in the theatre of Pompey at the third hour.'

Another cheer.

'Greek actors at the theatre of Marcellus at the fourth hour.'

'Is there no end to it?' said Whisper.

The careful scheduling allowed Octavian and Agrippa to be present at the opening of each of these offerings to the people. They were received like gods amongst men. There was no one in Rome who did not love those two men amidst such a magnificent show.

And just when we thought it was all over, on the last day of the seven promised, another edict was declared.

'There can't be more,' exclaimed Whisper.

But there could.

'The Fifteen' were going to present us with a day of wild beast hunting and chariot races in the Circus Maximus.

'Would it ever end?' I wondered.

But unfortunately, as with all good times, it did.

Rome felt strangely subdued and deserted the day after those final races. Everywhere, people were cleaning the aftermath away, or deconstructing the temporary structures. The routine of daily life would return all too quickly.

This lull in the mood of the city was lifted by the announcement of a third child for Agrippa. Lucius Caesar was born only a month after the games had finished.

One morning, I was surprised to receive a summons to meet Agrippa at the steps of the Pantheon.

'In public?' Whisper asked.

'In public,' I replied. 'Octavian knows who I am now. There is nothing to hide.'

'What does Agrippa want I wonder?'

'I suppose I will soon know,' I said.

Agrippa was surrounded by his lictors and by a large crowd.

'Can't go anywhere these days,' he smiled broadly.

'Congratulations on your son,' I replied.

I should have spotted then. There was something in Agrippa's reaction. I do not know what, but some involuntary movement before the customary thank you came.

'Are mother and son doing well?' I asked.

'Very well, thank you.' Agrippa replied. 'The gods have been kind to us once again. How is Whisper, and little Cornelia? Not so little now I would imagine.'

'Growing too fast,' I replied. 'But they are both

wonderful.'

'Come,' said Agrippa. 'I have something to show you.'

Agrippa led me through his amazing building works, through his beautiful gardens, alongside the stunning canal, past the aqueduct, to a new building site. It seemed to me that he was limping. I felt certain I spotted the occasional wince.

'You have transformed the place,' I said. 'Did you ever imagine it would look so good?'

Agrippa scowled at me. 'Of course I did. That was the whole point.' He looked about him. 'I'm just grateful I'm still alive to see it.'

'You're not old,' I laughed. 'What are you, mid-forties?'

'Old enough,' replied Agrippa. His tone seemed dark. He looked at his feet. 'My body is beginning to fail me,' he said. He lifted a foot. It seemed swollen and red. 'The pain is sometimes unbearable. I've tried everything. Even plunging my feet into hot vinegar. Anything to numb the pain.'

He gazed wistfully at the gardens and the water flowing freely to the people. 'But it seems, even for me, money cannot buy good health. Just as I realised that the people didn't need money,' he said. 'It's not coins which bring you good health. For them, it's the water. Water is the key.'

'And water you have provided. In abundance,' I said, uneasy at Agrippa's revelations. I did not know what to say to a man laying bare his weakness. 'So what will this be?' I said, pacing around the area which had been clearly marked out for a new construction.

'This,' said Agrippa, 'will be my tomb.'

'Your tomb?'

Agrippa nodded.

'Why are you building this? Are you ill?'

Agrippa shook his head. 'No,' he said, 'but it's best to start these things ahead of time. If not, you end up like

Cleopatra.'

I remembered Cleopatra's half-built Mausoleum. It was only because it was unfinished that I had been able to scale the walls and get inside to stop her killing herself.

'Something's wrong,' I said. 'What's happening?'

Agrippa pursed his lips.

'I'm off to the east again.'

'You're leaving Rome?'

'Well, if I'm going east, that's what I have to be doing.'

'Why?'

'The empire needs ruling.'

'And Octavian?'

'Augustus will also be leaving the city. He's heading west.'

'Why?'

'Same reason. The empire needs ruling.'

'But why this?' I gestured at the site. 'Why the tomb?'

'Many men do not return from the east. I am getting older Rutilius.'

'What do you want me to do? Oversee its completion?'

Agrippa shook his head. 'No need for that, my friend. The contracts are all signed. The work will be completed.'

'I know you Agrippa,' I laughed. 'You always inspect the building sites. You even rowed through the underground sewers to check the quality of the repairs.'

Agrippa chuckled, clearly recalling that journey. 'True,' he said, 'but, my mission for you is different.' Agrippa hesitated. He seemed to be struggling to find the words.

'What is it Agrippa? What can I do?'

There was a silence. Agrippa suddenly turned and gripped my shoulder. He looked me directly in the eyes. 'You must make sure I end up in this tomb.'

He nearly brought tears to my eyes. 'What do you mean?'

'Promise me,' Agrippa said fiercely. 'Promise me, I will

end up in my tomb.'

'I promise. Of course I promise. I will do anything for you, but I don't understand.'

Agrippa turned away from me and looked once more at the site. 'One day you will,' he said.

'Why me?'

'When the time comes, you will understand.'

We stood side by side for a quiet moment.

'Have you heard the news?' Agrippa said at last.

'What news?'

'About my sons.'

'No, what's happened to Gaius and Lucius?'

Agrippa seemed surprised. 'Of course,' he said, realising why I was ignorant, 'you don't attend the senate or the courts anymore. You would have heard all about it if you still did. "Lifted to nobility from the depths of my non-nobility" as some have said to my face, Augustus is adopting my sons.'

'What?' I exclaimed in horror.

'They will move into his palace and be brought up as his own.'

I felt rage consume my body. At first I could not speak.

'Why?' I blurted.

'They will be his heirs,' replied Agrippa firmly.

'But why did you let him?' I protested. 'Can't you see what he's doing?' He's stealing your glory. Whose name will they carry? Gaius and Lucius Caesar. Where is Agrippa in that?'

'In their blood,' he growled.

I shook my head.

'You truly don't see what he's doing do you. He's so clever, so cunning. All your efforts. All your glory. He takes it all. You are celebrated today, but tomorrow, the people will speak only of Octavian, of Augustus.' I spat on the floor in disgust.

Agrippa looked pained.

After a while he looked at me. 'Rutilius, old friend. Have I ever told you of the proverb I hold in this old head of mine as a guide to my life?'

I shook my head.

'It is something the king of the Numidians said to his sons as he was about to die. He had two sons, and a nephew. He told them he wanted them all to rule the kingdom when he died. He said, "I leave you a kingdom which will be strong, if you act honourably, but weak if you are ill-affected to each other; by concord, even small states are increased.' Agrippa fixed his eyes on me. 'But by discord, even the greatest fall to nothing."'

I fell silent. 'And what did they do?'

'They did not listen,' Agrippa said. 'The nephew assassinated one of the brothers. And he fought the other until they brought about the destruction of the kingdom at Rome's hands.' Agrippa shrugged his shoulders as if this explained everything he had ever done. 'I will not let this happen.'

It was later that very day that the Praetor was summoned to the palace and witnessed the adoption ceremony. Octavian symbolically paid for his grandsons to become his adopted sons. The pair of scales was touched with a copper *as* three times and so it was that Agrippa's sons became the sons of Augustus.

I began to wonder if this had been the arrangement from the first. Perhaps before Julia was given to Agrippa, Octavian had set these conditions. I dared not ask. It was obvious to me that Agrippa was making decisions which pained him, but they were the choices he felt were best for the stability of the state. And ultimately, he was right. It was his blood flowing through their bodies, his virtue.

Agrippa left Rome even before the games he had paid for

in September.

'You could come of course,' Agrippa said to me. 'Nicopolis, Athens, Asia Minor, Syria, Judea. We'll be visiting them all.'

'We?' I replied.

'My wife and I. The usual entourage.'

'That's a kind offer, but I will stay in Rome with Whisper and Cornelia. You will be away for years I fear.'

Agrippa smiled.

He embraced me.

'You remember your promise,' he said.

'I do,' I replied, 'and I look forward to you reminding me of it again when you return.'

'Farewell,' said Agrippa.

I would not see him again for several years.

I hesitate as I approach this part of the story. I have done many terrible things in my life, but what I am about to reveal, shames me to my core.

The episode began in the baths of Agrippa, a place I loved to visit. There, gossip is as present as steam. One conversation in particular caught my attention through the haze.

'You know who I came across the other day?' said a dark haired, over-weight man.

'Who?'

'Sempronius Gracchus.'

'What did he have to say for himself?'

'Oh the usual anti-Augustan rants of course, but that wasn't the exciting part.'

'What was?'

'He's been at Augustus' daughter.'

My pulse quickened. I felt sick.

'He's what?'

'You know, having his way with Julia.'

'Agrippa's wife?'

'The very same. In fact, he thinks he might be the father...'

How could this be? Julia was pregnant while she was away with Agrippa on campaign. Unless he meant their first son Gaius. Gaius had been conceived in Rome.

'He should be careful with comments like that. The wrath of Augustus is not something you want to bring upon yourself.'

'It's not surprising though is it? What with Agrippa being so old. He can barely walk on those ancient feet of his. A strapping young man such as Gracchus would be a temptation for any young wife I'm sure.

'Women have needs, especially that Julia. She really seems to have an appetite. There's something in the looks she gives which makes all men want her. Our very own Cleopatra.'

'There are always rumours about Julia. If everyone who claims to have had her, really has, then Augustus will have a lot of punishment to mete out. I'd heard the man she really wants is that Tiberius.'

The man laughed. 'Augustus the doting dad. Imagine if this is all true. Imagine Augustus' face. Imagine if she's been at it with his stepson. He stands there preaching all those morals while his own daughter is all over the young men of Rome with her legs splayed.'

For once, the chance for Octavian to be hurt did not inspire me or fill me with joy. I was horrified at the shame Julia was bringing to Agrippa. As I sat in the steam, rage boiled within me.

I formed a plan.

No woman would bring shame to Agrippa. It would be all too easy an opportunity for Octavian to show his superiority to the man. That could not happen. Julia had to be stopped before the rumours turned into truth.

I would seek out Agrippa and his entourage wherever they had reached in the east, and somehow, someway, Julia would not return. It was for the good of the state. It was for the good of Agrippa. And it was a just punishment.

Such were the arguments I convinced myself of. I shudder at how easily.

Of course, Whisper tried to persuade me not to go.

'By the gods, why do you think it's your role?' she screamed.

'Because someone has to,' I replied, 'The gods chose me to overhear that conversation.'

'Then you should pass it on to Augustus.'

'Don't you dare call him that name,' I raged.

'Don't shout at me,' she bawled. 'We're happy and now you're going to leave me and Cornelia here in Rome. What kind of husband are you?'

'We've got to protect Agrippa,' I shouted. 'It's my duty.'

'He can handle himself,' she shrieked.

But there was no stopping me. This mission gave me purpose. Had Agrippa not turned to me to ensure he would be buried in his tomb? Was I not his trusted friend? The gods had chosen me for this task.

I packed my hooded cloak and mask of Octavian and headed east. When I set out on that fateful day, I had no idea quite how far or how long that journey would take me.

When I finally reached Athens, Agrippa was, once again, long gone, but not before leaving his mark. In the centre of the ancient agora a new theatre was rising.

'It will hold twelve hundred people,' exclaimed a tour guide, showing off the new site to visiting travellers. 'There will be a magnificent stage and a marble paved orchestra for the guests. What a generous man Agrippa is, yes?'

A generous man indeed, I thought. When the theatre was complete it would dominate the centre of the city. Elegant columns with decorative Corinthian capitals lined what would be a covered walkway. Once complete, this would provide a space to wander about just like his porticoes and colonnades in Rome.

And even better. There was no mention of Octavian.

I learned that Agrippa had crossed the Aegean Sea. Before leaving I visited the Acropolis. I climbed the great staircase and opposite the temple of Athena Nike I admired a statue of Agrippa, pricey Hymettian marble, its white veins cutting through bluish grey slabs.

THE PEOPLE DEDICATE THIS TO MARCUS AGRIPPA, SON OF LUCIUS, THREE TIMES CONSUL AND BENEFACTOR

I touched the foot of the statue and prayed.

I needed to see him in the flesh.

When I reached Mytilene, I laid eyes on Agrippa again. Alas, in marble once more. A new statue of the great man with his wife Julia had just been put up to celebrate their recent visit.

In Mytilene, I learned that Agrippa and Julia no longer travelled together. Agrippa had joined King Herod of Judea to resolve provincial disputes. For safety, Julia had withdrawn to the comfort and sights of Ilium, the legendary city of Troy.

This was my opportunity. I had to reach Ilium, and quickly, before Agrippa returned from Amisos.

Long before I reached Ilium, I could see mount Ida. Its windswept summit, bereft of life, rose to the skies and dominated the hinterlands.

On that summit Homer gathered the gods and goddesses to watch the epic Trojan war. When I laid eyes on it, I understood why the poet might have been so inspired. It was so striking, so dominant.

Few mountains can have had more stories to tell. This

was the mountain on which Paris was exposed by his father, King Priam when Priam learned that the boy would bring disaster to his city. Somewhere on that mountain was the spring where the three goddesses gathered for Paris to judge who was the fairest. Trust a man to be bribed by the gift of a beautiful woman.

From Mount Ida across the plain through the city of Ilium, the Scamander River flowed. I did not know it when I first saw it, what dramas that river would hold for me.

I set off for the city walls. As I approached, the weather was ominous. The rains teemed down, heavy and long. It was hard not to feel that they were sent by the gods, a setting for my evil purpose.

The merchants and ferryman complained that the river was swollen. They were hampered moving their quarried stone or ferrying their goods and passengers.

'It's supposed to be dry season,' they muttered. 'What's upset the gods?'

I looked at the Scamander. It looked as if its banks would burst. The current flowed at pace, eddying and whirling in the wind, the surface breaking with each new deluge of rain.

'No more crossings today,' the ferryman shook his head, 'too dangerous.'

Bedraggled and sodden, I thought to seek shelter for the night. Then I heard a voice.

'What do you mean, no more crossings? I need to reach the city.'

There was something in the tone, in the confidence, in the self-assured manner, which revealed at once a well-spoken, well-educated, forceful woman.

'Do they not know who I am? I must reach the city. I'm expected for dinner.'

'But my lady, they say it is too dangerous.'

I was smiling. I knew exactly who it was. It had to be Julia. Who else would be speaking Latin?

On impulse, I grabbed the ferryman.

'You will cross this river tonight,' I said. I thrust a bag of coins into his hand. 'Is this enough?'

The ferryman stared at me. He looked at the river, then assessed the weight of the bag of coins.

'It will be a terrible crossing,' he replied.

'It will indeed,' I said.

I spun on my heel and marched to the gathering around Julia.

'My lady,' I called. 'I have a boat which is crossing. You are welcome to join me.'

'Ah,' replied Julia. 'Splendid.' She beamed a smile at me and I was at once struck by her beauty. She paced over and took my arm. 'A real man,' she said. I can still feel her grip on my forearm. She was at once sexual and innocent. Her eyes full of youth.

I shook my head and boarded the boat.

The crossing was rough. The oarsmen worked hard to keep the boat going forward, resisting the swell and tug of the tides. I leaned over the edge, staring into the fierce, flowing water.

Despite the tempestuous crossing, it became clear the boat was not going to wreck. I was going to have to act.

I made my way over to Julia.

'My lady, all will be well.'

Julia looked back at me. Her eyes settled on my scar. For a moment I wondered if she might know of me. Had her father ranted about Rutilius, the man with the scar?

The captain was shouting at his oarsmen, imploring them to increase their efforts. We were now in the middle of the river, but barely making any progress. Buffeted this way and that, the rains kept falling. All about us the clouds showed no sign of breaking.

I gripped the side of the boat and stood up to peer over

the edge.

'It's something to behold,' I said to Julia. 'A river in full spate. Why don't you take a look?'

Julia huddled down. 'Not a chance. I might fall in.'

'I'll hold you,' I replied.

But she refused. 'I just want to set foot safely on the other side. I don't care what the river looks like. I'm late already.'

I looked at her. I saw a frightened young girl, her hair the same colour as little Cornelia's. I wiped the rain from my eyes. This was no time to feel sentiment. The gods had provided me with this opportunity. I had to take it.

Nearly an hour passed and still the boat could not make the crossing.

'By the gods, why did the captain allow us to cross?' ranted Julia. 'It's obviously too dangerous.'

'We've started now,' I bellowed. 'We have to finish.'

The boat spun and suddenly we were heading at speed in the same direction as the current. We were swept away from the landing point we were trying to reach.

All about me, people lost their footing. The oarsmen grappled for their oars, desperate to recover some form of rhythm.

Julia spun and grabbed the side of the boat with her hand.

I fell beside her. I took one last look at her. The boat rocked. It seemed as if we might capsize.

I would love to say I did not grab Julia. I would love to say that I did not lift her over the side. I cannot remember clearly what happened. But I must have grabbed her, because the next moment I was hanging onto her for dear life. She was over the side of the boat and in the water, but I did not let go.

I could not let go.

I did not want to let go.

Even as what I had set out to do was happening before

me, I had changed my mind. This was just a woman, enjoying the lusts of life. Was adultery such a dreadful crime?

Suddenly I was completely certain that killing Julia was the wrong thing to do. Julia screamed.

Her eyes were wide with terror.

I gripped the side of the boat with one hand, and her wrist with the other, as tightly as I could.

But the boat kept rocking from side to side. Julia was plunged under the water, then dragged back up again, still clinging to me.

'Help!' I tried to call, but my shout was drowned out by the crashing water, the howling wind, the driving rain. 'Help!' I cried again. 'Gods save her!' I bellowed.

Julia was choking the water clear from her mouth. She screamed again. It filled me with horror. I can still hear the scream piercing above all the din around me. Loud, long and clear. Pure terror.

I felt her hand slipping from mine.

I gripped tighter. As tight as I possibly could.

My fingernails pierced her fair, pale skin, drawing blood.

Then my arm went light.

She was gone.

I fell back into the boat and began to shake.

What had I done?

At last, the boat crashed into the far bank. We scrambled from the boat.

'Is everyone here?' bawled the captain.

'Where is my lady?' asked her attendant. 'Where's Julia?'

Then the realisation. Then the scream. Then the scramble down the riverbank for the search.

I sat numb in the boat. I vomited. It would look like an accident, but I could not bear what I had done. In a daze, I disembarked. I sat on the riverbank and stared at the water rushing past.

Then cries, shouts, waving arms. They had found her, washed up on the riverbank.

I turned. 'Is she alive?' I asked, with a pathetic tone. 'Is she alive?' I shouted, angry that no one answered. I leapt to my feet. 'By the gods, is she alive?'

Julia was alive. Through strong will or good fortune, she had managed to flow with the water until she was swept up on the bank. Grimly she had clung onto a fallen tree.

I began to make my way towards the gaggle of people around her. Then I realised that she may believe I had pushed her overboard.

I hesitated. Should I wait to find out, or run? If I ran, it would confirm my guilt.

In the end, I did not move fast enough. I was summoned over.

Julia lay, her hair wet through, her clothes stuck to her body. She shivered and looked pale as death.

Her slaves were tending to her. Their faces were filled with anxiety.

'Thank you,' she said. 'For trying to save me.'

'She's pregnant. That's why she left Agrippa's side. A campaign was no place for a pregnant lady. Pray to the gods to spare the child.'

Guilt silenced me. Guilt which still lives with me every day I live.

Some misdeeds, I cannot wash away. This is one. Did I lift her out of the boat? Or did I grab her as she was already falling overboard? I still cannot answer that question.

But what I did know, as those fear-filled eyes locked onto mine, was that I had to come up with an alternative plan.

All that travel. All those weeks and months with one purpose driving me forward. All wasted. All destroyed in one climactic event which destroyed even the last vestige of belief I had that I am a good man. I confessed to you earlier in these scrolls, that I am not a good man. I am now old enough and wise enough to know that. But was I cold enough to murder? I hope I was not. I believe I was not.

But I cannot be certain.

When Agrippa learned of Julia's near death, he blazed into a fury. He threw the ferryman into prison and fined the city of Ilium for being so careless. One hundred thousand silver *drachmai*, a massive sum.

I had misjudged, again. I had nearly cost the man I love above all others, the woman he clearly loved above all others.

And I had literally cost a people more than they could afford. The people of Ilium at once sent a delegation to Amisos, to beseech Agrippa to change his mind.

I beat my head. 'Why are you such an idiot?' I cried. 'Whisper even told you.'

And then I remembered Whisper and Cornelia, still waiting patiently in Rome. I was missing Cornelia growing up. The whole escapade had been a complete waste of my life and theirs.

I returned to Rome in the winter of that year. I was so excited to see Whisper and Cornelia. As I crossed the threshold, Whisper burst into tears. I was staggered by how much Cornelia had grown. She was staring in wonderment at her mother, confused that she was crying.

I embraced them both.

'I'm sorry I was gone so long,' I said.

'Never again,' replied Whisper. 'It's not fair. You will have to take us with you next time.'

Not only was Cornelia twice the height she had been when I left, she was also talking fluently.

'She's an intelligent girl,' said Whisper proudly. 'She picked up reading and writing far quicker than I did.'

I told Whisper all about my adventures and confessed to the incident on the boat.

'Did you push her?' Whisper asked.

I did not answer. I could not answer. I tried desperately to remember. I would confess everything to Whisper. But I still could not recall whether the boat tipped Julia out and I grabbed at her, or had I shoved her.

'Surely you would remember pushing her?' said Whisper. 'I think you grabbed her as she fell.'

'Perhaps you're right,' I replied.

But I was still troubled by a lingering doubt.

In Agrippa's continued absence news of the birth of his fourth child with Julia, Agrippina, filtered through to Rome. Agrippina had had a dramatic life inside Julia's belly already with her exploits in Ilium. I hoped that both mother and daughter were fit and healthy.

When Whisper heard the news, she looked crestfallen. 'Do you think we will ever have a second child?' she asked.

I hugged her. 'Of course. The fates are just choosing their moment, that's all. And,' I added, 'our chances are vastly improved now I'm back.'

It was not until the following year that, at last, Agrippa returned to Rome. Octavian soon followed, after three years in Gaul and Hispania. I had to swallow my distaste at Agrippa's greeting Octavian at the city gates like a suppliant. But the whole of Rome was there, cheering Octavian's entry into the city. I spotted Julia beside her husband.

Was she being faithful? I wondered. There was such a visible difference in age.

Octavian, unlike Agrippa, did not seem to be aging as much. He looked fit and well, grey haired of course, and thinning, but were not we all. All three of us had lived longer lives than many. Who would be the first to die? Something in my heart told me, it was not going to be Octavian.

If I was to bet on our deaths, like I did on the chariot races, unfortunately I concluded, I would back myself.

The senate vowed to create an altar commemorating the peace that Octavian had brought to the empire. On July 4th, the sacred precinct on which the altar was to be built was marked out. It was sited beside the Flaminian Way, north of Agrippa's great works on the Plains of Mars.

'I think that's good, pater,' said Cornelia. 'Not many monuments celebrate peace do they...it's either for dead people, or for killing people.'

She had a point. Just like her mother.

While the senate were in the business of sycophancy once again, they renewed the powers they had given both Octavian and Agrippa for five years. They extended them for both men for another five years. It must have been a smooth enough process. The two consuls that year were Octavian's stepson Tiberius and Agrippa's son-in-law, Varus. He had married Vipsania, Agrippa's daughter from his earlier marriage with Marcella.

Not forgetting that Octavian was sitting between these two throughout the session.

I was delighted to see that the latest issues of coins showed Agrippa and Octavian as co-leaders. At last Rome was recognising Agrippa as Octavian's equal. The peace we were all living was as much his as it was Octavian's. The baths people washed themselves in, the gardens they walked in, the clean streets, all were Agrippa's doing.

And the rumours about Julia's infidelity were not gaining further credence. You heard no more about them than you did any plot or conspiracy against either Agrippa or Octavian.

Octavian was contained by Agrippa and with each month that passed, Agrippa's children became the likely heirs.

When Whisper announced that she had not bled that month, it seemed that, in all aspects, life was good.

News reached the city of trouble in the north of Illyricum. Marcus Vinicius had written to Octavian requesting urgent relief. Despite successfully quelling an uprising of the Pannonnii, another revolt would be too much to contain.

I suppose with Tiberius still as consul, there was only one man to go. Agrippa.

'He's nearly fifty,' I exclaimed. 'Can they not find anyone else? And winter is coming. It's too late to campaign. He should not be risking his life.'

But ever loyal and obedient, Agrippa departed the city for Pannonia.

As soon as he arrived, news spread of his presence. The Pannonii immediately approached the camp and sued for peace. That is how great a general Agrippa was.

So, as quickly as he had arrived, Agrippa set off on his return.

Rome heard of Agrippa's safe arrival at Brundisium. But after that the news went silent. Rome was distracted by another monumental event which upset my newly found happiness. Lepidus, Rome's chief priest, finally died. He had been exiled in Circeii for nearly twenty-five years, but was so sacred that even the devious Octavian refused to execute him, despite having good reason.

Now, at last, natural causes had taken him to the underworld.

Such a prestigious position was too great an opportunity for Octavian to let pass. And so he became Rome's chief priest. In taking up that priesthood, Octavian marked himself out as greater than Agrippa once more. It rankled with me. Chief bridge-builder to the gods? Not in my eyes.

Octavian was now custodian of the sacred law, the calendar, the statutes relating to all the temples, all things religious. It was the final element of power he needed to become all supreme. It was opportune in the extreme that Agrippa had been out of the city when it all happened.

A few days later, a messenger arrived at my door.

'You must come at once.'

'Where to?' I replied.

'Agrippa's villa in Campania.'

'Why?'

'No time for questions, just come.'

'But my family?'

'Bring them, as long as you come immediately. There is not a moment to lose.'

I doubt we have ever ridden so swiftly. The messenger refused to give me further details. Just that Agrippa himself had sent for me.

As we arrived at the villa, I realised something was not right. It was in the concerned expressions of everybody I saw.

I was greeted by Agrippa's sister, Vipsania Polla.

'Thank you for coming so quickly,' she said.

'Of course. I came at once, but please, will somebody tell me what's happening?'

'It's Agrippa,' Vipsania Polla's eyes welled up with tears. 'He's unwell.'

'Unwell?'

Vipsania Polla just managed to nod.

'Where is he?' I demanded. I was immediately trying to remember all the teaching I had had from Musa. 'Perhaps I can help?'

We were led into Agrippa's bedchamber. As soon as we crossed the threshold, I could smell sickness, illness.

Agrippa was lying on the bed. I rushed to his side.

'Agrippa,' I said.

His eyes slowly focused on me. He smiled. His lips were cracked.

'Hello, old friend. You came.'

'Of course I came. What's happened?'

Agrippa let out a gentle cough. 'Not sure,' he croaked. 'Came back from Panonnia and felt peculiar. Thought it best to avoid Rome, and rest here...'

Agrippa's speech was slow. Each word an effort.

'Who's treating you?' I asked, looking about me.

'Oh, everybody,' Agrippa smiled. 'They're all trying.'

'Can I try?' I asked.

A physician tried to protest, but Agrippa raised his hand. 'It's alright. Musa taught him. Do what you can,' he said. He lay back and dozed off.

I prepared cold poultices just as Musa had taught me, but trying to bathe Agrippa in cold water proved impossible. The man, even weakened and ravaged by whatever illness and fever he had, was still a massive frame. And he did not want to move.

'Fifty eh?' Agrippa croaked. 'That's pretty good. I nearly made it to fifty one. It's my birthday soon.'

These words filled me with dread. He was preparing for the end.

'Have you informed Octavian?' I asked.

But Agrippa was asleep.

Vipsania Polla shook her head. 'He refused,' she said. 'He doesn't want the *princeps* to think he is an invalid.'

'Invalid? By the gods,' I cried. 'Send for the *princeps* at once.'

An unlikely outcome was it not, me being the man who sent the messenger to summon Octavian. Octavian, no doubt still beaming with joy at his new priesthood, was in the middle of overseeing contests of armed warriors, exhibits on behalf of his sons. The news will have drained the joy from him. He set off at once.

I would come face to face with him once more. But for once, that did not matter. All my attention was on trying to help Agrippa.

Whisper tried too, with Cornelia at Agrippa's bedside. Cornelia even managed to raise a smile from Agrippa.

'We're going to go out in your lovely garden,' said Whisper. 'As soon as you're better, you will be able to enjoy it again. Cornelia loves your garden. She loves the flowers.'

'Don't let her sneak away and pick one.' Agrippa winked.

Whisper turned to me. 'Well at least he's still got his sense of humour. That's got to be encouraging hasn't it?'

I hoped so.

'Goodbye Agrippa,' Cornelia said. 'I hope you feel better very soon.'

Agrippa rolled onto his side. He was becoming increasingly fidgety. His hands moving from place to place, trying to settle. 'Know how,' he mumbled. 'That's all I need. A little know how.'

Whisper left the room. Cornelia hesitated at the doorway. She smiled at Agrippa. Agrippa smiled back, and managed a short wave.

I tended to him day and night, refusing to sleep. Nothing anyone was trying seemed to be working.

Agrippa hauled himself onto his side. He beckoned me over. His breath smelt dreadful. His face was pale, his eyes sunken. The great general was dying before me, and there was nothing I could do to stop it.

He swallowed a few times, before trying to speak.

'Something's working Rutilius,' he said, 'my feet don't hurt anymore.'

I stared back at him.

I put my hand on his shoulder. 'Agrippa,' I said.

'Rutilius,' he replied, 'remember your promise?'

I nodded my head. 'I remember.'

Agrippa swallowed again.

'Keep it,' he whispered.

His head slumped slowly down. His eyes lost their focus. And then a last deep breath came from his great chest. I had hold of his arm as he died.

I reached forward and closed his eyelids over his staring eyes. Already his face and body had a greyish hue.

'Hail and Farewell,' I said.

I sat by his bedside and wept.

Epilogue

We have lost Rome's greatest son, the man without whom Rome would not be prospering. A man who, despite his wealth and power beyond measure, never lost his principles or morals and always remained steadfast to those he deemed worthy. A man who embodied the spirit of the Republic.

It is my greatest honour that Agrippa counted me amongst his friends, for I am not a great Roman. I am old enough and wise enough to know my place.

In my youth I objected to a man gaining power beyond his rank. Now, I understand that the best men can come from any background.

In Agrippa's position, many years ago, I would rather have died than support Octavian when he chose to take on sole rule and abolish the last traces of the Republic.

Agrippa, like me, was a staunch Republican. He, like me, was deceived by Octavian into believing that we fought to 'restore the Republic'. But when the Republic had fallen, he, unlike me, realised he could play a role in forging the new future of Rome. He could ensure the qualities of the Republic would be maintained in the new government.

Agrippa will be remembered in time to come without my help. His name is inscribed in marble all over this great city. Rome is filled with his works; temples, aqueducts, baths and gardens; all for the people of Rome, the common people.

Few will learn about Agrippa's integrity for I know the historians will speak only of Octavian. I hope these scrolls will give some essence of the man.

It is with great pain that I bear the loss of Marcus Vipsanius Agrippa. Pain Rome will share. For without Agrippa, there is no restraint on Rome's king. Octavian's power is total, self-centred and all consuming.

Once again, the people of Rome are in grave danger.

Thunder rumbles outside my window. A comet lights the night sky.

Octavian approaches. As I await the arrival of the *princeps,* I realise there is nothing and no one left to stand against Octavian.

Only me.

www.ingramcontent.com/pod-product-compliance
Ingram Content Group UK Ltd.
Pitfield, Milton Keynes, MK11 3LW, UK
UKHW042147020225
454580UK00005B/162